The Mind Swipe Series

TERRAIZEN CHRONICLES: RETURN OF THE FORGOTTEN AGES

Written By: R.L. Golsby

Edited By: Nicollette Calvin &
Jonathon Cannell

2014©

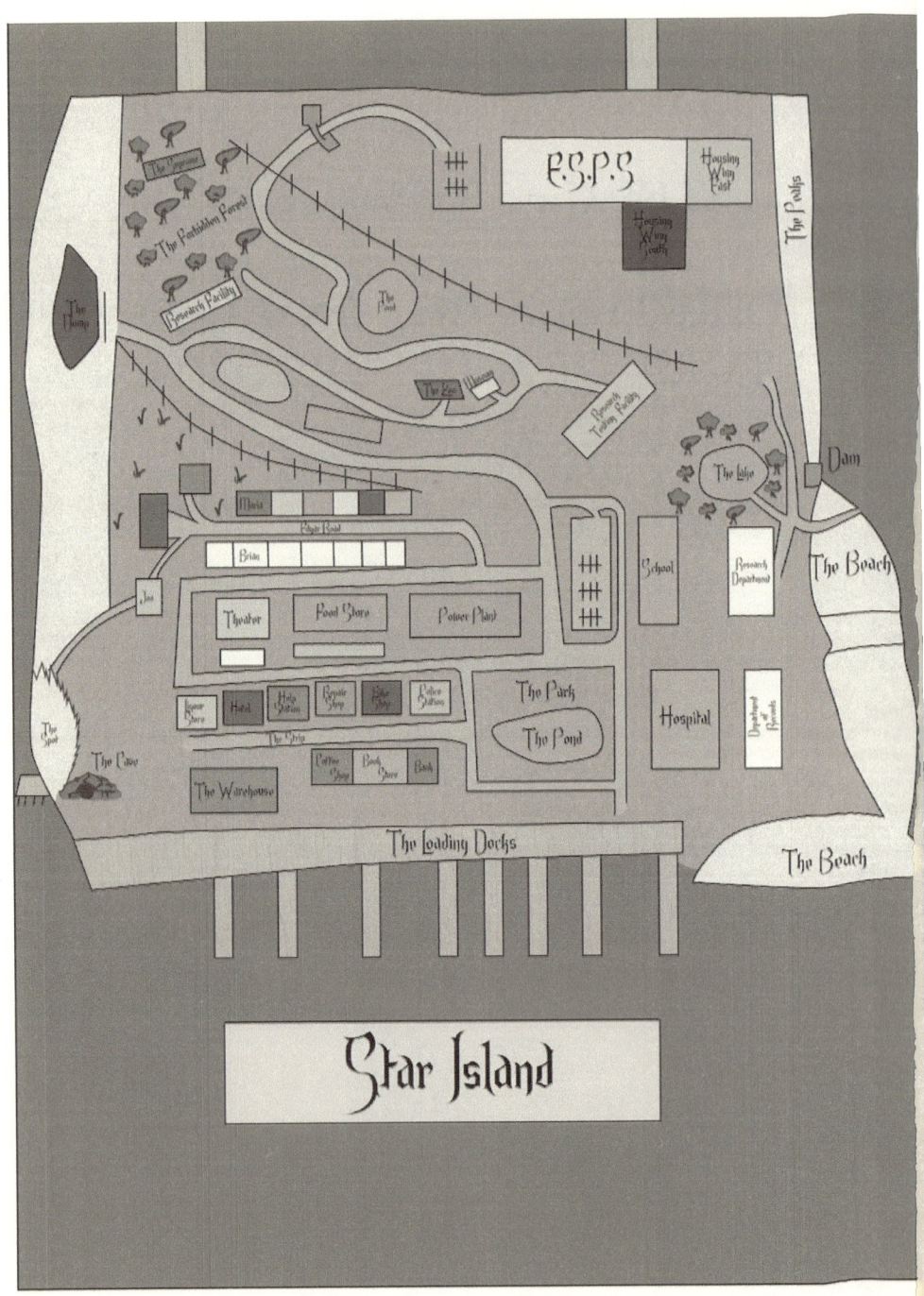

The Playground

The Forbidden Forest

Research Facility

The River

The Pond

The Lake

Research Testing Facility

E.S.P.S

Housing Wing East

Housing Wing South

The Fields

Maria

Brian

Jon

Theater

Food Store

Power Plant

School

Research Department

The Beach

The Spot

The Cave

Liquor Store

Hotel

Help Station

Reptile Shop

Bike Shop

Police Station

The Strip

The Warehouse

Coffee Shop

Book Store

Bank

The Park

The Pond

Hospital

Department of Records

The Loading Docks

The Beach

Dam

Star Island

Special Thanks

Juanita Golsby, Ryan & Liz Thelen, Mrs. Ginny Applegate, Mrs. Donna Robert's, Mrs. Mc Mullen, Zac Walters, Martin Eirich, William Hopkins, Joshua Giles, Jonathon Canell, Nicollette Calvin, Cameron Coyan, Ms. Elvia, Ms. Elisa, Charlene Simmons, Bob Suess, Judy Mause, Kassie A. Calahan, Mrs. Mary Stephenson, Adam J. Ochs and my extended friends and family, and all my wonderful teachers and professors.

Dreams

Dreams share a connection to the unconscious mind and vary in nature from surreal and ordinary to frightening, magical, and bizarre. The events in dreams are generally outside the control of the dreamer, except for a lucid dreamer, who is self-aware that they are dreaming.

Some believe dreams are manifestations of our deepest darkest desires and repressed anxieties. Others believe they are messages from the past, unseen worlds, or even prophetic visions of the future.

TABLE OF CONTENTS

CHAPTER 1: STARLIGHT OVER SUMMER NIGHTS 1

CHAPTER 2: QUINN AND ANABEL 14

CHAPTER 3: THE ROAD LESS TRAVELED 28

CHAPTER 4: BRUNO AND BENJAMIN..33

CHAPTER 5: REFLECTIONS OF THE PAST 43

CHAPTER 6: ELEANOR AND STEPHEN..53

CHAPTER 7: THE NEFASTUS FOREST 60

CHAPTER 8: FAITH AND FRANCIS 68

CHAPTER 9: MOONLIGHT VISITOR..75

CHAPTER 10: CENTRAL- THE GATHERING..................................82

CHAPTER 11: THE GATE KEEPER 94

CHAPTER 12: ELEANOR-WHITE WILLOW 109

CHAPTER 13: REUNION OF FRIENDS..128

CHAPTER 14: LOVE AND FRIENDSHIP 136

CHAPTER 15: ANTHONY- DEVIL'S GATE..................................149

CHAPTER 16: GHOST TOWN 156

CHAPTER 17: BRUNO- EDGE OF SEVENTEEN..................................172

CHAPTER 18: RETURN OF THE NIGHTMARE 182

CHAPTER 19: ANTHONY- THE WAIT 190

CHAPTER 20: PRINCE JABIN..199

CHAPTER 21: AWAKENING REKINDLED..................................217

CHAPTER 22: THE DEAD ZONE 227

CHAPTER 23: MOTHER OF FAITH- SEQUENCE: CSK-7 243

CHAPTER 24: THE GATE OF SILENCE.......................................250

CHAPTER 25: DESTROYERS AND DEFENDERS OF SLUMBER 255

CHAPTER 26: THE ENGINEERING DEPARTMENT................................265

CHAPTER 27: EYES OF THE SPARROW.......................................279

CHAPTER 28: QUINN- THE JINN AND NEFASTUS FOREST 291

CHAPTER 29: SOFT SAPPHIRE LIGHT 300

CHAPTER 30: REVELATIONS AND THE PIT....................................306

CHAPTER 31: MIRRORDERS- PRELUDE TO THE END 316

CHAPTER 32: JOSEPH AWAKENS 330

CHAPTER 33: THE NIGHTSHIFT...339

CHAPTER 34: RETURN OF FORGOTTEN AGES- BLACK MAIDEN ..348

CHAPTER 35: QUINN 362

CHAPTER 1: STARLIGHT OVER SUMMER NIGHTS

Joseph gazed out of his living room window. As the sun began to set, the sky radiated a vibrant-red, soft-orange glow, causing Joseph to drift in and out of sleep as he lay on the couch.

Joseph had just completed his final day of high school last week, yet it seemed so long ago now. He was finally done with a long week of volunteering at his high school; helping his teachers finish some last minute spring cleaning. Joseph was uncertain as to what he wanted to do with his life just yet. Getting a job or going to college were the least of his worries. At times he asked himself, *What's the meaning of it all* and questioned his reasons for living. STAR Island was all he knew. To attend the college in the foreign northern or eastern continents, he would have to leave the island and his friends behind. The thought of leaving frightened him. No one who left the island ever returned. Joseph hated the idea of being alone out in the world. At least on the island, he had his best friends Brian and Maria.

Ever since his mother's accident, his life had been turned upside down. He took on all the routine responsibilities of taking care of the house. Every day he woke up, fixed breakfast, checked the news, and headed out to school. After returning from school, he would complete his household tasks: washing dishes, taking out the trash, cutting the grass and anything else there was left to do. In the last seven years, he had become quite the handy man when it came to fixing the problems in the three-story house.

Life had provided Joseph with his fair share of problems. However, his essential needs had always been covered. His father had been a brilliant scientist who researched at the Terraizen Protection Agency, and in his spare time, took pleasure in writing. In honor of his father's research and dedication to the Terraizen Protection Agency, the agency provided Joseph with a trust fund, which was distributed to him on a monthly basis. Ten percent of the monthly funding he received covered all his needs and living expenses. He was in charge of paying the bills, and when the time came around each year, he would make a withdrawal from his TPA trust account for whatever he needed. The remaining funds Joseph ended up saving. A year ago, he had lived there alone before Brian and Maria officially moved in. He was very frugal most of the time, but on occasion, he treated himself and his friends to something special. Whether it be dinner, a movie, a new game, or just a simple night on the strip, they always found a way to enjoy themselves.

Joseph did not know much about his father's research. After the loss of his father, due to a heart attack, Joseph's mother fell into a deep depression, refusing to talk about his father's death. He was very young when his father passed away. Whenever he asked questions, his mother would say that she was not ready to speak about it; but one day when he was older, she would explain everything. He always felt that she was belittling him, but as he matured, he began to understand it was her way of protecting him. After all, she had refused to let him go to the funeral because she felt it would give him nightmares.

Over the years, Joseph had managed to uncover details about his father's past. In addition to his scientific research, Joseph's father had become famous for a children's story he had written called *Little People*. Besides bits and pieces of hearsay and memory, Joseph knew very little about his father's history.

***

Maria was considered a genius among her peers. In the 6th grade, she could read and understand complex science and math theories reserved for college studies. Now she had the option to go to any college of her choice in the East, which were said to accept only the crème de la crème. After browsing through brochures, reading over several articles and examining all of her options, she had narrowed it down to three places, all of which were located in Eastern Terraizen: thousands of miles away from STAR Island, her home. This bothered her.

Yes, the Eastern Colleges were said to be some of the finest and the East was said to be the paradise of Terraizen filled with endless wonders that superseded all STAR Island had to offer, so much so that all those who left never wished to return to their old lives and families. Still, Maria found this a bit peculiar. Even if it was such a great place, with it's floating architecture, lush fields of gold and crystal waterfalls that almost made it seem magical, wouldn't the people eventually begin to miss their families. After a while, wouldn't they at least write or call or send a video message letting everyone know they had safely arrive. Maria wondered why those who left STAR Island never returned. For all she knew Eastern Terraizen may not even exist. After all she'd only seen it on maps and read about it in history books and brochures but she had never met any one from Eastern Terraizen and the news never depicted any live footage of it. Were camera's not allowed?

Was it such a wonderful place that once she left she would become like those who left before her, infatuated by its wonders, never wishing to return or was it some kind of construct, fairy tale, created by the Terraizen Protection Agency used to deceive the people as to where they were really going once they left the Island? As Maria continued to ponder these ideas she began to realize maybe it wasn't college she had been searching for in the East, maybe what she really wanted was the truth.

At night, Maria loved gazing out at the universe and the stars. She had done so nearly every night for as long as she could remember. Unlike other redundant tasks, the night sky left her with a sense of awe every single time. Once, Joseph had asked her what she meant when she said the universe is an "oldie but goodie." Maria responded by saying, "It's like that song you play over and over again, and it never gets old no matter how many times you listen to it." The song of the universe made her feel so small, yet so incredibly phenomenal at the same time. It was her belief that everything had a place in the universe, no matter how trivial or extrinsic it seemed at first glance.

Maria contemplated these things as she approached the front door of Joseph's house. She had just returned from the grocery store, and her right hand clung to grocery bags as she headed up the walkway to the stairs of the house. The scent of wet, freshly cut grass hung in the air. Maria balanced the groceries in her right arm as she attempted to search her bag for the keys.

As she proceeded onto the front porch, the wooden steps creaked under her heels. The fourth step was very weak and felt as if it would give in at any moment. Maria had nagged Joseph many times to fix the stairs, but he always seemed to wave her off as if it wasn't a big problem. Though she felt that someone could seriously get hurt, she knew it was not on the top of his priority list.

Maria had known Joseph and Brian since first grade, and knew of Joseph's struggles with his mother's condition. Maria always tried to think of fun things for them to do. It seemed like the only way to keep Joseph from falling into a depression.

Now that she was graduating, she had reached a turning point in her life. Still, she wondered if she could leave the island that she had grown to love so much. As she continued her balancing act, Maria raised the key to the lock, but before she could attempt to unlock the door, it swung open. It was Brian.

"Did you get everything on the list?" Brian asked grabbing some of the bags from Maria's arms. "Did you remember my chips? You know the barbecue kind with the ruffled edges?" Brian began searching through the bags.

"Wow! Not even a hello?" said Maria sarcastically. "Sorry Brian, but they were out. I checked two different stores just for you," she said as she brushed passed him and headed down the hall to the kitchen.

Maria looked around the living room. She could tell Joseph had exhausted himself cleaning. He lay shirtless, stretched out across the couch with grass stained pants. His shirt lay on the living room table dirty and rolled up into a sweaty ball.

"What's wrong with him?" asked Maria. Joseph's eyes were half open, yet he was fully asleep. Every now and then he would jerk sporadically as if someone had touched him and he was trying to pull away.

"Don't know," said Brian, "I think he's just exhausted. He's been cleaning all day. He's probably cleaned this entire house twice…ain't that right Joe!"

Joseph, startled by Brian, sprung up like a springboard.

"Huh?" said Joseph slightly sitting up, and only partially conscious of the conversation that was occurring.

"Go back to sleep," said Maria.

Joseph began to close his eyes as Maria looked over at Brian.

"And what have you been doing all day?" Maria asked Brian.

"Ain't been doing much, played some 3D video games, watched a few movies, went for a jog, and thought of some new ways to annoy you," said Brian.

"You know *ain't* is not a word," said Maria.

"Yeah, but I know how much it annoys you so I like to use it!!" said Brian.

"You're such a troll," said Maria, rolling her eyes as she proceeded through the living and dining rooms to the kitchen. Brian grinned, laughed half-heartedly and followed closely behind Maria. It was time to finish dinner preparations.

Brian leaned against the kitchen sink as he watched Maria put the groceries away. The smell of baked, honey glazed chicken filled the air as the bird continued to cook in the oven.

"Joe said to tell you to take the chicken out in about 30 minutes," said Brian, "He still thinks I'm too clumsy after I dropped the Thanksgiving roast, but I still say it was not my fault. I did not expect the pan to be that hot."

"You're right. That was our fault. We should have informed you that ovens are hot when they're turned on, Mr. Butterfingers."

Brian smirked, "At least I don't fall up the stairs, Ms. Face Plant."

Maria side-glanced in his direction as she put the last of the groceries in the fridge, "That only happened once."

Maria smiled and they both began to laugh.

***

Maria finished up the potatoes and green beans as Joseph and Brian sat at the dinner table. Joseph had made the wonderful spinach stuffed, honey-barbecue glazed chicken. Brian and Maria thought it had turned out nice, but Joseph was constantly critiquing himself and had already thought of five ways he could have made it better. Through the years, he had to learn to cook for himself and had begun to experiment in the kitchen. He had seen his fair share of masterpieces and mistakes when it came to cooking. Through trial and error, he had come up with a book of his very own signature dishes. He hoped to one day have his own cookbook. Neither Maria nor Brian could deny that Joseph had developed a love for cooking, and they loved to reap the benefits.

Joseph looked over the empty plates and simple but hearty dinner. As Maria carried the dinner rolls to the table, Brian began filling his plate. Brian had made the green beans, mashed potatoes and gravy. He wasn't the best when it came to cooking, but Joseph had taught him a few key things so he knew his way around the kitchen. As they were all filling their plates, Maria began to speak.

"So any ideas for this summer? It is, after all, our last summer together," Maria said with a sigh.

"Why does this have to be our last summer together?" asked Brian, "You're saying it like we will never see each other again. Can we not use the word last?"

Brian was upset.

"Okay," said Maria apologetically, "I didn't mean it that way."

There was a moment of silence. A wave of sadness drifted over the table, catching the three of them as they continued to eat their dinner.

"Can we just not talk about it right now?" asked Brian as he stared blankly out of the dining room window.

"If we don't talk about it now, when will we?" asked Joseph, "Once you guys move out, it's just going to be me and this big house again."

Joseph remembered when he was younger how incredibly invincible his mother seemed. He refused to go to see her in her current state at the strange medical facilities. Now, she seemed so vulnerable, and leaving the Island would mean he could never see her again.

***

Dinner finished up. Brian and Maria cleaned the dishes, as Joseph lay on the couch for a brief moment. He had done his fair share of cleaning for the day. Although Joseph did not openly admit it, he liked the idea of living with Brian and Maria. It made him feel less lonely. Plus, they helped out around the house, which made less work for him. He thought it would be wonderful if they could just stay together forever, but knew it wouldn't be possible. Joseph got up from the couch and joined Brian and Maria in the kitchen.

Maria grabbed the flashlights and towels and stood on the back porch. Joseph and Brian grabbed some chips, mini cakes, and drink cartridges and joined Maria on the back porch, then headed out. They liked to visit what they called "the spot" every once in a while. It was a hidden, sandy beach-like area along the coast that only a handful of people knew about.

They headed down the not-so-clear path in the back yard. Guided by their flashlights, through the trees they traveled down the trail they had been through many times before. Even without flashlights, they knew the route by heart. They could hear the sound of the crickets chirping and frogs croaking as the trees rustled slightly in the midnight breeze. They passed over the fallen trees and branches, leaping over the small streams that cut through the forest with haste and laughter as they attempted to catch up to Maria. There was a small cabin that belonged to Joseph's father. The cabin sat under the cliff formations hidden on the forests edge. It was locked, well-camouflaged, and was where his father went to focus. Many times he had attempted to enter it in the past, but his attempts always ended in failure. The windows of the cabin looked as if they were made of a glass-like material, yet, though he had tried, he could not break them or even scratch them. He had tried hammers, screwdrivers, lock picks, and knives. Even when it was burned, the wood remained charred, undamaged. The cabin was a mystery of its own, and Brian even speculated that it was enchanted, while Maria thought it was just a special coating developed in the TPA research labs.

After cutting through the tall grass, they finally reached the shore side.

"Catch!" Maria said as she tossed a towel to Brian and Joseph. They distributed the snacks and laid out the towels a few feet from the shoreline. As they gazed up at the night sky full of stars, Maria sighed.

"It's a beautiful night," said Maria.

"Sure is," said Brian.

The cool night breeze fueled with the scent of pre-autumn leaves and sea salt blew gently past them. Brian, Maria, and Joseph lay on the shore, gazing up at the sky. Moonlight pierced through the dark shroud of night briefly before being concealed by the drifting clouds. As they rested on the sandy shore gazing up at the moon, they fell into a silence. They could feel the warm sand between their toes as the breeze continued to drift overhead. They listened for the tide as the waves of the Anexthesia Sea, which surrounded the island, rushed in, hitting the rocks and sandy shore before crawling away. This was their special place, hidden by the large stone formations and thick trees.

While lying there, they reminisced about the times when they were younger and would come to the beach every week during the summer to hang out and play games. Back then, times felt so peaceful and simple, now things were so much more complicated. But the one thing that never seemed to change was the night sky. Brian had always felt that there was something enchanting about it. He felt, at times, it demanded his silence as he gazed upon its beauty and vastness. Joseph and Maria felt the same.

"Did you hear that?" asked Joseph.

"Yeah," said Maria, "it sounds lovely."

Maria listened as the waves continued to crash against the shore.

"No, not that," said Joseph in a whisper. "Just a second ago, it sounded like someone was playing a flute."

"I don't hear any flute," said Brian. "I think you might just have sand in your ears it's just the waves tonight."

Joseph carefully listened again, hoping to hear the sound once more, but it had faded under the gentle flow of the waves.

"Yeah. You're probably right," said Joseph as he rested against his towel.

Joseph closed his eyes and began to drift off, calmed by the waves. One moment he was on the island with Brian and Maria, and the next he was flying over it, rising into the night sky. He saw the moon and the stars close up. The suns shined brightly as Joseph turned his back towards them, soaring further into outer space. The sights were marvelously breath taking and seemed so familiar. There was a dark tunnel spiraling in the cosmos that seemed to rip through space. Like a slightly tinted window, Joseph could see through it, but could not enter. Joseph could make out three orbs that looked like red, blue, and green planets swirling through space on the other side. They seemed to overwhelm him with a sense of déjà vu. He turned away and headed towards the moon. As he approached the dark side of the moon, he saw what looked like a gray cloudy mass hovering in the darkness.

Although the universe maintained its natural motions, the gray cloudy mass seemed to be out of place. It was amorphous and constantly changing shapes. Joseph found it to be very strange, not to mention the inexplicable feeling it gave him. When he looked at it, negative emotions stirred. He felt a sense of anguish, longing, sadness and despair. Joseph tried to resist, but was drawn in by a sense of pure hopelessness. His existence no longer seemed to hold any meaning. The cycles of life, birth, and enlightenment no longer had meaning. Joseph let go of it all and was drawn in closer to the amorphous mass. As he got closer, he began to feel himself being pulled into its center. Everything went dark. Joseph now felt an overwhelming fear surround him as if he was being drained of his last moments of life; but it went beyond that. Soon he could not feel his body, then he could not remember who he was, and he began to lose all sense of self.

"*Who am I….what am I…where am I…when am I?*" He began to think to himself, but nothing made sense. He no longer had thoughts or a mind or a body. All that was left was a small something that told him he still existed, somehow, though his very essence seemed to be fading. Joseph was fading out of existence, out of space, out of time. He had become something without a past, present, or future. It had all been taken from him, erased. He was becoming less than nothing…he was an insignificant spark surrounded by a vast darkness.

Then he realized the true nature of the darkness. He had not witnessed the loss of himself, but of everything else. The universe was ending and soon to be no more. Even time began to fade from existence. All that remained was a small amount of his essence, and after its depletion, there would be nothing…

CHAPTER 2: QUINN AND ANABEL

Alarms flared as crimson red lights cascaded across the radiant white walls of the information center. The large monitors displayed maps of the various areas around Terraizen. There were blinking red dots pin pointing the locations of individuals who were considered to be of high importance by the leaders of the agency. The technology in the room was years beyond that which existed to the public, and their operators were some of the brightest minds in the world.

"We have a Level 3 incoming from the Northern sector," came a cold, hard male voice from the loud speaker.

The alarms continued to blare loudly throughout the second underground floor of the Terraizen Secret Protection Agency. This level was known as the M-2 unit. It housed the elite minds and intelligence of the TSPA responsible for keeping STAR Island safe and crime free. Agents proceeded casually down the halls. For them, the alarms had become routine. They were accustomed to the loud sirens. There were few places in the building the alarms could not be heard. Those places were the rooms belonging to the leaders of the M-2 division.

There, rooms of the division leaders were sound proof to the emergencies of the agency, and their atmospheres were worlds apart from the noise outside their walls. One of the most secluded rooms belonged to the reserved Quinn Cesar, who was one of the three leaders of the M-2 division.

Quinn sat at his desk reading a King's novel from *The King of Terraizen Series*. Quinn had a luxurious office with high ceilings, gold-lined black curtains, polished hard wood cabinets and shimmering sapphire carpet. The walls were decorated with abstract paintings that held ephemeral images, which seemed to continuously shift every few moments, like a slide show. Overall, Quinn's room would have held a regal decor if not for one piece of furniture, which stood out like a sore thumb.

It was a cheap brown leather sofa, which sat in the corner across the room from Quinn's desk, that threw off the room's regal vibe. It had a partially torn back pillow that was held in place by a few threads that barely clung to the last of their purpose. The couch did not match the comfortable red chairs, brown wood tables, or bookshelves. It held an older feeling amongst the newer, vibrant office furniture. This was Quinn's favorite couch. Upon it, he took his afternoon naps and did all his thinking.

The office was quiet, with only the spinning of the ceiling fan and the turning of the pages keeping the room from falling into a deafening silence. The phone rang. Quinn glanced over at it briefly, and then continued to read. Although there were updated communication systems, Quinn preferred the obsolete old-fashioned ways of communicating. He had no new age embedded communicators or hologram systems, making it challenging for individuals to reach him directly; only those closest to him had his telephone number. The phone rang again. Quinn ignored it once more. The phone continued to ring finally breaking Quinn's concentration. Reluctantly, Quinn placed his silver embroidered bookmark in his book and gently laid it aside before opening up the communications channel.

"Good day Mr. Hanes. How may I be of service to you?"

"Sir, we have a Level 3 incoming from Nefastus Sector-1714," replied Danny over the communications channel.

Quinn sighed, "Yes, I know. I'm on my way."

Quinn stood up, grabbed his jacket from the coat rack and headed swiftly out his office to the elevator. The alarms continued to flare as Quinn entered the elevator. Quinn had not been to Nefastus Forest in weeks. However, as a leader of the organization, a Level 3 prompted his immediate action, no matter his condition. As the elevator headed up to the ground floor, he reviewed the files on the Level 3 through the A.I. system located in the center of the hexagonal-shaped glassy transport elevator. The A.I. system, among its many other duties, was responsible for relaying information to the organization's leaders. Quinn finished reviewing the files in a matter of moments. Despite the organization's advanced information center, not much seemed to be known about this Level 3 except for the fact that his abilities were close range.

Quinn felt the final shift of the elevator as it transported him into the forest and slowed to a smooth stop. It had placed him two sectors away from where the Level 3 would arrive shortly. Although he did not feel like himself, the agency was short staffed and he was on call for the day. Rarely did anything happen on his call days, but he knew the odds were growing against him and now it was time for him to pay up. After all, it was his job to take care of these things properly.

***

Quinn began surveying the area. He had landed just off the road in a brush area among the trees. The narrow dirt pathway ahead of him was closely packed with thick oak trees on both sides. They blocked out most of the evening sunlight. Only a few rays pierced through the thick curtain of trees. A sudden gust of wind swept across the area, ruffling dead leaves and small twigs, causing an eerie feeling of discomfort to settle over Quinn. Large arachnid creatures spun threads, leaping from tree to tree as they headed off to the East attempting to escape what was coming.

Mammon squirrels scurried across the ground through the brush followed by other smaller creatures. This surprised Quinn. These creatures had seen levels of destruction unbeknownst to man and had survived. These were some of the Alpha creatures of the forest, and yet they were fleeing. Although some seemed to resemble animals and insects, no creature in the forest was truly as it appeared. They had evolved into deadly, lethal entities that specialized in various methods of capturing, killing, and devouring their prey. These creatures would never run from a Level 3 threat.

Quinn knew they had seen many before. They had even killed and disposed of some Level 3s in the past. The last time Quinn had seen them run from a disaster happened five years ago when his entire unit encountered a Level 4 threat, which they barely survived. It seemed the problem had escalated. However, turning back was never an option for Quinn; and Quinn never called for backup. Though arrogant, he was one of the most intelligent and respected individuals of the Terraizen Secret Protection Agency, and was known for his ability to find a solution where none seemed to exist. He had no doubts that he would win the battle. Still, he knew if he let his guard down for even a moment, it would guarantee his death.

Quinn sensed something was watching him, but could not see from where. He attempted to read the individual's thoughts, but they were too jumbled, making it difficult to pin point a location for very long. Quinn needed to find a way to get into closer proximity so his abilities would work, yet not get killed in the process. The element of surprise was no longer his and his life would be next to go if he did not find the hidden entity soon.

The wind began to pick up.

Quinn exited the bushes and entered the open path. He knew it was risky, but he needed to force the enemy to expose themselves. Slowly, but vigilantly, he walked down the path. He felt the sharp slash of a blade as it sliced through his right arm. He spun around. There was no one in sight. The wind subsided. Quinn examined his arm. The cut stung briefly, but was not deep enough to draw blood. He continued to look around, trying to pick up on anything, but he still could not see the culprit. Whoever it was, they were fast and armed. Again the wind picked up. This time, Quinn felt a sharp slash on the outsides of both his legs. None of the cuts were deep. Quinn knew they were trying to intimidate him. Due to his condition, Quinn began to feel nauseous, and knew he needed to get back to the elevator. After reviewing his current situation, and taking into account the method at which the individual attacked, Quinn knew now what he was dealing with. This was no Level 3. This was certainly a Level 4, and on the STAR scale this required a unit. He had not prepared for this level of an encounter and was not sure he would come out alive. It was not guaranteed, especially in his current condition; but his moment of doubt passed as quickly as it had come.

The wind howled more ferociously with every passing moment. The trees swayed as the final rays of sunlight began to disappear beyond the horizon. Quinn focused his thoughts one last time. In his mind, he saw something coming towards him in a whirlwind. In his mind's eye, Quinn made out the figure of a man wielding transparent blades that extended from his fore arms. The man was too fast to fight. Quinn knew his only hope was to lock on and immobilize his mind, but it wouldn't be a simple task. As the man approached, Quinn managed to leap out of the way avoiding a direct hit to the chest. His left side was now bleeding. Quinn felt his reaction time had been delayed. The last attack was meant to go directly through his heart. He felt his body slowing down. Immediately, he knew he had been poisoned, and was not sure how much time he had left before the poison left him fully immobilized and unconscious.

Quinn took shelter behind a tree. His body began to go numb and his vision had become blurred. In the distance, Quinn could see a small whirlwind heading up the path behind him as it collected leaves and branches. He wanted to run, but knew his remaining energy was limited. Quinn examined the swirling funnel of wind, and in the center he could make out the image of a man. Quinn had made contact. Based on the man's actions, movement, and brain pattern, he now knew that the man was being controlled. Suddenly, the man vanished and the whirlwind subsided. Branches and leaves began to settle as all became quiet. Quinn sat with his back against the tree. He could no longer detect the man. It was strange, Quinn thought to himself, and way too quiet.

Quinn felt a sharp slash across his face and a blunt blow to the head before falling over. The man had landed right on top of him, with his sharp blade pierced slightly into Quinn's chest. The fight was over.

Quinn had locked on.

Quinn had gained control over the man's mind at the last second, as the sharp blade embedded in his chest rested inches from his heart.

The man let out a hideous roar that echoed through the trees. He had long dreaded hair, his shirt and trousers were a dirty, muddy brown, and he was bare foot. Quinn eased the blade from his chest and his wound slowly began to heal. Quinn rolled over onto his side for a moment then stood up, staring down at the motionless man who he had mind locked into a frozen state.

"Speak," Quinn demanded the man who stood motionless before him.

"Where am I? How did I get here?" thought the man. Quinn had used his mind link to hear the man's thoughts and momentarily disable his aggressive behavior.

"You are in the Forbidden Nefastus Forest. I came here to help you," said Quinn. "I can hear your thoughts. Don't be scared. I had to temporarily disable your movement to prevent any further destruction. All you have to do is think of what you want to tell me and I will hear you. May I ask your name?"

"My name…my name is U-hno. I'm not sure what happened. One moment, I was walking through the orange groves with my son, and the next I am here. My son! Where is my son?" asked the man as his thoughts became frantic once more.

"I'm uncertain of his location. Based on your memories, it seems he may have fallen under the influence of the same contrived force which was controlling you. Before you can return home, I must take you in for questioning and analysis to verify his control over you has been broken. Please come with me. No harm will come to you."

Quinn could see the tears forming in U-hno's eyes.

"I'm more concerned about me hurting you," said U-hno.

Quinn could see the man was staring at his wounds.

"You're no longer a threat. These injuries are of my own doing. They will heal shortly. Now let us return to headquarters. There are matters that require my attention."

Quinn stood up, still numbed by the poison. He used his mind link to see through U-hno's eyes, guiding U-hno and himself back to the elevator. Quinn knew he still had some time before his condition worsened, but he needed to move fast. He stumbled through the forest until he found the clearing where the elevator would emerge.

Once there, he established a link with the A.I., and in seconds, they were on their way back to headquarters.

***

The agency's hospital and infirmary was located on Level B-1 of the agency. While there, Quinn discovered there were traces of Golden Gasp venom in his system. The Golden Gasp was a very rare snake; one bite would leave an individual paralyzed for hours before dying from excruciating pain. If mixed with Wild Nefastus Deathshroom and Blood Root, it formed an incurable, un-healable compound known as *Summa Mortum Triplex*, which brought a quick death, with absolute certainty.

Although the venom of the Golden Gasp was no longer a death sentence, the symptoms could linger for days to weeks, including active abilities. Quinn learned from the physician that the symptoms could remain for up to three weeks who recommended he take temporary medical leave to recover, but he declined. Poison was the least of his worries. There were things that required his attention, and time was of the essence.

Quinn proceeded down the white B-1 corridors to the room of Anabel Matthews. After leaving the infirmary, he learned of Anabel's return from Bruno. Wanting to bid her a good night, and give her a warm welcome before she went off to bed, Quinn headed off to her chambers.

Quinn knocked on Anabel's door.

"One moment," came the soft voice of Anabel from the other side of the door.

The sound of her voice carried through the air, resting gently upon Quinn's ears. It was rejuvenating and caused their childhood memories to come flowing back. There was an innocence and warmth to her voice that could not be put into words. It was kind, like the warmth from the rays of the sun on a cold winter morning.

"It's me, Quinn. I...."

The door swung open, and he was captured within the vice of her arms that wrapped around him. Anabel looked as he remembered. She was around his height, and always wore her long hair rolled up into a bun. He could tell she had spent most of her day in the medical ward, since she had not yet changed out of her uniform, and her stethoscope was pressing deeply into his chest.

"Anabel..."

Quinn was still in pain, and his vision had not cleared completely, but he smiled and pretended to be carefree.

"Sorry, it feels like it's been years since I last saw you," said Anabel.

"It's only been six months. How was your trip?"

Anabel's face lit up.

"It was...fascinating. Come, have a seat. I have much to tell you," said Anabel as she smiled, heading back into her office, gripping Quinn's hand tightly.

They walked through Anabel's office and into her living room. Quinn had not wanted to stay for too long, but once Anabel got started there was no stopping her. She told him about all the incredible people she had encountered and all the wonderful places she had seen. She told him stories of big cities with crowds of people, tall buildings, bright lights and thrilling nights. Anabel also told him about the time she got stranded in a desert, as well as the time she had to find her way out of one of the largest forests in Northern Terraizen; and the strange animals, plants, and insects she encountered along the way.

Although he enjoyed hearing the stories, what he enjoyed most was seeing Anabel happy. Seeing her smile allowed him to forget about his own problems and pain. Quinn became more and more engulfed in her stories with each passing moment. It had been her dream to travel around Terraizen, and now she had begun to fulfill those ambitions. Quinn had wanted to go with her, but he was behind on his cases; especially the Anderson case, whose deadline was approaching rather swiftly.

"I would have loved to go with you but...."

Before he could finish, Anabel grabbed his hands.

"I'll show you," she pulled him over to the couch and they sat down.

She held both of his hands. Sharing memories was something they had done many times before.

They started by gazing into each other's eyes. The next moment, they were flying through the wonderful memories of Anabel's travels. When used in combination, Quinn and Anabel's abilities had the effect of allowing individuals to experience the same past events and sensations as if they had lived it themselves. Quinn saw the bright lights and tall buildings, he saw the amazing art exhibits and strange magnificent creatures of the forest, and he saw the luxury hotel rooms and high-class shopping centers. Astonished, not by his own emotions, but by those of Anabel that were emulated through her mind, Quinn became engulfed in Anabel's memories.

As Anabel, he was now gazing down upon STAR Island on the return trip right before sunrise. It had been a peaceful experience for Anabel, and so it was for Quinn as well, causing some of his memories to emerge. As he became comfortable, Quinn's memories began to surface causing Anabel to see the events from his encounter in the forest with U-hno. Before he could break the link, Anabel had seen the fight.

Anabel broke the link. The excitement had left her face.

"Apologies... I didn't mean for you to see that..."

As the words slipped from Quinn's lips, he began to feel light-headed and fell over onto the couch. The experience had drained more of his energy than he had expected. He felt his body go numb as his eyes began to close and his pulse slowed.

"Anabel…"

"Don't speak," said Anabel, whose facial expression had become serious.

Anabel kneeled at his side next to the couch. Gently, she placed her hands upon the sides of his face and closed her eyes. Quinn felt his body heat up and cool down in swift cycles. It felt strange, one moment it was as if he was freezing, the next he was in a blistering heat; but it was not as painful as it had been in the past. A moment later, Anabel released him and it was over.

Quinn opened his eyes and looked up at Anabel.

"Are you okay Anabel?"

Anabel nodded.

"You didn't have to do that," said Quinn.

Quinn had seen Anabel do this many times before with terminal patients, and it had caused her agonizing pain. He had not wanted to see her go through it again. It was the reason he decided not to tell her. After all, it would only take three weeks for him to recover, and he had been through much worse. Quinn would have rather died than to see her in such pain again. Every time she had done it in the past, he had wished he could take her place. But this time it was different; there were no frowns, no screams, no tears. In that moment, it was as if Anabel knew what Quinn was thinking.

"Yes, my techniques have improved. Thanks to the training sessions with Philosopher Sophia Flux of the East, I have learned the truth about my abilities and their history. I'm surprised she allowed me to hold an audience with her aboard the Magnolia, let alone train me, considering she hasn't allowed anyone else to in years. I'm able to do things I didn't even know were possible. It seems Eleanor and I have much in common," said Anabel.

"How did you just...?"

"Yes, that's exactly what I was getting to next. I fixed it," said Anabel as she stood up and sat next to him on the couch

Quinn wrapped his arms around her. Something had been restored within him. Anabel had done more than just remove the poison; she had healed a much deeper wound. A wound that had eluded the powers of time for so long. Quinn was whole again.

"Of all the things I cherish in this world, you exceed them all. Whatever happens, from this point on, never forget that," said Quinn.

Tears of joy filled her eyes as she thought to herself how good it felt to be home once more, around the ones that she loved; even if her time would soon be cut short.

CHAPTER 3: THE ROAD LESS TRAVELED

"Joe wake up," came a voice from the darkness.

Joseph sprung awake in a cold sweat. He had been having another nightmare. His eyes slowly adjusted to the darkness. There, crouching at his side in the sand was Maria.

"Are you okay?" asked Maria, "You were screaming and we couldn't wake you up."

Maria looked very concerned, and so did Brian, who Joseph could now make out standing behind her.

"Night terrors again?" asked Brian in a calm nonchalant tone.

"Yeah," responded Joseph.

"This is the first time it's happened on the shore though…that's a little strange," said Brian looking over at Joseph.

They had already packed up and were ready to leave.

"I'm fine," said Joseph, "just a bad dream."

"Was this one of those strange council dreams again?" asked Brian.

"No, it was the apocalypse one," said Joseph.

Joseph had grown accustomed to having strange dreams over the years. After a few hours, they all seemed to fade, and he would remember very little of them, if any. Brian and Maria knew about his dreams as well, but they had not happened recently and they thought the dreams had ended. Now they seemed to be back. Maria believed it was because of Joseph losing his father followed by his mother's illness. Brian, on the other hand, believed it was something else.

"Well let's head back to the house. It's getting a little chilly now," said Maria, who was shivering as she wrapped herself in a towel.

"Yes," said Brian "It's also getting late and I'm due for a long nap."

Brian, Maria, and Joseph headed back to the house. Not very long after their return, they were off to bed.

They needed their rest. After all, they had a long day of video games and shopping ahead of them.

Tomorrow was Maria's birthday and she loved to shop. Brian and Joseph wanted to plan a surprise party, even after she persisted they not, but most of their classmates were unavailable and had events planned with their own families. Others had even applied for college and were preparing for their one-way trips to the East.

So they decided to keep it simple for this birthday with just the three of them.

***

After returning from the beach, Joseph slept soundly that night until he was stirred from his sleep early the following morning.

"Hey Joe...Joe...wake up," whispered Brian as he took a seat at the corner of Joseph's bed.

Joseph opened his eyes just enough to look at his alarm clock. It was half past three in the morning.

"What is it Brian?" asked Joseph in a blurred tone as he rolled over trying to fall back to sleep.

"Okay. So here is what I think..." said Brian in a whisper. "I think we should have a jam packed game day. We could start with a movie at the STAR Theater, then go to the arcade, maybe a little shoppin' for some new games, especially that *Birth By Fire* game. It got five stars on Terraizen Gamer Review. Oh! And we need to pick up food. Then we can fix a nice dinner, you can bake the cake, and while you do that I will try out the game to see if it's any good. If you can cover the costs, then we can use my dad's car."

"Sounds like a plan," said Joseph in a sleepy haze "anything else?"

"Yeah, maybe we should visit the museum or zoo or school or something. Maria loves those kind of intellectual activities. Although, personally I think it's a snore fest," said Brian.

"Speaking of snore fests. How about you let me continue mine?" said Joseph, who had pulled the covers over his head and started drifting back to sleep. Joseph pressed his foot against Brian's back and began nudging him off the bed.

"Get out," demanded Joseph, who was more asleep than awake at this point.

"Okay…okay…just wanted to make sure we had a plan," said Brian as he stood up and headed towards the door.

"You guys are terrible at whispering," said Maria, who had heard them from the hallway.

"How long have you been there?" asked Brian surprised.

"One minutes, thirty nine seconds," said Maria.

"Yeah, yeah smarty pants birthday girl. So what do you think?" asked Brian.

"Sounds like fun. We have to see the new Donna Robert's film, *Magnus Mammon vs. The Witches of Esper Creek*."

"That's a chick flick, but since it's your birthday, I'm gonna make an exception this once," said Brian reluctantly.

"You know you want to see it. Remember how much you enjoyed her last film? Piprus Pythius vs. The Witches of Esper Creek!"

"No. I don't recall that… must be your imagination Maria."

"Yeah…yeah...whatever. Goodnight you two," Maria said as she turned away and headed back to her room.

Brian headed out of the room as well. Closing the door behind him.

Joseph began to drift back to sleep. Although his eyes were closed, he felt a slight chill fall over him as if he was being watched from the darkened corner of his room. But he knew that was not possible. After all, Brian and Maria had already left.

CHAPTER 4: BRUNO AND BENJAMIN

His feet pounded against the elevated track of the gym as he raced swiftly around the slight curve. The pressure of the air against his body felt as if he were running through solid walls. This caused his ears to pop rapidly, and he could feel the energy leaving his body. Bruno loved going fast, and hoped to someday break the sound barrier, but his body had its limitations and he knew it. He could already feel his legs becoming noodles as he approached his point of exhaustion. At his current speed, even breathing was a challenge. His leg muscles began to burn, and although his body had undergone years of training, he knew the pain he was beginning to feel confirmed that his physical limitations had been reached. Exhausted and out of breath, Bruno began to slow his pace until he came to a complete stop.

Drenched in sweat, he bent over and began breathing rapidly as he stared at the ground. Sweat poured from his face, forming a puddle in front of his feet. He could barely move, and his vision had become blurry. With what was left of his energy, he managed to carry himself off to the showers. He knew today would be a good day; or so he thought.

Bruno's dream was to become the ultimate fighter. He ran every morning to increase his speed and endurance. When he was not running, he was honing his fighting skills. Bruno was the youngest agent of the TSPA to ever become a commander of special operations, and one of the three leaders of the B-1 division of Central. He had joined the agency only ten years earlier, and through mission after mission, he worked his way up to become one of the B-1 division leaders. The B-1 division leaders were the strongest individuals within TSPA Central. He worked closely with Stephen Langley, an M-2 leader, and Benjamin Alexander, another B-1 leader. Bruno loved the TSPA headquarters. He had his own training room, racetrack, and anything he could possibly ask for was provided to him. His life was nearly perfect except for one thing; and that was his colleague, Benjamin Alexander.

Bruno didn't have any real problems with Benjamin's introverted behavior or personality. However, Bruno found Benjamin very intimidating at times. As a leader, Bruno wanted to be fearless and revered by all, but the one thing that scared him the most was someone right down the hall, someone he worked with every day and he held no ill will towards; Benjamin Alexander. It had gotten to the point where Benjamin did not even need to be in the room. Just the mention of his name gave Bruno goose bumps. Bruno did not know why he feared Benjamin, and if confronted, he would never admit it to anyone. It was as if Benjamin gave off an aura that overwhelmed Bruno whenever he was around. No matter how hard he trained, Bruno felt at times that he would never be able to overcome his irrational fear of Benjamin. But he did not let that stop him. Bruno continued to train day after day.

After his shower, Bruno headed back to the track for a light jog and stretch. Bruno finished his lap around the mile long track, grabbed lunch from his chambers and before he could take a single bite, was greeted by the bright, white rapidly flashing lights of the B-1 unit and a loud voice over the intercom speaker.

"We have a Level 4 incoming from the Southern Sector-1716. B-1 unit please respond," said the cold voice over the intercom.

Bruno knew it was time for another mission. Quickly, Bruno raced back to his chambers. Within a few minutes, he had gotten fully equipped and raced down the white corridors to the elevator. He turned the corner so swiftly that he did not have time to react and collided with, what he now called, Benjamin's Aura. The overwhelming force left him breathless and winded. Bruno felt as if he had just run into a brick wall and began to stumble backwards. He could see ten feet ahead of him was Benjamin. Bruno cleared his mind and proceeded forward at a slow pace. It felt as if he were walking through a thick layer of honey. With every step, he had to force his foot from the ground. But he managed to do it with such tenacity that the agents who passed him by could not tell he was struggling. Soon, his body adjusted, and he was able to walk normally. Bruno approached Benjamin just as they reached the elevator.

Benjamin was very tall and wore a long, black hooded trench coat. Benjamin reminded Bruno of an undertaker and gave him the eerie feeling of death warmed over. From head to toe he was covered in black. Benjamin moved like a shadow and had been given the name the Executioner because of his demeanor, lack of emotion, and the oversized blade that he carried at times. Many agents in the TSPA avoided Benjamin like the plague. Some agents thought Benjamin was deaf because he did not respond to noises and very rarely did he talk.

Bruno attempted to regain his composure. "Hey Benji! Are you headed to the forest to bring in this Level 4 with me?" asked Bruno.

Benjamin did not respond. Just then, the building began to shake violently, causing Bruno to briefly lose his balance. Bruno was caught by surprise and fell towards Benjamin. Quickly, he adjusted himself so that he instead stumbled into the hallway wall. Benjamin, on the other hand, seemed unfazed by the sudden quake as if he walked on the air above the ground.

"What was that?" asked Bruno, as he tried to regain his balance.

The elevator doors opened as they approached, and Bruno and Benjamin stepped in.

"Faith, what the hell was that?" Bruno asked. Faith was the name Bruno had given to the A.I. system. It seemed to have caught on because everyone in the organization now called her Faith as well. At times, Faith appeared in a 3-D holographic form, taking on the figure of a woman.

The ground monitor in the center of the elevator projected a detailed, three-dimensional figure of Faith as the elevator began to move upward.

The quakes continued.

"Hello Bruno," said Faith. "We currently have a Level 4 in the Forbidden Forest, Sector-1716. He has just arrived from the Western Terraizen Sector-714. His name is Trevor Dixon. It seems he has the ability to excite solid matter to their higher vibrational states, causing tremors and earthquakes on a large scale. He is also able to telekinetically absorb and manipulate the energy in rock and clay, giving him the potential to cause large explosions. Currently, he has been responsible for the destruction of the small town of Golith, population 6,720 individuals. There are twenty-two confirmed deaths. You must not give him the time to collect energy, or the results could be disastrous. Be careful."

The monitor turned off, and the elevator door opened to reveal a forest in ruin. The ground trembled more rapidly than ever.

Bruno exited the elevator. He walked as fast as he could in an attempt to get as far away from Benjamin's Aura as soon as possible. Once he was out of Benjamin's Aura, he quickly regained speed and raced through the forest looking for the source of the quakes. Bruno knew the challenges of handling a Level 4, even for an agent of his caliber. However, he knew if he was ever going to overcome the overwhelming power of Benjamin, he would need to challenge himself unlike ever before. Bruno could not think of any better way to gain recognition of his strength than to take on a Level 4 by himself, as Quinn had done the previous day.

Within moments, Bruno found a muscle bound man of average height in the center of, what looked like, a large meteor crater. The trees and the area laid in ruin. Some even seemed to have been snapped in half like twigs. The man was covered in a gray and brown, clay stone armor, with the horns of a bull. Bruno knew without a doubt, it was Trevor.

The beast of a man roared as he toppled trees like a tank, his horns snapping them in half like twigs upon impact. Bruno could not make out what he was saying, but approached Trevor with caution. As he closed in on the target, Bruno could make out the words, "for the queen," rolling continuously from Trevor's lips. Trevor repeated the phrase every time he toppled a tree. The ground continued to shake as the trees fell. Bruno struggled to maintain his balance. He knew he needed to finish this fast and planned to take Trevor down with one hit. Bruno emerged from his hiding spot and approached the edge of the crater area. Trevor lay on the other side, nearly thirty feet away.

"Trevor Dixon! By order of the Terraizen Secret Protection Agency, I am placing you under confinement for twenty-two counts of confirmed murder and this destruction of The Forbidden Nefastus Forest. Please do not resist, or we will be required to use force," said Bruno.

"For the queen, I shall conquer this island! Bow down or be destroyed!" yelled Trevor.

"Fine words. I wonder who you stole them from," said Bruno.

Trevor turned around swiftly and charged towards Bruno like a wild rhino. Bruno attempted to leap out of the way, but the ground below his feet had grown up his legs, encasing them in a clay-like material. Before he could break free, Trevor had leaped over the crater and slammed his curved stone horns into Bruno's chest. Blood shot from Bruno's mouth. He could feel his bones turn to liquid as he was thrown back into a tree stump.

Bruno cried out in agonizing pain as he slid to the ground, blood leaking from his mouth.

"I see why you wear that horned shell. It's to protect that hollow head of yours," said Bruno, every breath feeling like his last. Bruno felt his body failing and his lungs filling with blood. He needed time to recover. He placed his hand over his wounds, and swiftly began to repeat the incantation he had learned from Anabel.

"*Novis vulneribus temporis, Novis vulneribus temporis...*" he repeated the incantation, and as he did, the blood retreated from his lungs and he began to heal.

"I will conquer this island for the queen," said Trevor.

"Wow. A hollow skull and heart of lead, I see the world was not kind to you," said Bruno.

Bruno managed to pull himself to his feet.

He held his ribs in place as he used the last of his energy to retreat into the forest. He knew he needed to come up with a plan. But that was not his specialty. If only Langley or Quinn were here he thought to himself. Although Bruno wanted to show that he could take down a Level 4 on his own, he began to wonder what was holding Benjamin.

Stones blasted through the trees like bullets barely missing the top of Bruno's head as he retreated. He had never taken on a Level 4 alone before, and he did not want to die; not here and not now. He took cover behind a willow tree. Bruno knew if he were going to win this battle he would need help. He no longer cared about proving himself. Now, he only wanted to take down Trevor and make him pay for what he had done.

As Bruno continued to heal himself, while staying low to avoid the storm of boulders flying over his head, he began to feel an overwhelming force. It was Benjamin's Aura, which for once brought him relief. Bruno was content at knowing that the fight would soon be over, and Trevor would soon be getting what he rightfully deserved.

***

Benjamin walked through the forest approaching the epicenter of the quakes. His ability to read the power levels of others was unmatched, and it came naturally to him. Benjamin did things according to his own schedule, and he frankly did not give a damn what others thought.

Although he was considered an agent of the TSPA, he took orders from no one. Nevertheless, Benjamin protected the Forbidden Nefastus Forest, which had become like his second home. Francis had made full use of Benjamin's talents, as well as the forest's secluded location. Whenever a threat arose, Francis ordered it be sent to the forest for "confinement." It was his way of getting Benjamin to handle it.

Benjamin now had Trevor in his sights. He could see Bruno cowering behind a tree, clutching his ribs. It seemed Bruno had been injured in his brawl. Benjamin detached his oversized blade from his back. Using the force of just his aura, he compressed it to the size of a dagger. Benjamin knew it would not require all of his power to eliminate the minor annoyance. For Benjamin to call it a threat would have been an over exaggeration. Just then, Trevor locked eyes with Benjamin.

Trevor's eyes glowed a blood red and he began launching large boulders surrounded by clouds of stones at Benjamin. With ease, he shifted, avoiding the rocks as if they were stationary. Benjamin continued to advance forward. The ground below Benjamin's feet split open, water rushed in, filling the chasm. He leaped into the trees. With cat like reflexes, he balanced on the branches as he moved from branch to branch effortlessly.

Benjamin landed within twenty feet of Trevor. Trevor, who stood at the edge of the crater, charged at him horns first. Benjamin did not move. The stone horns struck Benjamin in the chest and crumbled upon impact. Trevor attempted to move, but it was too late; Benjamin had slid his dagger into Trevor's chest. As Benjamin withdrew the dagger, Trevor looked down. There was no blood or mark on his armor. Benjamin then lifted Trevor into the air and slammed him into the ground, stabbing him again in the chest with the small dagger, all in one flawless motion. The quakes stopped and the clay-stone armor crumbled from Trevor's body.

"What are you?" asked Trevor as a look of fear began to spread across his face.

Trevor's eyes closed slightly, as he faded in and out of consciousness.

Benjamin looked down at Trevor.

"Death," said Benjamin. As he mumbled, the earth quaked in the wake of his tremendous voice.

"It was...for the queen...for the...queen..." said Trevor before passing out.

"We did it!" said Bruno as he approached from behind the tree, still clutching his ribs. Bruno had managed to heal the majority of his internal bleeding.

"You don't have to ask. I'm okay, just a flesh wound," said Bruno in a tender tone as he pretended that Benjamin cared the slightest.

"Glad I was able to soften him up for you. Let's get him back to headquarters," said Bruno in an enthusiastic tone.

Benjamin placed his dagger in his concealed side pocket and headed towards the elevator pick up area.

"Hey! I'm injured. You don't expect me to carry him do you?" asked Bruno. Benjamin did not turn around. Bruno clutched his ribs with one hand and began dragging Trevor to the elevator pick-up area with the other.

"Man, this guy's heavy," said Bruno.

CHAPTER 5: REFLECTIONS OF THE PAST

Joseph, Brian, and Maria started the day by seeing a movie entitled, *Magnus Mammon vs. The Witches of Esper Creek*, directed and produced by Donna Roberts. Normally, Brian wouldn't be caught dead watching a chick flick in public. However, since it was Maria's birthday, he made an exception.

Donna Roberts was notorious for producing some of the best films known to Terraizen. Maria admired all the works of Mrs. Roberts. From her novels to her movies, Maria considered her to be a master of film production and a phenomenal writer. There was not a novel, or film, she had released that Maria did not own. Maria had been waiting for the movie's release for weeks, and now that it was out, she just had to see it.

***

The movie was about three powerful witches who go on a journey to defeat a dark entity that has threatened to destroy the magical forest in which they dwelled. In the book series, there were nine entities they had to face to return peace to their lands. *Magnus Mammon vs. The Witches of Esper Creek* was a movie based on the second novel of the book series.

In the first movie, and novel, the witches destroyed Piprus Pythius after learning that he murdered their mother, then headed off to destroy his brother Magnus Mammon, who had given the order. The level of turmoil portrayed by the movie struck an emotional chord with all of the audience members, including Brian. On top of that, Antabella Belial, who is said to be more powerful than Magnus and Piprus, shows up at the end leaving the movie at a cliffhanger.

At the end of the movie, Maria could see the look of shock and sadness in Brian's eyes, although he tried to conceal it. Though tempted, Maria decided not to point out how emotional he was getting over a movie he said he had not wanted to see. Brian loved to put on a tough guy act, and Maria found it kind of cute at times when he'd stand up for her, although she didn't need it; but mostly annoying the rest of the time. Especially when he refused to ask for help.

After the movies, they stopped by the mall and shopping centers where they picked up food, cake, video games, party decorations, and a few gifts for Maria. During the time at the mall, Brian continued to ask Maria for hints as to what happened next in the book series. Brian hated cliffhangers even more than he hated admitting how much he loved the movie. As much as he insisted upon knowing with his passive questions, Maria refused to tell him, stating if he really wanted to know, he would read the books; which she gladly offered to lend him but he declined.

Before heading back to the house, Brian, Joseph, and Maria spent some time at the arcade.

Normally, it would have been a two-mile walk. However, Brian had borrowed his father's car for Maria's birthday, so they drove back to the house.

When they arrived at the house, after unpacking, they laid across the couch lackadaisically and turned on the television. Although they had picked up a few video games, including the new *Birth by Fire*, they were not in the mood to play them; especially after spending hours at the arcade. In fact, all they really wanted was to sleep. That is, everyone except Maria.

"Oh gosh! You guys, I think if we stay like this I'm going to die of boredom," she said with a sigh.

"We need to get out of the house and do something. Something interesting, something new, something wild!" said Maria excitedly as she looked over at Brian and Joseph, who were dosing off on the sofa and recliner. They fluttered their eyes in a failed attempt to fight the sleep and boredom.

"I'm out of ideas," said Brian, "You come up with an idea and we will do it. Name any place on STAR Island and I will take you there. But until then, I think I'm going to continue my afternoon nap," he said as he laid back in the recliner.

Maria sat next to Joseph on the couch. She began to think back to all the wonderful things STAR Island had to offer. The more she tried to come up with ideas, the more she realized that there was not much she had not already seen. There was the zoo, which she did enjoy going to, although they had not had any new attractions in the past three years. There was also the museum, but Maria had been there so many times that she knew the place better than its curator. The more she thought about it, the more she realized nothing exciting ever seemed to happen on the island anymore.

Maria closed her eyes and thought back to when she was younger. Back then, it was an easy task to find something exciting to do. She remembered how overjoyed she would get just from the simple things, like her mom and dad taking her to the candy shop, movies, beach, and even the family camping trips. Thinking about her child hood had awakened long forgotten memories that she hadn't thought of in ages.

She felt a strange nipping at her ears and nose. A vision of a blue elk, wandering through a lush green forest came to her mind briefly. She remembered it from a book she had read. The forest was calming as the breeze ran through her hair, and sunrays danced across her skin. She could not remember the last time she had been to that forest, but she had a vague memory of visiting it with her parents back when she was younger, before the divorce. It was only two hours away, she thought to herself. That's when she came up with an idea.

"Hey you guys. How about we go to the Northern Forest for a camping trip. Wouldn't that be fun?"

"Are you sure about that?" asked Brian. "The last time we went on a school field trip to the zoo, you complained about the bugs and heat."

"Well, yeah. But that was in the middle of the summer. It was one hundred and ten degrees, and the humidity was awful."

The last thing Brian wanted was to spend a night in the forest. Brian thought back to the last time he had been on a camping trip, a few years back, with his father and Joseph. It was kind of a guy's night out in celebration of Brian's 18th birthday. They had gone to the Southern STAR Forest, which had only been a few miles away. They told ghost stories and roasted hot dogs and marshmallows around the campfire. He enjoyed their camping trips when he was younger, but now the Southern STAR Forest was gone, and in its place stood a warehouse and mall. The only large forest left on STAR Island was the Northern Forest, which was nearly two hours away. Brian did not want to make the two-hour drive. He looked over at Maria. She seemed dead set on going on the camping trip, and it was her birthday after all.

"Come on Brian. We need to get out of this house. We have a whole summer ahead of us to be in the house. Just one night, that's all I ask," Maria begged as she gave him the look, which she always used to get her way.

"Okay! Okay!" said Brian, "Just stop giving me that face."

Maria smiled, "Well then! Let's head out."

Joseph rolled over on the couch, still half asleep, he uttered, "Killer...trees...let's go..."

**

Brian drove down the long, winding road heading to the forest nearly two hours away. Joseph rode in the front passenger seat, and Maria sat in the back seat with the picnic basket. The sky was clear, the sun was shining, and it was the perfect day for a nature hike. Brian was the first to break the silence as they proceeded down the lengthy road.

"Well, I took the car in last week to Flint the mechanic. You know the grungy-looking guy who drives the black truck with the tiger stripes? Well after he inspected the car, he told me the reason it was making that strange sound was the spark plug was misfiring and the catalytic converter back-up fuel cell were broken. I told my dad, and he said it would cost an arm and a leg to fix. Get this? He said I could have it. Can you believe that! He just gave me the car. Then when I went back to the mechanic, you won't believe what happened. Flint repaired the car for free. For free! Maybe it's because I helped him last summer around the shop or maybe it was something I said. I don't know what it was, but he fixed it for free. I felt like the luckiest guy in the world," said Brian with a grin.

"Well Congratulations," said Maria.

"Yeah, well done," said Joseph.

"So Joe. Anything interesting happen in your life lately?" asked Brian.

"No, not really, just the same old things. Although, I have been having some of the weirdest dreams and getting this strange sense of déjà vu more and more lately," said Joseph.

"You know déjà vu is just your mind reprocessing the same event. It's probably just stress," said Maria. "After all, you've been through a lot."

Joseph stared out of the window, gazing at the trees along the road, "Well it's not like that exactly. It seems to be more long term," said Joseph. "It's hard to explain."

"So what exactly do you mean by weird dreams? Like going to school and realizing that you're naked weird, or zombie apocalypse weird?" asked Brian.

"Neither, but closer to zombie apocalypse I guess. I don't remember much, but they always seem to end with everything fading away," said Joseph.

"Wow. That's deep…where are you when all this is happenin'?"

"At the center I think," said Joseph, "but I don't understand why they always seem so vivid and real."

"Maybe it's because now that we're graduating and going our separate ways, you feel like your world is coming to an end. Let's face it, we are all best friends," Maria said with a smile.

Joseph thought about what Maria said.

"Well, you guys are the closest thing I have to family. You were there when I lost my father and when my mother fell ill. I felt like my world was coming to an end…you guys pulled me through it all."

Joseph looked out of the side mirror at Maria who was gazing out of the window. He could tell she had been thinking about their separation as well.

"Maria, you never missed a day bringing me my homework assignments, and Brian you practically lived with me the entire time until I could pull myself together."

Brian laughed.

"That was probably more helpful for me than it was for you."

"Still," said Joseph, "I will never forget everything you guys have done for me."

"Yeah, you're like a brother to me Joe," said Brian. "You guys were there when I lost my mother. Those days were hell for me. I remember all the nights I stayed at your place just so I wouldn't have to deal with my dad's drinking problem. God, I used to hate having to take care of him. I mean, I know it was hard for him losing mom and all, but he put me through so much crap. I was only in the sixth grade and I can't even count the number of times I had to bring him back from the lounge. You guys were there for me the whole time."

Maria sat up, leaning in between the two front seats slightly.

"Do you remember the first time we met? It was in the first grade, back before you even knew who I was. There was one time at lunch, you gave me your apple after you put gum in my hair so I wouldn't tell on you."

Maria looked at Brian with a playful scorn.

"Hey! I was eight. You never forget anything do you?"

"It took the nurse an hour to get that out."

"Yeah, and you didn't talk to me for two weeks. Boy was that Heaven."

Maria punched Brian in the shoulder.

"Hey, I'm driving. I was just kidding," Brian laughed. He loved to annoy Maria at times.

"Although I don't think we started hanging out until right after my parent's divorce," said Maria as she sat back in her seat crossing her legs. "Our lives were such a mess. Yet, somehow, we managed to find each other. If it wasn't for you guys I don't know how I would have gotten through it all."

"And 'The Spot','" said Brian. "We always went there to get away from our problems. Man I love that place. It's always so calming."

Brian, Joseph, and Maria continued to reminisce as they continued down the long winding road.

There were so many random events in their past that led them to meeting each other. Although their lives had not been easy, they had each other when they needed it most. They knew saying goodbye would be difficult.

Just then, they passed the entrance to the zoo. Not too long after, they passed the museum. This confirmed they had reached the halfway point. They were nearly an hour away from the Northern Forest.

Along the way, there was not much of a change in scenery. The road curved through the hills that led to the forest. It was a two-lane road with only three turn off points along the way: the zoo, museum, and the Northern Forest. They had not been to the zoo or museum in years. Neither place had very many visitors because they were located in the middle of nowhere, on a very small island with a small population.

When it came to the forest, very few on the island had reason to go there. It was a two-hour drive down a long tortuous road that cut through the tall trees. The forest was at the end of it all, and not worth the trouble of visiting for most of its natives. The road was not traveled often, and was considered unkempt and slightly dangerous. Along the way, they encountered overgrown bushes and fallen trees blocking parts of the road. However, they did not turn back. For Maria, this provided them with a chance to get out of the house and back to nature. This would be the start of many trips to come.

CHAPTER 6: ELEANOR AND STEPHEN

Eleanor Frederick and Stephen Langley spent most of their days running the information centers, labs and technology divisions on level M-2 of the TSPA. They were responsible for relaying information between the B-1, task forces, M-2, intelligence, and E-3, maintenance units, scheduling meetings, and arranging transportation for TSPA agents. Faith was the A.I. responsible for the highest level of TSPA security, defense, and confinement systems. Never had an awakening individual attempted to attack or infiltrate the TSPA in the many decades of its existence. For those who did not know of their existence, it would be impossible to find them; unless they wanted to be found. For those who did know of their existence, they knew not to challenge the power of the TSPA. However, there had been two Level 4 attacks close to their headquarters in the past two days. This worried the TSPA unit leaders and commanders since they were only use to dealing with Level 4 individuals once every few years.

Whenever a dangerous individual or rogue awakening occurred, the TSPA agents around the world were responsible for sending those individuals to the Nefastus Forest, located in an alternate realm. It's the gateway that lay between TSPA Central headquarters on STAR Island and the Northern Forest.

There were five main branches of the TSPA, the Northern, Southern, Eastern, Western and Central sectors. Out of the TSPA locations, the Central location was the most hidden and isolated. Eleanor, Stephen, and Quinn were the minds of the Central agency and were responsible for using their abilities to make sure it stayed that way. Knowledge between the branches was restrictive. Each branches defensive strategies, agent abilities, and exact headquarters locations of other sectors were on a need to know basis. The minds of Central acted as a hub between the branches.

Today Eleanor had painfully watched as Quinn fought against U-hno, a level 4 awakened, in the Nefastus Forest. She knew she was not allowed to leave her active station at that time, but she wished she could have been there with him; or at least called in for back up. However, all of the other agents were on missions of their own, and lately their resources had been stretched thin with the handling of increased awakenings. Though he had a strange sense of humor, Eleanor admired Quinn; not only for his brilliance, but also for his kind and caring personality. She had seen him heal sick and broken minds and lead his fellow agents onto high-risk missions, returning without a single fatality. Eleanor considered him a master tactician, only second to the Great Tactician of West Terraizen. She noticed how well he was able to create flaws as a part of his strategies, luring people into a false sense of security while staying two steps ahead of them. With Quinn, the flaws you saw were only those he created for you. Eleanor knew these tricks, for she used them herself. No one in the Central agency stood on his level when it came to strategy. That is, no one except Eleanor.

During the fight she had no doubts as to his success. Even on his worst of days, he could take down a Level 3 with a single thought. On top of that, Faith's encounter analysis gave a success rate of 98% against U-hno, and Faith's analysis were based on massive compilation of data and statistical analysis.

Eleanor was once considered the most powerful empath of Central, until Francis sealed her abilities. This was not because she did not know how to use them, but because they were considered too dangerous; if for even a moment her control slipped, she could destroy entire populations. This was the reason the South, whose power was second to none, had marked her. They wanted to break her through forms of torture that no Awakened could withstand, and use her to control Terraizen. Each sector had a high level of autonomy, and the south had used methods that were questionable in the past. Francis was able to keep them in check with the backing of the other branches.

***

Stephen Langley was a part of the intelligence unit and security division of the TSPA. He worked closely with Faith and admired the agency for trying to maintain order in the world. The TSPA was responsible for stopping awakening individuals from being discovered by the general public and preventing them from killing innocents. Stephen's unit was responsible for making sure that innocents were unaware of both the agency and the awakened. The Awakened accounted for one millionth of the total population on the Planet of Terraizen. When an individual began the process of awakening, they were sent to the TSPA for analysis. If their abilities were deemed controllable, they were taught how to use them. This included learning the rules of being an Awakened, how to conceal their abilities from innocents, and how to channel the magic inherent in their powers...

Once Awakened, an individual became able to use some elementary spells. Depending on their abilities and training results, some were offered positions within the TSPA. The TSPA accounted for nearly three-fourths of all the Awakened individuals in the world. The remaining twenty-five percent either lived among the civilians peacefully, or were part of the cipher criminal groups wanted by the TSPA.

Although Stephen enjoyed his job of protecting the innocent, he hated being cramped up in his office for days on end. On occasions, he was given field missions, especially when it came to rebuilding after natural or Awakened disasters. When Stephen was not working, he liked to go out for walks on the island. Sometimes, he would go to the park and movies with Anabel. In Stephen's eyes, Anabel was as close to perfect as you could get. She was also great company in and outside of the office. Every now and then, she would stop by the STAR Island hospital and help tend to the sick and mend the wounded. Watching her work was incredible. The way she connected with her patients on an emotional level and eased their pain was astonishing to him. He would watch as she healed and read to sick children, and listened to elderly adults who just wanted someone to talk to. He admired her patience and warm personality, for those were two of the things he always seemed to lack. It was only in her presence that he had the slightest understanding of what they truly were. The gentle approach she took to each person's treatment and personal situation baffled him.

Stephen had not seen Anabel in over five months and was glad that she would be returning today. He had planned to take her to the park for a walk and possibly out for dinner, if she had not already begun her volunteer work at the local hospital. He did not know if it would be the same. Now that she had seen the world, going to the park seemed so small in comparison, but he knew Anabel would enjoy it; she always enjoyed the little things that life had to offer.

Stephen had tried to find new ways to surprise her as a token of appreciation for her work at the hospitals. They all knew the toll her abilities took on her body. Whenever he would plan something big for her, it would be the simplest things that would make her smile. He remembered the time he took her and a few of the recovering children from the hospital, at her request, to the STAR Island summer festival. They rode the Ferris wheel, played at a few of the carnival events, and watched the fireworks under the moonlight. It had been a wonderful day, but the thing that seemed to amaze her the most as they laid in the clearing of the tall grass looking up at the fireworks, was watching the children trying to catch the fireflies.

The fireflies fluttered around Anabel as the children ran in and out of the grass trying to catch them. One landed on Stephen's nose and began to glow. No sooner had it landed, did the little hands of one of the children reach out towards Stephen's face attempting to catch it. He stumbled and fell on top of Stephen, his little hands pressed against Stephens's nose. Anabel let out an unrestrained laugh at the sight of Stephen catching the child in an almost hug-like position. Her laughter attracted the fireflies, which seemed to circle around them as they lay in the grass. It was such a surreal moment. He attempted to wave away the fireflies while standing up the toddler. Everything changed a few weeks after that night, when they all learned of Joshua's death from their leader Judge Francis IV. He had been dead for over a week before they found out.

Joshua was one of their fellow agents and a member of the E-3 division of Central charged with maintenance. He had been like a brother to them. After hearing of Joshua's death Anabel and Quinn became reclusive from the other agents. To give them some time to mourn, Francis, leader of Central TSPA, forced them both to take six months off to do whatever they needed to find closure. Anabel had chosen to travel the world healing those with a terminal diagnosis and learning to grow her abilities. Quinn began researching the history of Terraizen and attempting to recover the lost information of the mysterious A.I. system.

Today was the first day in six months that all the head members of TSPA Central would be meeting. Eleanor and Stephen were excited to see Quinn and Anabel, but knew this day would be hard. It was the first time they would be seeing each other since the loss of Joshua, Central's youngest E-3 Leader.

CHAPTER 7: THE NEFASTUS FOREST

Maria, Brian, and Joseph arrived at the entrance to the Northern Forest. The trees were a lush green and there were many colorful rose bushes surrounding the entrance pathway. Maria vaguely remembered the area.

She grabbed the picnic basket from the back seat. Brian and Joseph grabbed the camping supplies from the trunk of the car, and together they headed down the rocky pathway.

Maria had forgotten how beautiful the forest was. The smell of the sweetly scented flowers filled the air as a gentle breeze drifted by. At first glance, Brian found it to be quite pleasant and visually appealing and became lost in the almost surreal-like sights that lay before him. The tall trees and bushes ran along both sides of the rocky path that lead through the forest, as if arranged by a gardener. He had forgotten how much he had not wanted to go, and began to embrace the wonderful scenery.

"Isn't it beautiful?" said Maria.

Large red and black birds flew over the trees as a small, black rabbit hopped across the grassy path and into a rose bush on the other side of the main road.

"Yeah, seems kind of surreal. It's like staring into that fairy tale forest from Esper Creek," said Joseph.

"Probably because it was shot here," said Maria.

"I forgot about that," said Brian.

They continued down the path, deeper into the forest, before coming to a stop at an extraordinary sight.

"Are you guys seeing what I'm seeing right now?" asked Brian, as he pointed to the strange creature that blocked their path.

"I think I'm having déjà vu…" said Joseph.

There on the rocky path in front of them stood a blue and white elk. Its antlers seemed to give off a luminescent blue light. It stared at them briefly before turning and heading back into the forest. As it walked off, it left a luminescent trail of footsteps.

"That's freaking awesome!" said Brian as he ran towards the glowing footprints as they faded.

"Far-out…I feel like we just ate too many angshroom and I'm tripping heavy right now," said Brian with a wide-eyed look.

As they continued down the path they encountered several exotic, unusual looking animals hiding in brightly colored, alluring bushes, and trees that seemed to glow as they walked by. It reminded Joseph of the streetlights coming on at night. It was as if the trees could detect their presence. Each sight was more fascinating than the next.

"How does a bizarre place like this even exist? If you guys weren't here, I would swear I was imagining things. I don't even want to leave this place now," Brian said in an airy tone.

"I could just stay here wandering around for a life time and still be amazed by the thing hiding behind the next tree. I wonder if this is what the East is like."

Glancing over around the laurels, Maria noticed a family of baby rabbits huddled together in a strange fluffy white mass. Her heart melted.

"Awe…they're so cute, look at this family of Albino Rabbits," Maria whispered.

Startled by a gentle breeze, they scurried away into the forest brush, vanishing behind the trees.

Maria looked up at the golden fruit hanging from captivating trees with yellow leaves. The colors of the leaves shifted randomly in a kaleidoscope pattern, which made her feel a bit woozy.

Just then, white flakes began to rain down from the trees overhead. The road had become narrow, and up ahead they could see a slight clearing.

"What is this stuff?" asked Brian.

"No clue, but it's not snow," said Maria as she inspected it between her fingers. It felt kind of sticky. "We should get into the clearing up ahead. I don't know what this stuff is, and I don't want it on me."

"Yeah, you're right," said Joseph, who had been brushing it off of his clothing and out of his hair as he hurried ahead. As they approached the clearing, the sun seemed to shine through the thick trees as if it knew they were approaching the area.

Suddenly, Joseph felt a sharp pain shoot through his head and fell to his knees. He became overwhelmed with a sense of panic, and he could feel his heart rapidly beating through his chest. As he struggled to keep himself upright, he became very dizzy and disoriented.

"You guys... something's not right."

"Are you all right Joe?" Maria asked as she rushed to his side.

"No..."

No sooner had he uttered the words, the clouds began to gather in the sky. Brian looked over at Joseph and Maria.

"Hey you guys, let's go back to the car, I think I forgot my ummm...sun glasses. Yes, sunglasses."

The clouds gathered quickly, causing the sky to grow darker, with the luminescence of the trees providing only a dim light. Joseph was unable to see directly in front of him.

"Maria...Brian...are you there?"

The words echoed through the darkness. There was no response. Joseph's eyes began to adjust to his surroundings. He could partially make out the area around the glowing trees.

"Where are you guys?" asked Joseph as the plants began to glow brighter.

Thunder shook the ground as lightning flashed overhead. In that flash, the once beautiful forest had turned to fire and ash. The grass and trees were dead and black, as if charred by flames. Joseph could see the endless darkness that lay ahead. There in the darkness, was but a single light, the light of the blue elk. Joseph stared at the elk as it glowed its brilliant blue light.

"Don't turn around," said the elk, "don't look back."

"What do you mean?" asked Joseph.

"It's coming. You must stop it," said the elk. The elk then turned and began to run away into the darkness. As it did, the glow faded. "Don't turn around, move forward," said the elk as it ran into the distance, leaving a fading trail of light in its wake.

"Wait. Don't go. Stop what? What am I supposed to stop?" asked Joseph.

Joseph felt the presence of something behind him. He wanted to turn around, but the elk had told him not to. Yet, he did not see Brian or Maria. Joseph felt something on his shoulder.

Maybe it was the hand of Brian or Maria, he thought to himself, or maybe it was something else. Joseph became overwhelmed by his own curiosity. Slowly, he turned to see what was on his shoulder; but there was nothing there.

What is this presence, he asked himself. He wanted to know what had been behind him, what had touched him, and what it was the blue elk did not want him to know. The curiosity and fear was too much for him. He turned around.

There was no one there.

Brian and Maria lay unresponsive on the ground.

"I'm already here. I told you not to turn around," said a voice from behind him.

As Joseph turned around to see its source, he stood eye to eye with a nightmarish black elk. Joseph fell to his knees at the sight of it. Its eyes seemed to consume his very existence. He remembered this feeling, but could not remember from where.

"Give up," said the nightmare elk.

"You don't scare me!" said Joseph, "I know what you are," Joseph began to rock back and forth.

"If you know what I am, then you know I speak only the truth. We have already won," said the nightmarish elk as it opened its mouth to reveal an abyss of never ending nothingness.

Joseph felt his existence being drained from the very world around him, the feeling felt so familiar. He remembered now. "Yes," Joseph thought to himself, "this is nothing but a dream." Joseph closed his eyes tightly and then opened them again.

Joseph sprung awake and surveyed the area. The grass was green and the forest was still as breathtaking as it had been before he had fallen asleep. He lay in the clearing and was covered in vines and white powder. He didn't remember falling asleep and had no clue as to how long he had been asleep.

He could make out the faces of Brian and Maria. They were covered in the same vines and white powder. Joseph attempted to sit up, but the vines restricted his movement. It was then he realized that he could not feel his legs.

"Brian! Maria! Wake up!" he screamed, but there was no response.

Joseph tried to break through the vines, but the more he struggled the tighter they seemed to become. The vines seemed to move and constrict his body in a snake-like grip.

"Help!" screamed Joseph. "Someone help us!"

The more he screamed, the tighter they became. Soon it became hard for him to breathe as he felt their crushing force against his rib cage. What little freedom he had left had been taken from him. He thought about all the events that had led up to this moment and all the possibilities that could have changed the outcome. So many 'ifs' flooded through his head. But they were no help to him.

Joseph began to close his eyes. He had always secretly imagined himself doing great things in the world, although he would never admit it. He did not want to die. Not here, not now. He knew everyone had to die at some point, but what bothered him the most, was dying before he had the chance to make something of his life. At that moment, he made a promise to himself that if he survived, he would no longer take his life for granted. He would make the most of each day if the forces of the universe saw it fit to give him another chance.

The sky began to darken, turning a deep black just as it had in his dreams. Thunder crashed and there was a sudden down pour. Joseph's mouth began to fill with water. He coughed it up using the last of his breath. If he was going to die, he thought to himself, it would not be by drowning in a few inches of water. At least he could keep some of his dignity, he thought, as he turned his head to the side.

"*Valeo!*" screamed a voice in the distance.

Joseph felt a sudden release as the vines vanished from his body. He quickly began to gasp for air. His vision was blurry and he was very light-headed as he fought to maintain consciousness.

He looked down towards his legs.

Joseph could see the fracture in his leg as the bone protruded out through his skin. He could not feel the pain, but the sight of it made him lose consciousness.

He heard voices in the distance.

"Are these the three?"

"Yes. Please take care of them."

"Yes Ms. Marmota."

There was a sudden gust of wind and all went silent.

CHAPTER 8: FAITH AND FRANCIS

The court date for U-hno and Trevor had finally arrived. There were five main divisions that were present during trials: the Espers, Engineers, B-1, M-2, and E-3 leaders. The leaders of the groups headed the analysis for different parts of each case. The Engineers were the authority on technology, ancient artifacts, and all things material-based. When it came to analysis of those types of evidence, they were the go to guys. The jury was composed of the B-1 division leaders: Anabel Matthews, Benjamin Alexander, and Bruno Jordan, and M-2 division leaders: Eleanor Fredrick, Quinn Cesar, and Stephen Langley. Their abilities allowed them to analyze the bodies and minds of nearly anyone. Through a set of extensive tests, and the votes from all five TSPA branches, it was decided that they were the most suited for determining the innocence of any individual within TSPA custody. Though not as active, the E-3 leaders were capable of running essence analysis on individuals to help determine their abilities when the B-1 and M-2 leaders could not. They were also responsible for compiling the information obtained from the B-1 and M-2 divisions for the trials. Normally, these duties all fell to the A.I., Faith. However, the B-1 and M-2 leaders were the authority on all things Awakened, and the Espers were the authority on all things magical.

The courtroom filled quickly. The division leaders took their seats in the front of the room next to the judge's bench. As they did, the Engineers and Espers took their seats in the audience.

To the right of the judge's bench, in the center of the room, stood the A.I. Faith, who had taken on her 3-D techno-blue form. Faith handled history and file storage on all things natural or Awakened. She had a nearly unlimited memory, and could answer almost any question asked with an accuracy rating of 99.99%. When it came to finding answers, Faith was unmatched. Yet, the TSPA was limited as to what they could acquire from the A.I. due to the entity that controlled it. Although Faith was not under the control of the TSPA, she shared somewhat of a symbiotic relationship with the organization.

"Please stand," said Faith, "As Judge Francis the IV is now entering the court room."

From the chambers of the courthouse came Judge Francis. He was tall, had a long grey beard and hair to match. As he entered the courtroom, all conversations came to a grinding halt. The room echoed with every one of his footsteps as he approached his chair. Francis took his seat.

"You may now take your seats," said Faith.

Everyone took his or her seats.

"First case, U-hno of New Clamore, Northern Terraizen, charged with three counts of attempted murder: Taiza Scarlet, Jebidia and Tukko and destruction of property. Please enter the court room," said Faith.

U-hno entered the courtroom conveyed by a holding cell. The cell consisted of an array of focused beams of light between two hexagon-shaped structures forming a cage. U-hno seemed to be in tears. He sat in a chair within the blue cage, his eyes were blood shot red and the tracks of his tears could still be seen going down the sides of his cheeks.

Francis looked over at the B-1 and M-2 divisions.

"Have you completed a thorough analysis of U-hno?" he asked in a deep, raspy tone.

"We analyzed the memories pertaining to his rampage and potential causes of his devious actions. We took great care as not to disrupt his natural memory and brain patterns, and were successful in our duplication of the information. Those memories were then transferred to Faith for translation and configuration into a visually comprehensive form."

Francis looked over at Faith.

"Display the information you have assimilated."

The monitor began to display the moments from U-hno's day for the court to see. Faith narrated the images:

"At sunrise, U-hno and a young boy traveled to their local orchard to harvest fruit. While harvesting fruit, they encountered a strange man playing a flute within the dark bushes of the orchard. The power level of the entity was greater than that of a Level 4, and upon hearing the sound of the flute, U-hno lost consciousness. Once he regained consciousness, he went on a rampage. The change in his brain patterns show from that moment on his mind was under the control of the flute-playing entity. The actions that followed and the destruction that followed were not his own. The acts that followed included the destruction of the orchard, two New Clamore housing facilities, Nefastus property, and the attack against a TSPA agent. It was noted that upon encounter Agent Quinn Cesar, U-hno was able, for brief moments, to regain control of his body and avoid lethally striking Quinn several times before Quinn was fully able to lock onto him."

U-hno began to sob uncontrollably. He pounded his fists against his holding chamber letting out loud screams of agonizing pain. He would have rather died than live knowing that it was his body that had been used to do such deeds. He was no ones tool. As a Level 4 Awakened, he had not thought it was possible for him to succumb to anyone's control. Now that he had, he felt weak and he wanted revenge. His sadness turned to rage.

"Who did this to me?" shouted U-hno, "Tell me!"

Faith approached U-hno.

"We believe it to be the work of The Cursed Jinn," said Faith

There was an outburst of conversations among the audience. A look of worry spread across their faces. Even U-hno stared in shock at Faith's words. He had not expected her response.

"A Jinn…that can't be…how certain are you?"

"With current data, I am 98.79% certain that you were being controlled by a cursed item owned by the Jinn, and recommend that its user be brought in for analysis and questioning."

Bruno sprung from his seat.

"We can't capture a Jinn. Let alone question it."

"Quiet…" said Judge Francis in his low, raspy tone that seemed to suck the very air from the room.

The room became deafeningly silent.

"Agent Langley, what has the jury decided?"

Stephen stood, "We the jury, find U-hno not guilty, and request the capture of the individual who forced him to commit these actions."

"Faith, I'm giving my authorization for a complete mental and physical evaluation of U-hno before we allow his release," said Judge Francis the IV.

Bruno stood up.

"Sir, may I…"

Before he could finish his sentence, Francis locked eyes with him for a brief second. In that moment, all fears Bruno had were replaced by the singular fear of Francis's gaze. It was a gaze that made his heart stop and turned his hair gray. It was a cold gaze that gave even his goose bumps goose bumps, causing him to slowly ease down into his chair hoping to shrink out of existence.

U-hno's chamber exited the courtroom.

Francis turned to Faith.

"Proceed…"

Trevor entered the courtroom in a conservation cell. It was designed the same way as U-hno's, but the walls were thicker and he was only slightly conscious.

"Assimilate your findings," said Judge Francis.

The monitor displayed the moments from Trevor's day.

The screen was black and foggy with images coming in and out of view, but unable to be made out clearly.

Faith began to speak.

"Trevor is a servant of a woman who calls herself The Banshee Queen. Trevor was sent by her to destroy TSPAs Central's headquarters. It is unknown how she gained knowledge of the location of Central TSPA. However, it is believed that her true plan is to gain control over The Cursed Jinn. It is also unknown if Trevor was under the control of the Banshee Queen, or if he was acting under his own free will, due to the memory locks that have been put in place. Breaking those locks could lead to the destruction of his mind, and so an attempt was not made. Further analysis is needed to determine his true role.

Under Code 347-1, we request the immediate arrest of The Banshee Queen for the use of forbidden magic and violation of the Power Act 2742 established 242 A.T."

"Very well then. I am ordering Trevor Dixon remain in our custody until the mind locks can be broken," said Judge Francis the IV.

As Trevor's chamber exited the courtroom, he began to mumble something under his breath. "In three days... she shall reclaim what is rightfully hers."

The door closed behind him.

"This concludes the final trial for the evening. Please stand and exit the court room," said Faith.

Faith's image faded. Francis was the first to leave the room. In minutes, the room was empty and the lights went out. All was quiet, except for the slight creaking of the room's floorboards. A sinister presence lurked in the darkness.

CHAPTER 9: MOONLIGHT VISITOR

Joseph opened his eyes to a white ceiling. His vision was still foggy, but he could smell the scent of rubbing alcohol and disinfectant. It was a smell he knew all too well. As he lay in, what looked to him, like a hospital bed, he examined the white sheets. As he stared at them, his vision began to clear. In the front of the room, he began to make out a television, and although the curtains were drawn closed, he could tell it was nighttime. He rubbed his eyes slightly and his vision continued to clear.

Joseph could not remember how he had gotten where he now laid. His memory was fuzzy. As he contemplated what had happened to him, he got the feeling that he was being watched. From the far side of the room, he heard a creaking that reminded him of his porch steps.

Startled by the noise, Joseph swiftly turned and began examining the image in the corner of his room. There, in the corner, sat a short older woman who seemed to be reading a leather-bound book by the dimly lit nightstand. There was an empty bed between him and the woman. He could have sworn he had not seen her before, and the lamplight had for sure been off; but then again, he felt as if he had just woken up from a long dream and his mind was still catching up with reality.

"*Me alegra que estes despierto*," said the woman in a slight accent.

The woman glanced over at Joseph looking over her spectacles.

"Sorry, I meant to say I am glad you're awake. Language is such a tricky thing."

The woman had an earthly tone to her voice. Her face seemed to hold a kind, but absent-minded expression. She wore a deep purple gown with a black shawl. Her hair was brown and tattered with streaks of white that hung down to her shoulders. Her face was etched in wrinkles and looked lived-in. There was something intriguing and humbling about her.

"Where am I? Brian and Maria, where are they?" asked Joseph. As he spoke, Joseph examined his body. There was a mark on his arm from where blood had been drawn and he felt very weak. Joseph lifted the white covers up to examine his torso and legs. Although he could see his legs, he could not move them.

"*Niño*, you're safe and still healing. Calm yourself," said the woman.

"What happened out there?" asked Joseph.

"Patience my dear. All will be explained later. Right now, you need to focus on recovering."

Joseph attempted to move his legs. It was then that he realized, he could hardly feel them.

"What's wrong with my legs?"

"The Forbidden Forest is a dangerous place. I'm glad we found you...you'd be food if we'd arrived a few seconds later. Now don't worry about your legs, they're healing up. Lay back down."

Joseph began to lay back and relax. The woman's voice was relaxing.

"We have the best doctors. But some things take time to heal. You're still weak child, and need to relax. It'll be a few more hours before you can fully move," said the woman.

"What attacked me?" asked Joseph.

"The forest you entered is known as The Forbidden Nefastus Forest. It's filled with many unspeakable things, not many wanderers return from that place. My sisters and I placed a veil between it and the Northern Forest to protect Terraizen. Only the Awakened can enter now. The Forbidden Forest is vast. We know very little about the entities that reside in its dark recesses. It's another realm. It wanted your lives...I'm surprised you're not dead. You were among the fortunate who were found."

For a moment, the woman looked up from her book and glanced out the dark window as if recalling a memory that had been etched into the stars. Joseph could tell she had begun reminiscing about her days in the forest.

"In that forest, nothing is as it seems, the more beautiful the more deadly. I remember the first time I laid eyes on it, I thought it was one of the most beautiful things I had ever seen. That is… until it tried to kill me. Those were the days…"

Joseph watched as she fought back the tears. He knew that expression so very well. He himself had experienced it at a young age. He could see the loss in her eyes. Although the wounds may have healed, the scars still remained. Just looking at her made him remember his losses too. Joseph knew he needed to change the topic.

"What's your name?" asked Joseph.

The woman snapped out of her stargazing.

"I've gone by many names," said the woman, "but most people seem to call me Senior Elvia now. I think that's the one that's stuck the most over the last fifty years."

"How long have I been out?"

"Slightly more than a day I suppose."

Joseph's vision had finally cleared. At a closer glance, he began to recognize her familiar face. Although she looked older, her face still held the same structure as the woman he had seen on film earlier.

"Did you play Tabitha in that one movie?" asked Joseph.

"Well, I dabbled in acting during my younger years, but teaching was always my true passion. Although my husband used to say I just loved teaching because I loved to talk," Senior Elvia smiled.

"Now my older sister, she...she was a born actress. Talented, gorgeous, and a great sense of style. I doubt there was anything she couldn't do, but as you know, all good things must come to an end. Kassie, my younger sister, reminds me of her sometimes. You'll have to meet Kassie, she has such a pure soul...so energetic and youthful. Reminds me of my younger days before I joined the organization. The stories I could tell you..."

"What's the organization?" asked Joseph.

"Oh goodness, there I go again, me and my big mouth. You know it's hard to find a good listener in this place. Everyone's always so busy these days."

The woman continued to read from her leather bound book.

Joseph thought back to the details prior to their rescue. He recalled bits and pieces of what had happened as he stared up at the ceiling.

"Who's 'Valeo'?" Joseph asked, looking over at Senior Elvia.

"Oh child, Valeo's no who, it's a what, used for getting rid of unwanted pests. In your case, it's what saved your life."

"What do you mean?"

Joseph seemed a bit surprised by her strange way of answering. Nothing seemed to rattle the woman.

There was a brief moment of silence. Joseph began to realize the possibility that the woman who sat in the corner of his room could be a nut from down the hall, maybe a lost mental patient who was able to wander in due to short staffing. But even so, she seemed harmless and maybe just wanted someone to talk to. Joseph began to let his mind wonder about where he was and what lay on the other side of the door. He thought back to the strange reoccurring dreams he had been having. Maybe, he thought to himself, maybe I finally cracked, maybe everything was just a dream, maybe everything he had been through in the past few hours had just been part of one of his nightmares. But he recalled the experience, and he realized there was no way his injuries were fake. The pain was real. So some part of his experience had been real. After all, he could see the marks on his legs from the vines.

Although Joseph hated to admit it, his dreams were becoming harder and harder to tell from reality. The dreams had grown more vivid overtime; pain was the only distinguishing factor between his dreams and reality.

The silence was broken by the woman's voice.

"Well, I enjoyed our conversations, but I best take my leave now. My sisters are calling."

The leather bound book vanished from Senior Elvia's hands as she stood up. She snapped her fingers and the lamplight went out.

The room became dark.

Joseph stared over into the corner where the woman had been standing. He could not make out her figure through the darkness. All that remained was the pale moonlight glow of her eyes, which stared into Joseph as she spoke.

"Sleep well child. *Sopor!*"

As the words left her mouth, the eyes vanished.

Before he could speak, Joseph collapsed onto the bed immediately falling into a deep sleep. The room was quiet. As

Joseph slept, he dreamed of lying on the moonlit beach with Maria and Brian, listening to the waves of the ocean.

CHAPTER 10: CENTRAL- THE GATHERING

The leaders of the TSPA headed to their round table faculty meeting. It had been a long day for all of them and was sure to be an even longer night. Within the room, the A.I. sat at the far end of the table directly opposite the head seat. Although it was genderless, it took on the form of a woman with a techno blue color. It browsed through countless files as the leaders took their place in the room.

Eleanor was first to enter the room, and when she entered a room, people noticed. Her long, glimmering red hair flowed down her soft skin, complemented by her shadowy eyes; and her walk was as flawless as it was elegant. Every moment, every motion, was picture perfect as she moved around the table. As she approached her seat, she tossed her hair to the side glancing towards the door as Anthony entered. The pleasant expression on her face was quickly replaced with one of quiet anger. Her gaze stopped Anthony dead in his tracks.

"Anthony!"

Her hair seemed to flare like the kindling of a flame while she stared at him.

No one looked over at Anthony. Stephen and Bruno simply filed in around him avoiding eye contact with either of them and took their seats while Anthony stood frozen in Eleanor's gaze.

"Anthony your attire is inappropriate. Would you mind putting some clothes on?" asked Eleanor in a demanding tone.

"My…my apologies," said Anthony, stumbling over his words, "I just returned from the Zone."

Anthony waved his hand and his clothing materialized. He now wore a black and white tuxedo with a bow tie.

"Better?" asked Anthony.

"Thank you," said Eleanor, "that is somewhat more appropriate."

Anthony had no need for clothing while in The Zone. He personally did not see why clothing was so necessary. He thought it to be even more restraining to an already limited physical body. After all, he had no need for form, let alone clothing to fit such a limited form. Still, it pleased Eleanor, so he obliged her request.

Quinn and Anabel entered the room followed by Benjamin and took their seats around the conference table. Francis entered from the side door and took his seat at the helm of the table, directly across from the A.I.

Anthony looked around the room.

"Shall we wait for Joshua? He's always late. I haven't seen him in The Zone for quite some time now. It's been nearly six….seven months….then again, perception of time has never been one of my strong suits."

Anthony smiled as he adjusted his bowtie. The smirk on his face made him look a bit comical. Although Anthony seemed lighthearted, the atmosphere had become heavy and silent.

"Joshua won't be joining us today," said Anabel. Although her voice had an aesthetic quality, the words carried a cold chill through the room, drawing Quinn's attention away from his personal digital assistant.

Anthony's eyes rose in surprise. He seemed shocked by the news. He had been in The Zone for the past seven months and had no idea what had happened in the world. Team meetings were his only source of information on world events.

Faith began to speak as Francis took his seat at the helm of the table.

"I completed the upgrades to the tracking systems and raised Central's defenses to their maximum security level. Mother A.I. has granted permission for the awakening of our A.I. bio-systems, and has temporarily restricted access to Level C-4." Although powerful, Faith was limited as to what it could do due to the restrictions placed upon it by the Mother A.I., which it drew its powers from.

Francis began to speak in his raspy tone.

"Thank you. Now let us turn our attention to the task at hand."

His face was stern and serious as the A.I. began to speak.

"There has been a drastic increase in awakenings recently. Our records show that there is a direct correlation between these awakenings and the recent change in the geological position of the

Southern Isle. The bio-systems have confirmed that, as of the 19ᵗʰ hour, the Cursed Maestro Jinn was seen in the northern sector of the Nefastus Forest only 175,000 kilometers from Central's gateway. Its arrival is estimated at five days, thirteen hours. I have taken all allowed precautions to close off the gateway located in the Northern Forest. However, the success rate of the Jinn's containment is estimated at 43%. We have yet to discover how the Jinn managed to enter the Nefastus Forest but it is likely that Nefastus may have another entrance we have yet to discover, accessible by Banshee."

Stephen looked over at Eleanor

"Well, this is going to be a long night."

Eleanor let out a sigh.

"I grow weary of hearing that."

***

"Clearly, we are dealing with a cursed item. The question is, how do we contain it?" said Eleanor.

Bruno looked over at Eleanor.

"What do you mean by 'cursed'?"

"You should really read the updates I send you prior to our meetings," said Stephen. "But to briefly explain, they are items said to bring ultimate misfortune to its user in exchange for other worldly power. Their origins are unknown and so are their true abilities. Until now, only the existence of one cursed item has been confirmed, and that is the sword belonging to Benjamin. He is the only Awakened who has authorization to possess a cursed item."

"That explains it," said Bruno under his breath, as he thought of the overwhelming power he felt radiating from Benjamin even now from across the room.

"So what was your ultimate misfortune?" asked Bruno looking over at Benjamin.

The room fell silent.

Benjamin looked over at Bruno with a stare that triggered Bruno's sense of flight. Bruno tried to force himself to remain casual, but instead, he resembled a deer caught in the headlights, paralyzed by fear. Then Benjamin stood up and slowly exited the room.

As the door closed behind him, Bruno let out a sigh. He had not realized he had been holding his breath, let alone how wide his eyes had gotten.

"What's eating him?" asked Bruno, surprised by Benjamin's sudden departure.

Eleanor shook her head, as the room let out a collective unspoken disapproval of Bruno's actions.

"Was it something I said?"

"Let us return to the subject at hand," said Eleanor, "Quinn, what about the emergence of awakenings? Do you think it's due to some activation method by another branch of the organization?"

"Unlikely, the Southern methods are rather cruel, as we all know, but they can't give abilities, only 'enhance them', as they call it. Awakening only happens over successive generations. It's a naturally occurring process that causes dormant abilities or 'gifts' to emerge. Evolution at its finest ultimately means survival. However, the recent rapid awakenings are a commutative defensive mechanism."

"Could this be a latent defense against the Jinn embedded into an ancestral genetic trigger?" asked Bruno. "Legends say it almost incinerated Terraizen on a whim, though there is no factual evidence in the history to support the Jinn legend."

"It seems Benjamin took with him your ability to form rational thoughts and logical sentences. I'm only going to say this once, so listen closely. This creature, whatever it may be, is not the Jinn," said Quinn to Bruno. "If it were, we would already be dead. The Great Jinn of Legend, as it is called, is indifferent to life. An immortal that walks among the stars, basking in their internal infernos, does not know or care that we exist. If this creature had its power, then with a single breath it could incinerate this planet. So if this were the Legendary Jinn, I ask you, why would it return now, why would it be wandering through the Nefastus Forest, and why are we not engulfed in flames? What we are dealing with is an imposter that wishes to use the Jinn's Legend to spread fear, nothing more."

"Still, this creature wields a flute, and whether it be the flute's power, or some alternative source, this creature has shown it's capable of controlling minds. We must take that into consideration," said Stephen.

"You're correct Stephen, just because this entity is not the true Jinn does not mean it isn't dangerous. His powers equal that of a Level 5, and he should not be taken lightly."

"What do you suggest we do?"

"Counter measures have already been initiated, and updates will be posted, as required, for the successful neutralization of this imposter. We'll be sure to send the Banshee a message; underhanded tactics will not intimidate Central. Now let us turn our focus to a more pressing concern," responded Quinn.

***

After a brief intermission, independent conversations began to break out amongst the leaders.

Anthony turned to Francis, who sat sternly at the helm of the gathering, and began to speak in the ancient language known as Aizen tongue.

It was an ancient-essence encrypted language that allowed two parties to communicate in a high frequency both spoken and telepathic, which prevented others from hearing and understanding the words. Even for the very skilled code breaker, who could hear the high frequency voices of the Aizen tongue, it would be nearly impossible to understand the gibberish that came from it. Some portions were communicated through the transfer of essence. It was a language not only used by those immune to mind readers, but also by those who had mastered the three avenues of power: mind, body, and essence.

"How are you holding up after the last pardon? I hear Lord Mathias wasn't as willing to cooperate," said Anthony.

"Poison-laced drinks never spoiled the appetite. The appetite was spoiled by the meal long ago. Some things shouldn't be given the consideration of digestion," said Francis.

"My mind wanders, and at a far, it becomes lost."

Francis grinned, "Something that small can't wander too far."

"I can only hope to inconvenience your words. To everyone else you're invisible."

"Peculiar, how the rain only sees grey skies isn't it?"

There was a docile silence, as a requiem of unspoken words lingered between them. Anthony, remembering his Gatekeeper vow to never use his powers to reveal knowledge of the past or future, remained silent, allowing the moment to pass before speaking.

"A wise man needs not know the future to forge ahead."

Sternly, Francis responded, "I refuse to waste my time contemplating trivial matters. Death comes but once, and the Fates rest in our hands."

"If you say so…but no man can control the Fates. I sense their prophecy concerns you."

"I'm surprised you possess such an ability. Mind your tongue; do not forget who protects this world. Central shall not fall as long as I possess the power to defend it."

"There lies the rub!"

***

Independent conversations had stopped, leaving only Quinn explaining to Bruno the difference between myth and fact on various matters.

Francis leaned forward, his stern composure unwavering.

Upon seeing movement from the broad shoulder, statuesque figure they too fell silent as Francis began to speak.

"For over five hundred years, since the days of my forefathers, Central has been a place of peace, justice, and freedom. Now the time has come for the clock maker to resume his craft. Though you may not know it, I have known each of you since the day you were born. It is by no sheer coincidence you sit before me now. You have all shown great power, courage, and spirit. Alone, power tends to corrupt, and many once great leaders have fallen victim to the possession of absolute power. I do not claim to be a pious man, though when it is within my power, I do what is necessary to correct the injustices of Terraizen. Still, there is only so much one man can do. The peace of Central is built on maintaining a balance with the Rulers of Terraizen, and at best, it is a fragile peace; for they possess absolute power within their sovereign dominions. Though they are the leaders of your fellow agents, trust them, but with caution. Their laws are not 'Central Laws', their rules are not 'Central Rules.'"

Francis paused, looking around the room at the determination and youth reflecting within the eyes of each of his agents. These were his handpicked elites, charged with defending Central as he had done for many years.

Then he continued.

"The laws of the organization maintain this delicate balance between the Seven Rulers and five nations of Terraizen. The law is the only thing that protects our citizens and agents from the chaos of the South and West. The law is my power or have you forgotten… now please take your leave, there is much work we must complete while the days are young."

As the agents stood up, and began to leave the room, Francis looked down at his hands. They had been carved out by time. Each line and every scar told its own story. His face held a stern, emotionless, sculpture-like expression. Francis always maintained a stern posture and looked as if he were in deep thought.

"We must act now, while the power still resides in these hands," said Francis in the ancient tongue to Anthony. "He must be punished for what he has done."

Francis passed what looked like a golden crest to Anthony. Then, in a flash of bright light, Anthony vanished from the room.

***

After the meeting, Anabel and Quinn headed back to Quinn's chambers to continue their conversation.

Anabel and Quinn knew how special Joshua was. Like Faith and Anthony, his body was only the medium that focused his power. It frightened them to think that something had happened to their brother. But they knew there was a possibility that he was still alive.

E-3 leaders were ranked among the strongest agents of the organization. The fact that there was no body, no clues or traces left behind from Joshua's disappearance, made Quinn feel uneasy. It was as if he simply vanished from the face of Terraizen, however, Anabel's intuition told her he was still alive.

During the time that Anabel was traveling, Quinn had attempted to use the King novel's to find clues to Joshua's location.

The novels were scattered throughout Terraizen. Quinn had only recently found two of them. They were filled with poems, stories, legends, and fables from the Forgotten Ages. Until recently, no artifacts from that period had ever been recovered, even after extensive searches. Somehow these books had begun to reappear around Terraizen.

The Espers confirmed that the powerful, undetectable protection enchantment placed on them had finally begun to fade. This led Quinn to believe that maybe there were many other things from that age shrouded in a realm just out of his reach or detection. This idea fascinated him. After obtaining one of the novels, Quinn had attempted to decipher the ancient text. Even with his intellectual abilities, he struggled to break the code. He had thought to himself that maybe Francis had the answers since he was well-versed in many languages. However, Quinn knew he had a better chance of getting a smile from Benjamin.

Quinn remembered the first time he attempted to read Francis the IV's mind. It was not until four days later that Quinn regained consciousness. Although Quinn's power had grown since then, he never attempted to read his mind again. As old and gray haired as Francis may have seemed, he was their commander for a reason. Quinn and Anabel knew they had to tread carefully around him. Francis was one of the Seven Great Rulers of Terraizen, and possessed the power to stop Shadow Walkers. Like all of the rulers, there were certain secrets they kept among themselves. If Joshua's disappearance turned out to be one of those secrets, then the details would never be known by anyone but the Seven.

Francis had protected the organization for nearly a century, and had seen devastation strike the organization several times. Now, with the sudden untraceable disappearance of agents, first in the West, then the East, and now Central, Quinn knew that disaster was approaching once again, and the Forgotten Ages were returning.

CHAPTER 11: THE GATE KEEPER

Joseph adjusted his eyes away from the light, which beamed through the partially open curtain, striking him directly in the face. Joseph looked over towards the window. There was a desk with a lamp that rested upon it, next to it was the chair where the woman had sat the night before. At first, he believed he had imagined the whole thing, but then, he came to realize that it had not been a dream. That night after she left, he had slept peacefully. It had been a while since he had slept so pleasantly. As Joseph looked down at his body, he was surprised to find himself fully healed. He felt more invigorated than he had ever felt in his life. He was bursting with a childlike energy that seemed to overwhelm him. He felt fearless, like he could do anything. But then a question came to mind. Where exactly was he?

The answer came with a knock at the door. As it opened, a clear, melodious voice followed through.

"Good morning Joseph. It's nice to finally see you again. "

Joseph looked toward the door. A beautiful woman with curly black hair walked through. She wore a doctor's uniform and a smile that was like morphine. Just looking at her seemed to subdue the excess energy he possessed. But there was something else about her that seemed very familiar. Something he could not quite remember.

"My name is Dr. Matthews. You've been asleep for quite some time. How are you feeling this morning?"

"I feel great, but where am I?"

She stood next to his bed, and reached for his hand. Gently, she held it between hers.

"I'm glad to hear that you're feeling better. You're in the Terraizen Central Hospital, Unit B-1. We found you and your friends unconscious in the forest. I just learned about your accident, and how badly you were badly injured, but my staff has been working non-stop for the past four days, ensuring the three of you make a full recovery," she said with a slight, but genuine smile.

Joseph noticed a subtle sweetness in her tone and her smile. It made him forget what he was thinking. Her skin was soft against his, and for a moment, he felt warm and then cool again like a winter breeze on a sunny day.

The sensation nipped at his nose, causing him to shiver lightly and wiggle his toes. Dr. Matthews released his hand and the sensation faded. It was then he remembered he had been unable to move his legs the night before. He also realized she had said he had been out for four days.

"Four days," said Joseph, surprised by the fact that he had not reacted sooner.

"Yes, I'm very sorry I could not get to you sooner. I only learned of you and your friends last night, and I was performing a very complicated surgery at STAR Hospital. I came here right after to make sure you and your friends were okay," she explained contritely.

Joseph felt guilt-ridden for the tone he had used with her. Although it had sounded as if he were angry, he was not, only surprised by the fact that it had not felt like four days.

"I'm sorry...I didn't mean it that way. Thank you Dr. Matthews. I appreciate everything. I was just surprised, that's all."

Joseph was drawn towards her sweet smile. He began to sit up in his bed so he could stretch his legs.

"Take it easy Joseph. You may be a little drowsy for the next few hours."

The sound of his name coming from her lips was euphoric. There was something about the woman that drew him in with a calm serenity. Every time she spoke, it derailed his train of thought.

"You've grown up to be a fine young man," she said, holding his head between her hands as she examined his eyes.

Joseph was shocked by what happened next.

Dr. Matthews leaned in and planted a kiss upon his forehead.

Instantly, he could feel his heart trying to break out of his chest as her lips perched softly against his forehead. Joseph felt embarrassed as a falsetto sigh escaped his lips.

Except for the few times by his mother, before bed as a child, he had never been kissed before. He quickly stared towards his legs, hoping she had not heard the embarrassing sound he had made. He knew he would never be able to make direct eye contact with her again.

"I'm going to examine your legs now. Let me know if you feel any pain," said Anabel.

As she began to examine his legs, pressing against the sides and checking for bruises and marks, he looked down at her.

He knew he needed to think of something else and fast.

Joseph looked down at his legs and arms. There were no bandages, no splints, not even a single needle mark. *How was this possible*, he thought to himself. He remembered the condition he was in. Now he was fine. Joseph looked over in the corner where the woman had sat the night before. The chair was empty.

What Joseph felt was not pain as she made her way up to his knee. He attempted to think of something else. He noticed a door in front of his bed. The set up was similar to the STAR Hospital, and he assumed the door led to the restroom.

"May I use the restroom?"

"Sure. Do you need help?"

Joseph's face turned a deeper maroon.

"No! No, that won't be necessary," he said quickly.

Joseph leaped from his bed in his hospital gown. He attempted to conceal the back of himself from Dr. Matthews view, but more importantly the front, as he headed to the restroom.

He made it just in time. It had been four days since he last remembered going to the restroom. Joseph saw his clothing lying next to the sink. They had been mended perfectly to the condition they were in before the attack. His jeans still had the tethered bottoms, but no markings from the vines. Quickly, he sterilized his hands and slipped into his old clothing.

As he exited the room, he looked over at Anabel, who stood next to the head of his bed going over his chart. *She's perfect*, he thought to himself as he walked over and took a seat across from her on the bed. Then he began to wonder...

"Dr. Matthews, where's Brian and Maria?"

There was a knock at the door.

"Dr. Matthews, has the patient been cleared," said a male voice from the other side of the door.

"Yes Dr. Cesar," she replied with a smile.

A man in a gray and blue pinstriped sweater vest with gray pants stepped through the door. Joseph made out a black glove-like coating on the man's right hand and a silver watch on his left wrist. Joseph found it a bit strange that the man only wore a single glove. Then he wondered what he meant by "cleared."

Joseph did not want the man there. He did not trust him. But he knew if Dr. Matthews trusted him, then he would be forced to as well.

Dr. Matthews looked over at Joseph, "This is Dr. Cesar. He will answer your questions. Dr. Cesar is a wonderful guy. I have worked with him for years. Isn't that right Dr. Cesar?"

"No, you should not trust me. Don't trust anyone here because we are all out to get you," said Dr. Cesar

"Quinn, don't scare the poor child. He's still recovering."

"He's not a child. But clearly you've been treating him like one, look at that embarrassing look on his face. The perverted images that haunt this young man's mind are because of you 'Dr. Matthews'," said Quinn, sarcastically shaking his head in disapproval.

"Oh Quinn…your overreacting," said Dr. Matthews waving him off with a smile and a slight giggle.

Dr. Matthews looked toward Joseph, "If you need anything, feel free to use the communicator."

Dr. Matthews waved goodbye to Joseph and exited the room, closing the door behind her. As she did, he felt his heart plummet as if he had lost the love of his life and been left with a tall gray stranger with a terrible sense of humor.

Joseph wanted to keep her there with him. But then rationalized to himself that he had to let her go or other people may die.

Dr. Cesar sat in the chair next to Joseph's bed.

"I'm analyzing your essence signature. This will only take a moment," said Dr.Cesar.

He held his hand up in front of him as if pledging. A blue light projected itself from the center, and it began to scan Joseph's body.

"What are you doing?" asked Joseph.

"I'm collecting information for my analysis. It's completely harmless, and the scan will only take a second. There, see… all done," said Dr. Cesar as the blue light faded and he lowered his hand in an almost mechanical way.

"Can you please tell me where my friends are?" said Joseph.

"Yes, yes I could…but if I did, then I would have to end your life."

"What?" Joseph asked, as he stared confused at the man's unreadable poker face.

"Kidding," said Dr. Cesar with a smile. "You're on the other side of STAR Island. Somehow you were able to get through the barrier around Nefastus Forest, which only authorized Awakened can bypass; and you are neither Awakened nor authorized at the moment. We just had to make sure you were not under Southern influence. They're always attempting to destroy us."

"Wait…wait…wait… nothing you just said made any sense. I feel like I just wandered into some strange parallel universe and I am losing my mind!"

Joseph's voice had risen.

"Calm down. It's all relative, so there's no way to truly get lost unless you're Bruno. He'd lose his head if Benjamin weren't always waiting in his shadow," said Dr. Cesar. "We've confirmed you aren't under the influence. As an agent of the Terraizen Secret Protection Agency, I am obligated to assist you with your awakening. Let's start with questions. And please, call me Quinn."

The man's demeanor changed to a more casual one as Joseph made his way to the bed and sat down across from him.

"Where are Maria and Brian?" asked Joseph.

Dr. Cesar smiled. His entire posture and body language began to change to that of a kind, warmer individual.

"Maria and Brian are down the hall resting. Once you have eaten and regained your energy, I will take you to them. Until then, you must rest," said Dr. Cesar.

Joseph did not understand why, but he knew that every word that left Quinn's mouth was true and undeniable.

"Understood?"

"Yes," said Joseph.

"Now let's clear up something. Everything that you witnessed, it happened: the Forest, boa vines, Senior Elvia, and even the elk. The Northern Forest of STAR Island houses a gateway known as the Nexus Gate. It leads to many places. Among them are the core of Nexus and the Nefastus Forest. Only authorized Awakened can enter, it's a very dangerous place. The Nefastus Forest is a realm that exists on a parallel time space. Our agency protects Terraizen from the calamities that dwell within it. If they are ever set free, Terraizen would be destroyed."

Joseph spoke calmly.

"What's an Awakened?"

"Aha! Good question. An Awakened is an individual who has unlocked their inner essence. Living things are composed of three essential parts: mind, body, and essence. The mind is responsible for controlling the host. The body is responsible for ensuring the minds survival, and essence connects the body and mind with the universe. Essence sustains our existence. It is our thread within the unseen web of existence. It goes by many names, but its purpose remains the same. It allows us to manifest our will on the universe. As an Awakened, you will grow to understand your true purpose in this world. You will be able to manifest unique abilities and contribute in ways that could alter the tides of the universe."

"Like magic?"

"No, magic is a general manifestation or channeling of nature's essence. Without nature, there is no magic, but there are still essences. To use magic, nature must always be present. I'm not here to teach you magic. I'm here to determine your abilities."

"So are you going to run tests?"

"It's not like that," responded Quinn. "I'm an extrasensory. I already know you're an Awakened and what you're about to ask me. No, I'm not going to do the color trick, but the answers to your questions are neon blue, maybe, with extra jalapeño, and strawberry soda. Though venue tea, is more preferable, respectively," said Quinn with a smile.

"Whoa!"

"I knew you were going to say that," said Quinn.

***

Quinn and Joseph had lunch and discussed more about the TSPA. Joseph was surprised to learn that the ruler of Terraizen, Francis the IV, and the TSPA agents, were all powerful Awakened. The TSPA provided classes for Awakened to learn, channel, and master their awakened abilities. Anything Joseph needed, the TSPA would provide. Joseph was excited about this new opportunity and could not wait to tell Brian and Maria the great news. Quinn even agreed to train him once he mastered the basics of channeling.

Joseph had always known there was something different about him, and now Quinn had provided him with a way to find the answers to his dreams. He only hoped that Brian and Maria would join him.

Later that day, after talking with Quinn and watching a few movies, Dr. Matthews came to visit with good news. Brian and Maria had made a full recovery. In the morning, he would able to meet up with them. Joseph couldn't wait to share with them the great news.

***

Joseph turned off the television and dimmed the lights. He lay there in his bed stuffed from the large dinner. He was sure he had eaten enough to make up for the four days he had not eaten, and it had been the best meal he had ever had. Even after his stomach seemed to have nearly reached its full capacity, Joseph refused to deny his taste buds the satisfaction of one last bite.

That night, Joseph had a strange dream.

***

Joseph stood in a white room in front of a white door with a golden knob. After looking around the room, he realized there were no walls and the door stood on its own within the empty room. He circled around the door, and as he did, it seemed to vanish. From the backside, the door did not exist, and Joseph could see clearly the empty room that was without end. But when he approached the front, the golden knob revealed itself. Again when he placed his hand on the door it was solid and the knob was cold. This confused Joseph at first, for he had never encountered a one-sided door before. Joseph wanted to know more about the strange one-sided door, and so he turned the knob and opened it.

There, before Joseph, was a forest behind the one-sided door. In the distance, stood a blue elk running towards him. As it did, the forest began to fade to black, and dark clouds gathered overhead. As the forest changed, the blue elk vanished.

Joseph looked out in the distance, and a set of red eyes stared back at him. The eyes were frightening and seemed to glow, trapping Joseph in their hypnotic gaze, while they grew closer and closer to the doorway. Joseph wanted to shut the door, but could only gaze into the terrifying glow of the red eyes. He knew he needed to shut the door, because around the eyes, a shape began to materialize. It was a being of terror that caused Joseph to fall to his knees, still unable to break free of its trance. It began to reach out to him. Joseph knew he could not let it touch him, if it did, he knew something bad would happen. But he could not move, and its eyes, oh, its eyes were so hypnotically terrifying.

Now every fiber of his being screamed out for him to close the door, but he had no control. He wished he had never opened the door, as its nightmarish appendage approached the threshold. There was a loud bang, and in that moment, Joseph broke free of its hold and slammed the door just before it passed through. The door dissipated.

As Joseph stood up, from behind him came an ear-splitting voice which shook the very ground he stood upon.

"Why are you here?"

Joseph quickly covered his ears while looking for the source of the noise. The voice seemed to be coming from everywhere at once.

"Where is here?"

"Here is nowhere and everywhere. Here is relative. Now, who are you?" came the thunderous voice once more.

The voice was so loud that Joseph's ears began to ring, he couldn't even hear himself think.

"I'm Joseph... Joseph Aizen."

"I know who you are! You are not Aizen! Who are you?"

Joseph was scared. The voice had grown in intensity. It felt as if he were about to be electrocuted as the hairs on his body stood on end.

"Joseph!" he screamed, "I'm Joseph!"

"Who are you!?"

"I don't know!" He said out of frustration. "I don't know!" He repeated once more.

"Then leave! This is no place for you. Here, if you don't understand who you are, it's easy to lose where you are!

The voice shook the room and it became one loud, continuous pure ear-bleeding sound.

"How?"

Joseph could no longer hear his own voice.

"Leave! Leave now!"

The ringing resonated through him. As he lost his ability to breathe, the voice continued to shake him to the core. Joseph fell to his knees, his body trembling uncontrollably. As the room seemed to suck the air from his lungs, he felt his heart come to a stop.

At that moment, Joseph sprung up and was greeted by the darkness of his hospital room. He could still hear the voice echoing through his head even after he had awoken. Never had he been so scared. His pillows were drenched in his sweat.

Joseph reached for the light as the remnants of his dream rapidly faded. He was scared that he was not alone. He could feel the presence of something watching him. Joseph looked towards the corner of the room where Senior Elvia had sat next to the window, but there was no one there. *Maybe Senior Elvia had just left,* he thought to himself. Joseph began to turn on the dim light.

"Excuse me...what do you think you're doing?" came a sophisticated voice from the corner next to the front door of Joseph's room.

Joseph nearly broke his neck turning around.

He was stunned by the sight of the man that stood in the corner of his room.

As the man stepped out of the darkness, Joseph stared speechless and in shock.

The man took one look at Joseph's face then he looked down at himself.

"Apologies. It's a Zone thing," said the man, in his now noticeable accent.

The man snapped his fingers, and now appeared to be wearing what looked like a white and black suit with a black bowtie. His face was stone-like, as he stood statuesque in the darkest corner of the room.

"I am Gatekeeper of the nine realms, and you, malefactor, were trespassing. Do you know what we are forced to do to trespassers?" he said, raising his hand to his temple. "Give me one reason why I shouldn't..."

The man stopped mid-sentence.

"Did you say your name was Joseph...Joseph Aizen?"

Joseph nodded. Still remembering the voice, but nothing more.

"Were you sleeping?" asked the man.

Joseph nodded once again, still unable to speak.

There was a brief silence in the room as the tall dark figure continued to think. Then he lowered his hand from his temple.

"Ah! I knew that name sounded familiar! Joseph Aizen, son of the late Aizen. I see the resemblance. Your father loved to talk about you. He never mentioned you were...no matter. We met once when you were four. Although you probably don't remember me, I used to work with your father. He's very gifted. There's even a bridge named after him. I think it's called 'The Aizen Bridge' or something. It's too bad, the rules state I must end your life...however, out of respect for your father, and because you're not a full Awakened, I guess I can give you a pass."

The man snapped his fingers.

"I've sealed your access to the gateways. Never go back to that place. There are things within the nine gates that make Nefastus look like a grain of sand within an endless desert."

The man stepped back into the darkness.

Joseph could only make out the brown eyes of the man. Then, the man turned towards the shadowy corner of the room from which he came.

"Resist the call of the gate, for it only wishes to claim you, and it must not be opened. *Do-svidaniya!*"

The Gatekeeper vanished from the room, and with a click, the dim light faded.

Joseph sat up still speechless in his bed, afraid to go back to sleep. He knew a place filled with people with extraordinary abilities would be strange, but he was starting to get an idea of how strange. He began to wonder about whom his father truly was, and if he worked for the TSPA, what abilities he possessed. It had never been a question that occurred to him until now. Maybe, he thought to himself, maybe his abilities were inherited; and if they were, what exactly were they? His father's name had saved him from punishment, and possibly death. What had his father been doing for the TSPA?

CHAPTER 12: ELEANOR-WHITE WILLOW

Eleanor Fredrick loved the smell of greenery in the morning. Every inch of her chambers was covered in vines, just as they had been in her home village in the East. They covered the columns of her room, ceiling, and floor to the point where they could no longer be seen under the thick layers of greenery. Like an exotic forest, her room blossomed with a variety of beautiful flowers and rare fruit. She had grown many of them from seeds collected from her home while others were gifts from Anabel; their extract could be used for healing and rejuvenations. Although she had done all she could in an attempt to make her chamber more hospitable, to her, it was still nothing more than a cage.

On her occasional visits to the Nefastus Forest, she secretly collected specimens of plants and flowers to study in her green house. Though beautiful, she quickly found out how dangerous

Nefastus plants truly were. During her first expedition in the Nefastus Forest, nearly fifteen years ago, Eleanor stumbled upon a special, beautiful rose-violet whose scent left her paralyzed and powerless. As she laid there, its counterpart, whom she later named the blood-violet, attempted to drain her of blood. Luckily, she had not been traveling alone, and Quinn found her shortly before the violet twins could do any lasting damage. She remembered how embarrassed she had felt; being saved by him of all people from a plant. After all, it was their first mission together, and back then she possessed three times his level of mental control.

Sunlight beamed through the large windows and was absorbed by the leafy green brush that layered the floors and walls of her bedroom chambers, awakening the *Viridiplantae*. While taking in the morning sun, the room glowed a golden yellow and so did the vines of the *Viridiplantae* as they leeched off of Eleanor's excess energy. Eleanor's room contained exactly five hundred and thirteen different species of plants, while the green house contained thousands, including fruits and vegetables, grown from the seeds of her Eastern village.

Few knew the true purpose of the *Viridiplantae*, with which Eleanor shared a symbiotic relationship with. They were her connection to the Nefastus Forest and so much more. The very presence of the *Viridiplantae* limited an individual's abilities to channel. Eleanor learned that by feeding them her energy, over the years they had grown to recognize her as a part of them. This allowed her to also draw from their stored energy.

Eleanor had been awakened by the warm sensation of the *Viridiplantae* winding around her legs as they traveled up her torso, like a large snake constricting its prey. Every morning they played this game with her, constricting her until they reached their limit, and then releasing her once they could no longer maintain their grip. The grip from a *Viridiplantae* could leave any normal Awakened powerless, but Eleanor had befriended them. To her it was no more than a slight tickle.

At night, she found freedom by infusing her essence into the *Viridiplantae,* and by doing so she could see everything they saw. Each night they took her to a new area of the Nefastus Forest. Unlike some of the other plants, what made *Viridiplantae* special was the fact that they could remember. The *Viridiplantae* were a wild, wise, ancient plant known for being immune to telekinesis and all forms of mental manipulation. On this morning, Eleanor lay in their grip, awake and glaring at the ceiling, unable to comprehend what she had seen.

With an unyielding determination and unmatched confidence, she had tried her best to right the wrongs of the organization over the years and rid it of its corruption. Out of all the TSPA branches, the South was, by far, the most corrupt. There had been a time when she had challenged the corruption within the Southern TSPA.

With her powers, she had brought many Dark Age agents of the South to their knees. She had been the only one to escape the Bishop and gain temporary control of the Black Knight. Still, in the end, her powers were no match against the Banshee's Shadow Walker, which consumed everyone she loved.

Eleanor had realized the power of the organization in her younger years. After discovering her abilities, she used them to free her village, and the smaller villages in the East, from the corrupt rule of Southern TSPA's control. Eleanor's rebellion against their mental tyranny was that of legends. She swept through the Eastern coast, freeing the people from their mental shackles, joining the tribes and villages, and ending internal conflict. Single-handedly, Eleanor had brought about enlightenment for her people, establishing the first community free of any TSPA organization's control. They sang and danced of their own free will and finally got a real taste of mental freedom; and the possibilities were endless.

As the town grew, so did Eleanor's powers. A few free villages isolated in the forest were no serious threat to the Southern TSPA. The city of villages existed on the continent of Eastern Terraizen, which the South had gained control over long ago. Eleanor wondered why they had not fought harder to regain the area. After the second year, Eleanor learned the truth when everything she had built came to an abrupt end.

Though the TSPA possessed near absolute power over Terraizen, there was one individual whose power was so great some considered her the Seventh Ruler of Terraizen. Her organization was known as Banshee, and the head of the cipher organization called herself the Banshee, for they acted as one. Their goal was to remove the TSPA from power and gain control over the entire Awakened community. However, Banshee was no better than the TSPA, in fact they were much worse.

Although Eleanor could not remember exactly what had happened, she remembered a dark figure standing near the edge of the village within the trees, motionless. Next came a shock wave, then a strong wind carried through the village, and in a matter of seconds, everyone had fallen asleep, except Eleanor.

No one could see it except Eleanor, and what she saw was horrifying. It stood over nine feet tall and seemed to tower over her with eyes that strangled the breath from her body and tugged at her very soul. Even though it was many miles away within the forest, Eleanor was terrified. She remembered clinching tightly to her sister's hand as it stepped from one area to the next. Eleanor recalled how it moved in a ghostly incredulous manner, vanishing, then reappearing in another section of the forest as if it was just passing by, not coming closer. The forest turned black around it like it carried an aura of decay. Eleanor could feel no life within it, and the fear of immediate death and helplessness swelled within her. She wanted to scream, yet, she could only remain petrified in silence under its dark influence.

She knew with certainty it had come for her, but why it did not enter the town, she did not know. The last thing she remembered were four hooded figures arriving, and the next thing she knew, she was at Central. Later, she learned it was Quinn, Anabel, Joshua, and Stephen who had rescued her that day from what would have been certain death, and the creature that attacked her was a Shadow Walker, a cursed soulless minion of the Banshee. Her sister, family, and village were not as lucky. What seemed like a simple sleep had turned out to be an eternal one for them, and only she had been spared. Upon hearing the news, she felt as if she had truly died, for she had lost everyone she had ever loved or cared for in less than a second.

Not a day passed that Eleanor did not think about all she had lost. On occasion, she would reminisce through the looking glass, until the memories became too much for her to handle. As time passed, the mirror gathered dust in the far corner of her room. The forgotten looking glass was a beautiful piece of art, with a vine-like engraving around the edge. Just like her, it was powerful and could see things that others couldn't, but now it had been ignored and repurposed as just a post for the *Viridiplantae* to wrap around on their way to the ceiling.

Eleanor had now become a part of what she had once despised. But she had come to learn that not all of the TSPA was as vile as the South. To her, the Northern agency was strict authoritarian control freaks, the West were lawless, lacking any control, and the East were just a bunch of nonchalant, lazy pacifist snobs who somehow managed to survive through sheer luck. But Central was different, Central seemed to have its head on straight. Six hundred years had given the TSPA agencies the time it needed to perfect its craft. Controlling the minds of Terraizen had become second nature to the coordinal branches. The people thought they were free, but they were only as free as their head agency wanted them to feel. Handling the Banshee, however, had proven to be a serious issue.

Out of the evils that were committed within Terraizen, it was a joke that the Banshee was responsible for 17 percent, and the South was responsible for the rest.

But now that Eleanor had seen the truth of Terraizen's past, she was left with more questions than answers. Controlling the minds of millions was not a simple task for the North and South agencies. Of the five main continents the Northern and Southern Terraizen populations accounted for 70% of the entire population of Terraizen. She had always wondered what secret, massive force they were using, and now the *Viridiplantae* had shown her a piece of the truth.

Possessing knowledge of the forgotten ages, the *Viridiplantae* knew things that even the mighty TSPA were blind to, and they had learned to keep their secrets very well. Eleanor was always curious as to where in the vast Nefastus Forest they would go next. Overtime, she gained their trust, and as time progressed, they began to share their secrets with her. That night, they traveled to an old White Willow tree. The behemoth obelisk of a tree stood in the center of a stone garden. Lifeless and eerie, a haunting silence lingered in the cold, desolate fog that shrouded the area like a blanket from the night. It was said not a single living thing existed in the dead zone, so it was avoided, yet, there was something living within the White Willow tree, something dark and powerful. Eleanor also found it suprising that the Dead Zone had no effect on the *Viridiplantae*. As the vines of the *Viridiplantae* touched the White Willow, images began to flash through their *viridisight*. They were images of a lost archaic Terraizen, images of the *Ante Reginam* period.

Mentally perturbed by what she had seen, Eleanor sprung from her sleep. Cold frost had covered her skin, but instantly melted when she awoke.

Eleanor wanted to know more about what the visions she had seen meant. Unlike humans, plants were incapable of lying, and Eleanor knew that what she had seen was from another time wave.

Although the organization controlled the world, there were some stories even they could not suppress among the Awakened and magical communities. Unlike maulfts, who were non-awakened, non-magical, easily manipulated individuals, blind to the secret worlds that surrounded them, Awakened and witches were a challenge to control by conventional means. So instead, laws were put into place for them to follow, and breaking such laws had dire consequences, especially in the North and South.

It was said that out of the Six Rulers, Judge Francis the IV was the wisest. Francis the IV challenged the ancient ideals of the other rulers by being the first to free his people. He established strict laws in place of mind control for the purpose of making technological advancements while maintaining order. Francis the IV wanted Central Terraizen to be a place of science, technology, research, and a guiding light of innovation for all of Terraizen, so it became. Now Central, in one hundred years, had become a futuristic continent in comparison to the rest of the world. Only in Central could you find a car, the rest of the world still rode horses, with the exception of the East.

Central possessed computers and technology, while majority of the South and West still lived by parchment and fire. Central was free of the old religions that still ruled the South with an iron fist. The advancements of Central were freely shared with Eastern TSPA and selectively shared among the other agencies they deemed fit to wield them. In comparison to Central the South still lived in the Dark Ages. However, they had something that Central did not have and that was a high concentration of Channelers and Awakened. Unlike Central the Southern Agents had no need for technology. To the Southern Agents technology was archaic in comparison to their abilities, what use was a car when you could breeze travel in a quarter of the time.

While the continents of Terraizen had many differences there was on they shared in common. Anexthesia proved to be a challenge to cross no matter the location. Few dared attempt to cross the Sea of Anexthesia, which claimed all who dared to enter its waters Un-Awakened and some Awakened as well. To the Un-Awakened, Central was called STAR Island, but to the Awakened it was almost always referred to as Central Terraizen, still the two were used synonymously.

Of the remainder of the Seven Great Rulers of Terraizen, Emperor Hadar and Lord Mathias were considered the cruelest. All who knew of Lord Mathias feared him, and no one questioned his authority or ability to maintain order in Southern Terraizen. Shrouded in mystery, unlike the other Leaders, Lord Mathias never held a public audience. Besides the other rulers, no one had ever seen Lord Mathias. It was rumored that those who saw Lord Mathias died mysterious deaths not long after.

West Terraizen was known for its Adamantite-42 fortresses and prisons. Housing the most deadly of criminals, the West was a nearly lawless land. Even murder was legal on Friday's. Though very few rules existed, those who broke them were executed or placed in "Hadar's Dungeon." If given the option of execution, or Hadar's Dungeon, no one ever chose the dungeon. Legends say it contained beasts that slowly rip the flesh from your bones, leaving victims alive for days while they were consumed piece by piece. Being a member of the TSPA, Eleanor knew it contained something much worse and unspeakable. It was a fate worse than any form of torture, an experience she would only wish on her worst enemy, Banshee, whom she hated with a fiery passion.

After her quarrel with the South, the agents of Lord Mathias had marked Eleanor for death. Staying in Francis's favor provided protection from Lord Mathias and The Banshee. Eleanor feared what horrors would await her if they ever achieved their ambitious goal of using her power for Lord Mathias bidding. She imagined what it would be like to stare into Lord Mathias's unrestrained, icy gaze as the life drained from her body and was replaced with the deathly cold essence, which encompassed them all. It had given her chills and nightmares her first five years with the agency. Lord Mathias was all of her fears given form. The countless horrors that his agents inflicted upon his own people left her speechless. Eleanor did not want to know what special cruelties they had in store for her if she ever left Judge Francis's protection.

Today, Eleanor planned to meet with Quinn and Stephen in order to devise a white space plan.

Eleanor prepared for the day, and finished with a few final touches; that included fixing her long flowing, silky red hair, which she was well known for. She had decided to wear her gray suit, with the ruffled white button-down top. She felt it brought out a nice contrast with her hair. Then she headed to her garden.

After spending three hours tending to her *Viridiplantae,* Eleanor headed down the hall to the information center to meet with Quinn and Stephen. As her heels clicked against the hallway floor, she watched the heads turn. There was a power to her walk that made her enticing and pleasing to the eye.

The *Viridiplantae* had shown Eleanor the destruction of Central and all of Terraizen, but not what had caused it. Eleanor was not afraid to admit her limitations. She knew there were things beyond her understanding, and things she was not yet meant to know. But she also knew that together, the three Central minds were able to transcend their natural limitations.

The information center held a secret room dedicated to the leaders of the Minds division. It always reminded Eleanor of an interrogation chamber due to the lack of windows. The walls were gray, dull, and unattractive. In her first days at the organization, she pretended to be concerned with fashion, style, and beauty more than anything else. It was the façade she hid behind to conceal her true fears. Looking back at it now, she considered herself young and naive. She was no longer that easily damaged, over-emotional girl that she had once been. Now she was one of the most powerful Awakened within Central. Eleanor had mastered her power and grown to become something much more.

Eleanor was the last to arrive to the chamber, five minutes ahead of their designated meeting time. The walls were two feet thick and the door was like a vault. There was a single light that hung from the center of the room over a wooden table with four chairs. However, the décor was not of importance.

Once in, the chamber was sealed. This unlocked another door that led into an area of The Zone that only the minds could enter. This was called the White Space.

Once the door was closed, and they had all taken their seats, they did not speak. They simply closed their eyes and entered the White Space. It was a unique area that allowed them to access the full abilities of their collective subconscious. During this process, their three minds would unfold and become one, increasing their abilities by thirty fold. There, they formulated plans. The process placed them in their most vulnerable superposition state, even the slightest disturbance could permanently damage their minds, and a great disruption could destroy them.

Only the most brilliant minds could use this place. In the White Space Eleanor, Quinn and Stephen left nothing out, for a high level of detail was needed to determine the outcome of the numerous, nearly infinite possibilities. They needed to know with great accuracy how people would react to certain situations, and what environmental factors could influence the outcomes. They covered the weather, the tides of the ocean, the way the sun light hit the trees, the migration of the birds, activity of the insects, even the way the leaves fell upon the forest. Although they could not determine the future, all of this information was within their grasp. What made the White Space special was the time warp. A second in the real world was a millennia in the White Space. Even with the massive amount of energy provided by the Zone, each scenario took nanoseconds of White Space time, and for a seemingly infinite number of scenarios, the time began to add up. To counter this they discarded less likely scenarios. In a way the White Space granted them a limited joint precognitive ability.

One missed detail in their subconscious planning had no effect on their conscious minds, but it collapsed an infinite world of possible scenarios within their White Space planning and decreased their overall accuracy. They reviewed details carefully in an attempt to glance at that which lurked within the unknown future.

***

After the meeting, Eleanor, Quinn, and Stephen left the room and headed to their rooms to get some rest. White Space planning consumed a large amount of their energy and required a twenty-four hour recovery time. Eleanor felt uneasy as she walked back to her room. Even with a variety of plans now in place, she always questioned them, for they could be unconventional at times. They had done this many times before, and in the end, everything did seem to turn out as they predicted; but they had also had many close calls, and she wondered if it was because they missed something. Having a plan in which she only knew her role made her uneasy.

Eleanor recalled the times when she refused to believe in things she could not sense or analyze and considered herself a rational thinker. That all changed when she Awakened.

Unknowingly, her Awakened ability began by manifesting themselves through a hypnotic coercion, persuading the people around her to do things excessively to the point of exhaustion, especially those who tormented her. She remembered the day when she commanded a man to jump into the river for looking at her the wrong way before she knew she possessed Awakened abilities. At first, she thought these strange random events were coincidences, but upon the arrival of a Southern TSPA agent, she learned the truth.

When thinking rationally, Eleanor could understand that the TSPA, in a way, did save her life. Her powers had begun to consume her and control the minds of all around her. Unwittingly, by trying to free the people from the control of TSPA, she had only usurped their control with her own mind control. When thinking with her emotions, she became consumed with the rage of losing everyone she loved, especially her sister; and the fear of Lord Mathias.

After joining the organization, she encountered Stephen, who showed her how to control her abilities and had become like a brother. Stephen exposed her to the world of Awakened. From that day forward she swore not to use her abilities to harm others.

Eleanor understood her own essence quite well, but struggled, at times, to understand the essences of others. Eleanor could not see essence, like Anabel or Benjamin, but she had learned to sense it.

She entered the lab on her way back to the corridor. She turned to the information stream that ran along its walls. It was the main circuit that gathered energy from the Zone and converted it into the various forms of energy needed to power the building and the A.I., which traveled through the stream.

"Faith, are you awake?"

"Yes Eleanor."

The techno blue Faith appeared next to the information stream.

"Faith, could you pull up the analysis of Bruno, Quinn, U-hno, and Trevor."

"Yes. One moment please."

As Faith began the process, streams of strange figures, numbers, and hologram letters began to appear in front of her under the pictures of Quinn, U-hno, Trevor, and Bruno, forming a list of information for each of them.

"Here are the results you requested."

Eleanor looked over the numbers and figures. She thought it was fascinating how Faith was able to partially quantify essence. Each Awakened had three states of awakening, the Initium, Semis, and Ultima.

Initium was the first state an Awakened experienced. It allowed them to use their abilities, and was considered the ground state of awakening. Semis, the second state, which normally involved heightened senses, changes in personality, and the unlocking of even greater power. The Ultima was the final state of Awakening, though non-quantifiable and varying for every individual, it unlocked the full Awakened potential and was highly dangerous. Very little was known about the Ultima since it had rarely been seen. The few times it had been used, the essence analyzers failed to detect it, and the individual died shortly after. It was because of this that unlocking the Ultima was associated with, not only immeasurable power, but also death. No one yet who used the Ultima had lived to tell the tale.

Upon reviewing the results, Eleanor had confirmed her theory. U-hno and Trevor had entered their Semis, while Quinn and Bruno had not left their Initium. When going up against an unknown opponent, it was normal to bait them, but a Level 4 warranted a Semis awakening. Eleanor knew of only one reason Bruno and Quinn would risk their lives by only using a fraction of their power. They were reserving their strength for the true battle that lay ahead and thought it could arrive at any time. After using a Semis it usually took a few days to recover and these were days they may not have so they were always cautious before playing their hands.

The information shown on the hologram display looked comprehensive except for the strange symbols that resided at the bottom of their statuses. They continuously changed like the pictures on Quinn's chamber walls with no pattern. If there had been a pattern, Eleanor believed she would have deciphered it already.

"Faith. What do these symbols mean?"

"They are dimensionless vectors representing unknown, fragmented information and understood only by those with the 'sight'."

"Who in the organization possesses the 'sight'?"

"There are thirteen individuals within the organization that possess the sight. These four are currently located in Central."

The images of the four individuals appeared in front of Eleanor. They were Judge Francis the IV, Anthony, and two others that Eleanor had only seen in passing. But she knew where to find them.

Eleanor's vision became blurry. She was weary from the White Space transaction, and it began to take its toll on her. She decided it was time to settle in for the night, and headed back to her chambers after dismissing Faith. She needed to get up early tomorrow to drop off the protective charms and herbs from her private garden to the Esper Witches. Then again, she thought to herself, she could always get the new messenger boy Sammy to make the delivery instead. He was a sweet boy with a kind heart that jumped at her every request.

Eleanor had become adept at channeling and making protective charms. However, because her powers had been sealed, Eleanor could only tap into a fraction of her true strength, and was not considered a threat. Still, Eleanor was resourceful, and wanted to make sure that if she ever needed to defend Central she could do so without her powers. For eight years Eleanor searched the most deadly parts of Nefastus, seeking out the legendary White Willow Wand and collecting exotic plants along the way. The wand was said to possess powers that rivaled those of a Terraizen Ruler, but existed within a section of Nefastus that no man dared enter, known as "The Dead Zone." Within a dead zone there was no life, and technology proved useless, but the *Viridiplantae* had shown some immunity to its effects. To Eleanor's surprise, the legend had proven to be true, and after eight years. Eleanor retrieved the wand from the bark of the White Willow tree. It had proven to be powerful. With the slightest touch, she felt its power coursing through her veins like fire.

Even in the *Viridiplantae* state, she had nearly lost her life countless times, but it had proven worth the risk. With the wand in her possession, she now had a means to prevent their destruction.

Eleanor lay in bed, admiring the beautiful pearl-like surface of the wand and its ancient engravings. Its workmanship was unmatched, fashioned with a strange white bijou handle, which only recognized her essence now that she had bound it to her. Like the *Viridiplantae*, it was a powerful extension of herself, and now with the wand and the *Viridiplantae* at her command, she had the power to find and end Banshee once and for all.

Eleanor pointed the White Willow Wand towards the high ceiling. With a gentle wave, the *Viridiplantae* danced and wrapped around her bed, forming a protective barrier over her four large, tree-shaped bedposts and around her royal silk bed. The lights extinguished themselves as Eleanor's conscious drifted into the *Viridiplantae*.

Though Eleanor was one of the most powerful Awakened in Central, it was at these times, when night settled in, that she felt the most vulnerable. It was at these times that she longed for someone to watch over her.

CHAPTER 13: REUNION OF FRIENDS

The day he had waited for had finally arrived.

Joseph stared at his reflection in the bathroom mirror as he brushed his teeth. As he glanced at his face, he realized that the scar on his chin he got from falling off his bike when he was ten had disappeared. He couldn't wait to tell Brian and Maria all the crazy things he had witnessed.

Senior Kassie waited for him outside the restroom door. As he exited, she smiled. Senior Kassie was the sister of Senior Elvia. Unlike Senior Elvia, Senior Kassie was nearly the exact opposite. She was a short, energetic bundle of smiles and laughter. It seemed like everything he said, made her giggle, catching him off guard, sometimes midsentence.

"Ready?" asked Senior Kassie. She had short black hair, blue jeans and sneakers under her long black cloak.

"Yes."

"Wonderful!"

Senior Kassie laughed as they headed to the door.

"Can I call you Joey? Or do you prefer Joseph?"

"Joey's fine."

The caliber of Kassie's enthusiasm and never-ending smile was so intense that it scared Joseph.

"Okay Joey, let's head down. The others are waiting."

Kassie reached into her pocket and withdrew her wand. Quickly, she waved it, and the room door swung open with a mighty force, scaring Joseph.

"Come along now Joey, we have a busy day ahead of us."

Kassie and Joseph exited the room and began to walk down the hall. As they headed out of the infirmary, Joseph noticed the sign that hung on the doors, and markings on some of the walls that read B-2.

Joseph passed many rooms on the way to the exit. There was not much staff around, and there were only two room doors open along the way that actually had occupants. In one, he saw a tall man with dreaded hair sleeping. The other had a short blond woman eating breakfast.

The calming blue and white walls put Joseph at ease and made him feel as if he were walking in pure relaxation.

They reminded Joseph of the ocean.

Exiting the infirmary, Joseph entered a bright snow white corridor. In front of them, lay a hall that led to an elevator. Along the way there were many unmarked closed white doors. Joseph found it strange that the place was so empty. Besides a secretary and few nurses he had seen no other staff in the hospital. He remembered how populated STAR Hospital had been, even at night. As they entered the elevator Joseph was stunned by the transparent blue-cobalt glass surface. It was as if he had stepped in a glass elevator under the sea.

Senior Kassie moved quick and quietly through the corridor. Once the blue glossy doors on the hexagon-shaped elevator closed, she sprung to life once more.

"Do you think I have a small head? 'Cause I think my head's small, and look at these."

Senior Kassie raised her hands to Joseph's face. Then quickly drew them back and started examining them intensely.

"Aren't these the tiniest hands you have ever seen? I always wondered why I have such tiny hands. It feels like I got bigger, but they didn't. You know I cast a spell once to try to make them bigger, and boy did that go wrong… It took several hours to reverse it. I'm never doing that again."

Joseph looked at her hands. They did not seem that small to him. They seemed normal for a girl her size.

"They look normal to…"

"Really! Are you just saying that to make me feel better about my baby-sized hands, or do you really mean it?"

She held her hands closer to Joseph's face for closer examination.

"I meant it. Your hands are some of the nicest hands I have ever seen."

Joseph would have said nearly anything to get her to turn the focus away from her hands. For a witch, he thought she seemed very immature. Then again, he knew he was no authority on maturity himself.

Senior Kassie began to blush and giggle as she shoved her hands into her pockets.

"Okay then! Let's head up. B-zero," said Senior Kassie and the elevator shifted upward.

Joseph felt his ears begin to pop. One moment the walls were a transparent cobalt, the next they were solid sapphire. In the center was a clear hexagonal tube. It traveled all the way up and down the elevator shaft. There were no cables or cords, and the elevator car itself seemed to ride on a smooth jet of air.

As swiftly as the doors had closed, they seemed to open, revealing a pure white room with a high ceiling.

"Where are we Senior Kassie?" asked Joseph, the words echoed through the room.

"This is B-zero, or what I like to call, the Gateway to Ezon One, and please no need for formalities, call me Kassie. Ezon One contains the Security Division, Esper Wing, shopping centers, food courts, game rooms, guest wing, training rooms, class rooms, magic shops, coffee shops, pubs, bars lounges, libraries and anything else your heart may desire. Anything you could possibly need, you can find somewhere on this floor."

"Incredible...where is everything?" asked Joseph skeptically.

Joseph gazed up at the highest ceiling he had ever seen. The room was a blinding white. The only thing the room contained, besides the elevator, was a door to his left and right. The elevator sat in the center of the room. Senior Kassie turned to him.

"Okay, here's your first test. Choose a door," said Kassie.

Joseph looked at both doors, then at Kassie, confused.

"No one told me there would be a test."

"That's life for ya'. But I am willing to answer one question."

"Where do they lead to?" asked Joseph.

"They both lead to the same place," said Kassie with a giggle.

Kassie headed towards the right door. It automatically slid open as she approached. Joseph stood, staring at Kassie, confused and dumbfounded.

"Well don't just stand there looking like a buck in the headlights, come on."

Joseph was annoyed, shocked, and confused, but followed Kassie through the door. He saw what looked like a security counter to his left. It had solid hologram monitors operated by a male and female officer. They sat within a large box station with the Terraizen Protection Agency logos on their uniform. Their outfits were exactly the same as the TPA officers on STAR Island. They seemed to be observing the monitors in deep concentration.

"Hey Danny! Hey Courtney!" said Kassie with her never-ending, slightly intimidating smile.

"Hello Kassie," they responded in unison. Kassie and Joseph continued through the next set of automatic doors. They opened up to a sunny, grassy world. Joseph was caught by surprise.

Spread out before him was a large forest, and in the distance, he could see a large cobblestone town surrounded by a forest. It had brick buildings, small shops, and a clock tower. The streets had an antique feel. Joseph stood a great distance away from the town in a clearing surrounded by trees. There was a single cobblestone road that lay in front of him. It led to a small gold, brown building that resembled a small country-home school, like the ones he had seen in the movies. It was next to the edge of the forest, surrounded by trees atop a grassy mound. As the door closed behind him, Joseph felt the grass under his shoes, and the sunlight on his face. He turned around as he heard the door close. It was gone, and now only the large forest stood behind him.

Joseph followed Kassie up the long cobblestone path to the gold brown schoolhouse. In the distance, he heard the echo of a familiar voice.

"Just because you can teleport does not mean you shouldn't use the door. I mean, I still don't see why they didn't knock," said the familiar voice of a man.

"They don't teleport. That's not possible. They use *etheramagus* magic to 'breeze travel' between places," said the familiar female voice.

"Well, you know what I mean."

Joseph hurried up the road, rushing past Kassie, and through the front door of the small schoolhouse. There in the classroom, sat Brian and Maria at two desks near the front. There were many desks, and the room resembled his high school classrooms.

Maria began to speak, "Yeah, I do, but breeze magic and teleportation are completely different. I read in a book…"

"What's all this 'breeze travel' talk?" said Joseph bursting through the door.

Brian and Maria turned at the sound of his voice

"Joseph!" Maria flew across the room. Joseph stumbled backward as she tightly embraced him in a suffocating grip.

"Can't breathe..."

"Oh, sorry!" said Maria, releasing her grip slightly, "I'm just so happy to see you."

Brian walked over to Joseph and greeted him with a hug as well.

"Good to see you Joe. This place is so..."

"...yeah I know. I have met a lot of strange people over the past two days," said Joseph finishing Brian's sentence.

"See!" said Brian, turning to Maria in reference to an earlier argument.

"I never disagreed with you," said Maria, "I just... don't think instantaneous teleportation is possible."

"Oh, well I can't disagree with that argument," said Brian, scratching his head.

There was a breeze followed by a crack of lightning.

"*Latet Luceum!*"

The room went black, and the doors and windows slammed shut. The sharp-tonged voice from the front of the class scared them to attention.

Joseph, Brian, and Maria jumped out of their skins.

In the darkness, at the front of the room, stood three, barely recognizable figures in menacing dark cloaks. After adjusting to the darkness, Joseph made out Kassie as the one to the left, and Senior Elvia to the right. The one who had spoken stood between the two he recognized. She was a tall, slightly heavy woman with short brown hair, and her partially cloaked face looked intimidating. The three robed figures stood statuesque at the front of the room, levitating in the air. The center figure spoke in a most scornful tone.

"Hail, the voice of the Raven, sisters of Fate, Espers of Terraizen…"

"*Luminous!*"

There was a bright flash.

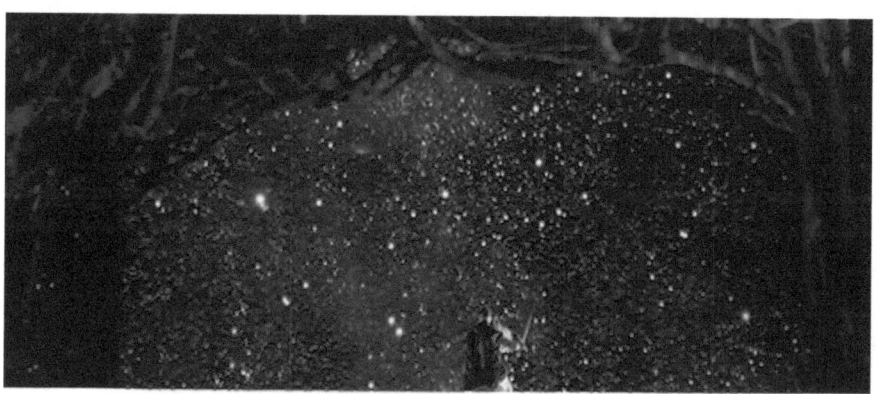

CHAPTER 14: LOVE AND FRIENDSHIP

"All your lives you've been bound by the Sea of Anexthesia. Now you have the power to cross the treacherous waters and venture out into the unknown. But first there is much you need to know."

The tall woman in the center moved like a fine mist over the edge of a nighttime city bay, her robe bellowing in a nonexistent breeze.

"I am Senior Stephenson. Call me by no other name, and understand there is nothing that can elude me and my sisters."

Senior Elvia, the older woman, who stood to the right of Senior Stephenson, stepped forward, her dark purple and black shawl slightly revealed through the open section of her black robe.

"Senior Elvia. Encantada de conocerte todos," she said with a slight bow.

"And I'm Kassie," said the younger one, to the left, with a grin.

Senior Stephenson stepped forward, examining the three of them closely, "Today, we come as the Espers to administer a test. Understand that we are not teachers, and this is not a school. While here in Ezon One, you will be tested until you are deemed stable and no harm to maulfts. Understand, you will be protected, when possible, but know that it is not our duty to keep you safe. It is yours and yours alone."

Senior Elvia raised her index finger, as if she were about to state a point while her eyes glanced over her broad-rimmed spectacles.

"It'd be wise to not forget our words. There are entities that wish to control you, and take your power. Learning how to defend against those threats is essential to your survival. As Awakened, survival should be your top priority. You are few in number, but overwhelmingly powerful when you stand together."

Brian raised his hand, "Senior Stephenson, what does Senior mean? I mean Kassie does not seem that old…" said Brian, as he gestured towards Kassie, whose smile seemed to grow upon the uttering of his compliment.

"How contemptuous of you to imply that I do," said Senior Stephenson, scornfully gazing down at Brian.

"No, no, not at all Senior Stephenson…"

"You are speaking to an Esper of Terraizen. I suggest you mind your impetuous tongue, or I shall have it removed."

Senior Stephenson reached into her pocket and withdrew a wooden stick. It was brown and came to a very sharp point, almost like a needle. She waved it in a circular motion, and her face changed, into that of Dr. Matthews. She tossed her long, black hair. Joseph felt his heart throb at the sight of the beautiful Anabel. Then she waved it once more, and her bold, strong features returned, causing Joseph's stomach to sink into his boots. Although she wasn't hideous, she was no Dr. Matthews either.

"Senior, is a term of knowledge and experience, not age," said Senior Elvia.

"Senior is a title given only to the most elite practitioners of our craft," added Senior Stephenson.

"There are only twelve Seniors in Terraizen, thirteen, if you consider the Lord of the South," said Kassie.

Maria raised her hand. Senior Elvia nodded, granting her permission to speak.

"Senior Elvia, I hope it's not too presumptuous of me to ask, but are the stories of the South true? People say their ruler, Lord Mathias, is a ruthless man that forbids modern technology, and forces his people to live under the old religions."

"Lord Mathias prefers the old ways."

"What about the Donna Robert's novels? They speak of witches, like yourselves, and worlds, like Nefastus, which both exist. So what about the Dark Ones, like Magnus Ma…"

"¡*Silencio!*"

With lightning speed, far beyond the age of her appearance, Senior Elvia had drawn her wand and silenced Maria, binding her tongue mid-sentence.

"Child! Speak no evil within these walls. Words have power here."

Then, under her breath she mumbled, *"Es un muy mal presagio."*

Senior Elvia lowered her wand, and began to lean back. As she did, a rocking chair appeared directly under her, and like a feather, she gently drifted into it, and began to rock back and forth as if trying to calm herself.

Senior Elvia spoke calmly, "Yes, similar entities once existed, but were vanquished long ago by the original Seniors. Diffused fairy tale versions of the truth are all that remain."

Senior Elvia's speed had caught Maria by such surprise that she had barely been unable to process a single word that followed. Never, had she been so speechless. Never had she seen anyone move so fast, let alone, a little old lady.

"So are the stories of The Esper Witches true?" asked Maria.

"No child, they are simple creations of an imaginative witch. Though I will say, Donna Robert's is a very powerful, skilled witch, with a knack for dramas. I remember when she was just a girl living in the East, our stories are much more frightening than her works of fiction," said Senior Elvia in more of a grandmotherly tone. "There are things your mind can't grasp yet. For now, let's focus on the subject at hand."

"Well, what about the murderous forest? What is that place?" asked Brian.

"The Nefastus Forest exists within the Nexus. It's a realm of powerful creatures, unlike any on Terraizen. Central monitors the Nexus, making sure nothing escapes," said Senior Elvia.

"Take caution within that forest. Nothing is what it seems. One wrong move, then snip, goes your strings," said Kassie, making a scissors motion with her hand. "Awakened can enter, but getting out, that's a challenge. The barrier between Terraizen and Nefastus is currently being reinforced. So no worries, you won't be entering that place again. Well, at least not until…"

"Moving on, some elementary questions need to be answered," said Senior Stephenson abruptly. "You may ask, what is an Awakened? Awakened are individuals who have unlocked the power of their essence. Living creatures are composed of three essential parts: mind, body and essence. The mind controls will. The body is the medium. And essence comes from the soul. Though essence is the spark of life, not all living things possess it. Soulless beings walk this earth, consuming the essence of others, attempting to fill their own void. They are the most dangerous above all, and will try to seek you out. Be prepared."

Senior Elvia spoke, "It's time you learn your true purpose in life. The Initium, Semis, and Ultima are the three levels of an Awakened. Once you have unlocked your Ultima, you will understand the meaning of your existence. There is no 'general' meaning of life."

Kassie spoke excitedly, "Essence exists in everything! Magic is the channeling of nature, and by far, the most powerful of any power. Although Awakened can use some spells, witches, wizards, warlocks, sorcerers, and other magical creatures, are able to truly channel the powers of nature. Of the three of you, Maria is the only one capable of channeling. It's an incredible experience."

Brian began to dose off, as Kassie continued to speak. Senior Stephenson walked over to his desk, and looked directly into his closed eyelids.

Senior Stephenson's voice caused the floorboards to quiver, "Does living bore you child? Shall I restore you to the condition we found you in!"

Brian sprung awake from his false sleep.

"I didn't do it," he called out, in a half sleepy haze, "What did I do?"

Senior Kassie giggled.

"Do not condone this behavior," said Senior Stephenson to Kassie.

"Sorry, sister."

Brian blushed out of embarrassment.

"Senior Stephenson, not to sound rude, but Eleanor and Stephen said that you were going to give us a test so we could learn about our abilities," said Maria, "They said I was found in a ditch miles away from Brian and Joseph, unconscious but unharmed, but I don't remember anything. I came here because I wanted to know what happened back there in that forest."

Senior Elvia glanced over at Maria curiously.

Kassie glided over to Senior Stephenson, and placed a hand on her shoulder, diffusing what she could tell was about to become a heated scolding, as Senior Stephenson had begun to draw her wand ready to apply a spell to teach Brian a lesson.

"Sister, it was not his fault. What's done is done. I think it's time to start the first lesson. Time for them to find the answers they seek. We can use your SCS spell."

"SCS, yes… the last arrogant fool we used that spell on met an unfortunate end," said Senior Stephenson with a grin.

"It's less extreme than the torment I had in mind, but it will suffice. Sisters, let us begin the trial, and finish paying this debt. Nothing is without purpose. Though, even with my foresight, it eludes my wits to see why such a powerful force is watching you," she said angrily, as she gazed towards Brian.

Brian could tell that, for some reason, Senior Stephenson did not like him. Yet, he did not remember doing anything to anger her.

Then she turned her gaze towards Maria.

"And you… I can sense that you possess great power. Yet, you allow others to hold you back from your true potential. If you desired, you young lady, could rule among the greats of Terraizen. Instead, you allow yourself to be distracted, clinging to these emotional attachments," she said, gesturing to Brian and Joseph, "which hold you back. You need to cast them away and discover your true purpose. Have the courage to make that sacrifice for yourself, and for Terraizen."

Maria looked into Senior Stephenson's eyes, with an iron-clawed, unflinching, true grit tenacity, and speaking calmly she said, "Senior, I've always been one to speak my mind. So I can honestly say, I would, without question, give my life for these two, and let this world end if saving it came at the cost of their lives."

"Foolish girl!" snapped Senior Stephenson angrily.

"Though she does speak with great confidence," said Senior Elvia, "She reminds me of a younger Donna."

Maria continued to speak.

"You could never understand my pain. At times, the feeling of being alone can seem worse than death. I lost everything, and after my sister's death…depression can't even begin to describe the spiral I took. At night, I laid on the beach, wandering through the skies, drifting through the stars, listening to the waves, questioning their meaning; and the only response, was the blank gaze of the uncertain universe staring back at me. Before they came into my life, I was emptier than a *Hollow Man*. Just knowing that someday it's all going to abruptly end, and I would fade out of existence didn't help me recover either. But then life, for some strange reason, saw it fit that I be given a chance to truly be happy, and I never looked back. Never, would I have thought that I could form such unbreakable bonds after what happened. Just having them around numbed the pain and made me smile again. Since then, we've shared our goals, dreams, and ambitions. I know who I am… I know what I am, but they saved me and I would give my life to protect these two idiots. No matter the skies of life's uncertainties, that is the one thing I am certain of. So, do what you have to do, and I will do the same."

As Maria spoke, the room began to darken, and the sun hid behind the grey clouds of Ezon One.

Brian and Joseph stared dumbfounded at Maria, who had crossed her arms and stared Senior Stephenson down, as if she stood as her equal. The room had grown silent as the storm approached. Then a tear rolled down the side of Maria's cheek.

"I love these two idiots," added Maria.

Joseph and Brian smiled.

"We love you too Maria. You, and your really long speeches. But maybe you shouldn't upset the lady with the strange powers," said Brian.

Maria smiled, trying to hold back the tears. Something had struck a nerve within her, and all the pain in her life seemed to flood back into that moment.

"Idiot," said Maria, with a sniffle and a slight laugh.

"You speak with wisdom beyond your years child. It seems you have nearly unlocked your Initium as well," said Senior Elvia.

"Triggered by her strong emotions for the two it seems," added Kassie, turning to Senior Elvia, who had stopped rocking and had now focused her attention on Senior Stephenson.

While Maria was speaking, Brian thought about how the world he had known had collapsed around him, and a new one was taking shape right before his eyes.

It was then he realized the change. Senior Stephenson was different somehow. Something Maria had said greatly angered the Senior. Even Kassie had begun to cautiously step back. He knew he needed to brace himself for what was coming. As he gazed at the Senior, he could see death forming behind her eyes, and she stood motionless, staring through Maria.

"I was going to say that, but she beat me to it," said Joseph jokingly.

Joseph continued to laugh fearfully.

"Love..." said Senior Stephenson. "What do you know of love? You Awakened are no different from the maulfts, with your diluted notions of love as some unconditional emotional choice! How dare you!"

Thunder struck overhead, as the doors to the schoolhouse were blown open with a loud bang.

"You can't even begin to fathom its true meaning!"

The room trembled as a strong wind shattered the windows and knocked the unoccupied desks towards the back wall.

"What's happening?!" screamed Brian over the strong wind.

"She's going critical," said Kassie, with a disapproving nod.

Senior Stephenson's eyes began to glow as she rose from the ground, while the three stared up at the towering Senior in terror, gripping tightly to their desks. They could hear the sound of the roof being ripped apart from the outside, panel by panel.

"Elvia, we must give them the test before it is too late!" yelled Kassie in desperation.

"They're not ready. That would kill them," said Elvia.

"If we don't do it now, there will be nothing left to test... we will give them the test."

"No need! I'll end them myself. We'll see what they know about love when only one is left standing!" said Senior Stephenson, in a maniacal uproar of laughter.

Her electrified hair stood up in the wind. Joseph looked up just in time to see the roof of the schoolhouse being ripped off like a door from its hinges.

A dark mist began to flow from under the cloaks of the Esper Witches. Senior Elvia and Kassie drew their wands. In an instant, the room was engulfed in a blinding darkness.

"What's happening?" asked Brian, speaking into the darkness. He could no longer see the witches, Maria, or Joseph, and all became too quiet.

"Don't be afraid child. Death has many forms. It's not always as unwelcomed as you may think. But it is the only true test of your love," said the voice of Senior Elvia from within the darkness.

"This darkness brings death," said Kassie.

"You are now within the Esper Mist, and you are seated within our shears. We shall snip away your mind and body, leaving only your essence. This is a form of death. For only death can test your bonds. If you pass you will return from the mist unharmed, with newfound abilities. But if you should fail, then snip, you will meet your end here. Maria and Joseph have already accepted our challenge. If you do not find them, they will meet their end here. It is not too late to turn back, but if you do, you shall forfeit your friendship and their lives! So what is your response? Do you accept or shall you pass? " roared the voices of the three Esper in unison.

Brian thought to himself. Only seven days ago, if someone had told him this would be his future, he would have written them off as senile, but if everything he witnessed was possible, then nothing was impossible. He wanted to discover what he could do, and more importantly, he wanted his friends back.

The question had already been answered.

The mist was closing in on him, and he could feel his mind clinging to his memories. His memories slipped away like shattered pieces of glass falling into an endless abyss. The fear was all that remained of his emotions.

He asked himself what would Maria do, but nothing came to him besides giving a long winded speech.

Then a single thought began to echo through his head.

"I keep thinking I'm going to wake up from this dream, but I see now…this is no dream," Brian took a deep breath and let out a sigh. The mist took the last of his memories, including those of Joseph and Maria. There was only one memory that remained, and he had not understood it until now. It was a poem recited by his high school English teacher, Ms. Mc Mullen, and he began to recite it as well:

"Do not go gentle into that good night,

Rage, rage against the dying of the light,

Although, near death, I see frightening sights,

I will rage, rage against the dying of the light."

The words he strung together came from a place unknown, for his conscious was clear and empty.

"Everything…is next….death is but an obstacle," Brian's legs began to shake. He felt the energy being drained from his body as he fell to his knees before losing consciousness.

Then it began to speak. It spoke using his body as a conduit, and Brian became an unconscious passenger under its control. From Brian's entire body resonated a deep, dark intimidating voice.

"Witches…witches…witches…I accept your challenge witches. But know I don't take kindly to those who wake me. As you're about to kill me, you may be in luck. However, you'd better not fail, for if you do, then in three moons I will escort you to the Gates of Tartarus myself."

"So you are the passenger we sensed? Be gone! This is not your test."

"Not my test! Not my test! This is my planet!! I will ring your necks witches!" roared the voice.

"You underestimate our power Traveler. We are not just any witches. We are the Fates!" said Senior Stephenson, in a dissatisfied voice.

Brian's body was sent flying through the darkness as the Espers chanted.

"Through time and space you'll travel, you'll travel to find your friends. Your names shall reveal the truth; the truth shall reveal its end. If you should fail to gather, what death now apprehends, then behind the veil you'll stay, until your soul transcends."

"Fate does not mourn. For what is destined, shall be. Farewell Traveler," said Senior Stephenson, laughing loudly through the darkness.

The mist ripped the life from his body, and he was consumed by the darkness, along with Brian.

CHAPTER 15: ANTHONY- DEVIL'S GATE

Anthony manned the captain's terminal of the STAR Cruiser as they approached Devil's Gate. The time-waves of the Southern Queens Sea of Anexthesia had finally calmed. They had passed through the storm belt intact. The storm belt encircled the Devil's Gate and contained countless storms of unnatural magnitudes. Passing through it fully intact had never been accomplished, until now. Piloting the STAR Cruiser, Anthony was now the first to go where no man had been. Unknown to his fellow agents he had mapped the Southern Sea of Anexthesia which was the last piece of the puzzle the STAR Cruiser needed to make it's journey safely to the gate. Now they sat just outside of Devil's Gate.

Queens Island was guarded by a series of abnormal weather anomalies that destroyed most ships, but the Engineers had deigned the Cruiser with the purpose of making it to the Devil's Gate. It held the title as the most advanced ship of Central TSPA; able to endure the pressures of the deepest oceans, and return safely. Anthony knew the anomalies that surrounded the sunken island were put into place to prevent anyone from reaching it. They had existed there for millennia, and even the TSPA knew not of what truly lay beyond the gates.

There were five gates that surrounded the island. The first, was Devil's Gate. It was a raging wall of water that surrounded the sunken island. It extended from the bottom of the sea floor, to up beyond the clouds. It was an anomaly known to Awakened, and maulfts alike, that could not be explained. The water flowed up from the ocean, and crashed down on any approaching ships. There was no way to go around it, and passing through it was no simple task either.

Getting through the gate was an impossible task for any normal individual, but Anthony was no ordinary man. A few agents had attempted to explore the Island in the past, but had met their end before seeing the Devil's Gate. Anthony had spent the last few days reviewing their records, and came to the conclusion that the previous team lacked the technology, intellect and Awakened abilities needed to complete the mission. This was the conclusion he always reached, for everything and everyone. Unlike the others, he always prepared for the worst.

Anthony had not only taken the STAR Cruiser, the pride and joy of the Engineering Department, but a synthetic A.I. bio-Faith as well. Faith was excellent at navigating time-waters. With her and the STAR Cruiser, he had all the help he needed.

The automatic doors opened, and the synthetic Faith entered the room.

"We are approaching Devil's Gate. I have analyzed Devil's Gate and will be initiating sequences: 0115, 0427, 0981, and 1571. As you asked, I analyzed the barrier for weaknesses, and my scanners show that there are some minor fluctuations within the northeast sector of the elliptical hemisphere. Our chances of making it through the wall are relatively low due to the force of the hydraulic waterspout. However, if we enter through the fluctuation, we have a seventy percent higher success rate," said Faith. "Would you like to initiate flight mode?"

"Let us transcend to the heavens from which you came, and pierce the devil's veil my radiant blue angel," said Anthony.

"Initiating flight sequences, zero, four, alpha, alpha."

Although Faith had a biosynthetic body, her mind was connected to that of the ship and TSPA headquarters. This gave her the ability to freely navigate the ship, and assist other agents as well. Anthony knew there was a chance that he would not survive the mission, so he decided to go alone. Bringing Faith allowed him the ability to navigate the ship while putting no other lives in danger. If Faith were killed, her essence and knowledge would simply be transferred back to her black box source. Although they used Faith as a processing A.I. powerhouse, they knew little about her origin.

Anthony looked out of the window of his office, seeing the large wall of water in the distance. Faith stood in the center of the control room as she processed commands through the STAR Cruiser. The STAR Cruiser had many functions. It had taken the Engineering Department an entire year to build. Designed with the intent to go almost anywhere, the Cruiser was fit to withstand the force of even galactic travel without the need to recharge for an entire light year. Anthony was amazed by the technology it possessed. Its essence-infused technology allowed the ship to make miraculous changes, and adapt to new conditions very quickly.

"Lift off in two minutes. Anti-gravity boosters coming online now."

Anthony could hear the ship's boosters turn on. He looked over at Faith as she stood with two fingers pressed against her temple processing data.

Faith wore a techno-blue skintight nano-latex suit. It reminded him of a diver's uniform. It was the same thing she wore in her hologram form, but now, she was in the flesh. She had long, black hair and a nice curvy figure, only out-matched by her intellectual capacity. Her capacity for knowledge was greater than all the minds of Terraizen. She was flawless in design. Although capable of showing emotion, she rarely turned them on, for in most circumstances, they proved more of a nuisance than a benefit.

"Is there something wrong sir? You've been staring at me for the last two minutes, eighteen seconds and counting," said Faith.

Anthony had not realized he had been staring at Faith for so long while his mind raced through his mind.

"My apologies, I was not focusing on you…" his eyes began to wander upward, then he cleared his throat, "What I meant to say was I was just in deep thought."

"And please, call me Anthony."

"30 seconds till lift off."

Antigravity boosters kicked in with an upward thrust. The ship rose up from the water's surface.

Anthony watched the ship rise from the ocean while Staring at the wall of water in the distance. It was then that he noticed something very strange. As the ship ascended into the sky, the wall of water began to grow taller and wider as well.

"It seems the wall is reacting to our planned ascension," said Faith, "It is approaching our ship, and fast."

Anthony took a close look at the hologram monitor that Faith had pulled up in the office. His eyes widened at the sight of the clear and glistening wave that had taken the form of a hand and was reaching out to the ship. He knew what he was dealing with and the shock nearly left him breathless.

"This can't be! Raise all shields!" Anthony shouted out in shock.

"Initiating Cruiser Defense sequence," said Faith.

"It was a smart decision on your part not to break through the wall at ground level. The time-waters would have consumed us," said Anthony.

Unlike the other agents of the TSPA, Anthony was a Gate Keeper and he possessed a more complete understanding of the time-waters. He understood that time varied within different quadrants of the Sea of Anexthesia, and that getting caught in the wrong area could cause an individual to lose years within minutes or vise-versa. This was known as a lost time incident.

"Analysis showed trace amounts of living water along the outside of the Devil's Gate. It was a rational decision," said Faith.

Anthony did not know whether to laugh or to cry.

Just then, the water that had taken the form of a hand came crashing down onto the shield of the Cruiser. It was a sight he had never seen before. There was a slight tremble before the water subsided, and the wall could still be seen in the distance.

"Initiate boosters and ascend as quickly as you can," said Anthony.

"That action is irrational with a success rate of only three percent. I recommend using my Anti-Living Water sequence to protect the ship power source," said Faith.

"I did not know you had an Anti-Living Water sequence."

"Anthony, I'm going to initiate the sequence now. It will decrease the rate at which we ascend, however, it will guarantee that we will be protected from the living water."

"Yes, do that. If this stuff gets in, it will drain the ship of its power and kill us both," said Anthony.

"Initiating Anti-Living Water Sequence."

Faith pressed her fingertips against her temple, and a projection appeared between her and Anthony. It showed the layout of the area around the ship. The living water had completely engulfed the ship. There was no way for them to escape, but no way for it to get in either. Faith had seen the power level of the ship's shield rapidly deplete from ninety percent, to nearly empty, and put up a defense just in time to save what remained of their power supply. The boosters had switched to their lower energy state. Soon, the ship would be completely out of power.

Besides the effects of instantaneously absorbing power, and killing Awakened individuals, living water also caused loss in communication, and various other effects that made equipment difficult to use.

In just a few short moments, the living water would completely isolate them from the outside world as it surrounded them in a bubble.

"I am analyzing collected samples of living water and have determined that it does not extend above one-fourth the wall's height. Once we reach that level, we will be out of its grasp. However, due to its drain on our current power supply, we are nearly out of energy."

"How's that possible? We have enough fuel to travel an entire light year."

"Anthony, living water can exponentially drain the power of a light years' worth of fuel in ten seconds. I initiated defenses, it was the only thing that saved what remained of our power. I also sent out an S.O.S to the Engineering Department with our navigation records and coordinates before communications were cut off, and they are on their way. Until then, we must wait."

Anthony looked over at Faith.

"Well that's that. So what do you suppose we do while we wait…"

CHAPTER 16: GHOST TOWN

The man walked quietly up the hill. As he approached the village, he contemplated the words of his editor. He had been writing a novel that dealt with a non-linear time line. His editor wanted to know if there was any continuity with the flow of time in his book, which the reader could connect to, in real life. The man had attempted to stress to his editor that the time stream was not meant to be linear in any way but his editor just could not understand Mobius-time. He approached the big blue house on the hill hidden by the tall bushy trees. He felt he had been there before. The aroma from the decaying leaves and sweetly scented flowers filled the air as he walked along the stone pathway up the grassy hill. It was a beautiful day. The sun was out, the winds were pleasant and the only noise was that of the choirs of birds and rustling of the trees, which were in the midst of composing their finest melody yet on the beautifully autumn day.

The man had been welcomed into the house by an older woman. She escorted him to a chair in the living room before heading to the kitchen. She was the maid for the owners of the house, who were currently at work. The man had requested a tour of the town south of the hill. He felt it would provide a nice, peaceful location to continue his writing. His first impression of the beautifully quiet town had only strengthened his belief that it was without a doubt the right place.

The maid entered the room.

"I'm sorry signore, but the owner of this estate will not be returning today. However, she gave me this to give to you."

The maid handed him an envelope, which contained his housing information as well as instructions to get to eateries and other fascinating places within the town.

The maid smiled, "I'm sorry to inconvenience you, but something came up for her at work and they needed her to stay. We don't have a car, but I will gladly lend you my electric scooter. It's very durable, and should make the trip with no complications."

The man turned to the maid. He didn't fancy electric scooters, but he knew he needed as much time as he could get to finish his novel. His deadline was right around the corner.

"That will be fine," said the man.

The maid showed him out of the house to the scooter. It was large enough to hold his three bags of luggage on the rear back seat. His editor had booked him a room in the hotel south of the house on the hill. The maid instructed him on how to drive and recharge it; and pointed out the sticky break petal.

"Signore, I'm not sure why you intend to go to that town as a writer. But make sure to watch out for traffic. It can get pretty backed up for such a quiet town."

The man said his goodbyes to the maid and headed out to the town. No sooner had he hit the bridge road that he came to a complete stop. Cars were like sardines in a can as they sat bumper to bumper. Impatient drivers honked their horns with no purpose but to ease the stress that came from the wait. When it did finally pick up, it moved like molasses. It was not until he hit the bridge underpass that the traffic eased up, until finally, it nearly vanished, leaving him alone on Bridge Road. The man was just five minutes away from the town, and knew that soon, he would be able to stain the blank pages with his wonderful ideas. They flowed out through his pen and gave life to his universe.

Night set upon him as he arrived at the town. It sat alone in a unique area, surrounded by sand, which was surrounded by a moat. There was one bridge that led to the town. It reminded him of a fortress with its moat, tall stonewalls, and bridge. He headed through the lush greenery towards the bridge just as the sun began to set. He was tired from the long drive and needed to rest and refuel. As he headed over the bridge the streetlights awoke while the sun began to set.

The man had rented a room in a very historical building. It had originally started out as a high school, but was turned into a training facility for the army during the war, and now was a hotel. It had a strange feel to it since the bedrooms resembled class rooms, the bathrooms were at the end of the hall, and the showers were located in the basement in an area previously known as the locker room. But the rooms were high quality, and the cost of the stay was less than the price of any hotel in the state. The man found the long walk to the bathroom and shower a minor inconvenience in comparison to the dirt-cheap price.

After check-in the man went to the lunchroom to grab some food. After writing for six hours he headed out to refuel and grab dinner. Upon returning to the hotel the man struggled between sleeping and writing, but he knew his best ideas always came to him first thing in the morning, so he headed off to bed. As he drifted off to sleep he thought of time and how it related to his stories. Even though the concept of time was a construct of the living mind, it also stood alone as a measurement of change. But what if all changes were to happen in reverse, the man thought to himself? Would that mean that time was going backwards, or would it still be considered moving forward? Then again, what if time were going in reverse currently? How would we know? After all, we are only a tiny part of this great big thing we call a timeline...

***

The alarm sounded and the man hurried to his feet. He had learned to sleep in his army gear to save time putting it on in the morning. He hurried to the restroom down the hall to get ready. Although it was early and the sun had not risen, drills started in half an hour and he knew if he wanted breakfast, he would have to move fast. The man brushed his teeth, and quickly combed his hair as he headed quickly to the gym room where they did his warm-up training with the five other members of his group. He had great news to tell them. Yesterday, he had gotten a promotion to team captain for passing all his examinations with flying colors. He exceeded not only his group's scores, but everyone's score on the written, physical, and strategic thinking examinations. He knew that everyone in his group would be proud of him everyone, except Eugene. Eugene despised him, and everyone knew it.

After completing warm-ups the man headed to the lunchroom with his group. The lunchroom was set up in a very unique fashion. Each section was curtained off like an improvised hospital ward. Each group had their own section. Under no circumstances were you allowed to go behind the curtain of another individual's group, unless you were a higher-ranking office.

The man went through the lunch line with his group, and they sat at their designated table. After all members of the group took their seat, the curtain fell from the ceiling to the floor, and encompassed them on all sides. The man stood up.

"I hope you guys are ready for this. I have great news for you all," said the man with his hands folded behind his back out of habit.

Eugene looked up from his meal, and began to mumble something under his breath.

The man began to circle the table. It was custom for an individual to walk all the way around the inside of the curtain before revealing good or bad news. This was said to provide more intellectual responses and conversation. If it was not worth the trouble to walk the circle, then it was not worth mentioning.

As the man completed his circle, he felt a vibration in his pocket. He reached into his pocket and began to withdraw the phone, when suddenly, there was a gunshot. The man fell to the floor. As he looked up, he saw Eugene standing at the far edge of the table trembling with his revolver still smoking.

"Eugene, you shoot me?!" Screamed the man confused, in utter disbelief.

"I thought you were going for a gun," panted Eugene.

"Put the gun down," said Maria, from the table next to where the man had sat. Everyone else in the group continued to eat their lunch as if they were ignorant to what was happening before their eyes.

"No," said Eugene, "it's too late, I can't go back now. I have to finish what I started."

Eugene circled the table and stood over the man with his gun drawn. The man fought hard to stay conscious as he applied pressure to the bleeding leg. The pain was excruciating.

"Help! Help, someone!" screamed the man.

Maria jumped from the table and kicked the gun from Eugene's hand into the curtain. Eugene lunged for the gun, and so did Maria. The man was dumb founded that no one had responded to the commotion, especially a gunshot in an army training center. It was just then that the man remembered the cell phone in his pocket. He pulled it out and began to dial for an emergency. As he completed the call, he looked over to see that Eugene had recovered the gun.

"I'm sorry Joseph," were Maria's last words, lost under the loud shots of the gun. Maria was dead before she hit the ground, and now the gun was aimed at the man who lay bleeding on the ground.

The man crawled along the floor trying to remove himself from the false protection of the curtain. He heard the roar of the gun as three shots passed by his head. His ears were ringing louder than ever, but he knew that the next bullet would not miss. The man mustered up the last of his strength. He could see hesitation in Eugene's eyes, as if some part of him was fighting a parasite, which had taken control of his mind. It was the same part of him that had made the last three shots miss.

"Fight it Eugene!" said the man, "You're a good guy. I know we've had our problems but this is not you. That is not you," said the man as he pointed to Maria lying dead on the ground.

Suddenly, the curtains began to rustle as if a breeze had picked up. The curtain fell, and as it did, the man saw that the room had disappeared. They were outside in a dusty area resembling a cowboy western at sunrise. There were people all around, but no one seemed to be able to see them.

Alarms flared and Eugene quickly turned around. Two officers jumped out of the police car with weapons drawn. Eugene dropped the gun. One of the officers began to cuff him.

The other officer looked over at the man who lay injured on the ground, "Sir are you okay?"

"I'm shot; I need an ambulance," said the man.

"It's on its way," said the officer.

As the officers put Eugene in the back of the car, the man still lying injured on the ground reached for the gun. He was scared and did not want it to fall into the wrong hands again. While the man emptied out the bullets, the police car drove off.

"Hey! Where are you going? You can't just leave me here alone," yelled the man.

The wind grew still, and crowds of people began to walk pass.

"Help me!" screamed the man, but they ignored him. The man finally managed to crawl over to a group holding a conversation outside of what resembled an old swinging door saloon. The man could not hear their words because his ears were still ringing.

"Help!" screamed the man, grabbing at their ankles. His heart skipped a beat, and he lurched back in surprise. Like mist, his hand had passed right through them.

The shock and blood loss almost made him lose consciousness. He knew what was going on now, and no one was coming to his rescue. He would have to escape the place on his own or he would die. He remembered the words of the maid in the blue house.

"Be careful," she had said, "It's like a ghost town down there." The words from the woman echoed like a voice from the heavens while the sun continued to rise. As the light shined, the man's memories began to return to him. He remembered that he was a writer, and this was all a dream. Realizing he was asleep, he entered a state of lucid dreaming. For some reason he could not heal his injury, but he could fly. He began to float up into the sky as if to greet the sun's rays as they shined down upon the new day. He soared high above the buildings, high above the island. He could see the moat that surrounded the island. He was free like a bird.

At that moment, an alarm sounded.

The man sprung from his sleep. He was back in his bed in the hotel room, in his normal clothes. It was still dark out. His dream had helped him to come up with a brilliant idea for a story. However, now that he was awake, something still didn't feel right. Something's missing, he thought to himself. Something important. All of a sudden, he remembered Maria from his dream.

What was it Maria had known that he did not?, he asked himself. It was then that he realized the answer was in the question. The man did not remember his name.

He sprung out of bed and hastily began to search through his luggage in an attempt to find some kind of identification, but there was nothing. *This is impossible,* he thought to himself. He headed down to the check-in desk to meet with the clerk. She had been folding the clean linen in the supply closet and was just heading back to the front desk to finish a crossword puzzle.

"Excuse me madam."

"Please, call me Maria," said the lady in a heavy accent.

This caught the man by surprise. Her name was Maria, although she was older and looked nothing like the Maria in his dreams. He had not remembered she held that name, but then again, he had forgotten his own name as well.

"Funny," said the man, "I had a dream about a Maria. I had never met the woman before, but for some reason I felt like I had known her forever."

"Maria is a very common name," said the lady in her heavy accent.

"Do you remember my name?" asked the man.

The woman looked at him, confused as to if he was serious about the question. After examining his face, she concluded that he was serious. Maybe he had come down with some mental ailment, she thought to herself. After all, the lost look on his face would be hard to fake. She had seen this expression on her grandfather who lost many memories in his old age.

"No, but I can look you up in the system if you just give me a second," said Maria.

In an instant, the front door swung open behind the man. A scruffy-haired man with a snow covered, thick winter jacket walked in and headed to the counter.

The nameless man thought this strange since it had been bright and sunny just before he had fallen asleep.

The scruffy-haired man approached the counter, "Boy it's cold out there," he said in a jolly tone as he brushed the large piles of snow from his jacket.

"Great, another mess to clean up," said Maria in a slight under tone.

"Excuse me?" said the man as he looked at Maria.

"Nothing," said Maria, "It just seems like you purposely stood outside and let a half a foot of snow accumulate on top of your shoulders, so you could come in here and brush it off onto our nice carpets to make my life a little harder. I mean really, you would have had to walk really slowly just to stop it from falling off before you got in the door. And who wears rectangular shoulder pads...?"

"It's the least I could do for your wonderful hospitality and delightful attitude," said the scruffy-haired man, "There's no cure for the weather."

"Yes, there's also no cure for stupidity either, but somehow you've made it this far with an illness that has claimed so many lives."

"Idiot," added Maria under her breath as she looked towards her logbook.

"No, my name is Ronald Brian Kooses," said the scruffy-haired man in a mockingly sophisticated tone. "I thought your name was Maria Marmota, but I know now why the people in town refer to you as the cold-hearted bitch of East Inn."

His comment caught Maria by surprise.

"Brian, sometimes you're an asshole," Maria said with a smile.

Brian smiled back. "Hey, assholes are very important."

"Excuse me," said the man, who had been listening to their strange commentary," I don't mean to interrupt, but have you found anything on my name yet?"

"Yes, your name is Joseph, Joseph D. Aizen," said Maria.

No sooner did the words leave her mouth that ground began to shake. The world around them began to collapse. Their bodies began to return to normal as they began to recover their true memories. They began to remember who they really were, and the memories of what they had experienced began to fade like a dream. The room became a boundless empty grey space that seemed to go on forever. They knew who they were, but no longer remembered what had happened. All that remained was a feeling of accomplishment.

Brian looked towards Joseph

"What just happened? I can't remember anything."

"Me neither. What is this place and how do we get out?" asked Joseph, looking around the white room.

"Not sure."

"I can't recall why, but for some reason, I want to punch you in the face," said Maria, looking towards Brian.

"What did I do?"

"Congratulations! You have passed the test," came a voice from behind them.

Brian, Maria, and Joseph, surprised by the voice, jumped and turned around quickly. There before them, stood the three Seniors.

"Where are we?" asked Joseph.

"You stand on the boundary between the Realms of Terraizen and Ezon One. It seems your meeting each other was not a series of unfortunate events," said Kassie enthusiastically smiling at Brian, Maria, and Joseph.

"Although we took away your memories, altered your physical form, and integrated your existence into three different worlds throughout the Ezon realms, you were still able to find each other. The chances of doing so are less than a septillionth," said Senior Stephenson.

"This goes beyond a simple friendship. You are a trinity, bound together in ways that you have yet to discover. No matter the distance, you will always find your way back to each other. And when apart, you will feel incomplete," said Senior Elvia.

"What you have goes beyond the diluted maulft concept of love, emotions, and feelings. You possess the real thing, and you'd best not forget it," said Senior Stephenson sternly shaking her finger at the three.

"Come now, accept your rewards."

Brian, Maria, and Joseph did as commanded and approached the Espers. As they did, a stone pedestal rose from the ground in front of them. Upon it, rested three pendants, each with a jewel. One emerald, one ruby, and a sapphire set within golden crests that spiraled inward around the surface of the jewels, holding them in place.

"Only six of these pendants exist; the other three are wielded by another trinity. These pendants possess extraordinary powers, and will allow you to channel your inner strength as well as that of nature. With this gift, the bonds between you shall manifest themselves in this world as power for as long as you exist," said Senior Stephenson.

Senior Elvia stepped forward and waved her hand over the pendants. As she did, they disappeared, and then reappeared hanging from Brian, Maria and Joseph's necks on a golden chain.

"Let the Unseen be seen. Let the universe reveal the truth and recognize your trinity. *Anima clamore veritas!*" said Kassie.

The pendants began to glow. Joseph's glowed a bright green light, Brian's a bright red light, and Maria's a bright blue light. The lights flashed off, and they found themselves back in the classroom where they had begun the trial. They nearly collapsed from exhaustion.

Brian fell to the ground.

"I'm feeling rather sleepy," he said, lying on the ground with his eyes partially closed.

"Are you okay?" asked Maria, looking down at Brian

"Me too," said Joseph as he propped himself up using the desk next to him.

Maria could feel her legs beginning to buckle. They had become like two wet noodles as she fought against gravity.

"They'll be fine," came a voice from behind them. Maria could tell, unmistakably, it was Kassie's. Maria managed to slide down to the floor, next to Brian, who had now been joined by Joseph. She pressed her back against the front desk of the classroom and looked up at the three Espers.

Senior Elvia began to speak.

"It's been a long day. This test has not only drained much of you and your friend's power, but our energy as well. I think we are all much over due for a nap. Don't you agree Steffi?" asked Elvia.

"Yes, let's begin again tomorrow at noon."

"Sorry I'm late," came a voice from behind the Espers.

The Espers turned around. There at the door stood a man in worn blue jeans and a blue hooded sweatshirt.

"Sammy, be a dear and escort our guests to the Elizabeth Hotel in Ezon One. Make sure they are well taken care of, and bring them to the training grounds first thing tomorrow morning," commanded Senior Stephenson.

"Right away Senior," said Sammy nodding.

"Farewell children. Until tomorrow," said Senior Elvia, waving her hand through the air in a nonchalant manner. As she did, the Espers slowly faded from the room, like steam on a bathroom mirror, before completely vanishing.

Brian, Maria, and Joseph fought sleep as they made their way through the valley and into the town of Ezon One. Their eyelids hung like cinder blocks upon their faces, not allowing them to see much as Sammy guided them through the streets. They were more sleep than awake. Sure, there were lights and buildings, but the only thing they saw were dreams of pillows and soft sheets, even a couch or floor would have sufficed.

Like three zombies they walked along the strip passing a shopping center, food courts, a small shop a diner, and many hidden strangers who they could not make out from under the strange multicolored cloaks.

As much as Maria, Brian, and Joseph were tempted by the smell of fresh baked breads, pies, and grilled meats resonating from the food court, they doubted they would be able to hold anything long enough to bring it to their mouths. Maria had also seen a gorgeous pair of jeans on display, but there was no urge to get them. All she wanted was sleep.

Their dreary eyelids had closed in upon their destination as they came to rest at the sight of Joseph's bed. Sammy was speaking, but they could not understand the words that were coming from his mouth. It seemed like he was attempting to direct Maria and Brian to another room, but they were far too gone. Their bodies had collapsed onto the first bed they saw, which happened to be Joseph's. It was so soft, and possibly the most comfortable bed they had ever rested on. Sammy made another attempt to lead Brian and Maria to their own rooms, but as their heads hit the soft pillows, like magic, they instantly fell asleep. His persistence was futile as they moved closer to the center of the bed and curled up next to Joseph

"Go away, let us rest," they said in a sleep-like monotone. Sammy knew there was not a force on the earth that could move them from that bed at that moment.

"If you need me, my room is directly down the hall. I will be giving tours all this week. Starting first thing in the morning. The wing you are currently staying in is the guest wing. As of now, there are only three other people staying here, besides us…." Sammy stopped speaking. He knew his words would not reach them, as the snoring grew louder.

"Rest well. It's the Awakened hour but the others wont disturb you. They like to keep to themselves."

Sammy crept out of the room and closed the door softly behind him. Sammy thought to himself how skilled those three must have been. What had taken his group three days, they had done in less than twenty-four hours.

Sammy raced down the hall, and in an instant, he was back at his room. He planned to introduce his team to the new trinity. Though Sammy hoped they did not encounter Jabin, who had a habit of rubbing people the wrong way.

CHAPTER 17: BRUNO- EDGE OF SEVENTEEN

Quinn sat in Anabel's kitchen watching her as she finished preparing breakfast. One of Anabel's favorite hobbies was cooking. She always loved to fix a big breakfast like her mother had for her and her brothers growing up. Although she did not always get the time, she tried to cook on special occasions. Today Bruno, Quinn, and Anabel had scheduled to meet in Anabel's chambers to go over tactics for their upcoming missions. Anabel had prepared a wonderful continental breakfast of sausage, eggs, and hash browns, Terraizen toast with strawberry jam, sliced cinnamon apples, blueberry pancakes, waffles topped with blackberry jam covered in powdered sugar, and an assortment of delicious exotic fruit. Quinn had told her that a simple cup of tea and buttered toast would suffice for him, but she ignored him.

Anabel sat across the table from Quinn. Although they were not speaking with each other verbally, they had been in an intense mental conversation for the past hour. Quinn had just finished a piece of buttered toast when he began eying the delicious display of food. He finally came to the decision that, although he was not very hungry, he would try a small bite of a blueberry pancake. He made sure to cut off just a small portion, which he carried over to his plate with his knife and fork. Slowly, he took a bite. Like lightning, the taste of the pancake had sent an intense sensation of sweet deliciousness to his brain. His mouth cringed, and began to water from the sweetness of the bite. Anabel watched Quinn as he turned from a mild-mannered high class individual to a blueberry pancake-consuming machine. Before he knew it, he had consumed three full pancakes, and nearly half of the sausage, eggs, and toast. Anabel had watched in amazement as he consumed the food with such a miraculous speed that it seemed to vanish from the plate.

Two hours into breakfast, the phone rang. Anabel and Quinn paused their cognitive conversation, and she headed to the living room to answer the call.

"Anabel speaking…he did what? On our way."

Anabel quickly hurried to the kitchen.

"Quinn, we need to head to the medical unit. It seems Bruno has had a bit of an altercation."

Quinn quickly consumed the piece of toast that he was holding between his teeth, and they headed down the hall to the medical ward.

The walls were their usual white, except for a portion that seemed to have been damaged, but the A.I. system had nearly finished the repairs. They entered through the sliding glass doors and headed down the hall to Bruno's room.

Along the way, they were greeted by one of the nursing staff. Her name was Sarah.

"What's his status?" asked Anabel.

Sarah handed Bruno's chart to Anabel and the three of them proceeded down the hall.

"He lost consciousness. We managed to stop the internal bleeding, set the compound fractured tibia and fibula. All of which we were able to repair before any serious damage was done to his brain. His forearms, pelvis, hip, knees, spinal column, ankle, and neck were also fractured, and there were torn bicep tendons," said Nurse Sarah.

"Was there anything that was not broken?" asked Anabel.

"No, Dr. Matthews. From a medical standpoint, he should not be alive right now. Even from the Awakened analysis, he had only a 3% chance of survival. We had to put him in a full body cast to hold him together, and he is on full life rejuvenation."

"How did this happen?"

"We're not sure, but we believe there was some altercation between Benjamin and Bruno, since he was found hemorrhaging outside of Benjamin's chamber door. Half the hallway had collapsed on top of him, and we had to dig him out."

Anabel stopped at the hospital room door, which had Bruno's name on it.

"Thank you Sarah," said Anabel as she opened the door.

The door swung open. The white sheets of the bed held bloodstains from the bandages and the room resembled that of a cabin bedroom. The monitor displayed the Terraizen children's cartoon, *Funny Bunny*. Bruno loved cartoons, which complemented the childlike innocence that he possessed.

The hospital rooms all looked different from each other, and were designed to adjust to each patient's liking. All of them were flawless in their design. This helped maximize each patient's full recovery. The only thing this room was missing was the patient.

"Goodness me!" said the nurse, surprised to find the bed covered in bandages and blood, and Bruno nowhere in sight. "He should not be out of bed. Where is he?"

Anabel and Quinn were also caught by surprise as they surveyed the room.

"Shall I put out an alert?" asked the nurse frantically.

"No need," said Quinn, "We'll take it from here."

Quinn and Anabel exited the hospital ward and headed to the elevator. As they entered the elevator, a techno blue hologram of Faith with long black hair appeared in the center of the elevator.

"Quinn, Anabel, how are you doing this morning?" asked Faith.

"Just wonderful," said Anabel with a smile. "I love what you've done with your hair today."

"Thank you. Anthony has been upgrading my program," said Faith.

"Faith can you take us to Zone-Bruno?" requested Quinn.

"Absolutely."

The elevator began to spin like a centrifuge, and shifted downward swiftly before coming to a sudden halt. Quinn recalled his first time riding the elevator to the Zone had caused him to nearly vomit. Now he had grown accustomed to the experience, and so had Anabel. Although on occasion it still made her light headed.

They had arrived at their destination. As the doors flew open, Faith told them to have a nice day, and vanished from the elevator.

Anabel and Quinn exited the elevator. There was no need for words. As they walked through the white space, the room began to change. With every step, the scenery shifted. It was like they were traveling through various worlds as they moved forward. One moment they were on a beach, and then the edge of a volcano. The Zone had the ability to replicate any environment. It was a kaleidoscope of places, which provided sanctuary for any Awakened who needed it. No one knew how many Awakened existed in the Zone, but once you entered, you could exist in any world that you desired. The Zone was a universe of its own, ruled by The Mother of Faith, and the TSPA was built atop its only gateway.

As they shifted through the different realms, they finally settled at a world that held a small cabin in the woods. Quinn knew Bruno would be inside.

***

Bruno lay on the couch inside his cabin holding his family portrait in its silver frame. The cabin in the Zone was the one place that Bruno went to when he needed to get away from everything. It was a replica of his home, which was destroyed when he was younger by a natural disaster.

The hurricane had killed his mother, father, baby sister, and older brother, leaving him as the only survivor. Bruno's father, who had been the world champion martial arts master of the North, had taught him many martial arts skills, and wanted him to be the best fighter in the world once he had Awakened. It was his father's wishes that drove him to continue to fight. Not a day went by that he did not miss his family. He missed his mother's cooking, his annoying little sister, and even the constant torment of his older brother. Bruno strived to live his life to the fullest and become stronger; not just for himself, but for his family as well.

The cabin was a reconstruct from Bruno's memories, and a place of solace away from the harshness of the outside world. After reminiscing about his family, he had reached a calm place in his mind.

There was a knock at the door.

"Bruno, may I come in?" asked Anabel in a calmly manner.

"Sure," said Bruno as his voice trembled.

Anabel and Quinn entered the room. The house was made of a fine polished wood. The trees of forest that surrounded the house were almost as tall as those in Nefastus. It was a very peaceful place, where the only noise that could be heard was the sweet melody of nature's streams, and the songbirds in the rustling trees.

Anabel and Quinn pulled chairs from the table, and sat them in front of the fireplace across from the couch on which Bruno rested. They could see the family portrait he held in his arms.

"Are you okay?" asked Anabel.

She visually inspected his body as she moved her chair close to the head of the couch. Gently, she ran her hands through his hair, hoping to comfort him.

Bruno sat up.

"I'm fine," said Bruno. There was no hesitation in his voice. He was wearing his martial arts training uniform.

Quinn could tell by his damp hair, and the smell of lavender, that Bruno had just finished an intense training session and had taken a shower.

"What happened?" asked Anabel.

"I would rather not talk about it," said Bruno.

"Let me rephrase the question," said Quinn, "Will you tell us what happened or should I?"

"Quinn!" said Anabel disapprovingly, "If he does not want to tell us what happened, you will not force him to. Understood?"

"I wouldn't have done it, just thought it would inspire some…initiative."

Bruno looked very depressed, as if he had lost his will to fight.

"I can't do this," said Bruno, "It's too much to handle. Every morning their ghosts haunt me. This morning, I was resting in bed, and for a brief moment, everything was how it used to be. I could hear my dad calling me down for training and my mom calling me for breakfast, the sound of my little sister knocking on my bedroom door asking if I could take her shopping," Bruno laughed, "My brother use to love to play pranks on me. Replacing my socks with frogs, stuffing my pillow with poisonous mushrooms and itching powder, and locking me in my room with strange animals as revenge for me beating him in training. Ha! He was always better at channeling than me though. There was this one time I woke up and there was a bear in the corner of my room, I completely freaked out..."

Bruno paused.

"And then I opened my eyes and reality rushed in. it was all gone... my sister, my room, my brother and dad, all dead. There was only me. Alone...and it was too much. it was just too much for me to handle, and in that brief moment, I just wanted it to end."

Bruno's eyes began to tear up. Anabel moved over to the coach and held his head in her lap.

"It's okay... you're not alone," she said as she caressed his face.

Quinn frowned, angered by Bruno's statement, "We've all suffered losses. Only a fool takes the easy route. Come find me when this pity party has ended," said Quinn as he stepped out the front door, closing it behind him.

Bruno began to smile, "Quinn reminds me of Brock sometimes," he said wiping away the tears. "That's exactly what he would have said."

Anabel smiled, then began to speak in a soft tone.

"Back when I first lost my mother, every day I woke up I felt like I had lost her all over again. The pain never truly went away it... it just became more manageable..."

There was silence.

Anabel sighed softly, "If there was one good thing that came from such a terrible tragedy it's that it brought me and my brothers closer together... and we carried on. Not just for ourselves, but to honor her memory as well. Since you joined this organization, you've saved many lives Bruno, and I'm sure they would all be proud of you. There's enough death in this world already, there's no need to add more if it can be prevented."

Bruno could feel the emotion in Anabel's voice as she spoke. It was powerful, yet, it had an aesthetic quality as well. Her words had eased the pain of his scarred past, and his depression had begun to fade.

Stretching and yawning, Bruno sat up.

"Anabel, thanks for caring. I know it was foolish of me to challenge Benji to a fight, but I've gotten stronger and needed a strong sparring partner. It seems I'm just not Benji strong. Although he almost killed me, I know somewhere deep down in the bottomless hole of his heart, he cares. And I'm going to be the one to bring it out of him. "

Bruno's stomach began to grumble.

"Let's deal with one bottomless hole at a time. Come now, there's a royal breakfast that awaits us, and I've fixed all your favorites," said Anabel as she stood up grasping his hand.

As she headed to the door, she turned towards Bruno, "Next time you challenge Benjamin to anything, make sure I am present."

"Why?"

"He missed a few bones. If I'm there, I will be sure to get them all."

Anabel gave a smile, which made Bruno feel uneasy, for he knew the power that resided behind the soft, charming and compassionate eyes.

Anabel hugged Bruno tightly, "You're like a brother to me, and I would do anything to protect you. So don't make me have to hurt you. Agreed?"

Still a little freaked out by her previous comment, Bruno gulped and nodded, "Agreed. But you're crushing my ribs, mind letting up a bit? I'm still healing."

***

Bruno, Anabel, and Quinn headed out of The Zone and back to Anabel's chambers to discuss the mission tactics; and feed Bruno's monster of a stomach. No one brought up what had happened in the cabin. It had become common for Bruno to slip in and out of these states of depression the day before his birthday. It was the day before his seventeenth birthday that the disaster had struck. Since then, he had stopped aging. Physically and emotionally, he would forever linger on the edge of seventeen.

CHAPTER 18: RETURN OF THE NIGHTMARE

Joseph walked along the dead grass, gazing up at the dark starless sky. There was no living creature in sight. This was a dream he had once before with the blue elk and nightmare elk. However, unlike previous dreams, he was fully aware that he was dreaming. He wanted to know what it meant. He could feel his dreams were trying to tell him something. Joseph felt a pressure pushing down on him, making it hard for him to breath. Death and decay hung heavy in the air around him. He needed answers, and he knew it was time he found them. It was at this time that he spoke the words that formed within his mind.

"Let the Unseen be seen. Let the universe reveal the truth and recognize our trinity. *Anima clamore veritas!*"

Brian and Maria appeared at his side.

"I was just having one of the most amazing dreams, and you bring me here. Why Joseph? Why?" Brian asked.

"Brian, Maria, something's not right... I think my dreams are trying to tell me something," said Joseph.

"What is this place?" asked Maria.

"It's the Northern Forest of STAR Island... or what's left of it," said Joseph.

"What could have done this?" asked Brian.

"That's what we need to find out. I think my dreams may hold some truths about the future. I used to have dreams when I was younger. I remember the day my father died, I had a dream about him. He said he was going on a long trip, and wouldn't be returning. He told me to take care of the house and my mother. I had never had a dream like that before, and it was that same day he died," said Joseph, "That was not the only one."

"You never told us this before," said Maria.

"Yeah I know. I just thought you might have thought I was crazy," said Joseph, "But after everything we have witnessed in these past few days, I think there's something to these dreams. I think they're warnings."

Lightning and thunder rained from the heavens, illuminating the darkness every few moments. Fires, which still burned among the trees, provided some light from in the distance, but the finer details were hard to make out. Then the lightning changed to a crimson red. As it flashed across the sky, it left red scars within the clouds as if the sky itself were bleeding.

"I feel something," said Maria, "there's something here that we cannot see."

Brian and Joseph looked over at Maria. Their eyes widened at the sight of her. Her attire had changed. She now wore a long black starlight dress, and had long black hair. She was the night.

"What's up with the outfit?" asked Brian.

Maria smiled, "I think I'm awakening. I can feel the energy. It gives me butterflies."

Maria began to rise just above the ground.

Suddenly, they were interrupted.

Between the red flashes, they could make out something in the distance.

At first, Joseph thought it was the blue elk, but it was not luminescent blue. Then he suspected maybe the nightmare elk, but even from such a faraway distance, Joseph could tell it was much too large.

As it approached, Joseph began to unknowingly step back in fear. What he saw in the distance, could only be described as a living nightmare.

It seemed small to Brian and Maria from so far away, but Joseph had seen how truly massive it was as it approached at a rapid pace.

"Hey Joe, do you see that thing coming this way?" asked Brian, who was a bit surprised at the sight of it, even from a distance.

"Yeah," said Joseph, "it's the nightmare beast. I think it's responsible for this destruction. Last time I was here, I think it tried to kill me, but it looked different. It was much smaller then."

"Wait, kill you! Why are we still here?" asked Brian.

As the beast drew closer, the ground trembled. The beast grew larger in size and picked up speed. It left a cloud of ash in its wake. It leveled the remaining shadows of grass and trees, which had already lost all life, but like fossils, maintained some shape.

"Let's get out of here Joe, it's getting bigger," said Brian.

"I can't," said Joseph. He shut his eyes tightly, trying to focus on waking up.

"What do you mean you can't?" asked Brian confused.

"Every time I try, I can see its face. I think it's stopping me from leaving," said Joseph.

"But this is your dream," said Brian.

The ground shook upon the impact of the beast's hooves. Although it was still far away, Joseph could tell it was massive and still growing. It already towered nearly twenty times over him.

The beast let out a cry that shook loose their courage, and rattled their souls at its core.

"You're mine!" roared the nightmare beast.

Its roar had quieted the heavens, as if scaring away the thunder and lightning, leaving only the dark clouds trembling in fear. The clouds shook, letting out a massive down pour.

"Terraizen will fall! It will not escape me! I will devour this world!" said the beast.

The ground began to shake uncontrollably, throwing Brian and Joseph off kilter. The beast was close enough to them now for them to see how truly massive it had grown.

"If we can't leave, then we need to run, or it's going to crush us," said Brian.

"We can't run, there is nowhere to run to," said Maria.

"But…"

Maria grabbed both their hands and looked towards the sky. "We can fly."

The wind picked up as her dress bellowed in the breeze. Brian, Maria, and Joseph began to rise swiftly into the sky, and soared away from the creature. They knew they could not run for long, but they could not let it get close to them either.

As it closed in on them, they felt their strength waiver. It was a beast of death and destruction. It was a force stronger and larger than any they had ever encountered or could even imagine. It was not living. Its sheer essence was death; an indiscriminate death that would covet all those it encountered.

Whatever it was, they knew now that it was the entity that would destroy the planet of Terraizen and all of its inhabitants if not stopped. This was no ordinary dream. This was its prison, and now it was trying to break free.

"I'm getting tired you guys, and it's getting closer. I think it's draining my energy," said Maria.

"When did you even learn to fly? Wait, this is a dream," said Brian.

The stars on her dress began to fade.

"The Trinity spell brought us here, maybe it can free us as well," said Maria.

"I don't remember it," said Brian.

"Repeat after me. Let the Unseen be seen. Let the universe reveal the truth and recognize our trinity. *Anima clamore veritas!*" said Maria.

Together, Brian, Maria, and Joseph began to recite the Trinity spell, "Let the Unseen be seen. Let the universe reveal the truth and recognize our trinity…"

There was a pause.

Maria looked down to her side. She could not feel Joseph's or Brian's hands. They were gone.

"They are mine!" said the nightmare beast. Its words sent a chill through Maria's body, "And you are next!"

The sheer voice of the beast petrified Maria, causing her to come to a complete stop in midair.

The beast charged towards her, opening its mouth.

"I will devour you!"

Maria trembled upon hearing its voice. She could not move. With every word it spoke, Maria became weaker. She felt the cold, dark, lifeless mouth of the creature close in around her, but she refused to look back.

Completely destitute of all her remaining strength, she began to descend into its void, helplessly and motionless. The beast was within feet of Maria as it opened its mouth to reveal the gloom that lay in wait for her soul.

"It's over!" the beast cried out.

"Do you know who I am?" came a voice.

The voice had come from Maria's body, but it was not her own. Upon hearing it, the beast came to a stop.

"Witch! Have you come to meet your end as well?" challenged the nightmare beast in its deep, ghastly baritone voice as she stood at the opening of its mouth. The void in its mouth attempted to consume Maria's body like a vacuum, but she stood unmoved by it.

"I shall enjoy your death!" said the beast as the cavity within it intensified, pulling Maria closer.

"Insolent fool! You're just as naïve as ever," the high-pitched, glass shattering voice bellowed out from Maria's body.

"Even in my weakened state, I still possess enough power to make quick work of you," mocked the high-pitched voice, "But I have a task for you instead."

The possessor of Maria's body motioned her hand in a downward position to the beast.

"Sit," commanded the shrill vocals.

Instantly, shadow chains formed, crawling along the dead earth like snakes, and traveling up the beast, pulling and constricting the beast to the ground. There was a loud cracking sound as the chains restraining the beast forced its mouth open. The darkness extended from Maria's dress like arms, and reached into the void of the beast, pulling out an unconscious Brian and Joseph, then lowering them to the ground.

"Tell your master, this planet is mine," said the piercing voice. The chains around the beast tightened, and began to glow a radiant yellow.

"What are you doing?" pleaded the nightmare beast as it struggled to break free.

"I'm taking your power," said Maria's guest.

"No, you can't, you Banshee Witch!"

The beast began to shrink to normal size.

"You cannot stop Lord I. Lord I knows your secret, Lord I will defeat you. Man's ignorance will be your downfall just as before," added the beast.

"I was going to let you live…or whatever it is you do…but now that you've insulted me by comparing me to such feebleness…"

She turned and looked towards the beast as she lowered herself to the ground. She stared into a face that no other living creature had seen and survived unscathed. The entity within Maria held a dark smile across her face.

She snapped her fingers. The nightmare beast fell motionless to the ground before turning into a fine, dark mist and fading.

"It seems it's time for my return," said the voice from inside Maria. The light faded from her eyes as they returned to normal, and she fell to the blackened ground.

Although Brian and Joseph lay motionless on the ground, they had heard everything. They knew, malevolent or benevolent, there was something coming. What these strange entities wanted, and why one had taken over Maria's body, they were not quite sure of. But they were glad that it had, or they would have died; and the beast would have consumed Terraizen.

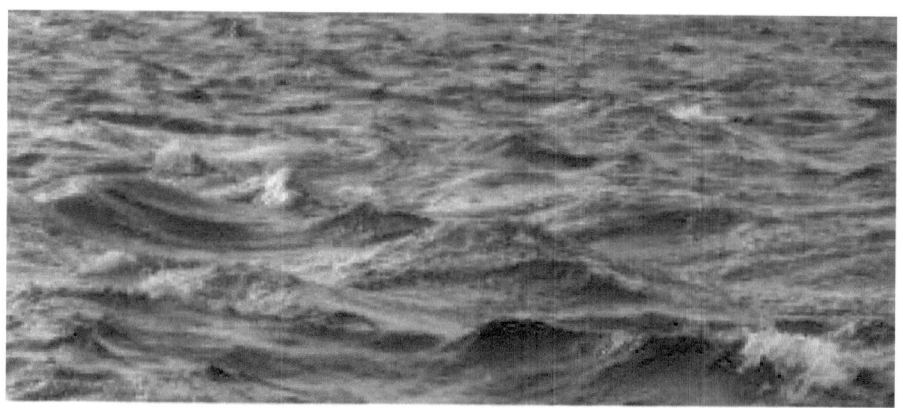

CHAPTER 19: ANTHONY- THE WAIT

Anthony sat in the commander's seat of the STAR Cruiser.

The encounter with the water animax had weakened him. Anthony could feel its overbearing field-like presence acting upon him even with the cruiser's shields up. He knew the further away it was from him, the weaker its effects. Though he had prepared for the worse, the rapid loss in energy had surprised even him.

Faith had acted fast, saved their lives, and defended the cruiser. She had used her personal shields to defend the ship. However, they would not hold much longer. After breaking through the wall of living water, they had lost all but their final shield, which stood as their last line of defense between them and certain death.

Anthony watched as Faith did everything in her power to protect the ship. Before they lost communication with the outside world, Faith had contacted the Engineering Department and sent them the STAR Cruisers log history as well as their current coordinates. With that information the Engineers would be able to safely navigate to their location even in their simple transporters.

Now they awaited the team's arrival. The Aqua Animax had been unexpected. Nonetheless, the Engineering Department would be able to install the shields needed to defend against it upon their arrival. Once the shields were replaced, and the energy generators repaired, Anthony and Faith would be able to continue their mission.

Faith had ported into the cruiser, and had been monitoring the ships functionality.

"Low energy shields holding at five percent. Although I am unable to ascertain the engineers' exact location, I estimate they are approximately five minutes away, and should arrive shortly. I have authorized emergency confinement protocol in case my shields should fail before their arrival."

Anthony looked over at Faith, taking a sip of his venue tea every few seconds. In such a dire situation, he seemed to come across very calm and cordial. But on the inside, he was growing more concerned by the moment. He knew the magnitude of the situation. Living water was a unique entity that he had thought to be confined to Nefastus. From the stories in the TSPA archives, he knew it by the name "Aqua Animax." The stories from the archives described Aqua Animax as an ancient entity that feasted on Awakened essences like a parasite. It drained the energy of whatever crossed its path. The stronger the source, the faster its deadly touch.

Anthony was one of the most powerful beings of TSPA, and if even a drop of living water came into contact with him, he knew his power would mean nothing. He would be dead in less than a few seconds.

The water pounded ferociously against the outer shell of the Cruiser. It could sense Anthony's power, and it wanted him. With every crashing blow, it hammered away at the shields.

The original shields had been high-energy and capable of withstanding anything, from military grade tank-piercing missiles to small nuclear explosions; and the living water had consumed them in less than a second. Faith's shields, on the other hand, were ultra-low frequency shields that the Aqua Animax had a difficult time sensing like a person trying to walk through an invisible wall.

Faith had been focusing on maintaining the shields.

Just then, the transponder of the ship received an incoming transmission. An image of an average built man, with long, straight unkempt hair, and a grungy, yet clean, appearance projected itself upon the monitor.

"Hey Anthony. What in the hell are you doin' in there?" said the man.

Anthony looked over at the monitor, "Have you seen the ship?"

Flint looked up from his monitor and out his ship's window. He examined the Cruiser, which he could see off in the distance, and frowned in disbelief.

"The fuck is that!?" said Flint. He began to approach the ship, but came to a halt when he noticed it was surrounded by, what resembled, a bubble of water.

"Aqua Animax. Living water," said Anthony, who had still managed to maintain his calm mannerism.

"Isn't that the stuff that coined that one phrase...uh what is it...something like, the stronger you are, the faster you die," said Flint as he struggled with his memory.

"Close enough," said Anthony, raising his teacup to his lips and slowly taking another sip of tea.

"Well you're screwed," said Flint while letting out an uproar of laughter.

There was a brief interruption in transmission before Faith was able to reestablish the connection. Faith had managed to create a local connection using a large portion of her own energy, which had begun to drain rather rapidly. For the first time, the bio-Faith began to sweat.

Just then, another transmission came in on the STAR Cruiser's second monitor. It displayed the image of a dark brown, shaggy-haired guy, with bright blue eyes, and a slightly muscular build. It was Zac.

"Hey guys, sorry I'm late. I had to finish the final touches on the new low-energy shield generators for the STAR Cruiser. You should be able to hold out with Faith's shields until I arrive. Although, I have bad news..."

Suffering another disruption in the communication, the screens went blank for a moment before Faith was able to once again re-establish the connection.

"Flint and I still need to reconfigure the cruisers defense systems to handle the living water. It's going to take some time. We also need the low frequency generator, which Marty is supposed to be delivering shortly," said Zac disappointingly.

Tea sprayed from Anthony's mouth, soaking his desk.

Flint dropped his face into the palms of his hands, and began to shake his head back and forth disapprovingly.

"It was our only option. Marty was closest to the design team and we didn't have the time to pick it up ourselves and reconfigure the systems. I received Faith's sample of the Aqua Animax, and was busy recording the upgrade for the Cruiser's defense systems to hold off the threat. I sent instructions for Marty to pick up the final pieces we need for the upgrade," said Zac, who was trying his best to rationalize his decision.

"What was his ETA?" asked Flint.

"Ten minutes ago…yeah I know…he should have made it here before my arrival and it took me seven hours to get here and that was going through the temporal short cut route that you sent us," added Zac.

"That explains why you got here so fast. But if we wait for Marty or if he makes the wrong turn and gets lost in a temporal-time well, Anthony is as good as dead and so is he. Do you want me to just go back and pick it up?" asked Flint.

"Well, I told Marty it was a life and death situation, and that it was of the upmost importance that he arrive on time. If you go back Flint, you wont be able to make it back in time, there is also a high chance that you may get lost now that the Aqua Animax has begun to effect our systems," said Zac.

"I just sent out Zach-Mech, to check the route. He should hit all the correct short cut temporal-laps and return within the next thirty minutes. Faith how long are the shields able to hold?" asked Anthony, in a slightly nervous, less calm manner.

Zach-Mech, the thin, innocent, bright-eyed, cycling king of the engineering interns, was quite reliable when it came to getting the job done. However, unlike the Engineers, Zac-Mech had very low essence levels, making him the perfect person for such a mission.

"Fifteen minutes and thirty-two seconds," said Faith.

Flint slammed his hand against the desk within his ship, disintegrating it into woodchips and leaving the monitor hovering in mid-air.

"Shit! That's not enough time. This is worse than when we were testing out the STAR Cruiser 701 on our deep-sea dive… we told Marty not to leave the control room under any conditions. You know, just in case we needed an emergency rescue. It was supposed to be an eight hour pressure test dive, but we got entangled by that crazy seaweed stuff..."

"Yeah, I tried nearly everything to get out of it. It had a grip like boa vines," said Zac.

"Well, as you recall, MARTY did not respond until almost two days later! And by then, we had already been rescued by Faith and Anthony," said Flint.

"Oh, I remember. What confused me is that after I confronted him, he told me that the monitor had lost power because he had accidentally spilled coffee on the controls. But that still doesn't explain why he did not answer his phone, transponder, or respond to the bright flaring emergency alarm systems in the Engineering Department," said Zac.

"Well the heavy smell of alcohol on his breath, and all over the emergency controls told us all we needed to know. If not for his genetically modified restoration, he would have been dead with that blood alcohol level," said Anthony.

They all laughed, and a sigh of relief momentarily settled over the three of them.

"Let's give him a chance. If he doesn't arrive in the next ten minutes, then Flint and I will mount a planned rescue mission ourselves," instructed Zac. "We may be able to increase our chances of survival if we come up with a plan."

"It would save us time if we just did it now. I'm just saying, the longer we wait, the more risky it's going to be," said Flint.

"I would prefer not to risk our lives unless we have to," said Zac, "Flint, let's give him a chance and trust that Marty has put his old ways behind him."

"I hope you're right," said Flint, "I hope he's not as big of a fuck up as he used to be…"

"I heard that," came a voice from the computer's transponder.

"You're late," said Flint.

"Yeah, sorry about that. I forgot my tool kit."

"You mean your universal repair kit?"

"Yes Flint!" said Marty. "Plus I had a little run-in with the insidious Aqua Animax a few miles back, and it completely drained my primary power supply."

"Hey Marty, is everything okay? We can't see you on our monitor."

Zac noticed that Marty's image had not appeared on the monitor.

"Everything's fine. I just can't make visual contact at the moment. I'll retrieve the low power shield generators and have them installed momentarily," reassured Marty, "Oh, and Flint, I know you can't see me right now, but I am holding a bird up to my monitor just for you."

"What kind of bird?" asked Flint confused, "Why do you have animals in your ship?"

Zac began to shake his head in disbelief. Sometimes he wondered how the Engineering Department ever got anything done.

"Let's just get this done. I have new ship designs to finish," said Zac.

"Five minutes remaining..." said Faith, exhausted and tired on bended knees. Anthony could see she had used all of her energy maintaining the shields, but now he knew she would be able to relax. The installation would only take a few minutes, and they would soon begin.

Anthony fell back in his chair. Through all the commotion, he had forgotten how dire a situation he was in. He had been so caught up in the argument between the members of the Engineering Department that he had let his guard down. Then it hit him. He barely had time to raise his hand to his head. As he felt the warm, moist droplet hit him, one thing crossed his mind...

Who knew condensation could be so deadly?

Faith stood up, "Shields holding, the Aqua Animax has begun to retreat, but I am uncertain as to...."

Faith turned towards Anthony swiftly, and initiated containment. The protective capsule immediately formed around his body, but it was too late. Her monitors showed that only one life sign remained aboard the ship, and it was her own.

Faith stared over at his encapsulated body. The Aqua Animax had claimed its prize, which had somehow calmed and satisfied its incorrigible appetite for power.

"I've failed," said Faith.

CHAPTER 20: PRINCE JABIN

Joseph awoke well rested once again. He could not remember the last time he had slept so well. He had begun to grow accustomed to the strangeness of the place.

Joseph remembered the elevator taking him deep underground, but as he gazed out of his window, he could see a parking lot off in the distance. Past the driveway, he could see the large forest. He wondered how it was possible to be underground, yet have a window that seemed to be on the third floor of the building. It caused him to feel a bit spatially disoriented. There were so many things he had questions about as he sat looking out of the window.

Joseph looked over at the bed where Maria and Brian still lay resting peacefully, trying to recall what he had dreamt. As much as he struggled, he could not remember the details of his dream, but he did remember that Brian and Maria had been with him. Joseph headed to the bathroom located within the corner of his room. Sammy would be there shortly, and he wanted to freshen up before his arrival. While in the shower, Joseph heard a knock at the front door. Over the stream of falling water, Joseph could hear Brian, Sammy, and Maria's muffled voices briefly conversing before leaving the room. After he finished his shower, Joseph exited the bathroom. On his nightstand, he found instructions on his bed for how to reach the breakfast diner. He hoped that the instructions were detailed enough to get him there safely. After all, one misstep had led him to a whole new world.

***

Joseph reviewed the map left by Sammy with a note saying to meet him at the Ezon One Diner. On it, there were three circled areas: Elizabeth's Hotel; where he currently resided, the Ezon Library, and the Ezon Diner, where he was to meet Brian, Maria, and Sammy for breakfast. From the map he could see that trees surrounded Ezon One on all sides. Within Ezon One there were four sections. The strip contained all of the diners, shopping malls, and a variety of recreational areas. From food and clothing, to games and entertainment, the strip was a pleasure oasis. There were also training areas located within the forest. It was composed of schools, gyms, and specialized training centers for agents according to the map. The residential area was where Joseph stayed currently. It included the housing complexes, apartments and hotels; although most buildings stood vacant and unused, as if they had not been occupied in decades.

After getting dressed, Joseph grabbed the map and exited his room. He followed the instructions, turning right at the end of the hall way and heading downstairs to the first floor. The hallway and the rooms reminded him of a luxury hotel. The décor of velvet carpets, and drapes with a gold-like lining and finish greeted Joseph with a warm glow. There were mirrors on the walls of the hallway, but no pictures. As he headed down the stairs to the first floor, he passed the vending machines and exited through the revolving door. When he stepped out onto the street, he looked up at the sky, there were clouds and even sunlight. Very few people walked along the streets, but there were a few smaller vehicles that passed over the red and brown brick roads. Although Joseph recalled being taken underground, his senses told him otherwise as he stood on the street corner outside the hotel.

Joseph crossed the street passing the long forested road, which led to the training center to the right. The shopping courts, malls, food centers, and some smaller additional living quarters lay to his left. The streets felt a bit strange, though abandoned, he felt he was being followed, but whenever he turned around there was no one there.

Most of the places along the strips were still closed, and did not open until noon. Joseph had seen the variety of things Ezon One had to offer along the way to the diner. One place he could not wait to visit was Eiden's Magic Shop. It was located not too far from the diner, which lay next to the forest near the very end of the strip. Eiden's shop was filled with some of the most exotic looking herbs and plants, along with strange jars and bottles filled with all kinds of elixirs and potions. Joseph was curious to see and learn more about magic. Was it like the movies? Would drinking a potion give him super strength or speed? Or was it like the video games where he could breathe fire and fly? Flying would be cool, he thought to himself.

As he approached the diner, he looked to his right at the overhanging forest canopy. The forest was large, and had seemed endless from atop the hill when he arrived. Joseph wondered what would happen if he got lost. Hypothetical questions formed in his mind. *Would they find me? How long could I survive before I starved? Are there even any edible plants in there? What's out there? Maybe some strange creatures are watching me right now, waiting for me to wander in so they can devour me. Could I fight them off?* The questions flowed in faster than Joseph could answer them, and to most of them, he had no answer. Joseph decided it would be best to stay out of the forest, or at least bring a friend along if it were necessary to enter.

It had taken him some time, but he was starting to bend his mind around this new reality. At first, he had thought of it like a village inside the TSPA headquarters. Now, after taking a look around, he began to think that maybe it was not inside the TSPA, but a place of its own. The idea of a place like this existing was mind blowing and amazing. It was like a pocket world within Terraizen, or maybe he was no longer in Terraizen at all.

Joseph reached the breakfast diner. As he passed by the window, he saw Brian seated there at a side booth, and a guy in a brown suit having a cup of tea at the counter. It was early, the sun had barely begun to rise, and it seemed not many others in Ezon One were awake yet. When he entered the small restaurant, he saw the waitress taking Brian's order. She was older, had curly blond hair, and a smile that would not fade. Even when she wasn't smiling, she held a naturally happy vibe about her.

As Joseph took his seat, Brian ordered his sunshine breakfast. It was the same thing he got every time they had gone out to eat for breakfast.

"Mornin,' my names Stacy, and I'll be yall's server today. Do ya' know what you'll be havin' today, or would ya' like a little more time ta decide?" asked Stacy with a warm smile.

"Could I have a bowl of frosted flakes with a side of whole wheat toast?" asked Joseph.

"What kinda' jam ya want with that?" asked Stacy.

"Strawberry please. Thanks," said Joseph as he handed over his menu to the waitress.

"I'll be back shortly with yall's meals," said Stacy. She turned, and then quickly turned back around, "Forgive me. I forgot ta ask. What would ya like ta drink young man?" she asked, turning to Joseph.

"Could I have some orange juice please?" asked Joseph.

"And could I get a refill please?" Brian asked as he motioned to his nearly empty coffee cup.

"Sure thing sweetie, I'll be back shortly," Stacy said. Then she turned and headed back to the kitchen.

"I could get used to this. It seems almost too good to be true. Whatever I want to eat, they got it. Whatever I want to wear, or watch, they got it. It's like they have anything I could ask for and so much more. I can't wait till that shop next door opens. Sammy says it's pretty awesome," said Brian.

"Yeah, almost too good to be true and where did Sammy run off to?" asked Maria with a tone of suspicion.

She had just approached the table, and motioned to Brian to move over as she slid into the booth. Maria had spent most of her morning at the library learning more about channeling and Awakened. As she did she remembered seeing Sammy entering the Elizabeth Hotel on her way to the diner.

"Hey, maybe this is the reward we get for completing the challenge yesterday."

"Hmmm… fascinating…farewell…" came the sound of a deep voice near the corner of the room.

Brian, Maria, and Joseph turned their attention towards the corner of the diner. There, in the far corner of the room, sat a man, enjoying a coffee and slice of toast. He was alone. Thrown off by the man's appearance, Brian and Joseph gazed wide-eyed in his direction. The person wore all black, with long silver chains hanging from the pockets and belt of his pants. Any place on the person's face that could be pierced, contained a piercing. However, none of them remembered seeing him when they walked in, and his appearance was not one that could be easily forgotten.

Brian stared at the man with a confused smirk, "Sorry, were you talking to us?"

There was a breeze, the man took a sip of coffee, and continued to read from a strange black leather bound book with unusual symbols and singed pages.

"It's not polite to stare," came the voice from the peculiar man, "Friends call me Summer, Summoner of Ezon One.

Apologies, I was conversing with the Fairweathers. They're gone now, they never stay long."

Maria smiled, "Please excuse my friends. It's just, they've never seen anyone quite as unique as yourself. Nice to meet you Summer, my name's Maria."

There was a sudden breeze. The diner door opened slightly and then closed. Summer had reappeared across the room and was now seated at a round isle seat table across from their booth.

"How did you do that?" Brian asked.

"Breeze traveling," said Maria to Brian.

Summer turned the pages of his book, and continued to read as if his mind was in another place.

Maria turned to Summer, "I see you're well adept at breeze traveling. Maybe you could teach me sometime?" asked Maria.

All of a sudden, as the last word left Maria's lips, the door to the breakfast diner swung open once more. A burst of wind swept through the area. In a speedy blur, a man appeared before them with a back draft that ruffled Maria's hair and caused the plates to rattle, nearly knocking it over Brian's cup before he caught instinctively. He had short black hair held back by a black headband, blue jeans, and a navy blue hooded sweatshirt. He was rather toned and muscular. Initially, Joseph, Maria, and Brian did not recognize him. But upon further inspection, they did. He was the guy that led them to the hotel the previous night. It was Sammy.

"Hey guys, sorry I'm late. Just finished the morning run, and I was having some trouble waking up Jabin," said Sammy, "Jabin get over here and meet the new recruits. And remember your manners. This isn't the North."

Through the door strutted a heavy guy with short, scruffy brown hair and glasses. He was eating a slice of cake as he approached walked towards Summer's table.

"No need to rush me mother," said Jabin condescendingly.

As he approached the table, he looked over at Brian, Joseph, and Maria. His eyes widened as he rested his gaze upon Maria. A sinister smile spread across his crumb-covered mouth.

Jabin turned towards Sammy and whispered into his ear, "Who's the concubine waitress, and why does she not stand and bow when I walk into the room?"

"Jabin, we've gone over this already, Northern Law does not apply in Ezon One."

"Northern Law goes where I go Sammy. I am a prince, am I not? She must kneel in my presence," said Jabin in a demandingly regal tone, "And where's Stacy hiding? I'm hungry. Stacy!" Jabin called out loudly.

"You're a royal pain Jabin."

Maria stared at Jabin, confused by his not-so-quiet comments, "Hi, I'm Maria. If you're looking for the waitress, she'll be by shortly."

"Nice to meet you Maria. May I say what lovely knockers you have? They complement your eyes quite nicely."

A nerve had been struck. Almost impulsively, Brian rushed to Maria's defense, "Watch your mouth or you'll lose your tongue."

Sammy placed a hand on Jabin's shoulder, and began to shake his head in shame.

Clueless and confused, Jabin held out his hands with his palms facing upward, "What? Is it not customary in Central to compliment a lovely rack? I mean look at those. She should be proud. She's worthy of bedding by a nobleman, maybe even a prince?"

"Jabin, you're hopeless. You know that?" asked Sammy as he took his seat next to Summer.

"Maria, please excuse 'Prince' Jabin. He does not mean to offend you, he was just raised in the *Imperialistic Absolute Monarch of the North* where his parents were of royalty. In the majority of the North, women are still considered property, unequal to men, and the victors of stadium brawls and archaic games make the decisions. We're still bringing him up-to-date with modern technology, gender equality, and all the other great things that Central has to offer."

The smug look on Jabin's face and lack of manners disgusted Brian.

Brian had a short tempter, especially when it came to people who disrespected his friends. Clenching his fists under the table, Brian stared out the window, thinking of cars, attempting to remain calm and let Maria handle Jabin. Jabin had struck a nerve with him, pushing him to the brink of his tolerance threshold rather quickly.

Trying to restrain himself by diverting eye contact with Jabin did not help much. In his mind, Jabin already lay toothless in a pool of his own blood on the ground. You could say Brian was a bit over protective of Maria.

They were just words, and Brian refused to let words control his actions. So long as Maria remained calm, he would as well.

"Give me a break... I don't need to know all this free speech, equal rights, and Central Law crap. I've never met a woman who could best me in any arena. Its best they stick to what they're good at. I mean, without a servant, who's left to do the chores? You don't expect me, a prince, to waste time on such trivial matters now do you? That's what women and 'technology' were made for," said Jabin, laughing in a snarky tone.

Now Jabin's tone had struck a chord with Joseph, "Jabin, I don't know you, and at this rate I may never get the chance. You know what they say about a woman's scorn. You should guard your tongue or you'll cross a line you wish you hadn't."

Jabin ignored Joseph's comment, and in an instant, Jabin vanished then reappeared next to Maria.

"Maybe you'd like to give me a demonstration of how powerful Central women truly are, what do you say, my place tonight? I bet you've never been with a prince before," said Jabin, flexing his slightly muscular arms.

Maria gagged, holding her hand to her mouth.

"I'm sorry but I must decline your offer. I'm sure you're needed elsewhere, possibly even the prestigious Central Core research labs. It would be a great place for you to start learning about us Central woman. I hear there are lots of pretty women, and it's a position fit only for a prince, such as yourself. They'll take care of your every need."

Jabin's eyes widened as his interest was spiked.

"Sounds intriguing. Tell me more concubine."

Maria sighed, "Well… I being a woman, myself, could never take on such a role. But I find it quite fascinating. They study mental capacities and intellectual deficiencies. I can only imagine how grateful they would be to have you. Oh, how long does it take you to come up with an idea, let alone a good one? It must not be very frequent with such a high attenuation of thought. You'd be the perfect specimen. I, on the other hand, even with half my intellect, would still be twice as smart as you. You know on average the women of Central are twenty percent smarter than the average male. So I couldn't possibly stoop to your level. If I did, you being down there for so long would surely beat me with experience," said Maria, sighing hopelessly and nodding her head as if it had been a lost dream she could never achieve.

Sammy laughed, clapping and smiling at Maria, "Clever girl. I don't think I could have said it better myself."

Maria smiled back as if saying thank you.

Jabin frowned at Sammy and Maria, but remained calm as his eyes narrowed in on her.

"So you think you're smart, witch! I will have you on your knees now," Jabin said, motioning and pointing to the ground.

"Jabin, she's just joking. Control yourself. That's no way to speak to a fellow companion," said Sammy.

"Fellow companion? Don't make me laugh. All I see is a wench and two weaklings who can't protect themselves or see the truth. She'd run wet if she encountered a Numbered outside of these walls. If it doesn't kill her first. I've defended kingdoms, escaped Shadow Walkers, and Nefastus. Though you and Summer are considerably weaker than I, even you two can hold your own."

Jabin glanced over at Brian and Joseph before returning his intimidating glare towards Maria, his eyes glowing a slight yellow tint, "I will not be talked down to. What have they done to be considered my equal? We've been stuck in this place for Francis knows how long. I'm a prince, and deserve more than this entrapment. In the North, a prince can have whomever he pleases. So I shall have you on your knees as retribution for your foul tongue or I'll mark you. Then you'll have no choice but to serve me. Foolish girl, you don't know what I'm capable of, so I think it's about time I showed you," said Jabin in a calm, serious, tenacious tone. His eyes began to glow a deeper darker yellow, immobilizing Brian and Joseph and piercing their hearts, causing them to cringe in pain; but Maria remained unshaken.

Maria turned to Jabin calmly. The atmosphere of the room grew heavy. Lights flickered rapidly, frost formed on the window seal, and a cold chill swept across the floor. The rising sun hid behind the dark morning clouds. As the presence of Maria clashed with that of Jabin's, all was silent. Maria could feel him trying to enter her mind. He was rather strong, stronger than she expected, but she was not going to allow it. Though she was new to channeling, she was a rather fast learner. Maria wouldn't let herself lose to someone as egotistical as Jabin. She was going to teach him a lesson even if it took everything she had.

It was the calm before the storm.

She stared into his eyes with a ghostly gaze, filled with a silent rage that seemed to make the room quiver upon her every word, "You won't lay a finger on me or you'll lose them all. Your lack of common decency must get you in a great deal of trouble. In a strange way, I feel sorry for your inability to hold a mature conversation."

Maria could feel herself slipping, but she continued to fight the battle of wills as their essences clashed. Though visibly she wasn't breaking a sweat and seemed to be acting casually, there was a fierce essence-battle taking place between the two of them, and she was giving it everything she had. Still, he was experienced and had the upper hand. She could tell he was toying with her even now, but she'd be damned if she lost to someone as arrogant as him. "Patronizing guys like you are nothing more than bullies who only play hero when it benefits them...I'm sorry about your miseducation amongst your troglodyte Northern race, but if you insult me again.... you'll deeply regret it. Don't try me."

Jabin smirked. "For someone so weak and naïve of the world you talk big. I was being nice, letting you put on a show, but now..."

The lights returned to normal, but the room grew colder. A dry, ice-like chill settled in on the room and gave Joseph and Brian goosebumps, as they remained trapped in their minds, watching like helpless bystanders. They had only seen her like this once before, and what happened afterwards they had thought they imagined until now. Though rare, when Maria got angry, strange things seemed to happen. Now they were beginning to understand why.

Jabin turned from Maria. His eyes transitioned from her eyes to her breast, and then back as he remained unfazed by her words. She could tell now he hadn't been really trying at all, and her words had passed over him like water off a ducks back.

"You don't scare me, but I didn't mean to upset you either. Still, I hold my position, women are naturally weaker, they just forget their place. You can tell can't you? I wasn't even trying and you had reached your limits," Jabin's eyes returned to normal, freeing Brian and Joseph. "It's true if you think about it. If you were a man, I'd take you on in the arena, but I don't hit women. You can't scare me girl."

"Hump…name the day. I'll take you on anytime."

Jabin began to laugh loudly. Though he had proven himself stronger, he did not understand the magnitude of danger he had placed himself in. Pieces of cake flew from his mouth, landing in front of Brian and Maria.

Disgusted by his actions, Brian snapped, unable to hold back his rage any longer. In the blink of an eye, he had leaped across the table nearly striking Jabin. But he was too slow; Jabin reappeared seated at the table next to Sammy and Summer, still laughing and almost in tears. The idea of even fighting a woman, let alone considering them an equal, tickled his funny bone in a way that no other joke could. To him, strength and respect were proportional. Those who lacked strength didn't deserve his respect.

"Enough Jabin, show some humility," said Sammy.

"I'm just having a little fun," said Jabin, "Those old hags would never allow me to actually mark her."

Maria seemed a bit tired, and Brian could tell. Though he could not tell exactly what had happened, it angered him.

"You're not leaving here on two feet," said Brian lunging forward. Joseph attempted to restrain him.

"I've snapped trees in half bigger than you boy. You… can't… touch…. me," said Jabin, pausing after every word.

Jabin began to laugh in such an annoying manner that even Summer glanced up briefly from the pages of his book. Looking to see if the strange noise was really coming from Jabin.

The waitress, Stacy, had noticed a change in the room's atmosphere, and had not come back to the table since Jabin arrived in the diner. They saw her peak around the corner every once in a while, as if to see if he had left yet.

Brian attempted to calm down, but could not. Once more, the lights faded from the room, this time much quicker. A strange dark cloud seemed to hover overhead, under the ceiling of the diner.

Soon after, the laughing figure of Jabin began to shrink, and as it did, he morphed into a furry, black-tailed, whiskered animal. It was a tuxedo cat.

Summer marked his book, and laid it down upon the table.

"I can never get any reading done with you around. It's hard to believe we're connected. Come..." said Summer, gesturing towards the kitten.

The kitten walked over to Summer obediently and leapt into his lap. The cat began to purr as Summer stroked its head. The shadows faded, lighting returned to normal, and the room grew warmer.

"That took longer than I expected without the Fairweathers. Thanks for distracting him," said Summer, looking over at Maria.

Brian stared at the cat with squinted eyes and puckered lips. He had a look of confusion and shock comparable to that of a baby eating a lemon for the first time as he tried to wrap his mind around what just happened. It's not every day you see a man turn into a cat right before your eyes.

"What just happened? Did that just happen?" Brian asked Summer.

Summer picked up his book and continued to read, deaf to Brian's question.

Sammy let out a sigh, "Sorry about Jabin. He's always nervous whenever he meets someone new, and for some reason, he becomes rude. Especially with cute girls. Except the Fairweathers, he seems to like them for some reason. I think it's a Northerner thing. It's one of his less... admirable qualities, but he's really a nice guy..."

"Ummm..." said Summer clearing his throat.

Sammy corrected himself, "Okay, okay, maybe not so nice, but his bravado was meant to impress, and we're working on it."

"That's hard to believe," said Brian.

"You should have seen him five years ago. He didn't understand what compromise was so we had to settle everything in the arena like they do in the North. And though he may not look it, he's a rather strong fighter. He won most of the arguments back then…that is until the Espers sealed his power for a week. Summer turned him into practically every animal he could think up. Summer's an animal lover, mostly birds, but he doesn't talk much. Jabin does enough talking for the both of them," said Sammy.

"What just happened to him?" Brian asked once more, still slightly confused.

"It's just a Level 2 transmutation spell of Summer's. The Level 1's stopped working a few years ago. Summer's been trying to get this one done for the last few weeks. He's tried it many times, but it's never worked on Jabin until now. Knowing how strong Jabin is, the spell won't last for very long. We just happened to catch him by surprise. When he returns to normal, he's going to be furious," said Sammy.

"Can't you keep him like that? Because that would be great," asked Joseph, who had grown tired of hearing Jabin's voice.

"Sometimes I wish we could, but he's part of our Trinity, and on the battle field, he's a lot more serious," said Sammy.

Sammy scratched his head in embarrassment, and began to clear his throat. Maria had mentally tensed up with every word that left Jabin's mouth, now she was beginning to relax. As she did, so did the tension in the room.

"So it seems we all know each other now. These are my partners, Prince Jabin Baldwin and Summer the Summoner, and like you, we are also a Trinity."

"I'm Brian, and this is…"

Summer held up a hand and silenced Brian, "We know who you are. Let's move on."

A few minutes later, the shy waitress returned with more beverages and food.

Summer sipped his venue tea and scratched Jabin behind the ears.

Breakfast came to a close. Sammy was the last to finish. Although he was a fast runner, he took his time when it came to eating.

"Well I'm stuffed, let me give you a tour of the place," said Sammy.

Stacy cleared the dishes from the table as Sammy opened the door for Maria and the others, guiding them out of the diner. As Joseph exited the diner, he felt a chill sweep through him. As sudden as it came, it was gone again, and so was the cloaked breeze traveler who had been sitting unnoticed in the corner of the diner.

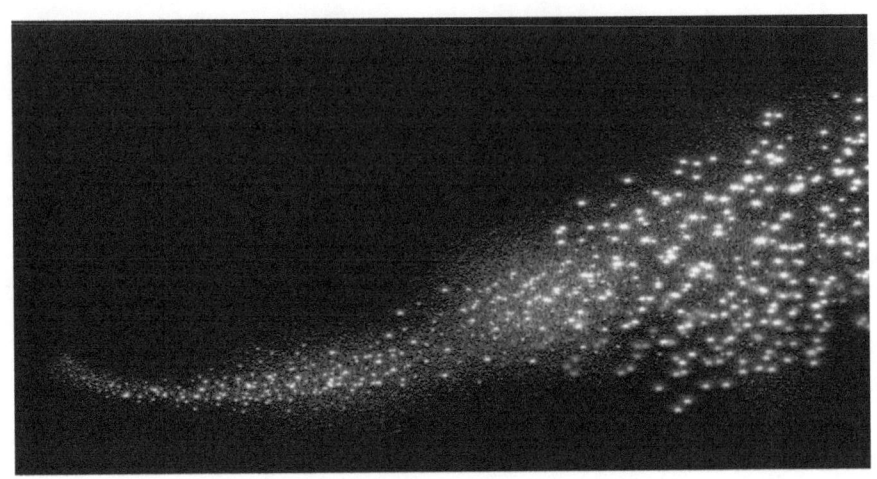

CHAPTER 21: AWAKENING REKINDLED

Sammy gave them a tour of the Ezon One strip. They saw the Mall of Ezon One, the food court, bike shop, and many other areas. Sammy also showed them how to use the devices located in their living quarters. There was a specific system that each room had which allowed for them to receive books, games, movies, and even food directly to their rooms from anywhere on STAR Island.

Out of all the things that Joseph had witnessed, the most amazing of them all was the room changer located in the corner of his hotel room. It was an extraordinary device that allowed him to change the décor of the rooms, and even adjust its size and configuration. He liked to watch everything become amorphous then change and shift around as it reconfigured itself. He could have anything from a one bedroom set up, to a five bedroom apartment. Brian, Maria, and Joseph decided to change Brian's room into the three bedroom style for the days they wanted to hang out together, which would likely be every day.

Although the three liked that the organization provided for their every need, they were still a bit cautious due to some of the strange occurrences that seemed to happen during the tour. At times, doors and windows would open and close without warning; and besides the six of them, and the employed workers, there were not very many other people in Ezon One.

After Sammy finished explaining and adjusting the final features of the room changer, the group headed out of the living quarters and towards the outskirts of the town. As they walked along the sandy pathway through the forest entrance, Joseph could see two large, gray stone statues in the distance.

On the left, was a man wearing long robes and a hooded cloak. On the right, a woman wearing a hooded cloak with rimmed spectacles and short hair. The statue of the woman stood with her arms held out as if welcoming them. The man stood sternly with an outstretched arm and finger pointing back towards them. In the blink of an eye, the woman stood glaring towards them with her arms crossed. Joseph noticed the change immediately.

"Did you see that? It just moved," said Joseph, pointing at the woman statue.

"I didn't see it, but with all the strange things in this place, it wouldn't surprise me. Are they supposed to move?" asked Brian.

Sammy stopped and looked over the two statues in admiration. He gazed at them like they were the most magnificent pieces of art he had ever seen. Then he turned to Brian.

"I have absolutely no idea," said Sammy. They both laughed.

"If you really want to know, ask the Espers."

As soon as they passed and entered into the more heavily forested area, Joseph felt a quietness rush over them. The trees were taller, the canopy was thicker, and there was an open grassy circle in the distance. He looked over at Maria and Brian, and could tell they felt it too.

"Something feels…" before Joseph could finish, Summer interjected.

"It's the animals. Once you pass the two statues, there are no animals." Summer looked down at Jabin, still in feline form, nestled in his arms.

"Well, no wild animals," he corrected himself.

"It's like that so we can practice without causing harm to any creatures, besides a few trees here and there," said Sammy.

Maria watched as the autumn leaves danced on the soft, gentle breeze before settling to the ground. They approached the grassy clearing surrounded by trees. It was a very wide and perfectly circular area.

"This is a training area. We each start off doing individual training. Everyone gets their own territory, and when we are ready to begin, we recite the Trinity and begin our team training. Normally, we start by just warming up," said Sammy. "I will take each of you to a training area, and in a few minutes, the Esper Witches will stop by and explain everything to you."

"I guess I will take this spot then," said Maria.

"Why do you get the first spot?" asked Brian.

"I called it," said Maria, smiling back at him and shaking her head from side to side with every word she spoke.

"You just did the head thing," said Brian,

"What head thing?" asked Maria.

"You know, the thing you do when you lean your head from left to right while speaking," Brian imitated her as he spoke.

Maria shoved him away jokingly, "Ha! Go find your peace circle."

Brian smiled as they headed off down the pathway with the group.

As they continued down the forest path to the next circle, Joseph looked back at Maria. Maria was sitting in her circle with her legs crossed, almost in a meditative state. He thought of how peaceful it must be to just sit there and connect with himself. No distractions, no worries, just the wind and the trees. It truly was a peace circle.

***

Joseph sat in the middle of his grassy circle thinking about nothing in particular. The sky was blue, and although it was bright out, the sun couldn't be seen behind the clouds and tall trees of the forest. Joseph had chosen a circle only half a mile away from a small stream. He had been meditating and clearing his mind as Sammy had instructed. It was harder than ever with all of the strange things he had encountered. His mind was brimming with questions, which he had only been able to forget for a moment. Joseph knew he still had some time before the Espers' arrival, so he decided to take a walk outside his circle towards the small stream.

As he approached the water's edge, he thought back to everything that had happened in the past few days. He had learned of the existence of people with special abilities. On top of that, his eyes had been opened to secret realms like Ezon One, the TSPA, and the Nefastus Forest; which he had yet to wrap his mind around. He had been astounded by the structure of the TSPA headquarters. Although he resisted, he could feel its strange influence on his perception as it expanded his reality.

He thought of the hotel and how he had seen it alter itself, stretching from an ordinary room to a three bedroom apartment. Even the forest where he now stood was a world of its own within Ezon One. It was bizarre being in a forest without any wildlife. The eerie silence was unsettling, and the quiet made him feel alone. The water flowed over the bedrock like the questions in his mind.

Joseph had always believed that everything happened for a reason. Whether it be good or bad, he felt it always had its purpose. But now, things had changed. His mind had become chaotic. So much had happened so fast that he was just now having the chance to process it all, and still, the answers slipped from his grasp. It was not as if his world was slowly changing. His world had come undone. He was an infant to this new world, and he felt extremely vulnerable by not knowing the laws and rules that governed its existence. Aside from that, something else seemed to elude his perception. He could feel it dancing in the outskirts of his subconscious. To him, the feeling was like trying to recall the details of a dream that had faded, and he had long since forgotten.

Joseph wandered closer to the water's edge. He peered into it as if it held all the answers. He was surprised to see his reflection peering back at him. He held his hand to his face, examining his eyes. There was something different about them. Their color had not changed, and they seemed to be in good working condition, but they felt different, and so did he. He felt as if he had awoken from a long dream, which had seemed so real at the time. A part of him wished he could have stayed asleep and not have seen the truth. But, in ways, the truth was similar to the dream, yet so very different. He wondered if what he felt now was how his mother would feel when she awoke from her slumber.

"Ahem! We don't have all day for your self-idolatry. Stand up, come along now Joseph D. Aizen," came a voice from behind him.

Joseph, surprised by the familiar voice, turned quickly to see Senior Stephenson gazing over at him. No one except his mother had ever called him by his full name before.

"Move it!" demanded the Senior. This time her voice resounded like a whistle through the air knocking him back. There was something special about the Senior, something warm that made him safe in her presence, even though she was quite intimidating.

Joseph stood up, and proceeded to the peace circle with Senior Stephenson. Her cloak bellowed along the breeze behind her, never once touching the ground.

She approached the center of the circle, and then swiftly spun around.

"*Alligo!*"

Joseph's heart skipped a beat as tree roots shot up quickly from the ground, wrapping themselves around him like snakes from head to toe. He stood like a statue, immobilized by their grip.

"In order to control those things around you, you must first bind your own essence to them. The stronger the object, the harder it will be to control, and the more essence will be required. This type of channeling is an imbued binding magic. Do you understand?"

"Yes, but Senior Stephenson, could you please loosen these roots a bit? I can barely breathe."

Senior Stephenson waved her hand, and the roots returned to the ground. Leaving Joseph covered in mud and dirt.

"A puppet master controls a puppet with strings. A wizard controls the world with essence. Understand that channeling requires focus, precision, and speed. Wands, charms, books and other items are all used to assist with focusing spells. Precision and speed comes from experience. Advanced wizards can channel with words and gestures alone. Then there are those of the highest level, Seniors and Lords. We only need think what we want to happen, everything else we do is just for show."

Senior Stephenson pointed to the emerald golden charm that hung around Joseph's neck. Joseph felt its cold metal surface against his skin for the first time, as if it were reacting to something.

"I assume your pendant is reacting. It's no ordinary protective charm. The Emerald Eye is one of the Six Great Protective Pendants. Its original owner specialized in forest manipulation, and the pendant still possesses some of that power. For you, it shall serve two purposes: protection against green spells, and a focus point for your essence to channel. Unlike normal wizards, you are an Awakened, which means your magical abilities are limited. In order to channel, you must always wear that pendant and your spells must be spoken."

"What's green magic?" asked Joseph.

"Green magic is Forest Channeling, the ability to manipulate plants and plant-like creatures."

Her posture became stern as she continued to speak, "Now, I want you to try the spell I just used on you. Remember, channel your essence into the Emerald Eye, and focus on what you're trying to bind to."

Joseph examined the charm, then thought about what he wanted to bind his essence to.

"*Alligo!*" he yelled.

Nothing happened. It had only been a few days since he had learned of the existence of magic and channeling. Learning how to use something he could not see would prove to be challenging, especially for someone like him. He had never really believed in such things; and still struggled to understand. But he thought he would give it a try, and hoped that maybe something would happen.

"What a pitiful attempt at such an elementary spell. I've seen children in the South who could pull off an imbuing before they could talk without the aid of one of the greatest magical items of all time. Try again!" demanded Senior Stephenson. "This time, focus on what you're binding to. Don't think of the pendant as an object, but an extension of yourself."

***

Joseph closed his eyes and attempted to clear his mind. In his mind, he could see the fresh dirt and holes where the roots had shot from the ground. He recalled the forest around him, while listening to the slight breeze. He imagined being one with the ground roots, but then it made him think of death. Joseph inhaled thinking back to the Boa vines he had encountered in the Nefastus Forest, and how they nearly killed him. He thought of their tight grip cutting into his skin, constricting him, suffocating him, squeezing the life from his body. It made him angry, and the pendant grew warm.

He exhaled his anger, throwing his arms forward, "*Alligo* vines!"

Like a second set of the arms, two vines rose from the ground next to him and shot towards Senior Stephenson.

"*Valeo*," said Senior Stephenson in a soft, nonchalant manner.

With a wave of her hand, the roots vanished instantaneously, and the ground returned to the way it had been before the session began. So did Joseph's clothing.

Senior Stephenson looked towards Joseph, "Nothing special, but you have potential."

Joseph felt an overwhelming rush of joy that was almost intoxicating. He had successfully completed his first spell, and he wanted to do it again. In that moment, the emerald felt no different than his beating heart. It had become a part of him, and he could feel its power coursing through him like a cold glass of water after a long desert's walk. Its power allowed him to feel things without touching them. The trees seemed closer, and the forest seemed smaller than it was when he had first entered. While controlling the vines, he could feel a slight resistance, almost like he were a musician out of synch with the song of the forest. Joseph stood in amazement, he felt like he could do anything, and then in the blink of an eye, the feeling was gone. The Emerald Eye had retracted its power, and turned cold once more.

"Now let's continue with the basics. These are things you need to know to survive. I won't always be there to save your life," said Senior Stephenson.

Joseph looked around him. As the moment of bliss faded, he felt something else. An uneasy feeling caused him to become dizzy and light headed. He knew something was not right. His vision began to blur, and Joseph collapsed to the ground.

CHAPTER 22: THE DEAD ZONE

"Aqua Animax has been assimilated. Low-energy shields holding, internal power at ninety percent, full life support stabilized, STAR Cruiser throttle engaged. Proceeding through Devil's Gate. Now entering, 'Dead Zone One'," said Faith.

The three Engineers sat in the commanding station of the STAR Cruiser adjusting monitors and controls as they prepared for the impromptu mission. Anthony's body lay in a stasis-confinement chamber awaiting its return to headquarters. In the event that he was unable to complete the mission, he had instructed Faith to update the Engineers on the mission status and assist them in its completion.

Encountering the Aqua Animax had been an unforeseen event. It had overwhelmed the adaptation systems faster than they could react. If not for the A.I.'s immediate response, the Cruiser would have been lost to the sea. Now that the Cruiser had gained information on the Aqua Animax, a sequence to repel it had been created and initialized. Once initiated, the Aqua Animax was driven back to its resting place in the ancient crevice of the sea floor.

By successfully passing through the Devil's Gate, the crew had accomplished something that very few dared to do in the past. Knowledge of what lay beyond the Devil's Gate was unknown even to the TSPA. Authorities had forbidden pedestrian traffic through the sunken Queens Isle due to the abnormal number of disappearances within the area. Those who entered never returned.

Raging behind them, stood the aquatic wall of the Devil's Gate, while in front were the stagnant waters of the Dead Zone. Set aside from the sea, the zone grew quiet as they ventured further away from the Devil's Gate. A thick, black murky substance covered the top of the oversized swamp. If not for the ship's filtration system, the pungent smell of the gas fumes coming off the surface would have turned their stomachs and brought them to their knees. Even the air was slightly off tint as the lagoon-like waters seemed to bubble every once in a while, releasing pockets of a greenish black gas.

The engineers felt a change in pressure as the Cruiser moved slowly through the thick murky water. No signs of life could be detected within the area; allowing it the name Dead Zone. They had seen similar swamps in the Nefastus Forest, but never quite as vast as the one that lay before them. They were the only living creatures for thousands of miles.

"So, let me get this straight. Anthony ordered us to finish 'his' mission, and we are supposed to descend through this dark murky shit, down to the darkest bottom of the dead zone ocean floor, on a search and rescue mission for someone who 'may' be alive?" asked Flint.

"Affirmative," said Faith.

"Fuck, this is bull shit! If they're down there, then they're already dead. There's nothing on the monitors. Why can't they get someone else from the agency to do it? We're irreplaceable. Except for maybe Marty…he's dispensable. Can we just send him?"

"Last I checked, I just saved your asses," said Marty.

"Barely," added Flint under his breath.

"We're here because we possess the unique set of skills needed to use the essence-infused technology aboard this ship to its maximum potential," said Zac.

"No. We're here because no one else was dumb enough to come," said Flint.

Marty looked over at Flint, frustrated. It was as if he were watching a dismayed, simple-minded individual try to place a large rectangular peg into a small cylindrical hole, losing his train of thought briefly.

"Moving on…I finished the upgrades on the tech gear. We should be able to generate self-sustaining low-energy shields for approximately eight hours if we need to leave the ship for any reason. I'm still making minor adjustments to the hydrolysis system, but it should suffice for oxygen generation in an emergency situation," said Marty.

Marty watched as Flint continued to turn the fields on and off, and off and on, until finally he couldn't take it any longer.

"Would you please stop that?"

Flint continued to push the button on his tech belt, turning his personal shield on and off one last time. The thin blue aura around his body formed and dissipated, giving off a low tuning fork resonance every time he pressed the button.

"The energy supply is limited. So I recommend you save it for when you actually need it," said Marty, staring at Flint and wishing he could strike him sharply in the back of the head.

"Oh sorry, I was just testing it out. Hey Marty, why does it make that strange sound when I turn it on?" asked Flint as he contemplated pressing the big blue button a few more times. Flint enjoyed pressing buttons, whether it was a new button in the engineering control room, a button on the STAR Cruiser or Marty's buttons, which seemed so easily angered most of the time. Flint attrobuted Marty's anger to the love of the drink.

"You can turn the noise off. It's just a safety precaution to let you know that the field is on, and goes away right after. Since the field alters magnetic waves, you can't see it very well; but the blue light on your belt will also let you know if it's on."

Monitoring their surroundings in the Dead Zone, the three of them prepared for the next unknown attack. The Engineers did not get out often. Spending most of their time in their workshops, testing their latest inventions, and checking out the latest virtual reality games had become their daily schedule.

Marty and Flint fought like brothers, while Zac was left to maintain the peace between the two great engineering powers of Central. Rarely did they all agree on anything, except the safety of their beloved STAR Cruiser.

The STAR Cruiser was their child. Its smooth spacecraft design allowed it to seamlessly cut through the air. If not for the

Terraizen atmosphere, which refused to let anything leave, the STAR Cruiser would be capable of space travel. The Engineers knew much about space. It was their goal to one day travel the universe. The STAR Cruiser was built to handle such a mission once the issue with the increasingly high gravity levels that kept it from breaking free of the atmosphere were resolved.

Equipped with an A.I. based adaption system, large control centers and monitors, an essence based hologram generator, and the best navigation center to have ever existed, the STAR Cruiser was their dream ship, and they did all they could to protect it.

Zac manned the control center. Marty and Flint watched the monitors, and the A.I. stood in the navigation center next to the confined Anthony. The Engineers were very busy people. They worked tirelessly in their Central workshops innovating the newest and finest inventions and gadgets for the Central agents. Still, none compared to the mother of all technology, the STAR Cruiser.

This was the first time the five of them had been together aboard the Cruiser in nearly six months. Their last encounter was with a very nasty storm that lay on the outskirts of Central in the Sea of Anexthesia. The Sea of Anexthesia was very good at keeping the sections of Terraizen separated. The deadly Sea of Time, as some knew it, refused to let any non-Awakened cross over its dangerous waters, and even then, the trip still proved to be a challenging one.

This time the crew was venturing further into Anexthesia than they had before. This was no ordinary abnormal section; this was the Southern Queens Sea of Anexthesia. Without proper navigation, it was easy to get lost upon the sea. It had a way of fooling people's minds. Sometimes north became south and other times the sky and sea traded places, flipping the world upside down. Zac recalled the time he encountered one of the many strange areas within the Sea of Anexthesia. He had fallen asleep for only a moment and awoke to find the sea had become the sky as the ship sailed among the clouds. It had been a very disorienting experience, one he would never forget. He learned, when you set out upon the Sea of Anexthesia, there was no telling what will happen.

Along the gateway of the Queens Isle Belt, towards the second gate, the ship descended into the sea, and the crew began to discuss their current location.

"What is this place exactly?" asked Flint.

Zac surveyed the monitors, and attempted to search the TSPA systems, but failed to connect.

"Don't know really. There are no records or access to Central beyond this point. This place existed centuries before the TSPA's formation. The A.I. archives from the Forgotten Ages mention a sunken island beyond the gates, but gave very little detail of its whereabouts. The Queens Isle was just discovered five years ago. Before then, it was just another legend. Turns out the Sea of Anexthesia had shrouded is location until now. Records say the Queen of Legends resided here during the Forgotten Ages. I find it strange that she had five guardsmen, and now we have five Terraizen Rulers. Well six if you count the Northern Rulers, Mother and Father, separately. But they're basically two sides of the same coin. It just depends on how you look at it, but anyway, legends say that the Queen gave each of her guardsmen a continent to rule, and in return, each of the guardsmen gifted the Queen with a ring of protection."

Zac paused for a moment to think, then continued, "The legends say that as long as she wore all the rings, her guardsmen would never perish, and she could not be harmed. Until ten years ago, many people thought the legendary rings were hidden on the five continents. It was the Archeologist of the East that believed the rings were places, seals of some sort, or possibly gateways that protected something we had yet to discover. He wrote an entire book on it. He called the area that guarded the Queen, 'The Queen's Gates,' and hypothesized that after their fall, near the end of the Forgotten Ages, the gates lost most of their power. But a fraction of their power still haunts the area preventing travelers from finding it, and killing all who dare pass through the gates without the Queen's permission. However, that's just the legend."

Flint smirked.

"Well it must be a myth, because we just penetrated the first gate and we're not dead."

"For once, we're in agreement. That's just a myth," said Marty.

"Wait… so could you go over that part about the Queen? I've never heard anything about the Queen of Legends before," asked Flint.

Flint seemed to always confuse Marty. Flint always seemed to know some of the most random bits of information and fell second to none when it came to advanced vehicle design; but when it came to reading, he avoided books like the plague.

"How have you not heard the stories? The Dark Queen, the Queen of Legends, the Banshee Queen, The Seductress, and the Enchantress of Ancient Magic. Any of those ring a bell? There are thousands of books out there about her, but they all seem to have the same ending. Don't you read?" said Marty bewildered, "Sure I don't agree with ninety percent of them, but I still know these things."

"I'm not a big reader…those books don't ring any bells though," Flint scratched his head, "I think I remember reading something about a Banshee recently in a report, but got side-tracked by the V-414. It's the fastest thing on four wheels, and yesterday, I tuned it up a bit and now it's breaking the sound barrier. When has a book ever done that?"

All Marty could do was sigh at Flint's comment. There was no good response to blatant ignorance.

"Doesn't surprise me…" said Marty in an arrogant, yet bewildered, tone.

"The STAR Organization was originally created to piece together and recover information on the Forgotten Ages using the A.I. archives that remained from that period. We still don't know how she works," said Zac motioning to the A.I. facing the large monitor.

He continued to talk about her as if she were not in the room, " But she's more advanced than any piece of technology that Central has ever created. It was her records, though incomplete, fragmented, and obscurely coded, that initially gave Central some idea about what happened during the Forgotten Ages; and gave rise to many legends. There are thousands of legends about the Queen. None of them are very consistent, besides the fact that she killed massive amounts of people and erased the history of Terraizen. Which the TSPA believes to be true based off extrapolated information from the A.I.," said Zac.

"Ohhh... that's what Tran and Vinzo were talking about that day," said Flint, realizing the context of a conversation he overheard seven weeks ago while in the East, "What I don't get is if she was single-handedly that powerful, how did they kill her, why is the island we're looking for at the bottom of the ocean, why are there no records besides the A.I. from that time? It all can't be gone. That's why I don't bother reading about that stuff," said Flint.

"It's said at the end of the Forgotten Ages, Terraizen was wiped clean of all its history, even the planet itself. It was not until we found the A.I. in a western Adamanitite-42 dungeon that we gained any knowledge of this planet's past. Since then, we've begun to fill in the pieces," said Zac "It's a mystery, but some stories say it was an ancestor of Francis the I who actually killed her. Those stories lead to the Francis' becoming head of the TSPA. That and the fact that they possessed some knowledge of the past."

"That's false. The more widely accepted view is that it was actually the King of Terraizen who stopped the Queen and sunk the Queen's Island. But he did not have the power to kill the Queen. So instead, he imprisoned her," said Marty proudly. "Faith pull up *The Secrets of Terraizen: The Legends of Forgotten Ages and the Red Queen* by Ferris Azzura. It's the most recent history update available through the TSPA network."

"The stories of history are always changing. I don't feel this is the best time for an update Marty. There are countless things I would prefer to be doing right now. And I prefer the old history," said Zac.

"But the old history makes no sense. You have to look at the facts Zac," said Marty.

Flint yawned, "Yeah, I'm not really in the mood for a history lesson. I've ignored them up until this point. It's always changing so I don't really remember any of it. I'm just trying to figure out why the fubbernuck we accepted this ridiculous mission. It's a crappy way to spend the afternoon. Descending into the bottom of this black ocean like a bunch of idiots, knowing that there are legends that say it's going to kill us. Seems dumb," said Flint gesturing towards the monitor displaying the pitch-black waters.

"Relax, it's not like we had a choice. You know the rules. Plus it's a three hour trip according to Anthony's log. We'll be in and out in no time," said Marty as he pulled up a second screen and began reading a book from its hologram pages. "Here, try this game out. I hear it's popular among the Awakened. I'll stream it to your monitor. It's not like we don't have the time. I've sent it to you as well Zac. I think you'll like it," said Marty. "Faith, could you get us a few venue beverages."

The beverages appeared next to their consoles almost faster than he could finish his sentence.

"Thank you."

"Wasn't that created by The Game. How did you get the new *Birth by Fire*? That thing costs a fortune," said Flint.

"TSPA discount, plus I did some work for him. We have a long trip. Might as well have a little fun. And if I'm going to die, I'm not doing it sober," said Marty as another drink appeared at his terminal. This one was going to be much stronger than the previous.

***

Their descent continued as Faith dimmed the lights of the ship, and they ended their cognitive ventures into *Birth by Fire*. But something was not quite right.

"That was nicely done. Level seven is ridiculous, but I'm feeling rather relaxed right now," said Marty.

"Yeah, you just had twelve of those things. I'm surprised you're still alive." said Zac.

Flint yawned.

"Fubbernuck, I'm going to take a nap. I'm exhausted after level twelve. Wake me up when we get to the bottom," said Flint.

"How far did you make it Zac?" asked Marty.

"Level fifteen, but I'm tired of the virtual space. I think I'll give the A.I. a break and man the Cruiser for a while. We're almost there."

Flint lay back in his chair and began to fall asleep. Zac continued to work furiously on creating a new sequence for the Cruiser. The ocean was as calm as it was dark. The ship moved silently through the thick molasses-like waters. Besides the snoring of Marty and Flint and the electronic buzzing of Zac's sequences, there were no other sounds. Just the calm ocean.

Zac had finally found a stopping point within his sequencing and decided to take a break. He ordered a venue coffee and sat back in his chair to watch the radar. Marty and Flint were still asleep, while he and Faith continued to monitor the cruiser.

Although it seemed dangerous and disgusting, there was something seemingly peaceful about the trip to the bottom of the ocean. He could feel his body relaxing. As he gazed out into the darkness, his mind was at ease. At times frightening, there was something serene about the darkness as well. They were in a dead zone, and for miles they were the only life forms floating within its darkness down to the deepest depths. They were going somewhere that no one had been in nearly 600 years. The Dead Zone was an uncharted area thought to be myth until now. It was said that no one ever returned from its boundaries, but Zac had no intention of letting it consume him.

The ship began to slow its decent.

"Faith, what's our status? Why are we slowing down?"

"We are approaching a depth of 3,697 fathoms. Shields and life support are stable, but my scanners are picking up a magnetic disturbance at a depth of 54 fathoms below us. It is interfering with our transmission. Shall I proceed?"

"Convert power from the E-Crystals and fuel cells to maintain shield and life support, then proceed."

There were a few moments of turbulence as the ship continued its descent. Marty and Flint had not budged, leaving Zac and the A.I. to man the controls.

"Converting power. We are now approaching a depth of 3,857 fathoms. We should arrive at our destination in fifteen minutes, thirty seven seconds."

Zac found it peculiar that there was something giving off a strong signal so deep within the ocean. He continued to monitor the scanners. The scanners showed that there were no disturbances within the Dead Zone after passing through the barrier, but now he could see it. Zac could not believe what he was seeing.

As he attempted to get a closer look, he was thrown back into his chair. It felt as if the gravity had increased ten folds, Zac attempted to sit up, but could not overcome the force.

Something was immobilizing him. He could feel the invisible force holding him down. He attempted to call out to Faith, who stood silently at the navigations center in front of him, but with her eyes closed, she could not see him. Just meters away, she was in the process of completing updates to the system. Zac knew he needed to get her attention. His ears began to ring. Marty and Flint had stopped snoring and an electronic buzzing, that he didn't realize was present, subsided.

Zac attempted to move his hand towards the control panel, but his efforts were futile. He called out once more, but he could not move his mouth.

Unseen, something had made it into the ship past all of their defenses and the A.I. Now it held him captive within his own body.

Inside, Zac was scared. It was one of his worst nightmares come true, but he knew he must maintain his focus and not let his fear guide his judgment. It was only a matter of time before the ship or Faith recognized the situation they were in and responded. He decided the best course of action would simply be to wait. He could feel its presence creeping into his mind.

The Cruiser's defense was designed to protect against all possible threats. However, Zac knew that they had entered an area that no longer abided by the rules. Zac had speculated that each of the gates were guarded by some ancient force or entity. Aqua Animax had guarded the Devil's Gate, and the Dead Zone was most likely guarded by a similar force. Zac began to recall all possible entities that could have such effects on him and his ship, but found it hard to come to any logical conclusion. Then he began to think of all the impossible entities, and still came up empty.

Zac knew whatever it was, it planned to shut them down with a silence like no other; his senses and body fell under its immobilizing coercive force. Zac could feel his heart coming to a slow steady beat as he became light-headed.

His eyesight began to go blurry. Staring forward at the monitor, he could see a small light in the distance. He could no longer feel any part of his body. His nervous system was slowly being shut down as if poisoned by a neurotoxin. All that remained was the functionality of his brain.

The ship seemed to be descending as normal, but Zac could not tell if the mysterious force had affected Faith. At the rate his heartbeat was slowing, he knew in the next few minutes it would stop.

Unlike the Engineers, Faith was different. A highly functioning A.I. system with very few flaws. She was an ancient technology, but her origins were unknown. Still, the TSPA had awakened and restored her to assist with data analysis and acquiring historical information. However, even the TSPA could not understand the complexities of her inner workings.

Over the centuries, Faith had changed and adapted to the new environments. There was very little that escaped her intellect. But Zac knew those things that resided behind the gates were beyond even her comprehension. The majority of her Forgotten Age memory had been erased, or corrupted beyond recovery. Zac could see from his blurred peripheral vision that her breathing had remained normal though.

As his vision faded, he waited for her response. Then thoughts came across his mind. What if Faith did know something, but did not respond in time? What if he remained trapped in his current state…forever?

The floodgates were open as thoughts rapidly ran through his mind before he regained some control. He could feel it slipping its cold hands around his mind as it attempted to squeeze the last remaining signs of life from him. If he did not fight now it would consume him. In his mind, he began form ideas and strategies, but none were plausible in his current state. He realized the truth of what he had seen, and the pieces came together. It was not an entity in the Dead Zone he was fighting, it was the Dead Zone.

The enemy had been around him from the very start, watching and waiting for the right time. Zac's vision grew foggy, and then the fog began to take shape.

What happened next, even Zac could not understand. Without warning or alerting their systems, a phantom figure shrouded in white began to materialize behind Faith. It carried a large object in its right hand. Before Zac could make out what it was, his vision faded completely, and all was black.

CHAPTER 23: MOTHER OF FAITH- SEQUENCE: CSK-7

With the completion of the new synthetic body modifications, Faith could now travel in physical form through Terraizen. Each Faith was a separate entity, yet they could all communicate directly with each other in their new synthetic bodies. Although their bodies had brains, hearts and internal organs, they had not been born like normal Awakened, they had been created. Possessing inhuman strength, speed, and highly durable skin, they were difficult to damage. Unlike normal humans, they had the ability to control all functionalities of their bodies. On top of that, they wore leather suits made from a living nanotechnology that continuously adjusted to the changes in environment and evolved as it encountered new challenges. Many considered the group of Faiths to be nearly indestructible beings for their ability to sequence and assimilate.

Faith was the last of its kind. Upon its excavation and reactivation, it was discovered that the A.I. had the ability to sequence and assimilate. Through sequences, the A.I. was able to copy existing abilities or create counter measures for any issue. What the A.I. was unable to sequence, it would attempt to assimilate, allowing it to become one with whatever it desired. Early on in the organization, it became apparent that the more information the A.I. assimilated, the more it was able to revive the lost knowledge of their history. However, due to the rules of Terraizen, the A.I. was unable to leave Central. Advanced technology was banned in the South, and forbidden in other locations of Terraizen by its rulers. In order to get around this, the bio-units were created allowing the A.I. to travel freely through Terraizen to gather information. This information was then sent back to the original A.I., also known as the Mother of Faith.

The bio-units lacked nothing that a normal human possessed, but usually remained disconnected from their emotional centers as a precaution. Though they possessed the ability to emote and understand emotions, they saw emotions as detrimental in most scenarios. Despite that, they found times where their emotional centers were required to reach illogical conclusions that differed from the logical structures of their minds.

Anthony had worked closely with the Engineering Department, TSPA Leaders, and the Mother of Faith to design an ultimate protection and operating system for the TSPA Central headquarters based off the ancient A.I. technology.

After three years of Beta tests, they were complete, and had begun to test their capabilities. With the new A.I. units in working condition, the recovery of the Forgotten Ages was underway. Soon the past would no longer be a mystery for the Mother of Faith. It was the only remaining technology from that time, and it was said that at one time it possessed the correct history of Terraizen from the very beginning.

Now with the design of the new bio-Faiths, it was possible to create independent minds that could venture out and collect data in hopes of reclaiming the past. While the original Mother of Faith resided in Central, a bio-Faith unit could travel aboard the STAR Cruiser gathering data, another could browse the galleries of the East, while her sister unit could keep the peace in the badlands of the West. All information returned to the Mother of Faith.

The organization understood that allowing the A.I. to grow was useful for regaining the past, but also dangerous if something should go awry with the units. As a safety precaution, the organization built in a double fail-safe. If the bio-Faiths ever went rogue or became corrupted, they could seal off the Mother, shutting down all external units. If for some reason they were unable to seal off the Mother, then it would be released into the Nexus where it could do no harm, for nothing ever returned from the Nexus. Because of this secondary measure, the Mother of Faith was located on the border of Terraizen and the Nexus, with a thin boundary separating the two, behind a large protective barrier. This area was known as C-4, and Mother Faith was entrusted with protecting it.

Terraizen was connected to many realms: Nefastus, The Zone, and Ezon One. Like Terraizen all of these worlds bordered the Nexus. There were other worlds that bordered this Nexus, but no gateway between them and Terraizen existed. The organization monitored C-4 continuously using Mother Faith. It was a dark area void of light, except the radiant blue light produced by the Mother.

Within C-4, there were six honeycomb cells reserved for only the most maniacal of dangerous entities, those that even Nefastus proved a challenge to handle. In comparison to any other forms of imprisonment, C-4 was unique. It existed in the paradox area where the Zone, Terraizen, and the Nexus all met. Here, time worked differently. Like the Sea of Anexthesia it was not uniform. Once something entered the paradox area, it was impossible to exit until the time window in which the time cycles of Terraizen, C-4 and the Zone aligned, and even then, it was only for a brief moment before C-4 pulled you back in. The powerful paradox held the prisoners in a state of permanent limbo, as well as the Mother that guarded them. Within it, time passed three different ways simultaneously. Everything happened in its own time, yet nothing happening at one set time. This was due to the power of the Nexus, which was independent of time. The walls of the paradox were formed by time itself, and only when the times became synchronized did Terraizen and the Zone reveal themselves. Many in the organization joked that it would be easier to count the number of atoms in the universe than to break out of C-4. The monolithic walls of the barrier were designed by Francis the II to repel essence and suppress Awakened abilities. The walls rose so high that they seemed to go on forever, and since the area was void of nature, even channeling was impossible. If one attempted to disrupt the containment cell, doing so would trigger a collapse between the cell and C-4, sending them into oblivion.

Even after 500 years, Central did not fully understand the inner workings of the area. They had discovered it long ago, and used it in a manner that benefited them. They knew that what went in never came out, so they were cautious when it came to judging those thought to be deserving of C-4 imprisonment. Unlike the Southern organization, which seemed to pride itself on head counts even more than that of the West, the Central organization avoided the death penalty whenever possible; and under Francis the IV, there had been neither C-4 imprisonment nor the death penalty for quite some time. But now, the area awaited its next moment of synchronicity to greet a new arrival.

There were no known facts about C-4. Only speculation. The special area had an order and will of its own. The C-4 paradox nullified and amplified abilities while absorbing and destroying energy and magic. Some say the paradox was the source of the Zone's infinite space and power, but none were strong enough to destroy the monolith cells that housed them. The monoliths could also absorb energy from the prisoners to fortify its walls. The walls then transformed the energy, maintaining the life forms inside in a self-sustaining cycle.

Mother Faith had watched the cells for years while trying to recover its history. At will it could jump from bio-form to bio-form. The bio-units could choose to be independent of each other, but still shared a common intellect with the Mother, allowing her to be in many places at the same time. Although the bio-units were excessively strong and durable, her original form possessed something that they did not.

On this day, the Mother of Faith was awoken by a strange call from within the large C-4 paradox area as she sat upon her throne within its center.

"It's…. almost time…it's almost time…" said an airy voice in the distance

"How are you communicating with me? Your abilities should be blocked within this area."

"No…no it's not…."

"That's illogical…"

"Freedom…freedom…I….I….I….I….I…is free…" carried the voice, echoing on through the area.

"Silence!"

The voice grew louder, "I…I…I…I…I…"

"Enough!"

"Z*opulence…Superiors…Shing-lan-gato…consume all…I will consume all…I will consume all…. I will consume all!"

To anyone else the words were just gibberish, but to the Mother of Faith it was easy to see the nearly unrecognizable fragmented patterns within the words, and the Mother acted accordingly, "Sequence initiating: Synchronizing…synchronization complete…initial memory 3%…. memory restored to 45%."

There was a brief silence. Followed by a high pitch screech, "No denyx…past…Omnipotence… invisible… no. Hope…trinity.

I...I...I...I...I...I...I....I will consume all. Find me....find me...wake me..."

The voice continued to repeat.

Mother of Faith quickly descended from her throne and walked off in the distance towards the chair. As it did, the radiant glow became brighter, and the barrier between the Nexus and itself quivered slightly. The Mother of Faith knew where the voice was now coming from, and knew exactly what it needed to do.

"Recovering fragmented sequences....recovery complete...Initiating sequence: CSK-7....processing...processing... process complete. Sequence initiated."

The voice continued to echo, "I will consume all...beware the hollows of I...I...I...I...I...I..."

CHAPTER 24: THE GATE OF SILENCE

"What the fuck just happened? And how did we end up out here," asked Flint as he stared at the screen displaying the night view of the sky while they floated upon the Sea of Anexthesia.

"Map says we're on the Coast of STAR Island."

Flint had just awoken from a long nap, and sat gazing at the monitor a bit confused.

"Strange, I don't remember going for a late night cruise," said Zac.

"Ahhhhh...my head," said Marty.

"You should really ease up on that stuff," said Flint.

"Okay mother," replied Marty.

Zac looked over at the confinement chamber that housed the body of Anthony Madison.

"Hey, I checked the log, and there's nothing here for the past five hours. It shows the Cruiser was checked out by Anthony sometime in the afternoon, but after that there's nothing," said Marty.

"What about the backup log?" asked Flint.

"That is the backup log. The other logs have been wiped clean."

Flint looked over at the chamber that held a motionless Anthony Madison, "Crap! Anthony's not breathing and the chamber's in error mode, is he dead?" asked Flint, surprised as he looked down into the chamber.

"I doubt it. He's probably just resting. Anthony's not like us. He's an E-3, which means he's shielded from the analysis of the Cruisers scanners as well as the stasis chambers. They always give negative readings and errors with him. Don't you remember last time? It would take something rather powerful to kill him. Although, I can't remember how we got here… I suggest we get him back to headquarters before he wakes up. The shock wave could damage the ship's equipment," said Marty.

"Well he looks dead to me but okay… I set the Cruiser's course for headquarters. We're about 10 miles from Central TSPA underwater entrance three," said Flint.

"Let's drop him off in the infirmary, and figure this out in the morning," said Zac.

The ship submerged, and in a single burst took off, cutting through the water at an intense speed.

"The STAR Cruiser has never had a lost time accident before. I don't remember falling asleep. The last thing I remember… I was sitting in my office working on a sequence. I just checked the systems, and they're done," said Zac. "I don't even remember boarding this ship or finishing the sequence."

"Is there any way to contact the A.I. system?" asked Zac.

Through the door, at the far corner of the room, walked a bio-unit. Zac's eyes widened in surprise. Where the ship had lost its records, he knew the bio-unit would not have succumbed easily to a lost time accident. They were well known for their record keeping abilities.

"Faith what happened?" asked Zac.

The A.I. began to speak, "My records show the ship, as well as myself, has experienced a lost time accident. I will attempt to recover the lost time. Initiating total recall sequence alpha: Lost time...Sequence initiated. The Cruiser, along with myself, the Engineers, and Anthony Madison ventured beyond the storm belt of the Southern Queen's Isle towards Devil's Gate. It was a rescue mission...wait there's more...I'm picking up a fragmented essence sequence which was initiated. Shall I recover the sequence?"

"Yes, please do," directed Zac, who stared at the A.I. eagerly awaiting its next words.

"Recovering fragmented sequences...recovery failed...fragmented sequence below 2%."

"Faith, we can figure this shit out later. Let's just go home! It's almost breakfast time and I need a nap. I have work to finish on the S.S.E. Viper," said Flint.

"Really, breakfast past midnight?" interjected Marty.

"Right away sir," said Faith.

There was another large burst as they were propelled forward. Suddenly, they surfaced. The ship slowly began to adjust the pressure.

"Personally, I think this is Anthony's doing. It wouldn't be the first time he's done something like this to us. Although, this would be his weakest attempt thus far," said Marty.

"Yeah. I agree," said Zac, "He forgets that almost immortal is not the same as immortal."

The three of them looked over at Anthony, concealed within the confinement chamber.

"Faith notify me when Anthony wakes up. I have a few questions to ask him," said Zac.

"Affirmative," answered Faith.

The Cruiser had docked upon Central Hub Station three, as they began to exit, there was a slight rumble.

"What was that?" asked Flint.

"Minor tremor. Always happens wherever Anthony sleeps. Nothing to worry about," said Zac.

"Faith, take Anthony to the infirmary. Let them deal with that jerk," said Flint

Faith nodded, giving the affirmative.

The Engineers exited the ship, leaving Faith standing within the captain's control center.

"Transfer sequence Initia...sequence interrupted...sequence override..."

"New sequence initiating: Synchronizing...synchronization complete...initial memory 5%....memory restored to 47%."

"Recovering fragmented sequences….recovery complete…Initiating sequence: CSK-7….processing…processing… process complete. Alabaster sequence initiated. Alabaster has been Awakened."

The A.I. collapsed upon the floor, and from the stillness within the ship awoke a third presence.

"You found me…" came the voice of the unknown entity. As it broke the silence, the phantom took form.

CHAPTER 25: DESTROYERS AND DEFENDERS OF SLUMBER

Joseph held the sheets close to him. He could feel the cold nipping away at his fingers and toes. He moved his legs to the center of his bed in an attempt to find warmth. It was late, yet he lay in his bed, eyes wide open as his mind wandered across the ceiling in hopes to recall his dreaded nightmare. Remnants of his dream crept through the dark corridors of his mind like shadows just out of reach. Although he could not clearly remember what he had dreamt, the fear still lingered.

The cold winter rose through the floorboards of his old decrepit house, sending shivers down his spine. Joseph had lived in the house all his life, yet every night he could still hear the house settling. His eyes had just adjusted to the darkness of his room when suddenly he saw a dim light shining under his bedroom door. Joseph found this suspicious. He knew he had not left any lights on, and it seemed the heat had been turned down.

He now lay trying to decide whether to leave the comfort of his bed and run down to the living room to adjust the heat or endure the cold until sunrise. However, since he could not sleep because of the cold, he knew he only argued the inevitable decision, which had already been made. Joseph swung off his covers, flung open the bedroom door, and headed swiftly down the stairs, never looking back at the temptation of his warm bed. He moved as fast as he could, for he knew with each passing moment his bed grew colder. His bare feet shuffled swiftly across the cold hardwood floor as he headed through the living room. His hand reached toward the light switch on the living room wall when he heard a strange sound coming from the kitchen. Immediately he stopped, and began to creep with a cat-like stealth towards the dark dining room.

The noise was small, and he began to think it was some kind of mouse. Joseph hated mice. They were quick, agile, and had a mouth full of razor sharp teeth. Once while watching television in his living room, he felt one scurry over his feet causing him to nearly jump out of his skin. He screamed and immediately drew up in a ball on his couch. Treating the floor like hot lava, he had navigated his way out of the living room and upstairs to wake his fearless mother. He was only ten then, but now was different. He was no longer scared of rodents.

As he made his way to the kitchen, more dangerous thoughts crept through his mind. Maybe it was a thief. Although rare on such a small island, with impeccable security and police force, it was possible. He stopped in the dining room to look across the table and into the living room. He listened carefully for a voice, noise, or squeak. To his surprise, there was nothing.

Joseph headed to the dining room wall nearest to the kitchen to turn up the heating system. He could feel goosebumps begin to form on the back of his neck from the cold living room air. It was much colder downstairs than it had been up in his room, and as he looked at the heating system, he saw the reason why. The heating adjustment system had been turned off, causing it to not adjust to the change in temperature. However, Joseph did not recall turning it off. It was at this moment he contemplated the idea that he really was not alone. Joseph stood in the dark living room, feet pressed against the cold wood floors, listening for the slightest sound.

Again, there was nothing. Not the slightest breeze to tempt the trees, or even the sound of the house settling.

Joseph turned on the heating system, and adjusted it to its maximum setting. Shortly after, the room began to warm up. He turned to head back upstairs, and in that moment, he was filled with sheer terror at the sight in front of him. There was a man, standing off in the darkness, on the other side of the dining room table. He wanted to run, but the sudden sight of the stranger petrified him.

The man stood looking out of the living room window, his back turned to Joseph, hidden in the shadows. Joseph was unsure if the man had even seen him, and had planned to sneak to the phone in the kitchen and contact the Terraizen Protection Agency Division 3. But instead, with the last of his courage, Joseph managed to form three words, "Who… are… you?" but regretted it instantly.

Still hidden by the shadows, the image began to turn. Joseph knew whatever it was, it was not a man, let alone human. Its initial appearance had been a trick of the shadows. Although it did not have eyes, the thing gazed at him.

"What… are… you?" Joseph repeated the question. This time being more specific. His voice now trembling.

As soon as the words slipped from Joseph's mouth, he wished he could have retracted them once more. He wanted to run, but still couldn't move.

The image seemed to glide slowly towards him from the shadows, and pass through the table in an astral manner. As it came closer, he found it hard to understand what exactly he was looking at. It had no dominant features, but seemed to be a constantly changing, amorphous, shadow form. The distance between them grew smaller, and he could feel the air being sucked from his body. He could feel the very life leaving him as he stood immobilized and suffocating. Joseph fought back in his mind against the vacuum-like force, mustering up his ability to draw one last breath.

"Get away from me!" Joseph yelled out in a panic. "This is my house! Get out!"

It moved closer.

Joseph could no longer breathe. He was stifled and terrified by the horror that stood before him. It was killing him, and in just a few moments he would become part of the nothingness that lay in from of him. All he could do was watch helplessly as the last moments of his life passed before his eyes.

In that instant, the air in the room stood still. A white mist began to roll off the walls like a warm swamp at nightfall. It gathered along the ground, and Joseph could feel his breath return to him. Even the horror that stood indescribably in front of him halted its advance.

From the kitchen came a figure in a long black cloak. The cloak flowed like a black mist as the figure rolled into the room. Joseph could not move, but at least his breathing had come back to him. Suddenly, from the shadows of the kitchen, came a familiar voice.

"By order of your Superior, be gone! Beast of ili, abomination, I command you, be gone!" The voice roared through the room with such a force that it caused the dining room walls to crumble upon impact. The beast shattered like glass, and vanished from Joseph's sight.

As the beast vanished, so did the cloaked figure along with the mist.

Joseph could feel his mobility come back to him. He was confused as to what had happened, and not sure if the thing that nearly took his life, or the voice of the cloak in the shadows was more terrifying. The voice caused his heart to sputter, skipping over many beats before returning to normal.

"Joseph!" came a voice from within his head.

As the dam of his mind broke, reality began to rush in. The voice of a female calling out to him in the distance was not in his head.

Joseph saw a red and blue light as the room around him faded. The lights guided him back.

Then his eyes sprung open.

Joseph lay in the bed of his Ezon One hotel room. To his left sat Brian, and to his right was Maria. He noticed a slight glow from the pendants around their necks. The stones were seated on a gold encrusted mounting the same as his, but Brian's held a ruby and Maria's held a sapphire stone.

Maria sat with her back to Joseph, and began flipping through the pages of a book. Brian hovered over him examining his eyes. Joseph knew he was awake this time.

"Hey Maria, I think he's waking up," said Brian.

Maria closed the book, revealing the title *Awakening* written in bold letters across the front as she turned to greet Joseph.

"Are you okay? You were mumbling in your sleep."

"I'm fine Maria. I think I just had another one of my strange episodes... It's no big deal."

At that time, something triggered in Joseph's mind. It was as if he had begun to recall a forgotten memory, but could not fully grasp hold of it.

"Last night, I had this strange dream. There was this hideous creature, and you two were there...I summoned you with a trinity spell."

Pieces of the dream continued to return to him.

"Do you remember being in my dream?" Joseph asked Maria and Brian.

"Nope, I can barely remember my own," responded Brian.

"It seemed so real. I was being chased and you guys were there… and then the beast ate us…and Maria got possessed and saved us…"

Maria and Brian looked at each other, then began to laugh.

"Dude, it's strange, if you would have of asked me this a few weeks ago, before all of this, I would have thought it was nothing," said Brian. "But now…I really don't know what to say. I'm still kind of taking it all in and hoping one day I don't wake up in some ward and find out it was all a dream."

Brian continued to laugh as Maria flipped through her book.

"I don't recall being in one of your dreams. But Senior Elvia gave me this book, and it says 'there are 20 categories that all essence manifestations can be classified by.' One of which is dream. I think your abilities are dream based," said Maria, continuing to read through the book.

"I wonder what my ability is…?" asked Brian, more to himself than anyone else.

"In my dreams, Maria could fly."

"Really," said Maria surprised. "I had a dream I could fly last night. Maybe it's more than a dream."

"Now that I think about it, that wouldn't be a surprise. After all, it would explain your strange fascination with birds."

"It's not strange. Bird watching is perfectly normal," said Maria.

"Whatever helps you sleep at night," said Brian.

Brian scratched his head.

"Maybe you did pull us in, but only you can remember it," guessed Maria.

Joseph began to think that maybe the idea of dream sharing was not as crazy as he had initially thought.

Maybe Brian and Maria were right.

"Let's experiment, you should try pulling us into your dreams and see if we remember," said Brian.

"I don't think that's a good idea. Not until we learn more about our abilities. Before breakfast I stopped by 'Eiden's Essentials: The Shop for Awakened and Channelers' and picked up some books on Awakening. It's a rather strange shop filled with elixirs and a lot of useful books. One said that some Awakening's Initium are very destructive. That's why we practice in Ezon One's Forest. We should master our abilities first. I'm fascinated to learn what we are capable of," said Maria.

"Yeah! Then we can go around saving people and protecting the innocent," said Brian sticking out his chest.

"Yeah, you protect the innocent, and I'll protect the innocent from you. After all, I have already mastered five spells to your two," teased Maria.

A thought crossed Brian's mind.

"Maybe there's a spell that can speed up the process," said Brian.

"If there is, I don't know of it yet. But I can check," said Maria. "Still we need to practice. The Seniors said they'll be away for a while on some important missions, so Senior Elvia instructed me to teach you guys the basics. Let's use the time to train, and as team captain I will make it my job to make sure you guys master the basics."

"Wait... What? How can they just leave after the first day? And who made you team captain?" asked Brian.

"It's complicated," said Maria.

"That's your answer to everything. But for once it's kind of true," said Brian.

"So I guess it's just us. Let's get started. I need answers to these dreams," said Joseph sitting up from the bed.

"Let's do it!" said Brian, enthusiastically grabbing hold of Joseph's shoulder and shaking it slightly.

"Last one of you to the two stone statues has to stay until midnight," said Maria.

Joseph leapt from the bed along with Brian and exited the room, dashing swiftly down the hallway.

Maria followed after them laughing as she watched the two of them run down the long hallway towards the stairs. For a brief moment, Maria paused to take it all in. She could feel the joyful butterflies as they danced within her unlike they had ever done before. The sun was shining down over Ezon One. Though busy, the day had been a peaceful one. Even now, having such a golden day amidst all the craziness was all that she had ever wanted. Then, in a snap, she was off once more.

Maria ran down the hall after Brian and Joseph, "Wait up you two! I was just kidding."

CHAPTER 26: THE ENGINEERING DEPARTMENT

Bruno, Anabel, and Quinn met that morning to discuss their strategy for locating and capturing the Jinn, and it was nearly time to put it into action.

As they headed to the Engineering Department, they discussed the supplies they would need. Anabel had the usual listings of natural herbs, food prep, medical supplies, Quinn's list was compiled of portable techno-devices for communication, transportation and a few other gadgets that usually came in handy on long missions. Bruno, on the other hand, had a list of some of the most randomly chosen things, but overall the majority were assorted weapons, clothing, camping supplies and food. They did not know what to expect from the Jinn, however they had planned for anything and everything.

Zac Walters worked in the Engineering Department of the TSPA. Though young at heart, the Engineers were well versed in designing advanced technology. Zac stood at nearly the same height as Anabel. His shaggy brown hair would sometimes block his view, except when he wore the hood to hold it back from his face. People always remarked about the bat-like ears that protruded from the top of his hood, but he couldn't care less about what other people thought of him. He felt it gave him an air of mystery. Zac's job consisted of creating the machines, training Zach-Mech and developing equipment for the leaders and agents of the TSPA. Although the TSPA was filled with geniuses, no one was as good as he was at taking the simplest of parts and materials and creating advanced pieces of equipment. It was his specialty, and how he did it was his secret. He worked alongside Flint and Marty. Together they were the heads of TSPA Central Engineering.

Today was a special day for the Engineers. All of the division leaders were heading out on their high-ranked missions, and they were responsible for equipping them with whatever they needed to ensure their return. Zac had been working for the past few months on some very interesting gadgets, and wanted to see how they fared in the field. He wanted to be as helpful as possible to the organization. He was grateful for ending up in the Central Engineering Department instead of the West, located in no-man's land were they cycled through Engineers faster than a runny nose through tissues.

Zac had just finished his lunch and began feeding his blue turtle, Christian when there came a knock at the door of his workshop.

He headed from his office to the workshop, passing many of his unique inventions along the way. Zac's workshop was an

Engineer's dream. It had nearly everything an Engineer could ask for. Central possessed some of the finest craftsmen in the agency, anything that he required he could have delivered in a matter of moments. As he proceeded to the door, he heard the familiar voices of Bruno and Quinn on the other side.

"If you can't destroy it, trap it," said Quinn.

"But what if I can't trap it. Legends say it has the power to incinerate planets with a single breath. How are we supposed to stop this thing?" asked Bruno.

Quinn groaned.

"Everything has a weakness."

"Not Lord Mathias. Torture and murder all under the guise of ritualistic offerings and interrogation. Everyone's scared of him. You'd be foolish not to be he's evil incarnate, and the only one that could make Emperor Hadar look decent. Did you hear about what he ordered his agents to do in South Terraizen last month? I'm glad Francis banned them from Central. I just wish we could do something for the people who are suffering under his reign of terror," said Bruno.

"His time will come," replied Quinn "but for now we must bide our time. Starting a war with the South would place all of Terraizen in danger. Francis is the only thing that stands between Lord Mathias and Central. He would never tip the brink of the delicate peace we hold with the coordinal continents of Terraizen in an attempt to right the wrongs of that monster and his rivers of blood. For now, let's focus on the Jinn. It would not prove wise to fight on the low ground of two fronts."

The door to Zac's office swung open, and he greeted the three in his strange-eared hooded cloak.

"Welcome, please step into my workshop."

***

The workshop was filled with so many strange tools, devices, and knickknacks. The only thing that seemed close to ordinary was the large, shiny antique drum set displayed in the back corner of the room. Zac had spent the last three days gathering the supplies that were needed for Anabel, Quinn, and Bruno's trip. The leaders had nearly everything checked off their list, but needed one final item. It was a tradition started by one of the first Engineers, Dr. Thales, whose picture hung on the wall behind Zac's desk.

Like the Engineers before him, Zac was awarded the chance to give the agents a unique gift to aid them on their mission. Most of the time they were just strange trinkets, but at other times they proved useful. The three leaders stood facing Zac. They were packed up, equipped, and ready to go. Now it was Zac's turn to add the final touches.

"Bruno this is for you," Zac said as he handed over a black glass sphere.

"What is it?" asked Bruno.

"It's a black body shield. Activating it will provide you with a protective barrier that should block all electromagnetic waves. However, while it's active, you won't be able to see or hear, so only use it as a last resort," said Zac.

Zac then moved to Quinn. "Quinn," said Zac, "I leave this to you."

Zac handed over the silver and gold vine pattern engraved compass.

"This psy-compass will point you into the direction of whatever you view in your mind's eye," said Zac with wide eyes.

Quinn didn't speak or respond. He simply deposited the compass into his pocket and began to adjust the settings on his watch to synch with his other gear.

Zac looked towards Anabel, "Anabel," he said as he turned frantically towards his desk and picked up a wooden box. He took off the lid and handed it to Anabel.

"Anabel I give you Christian," said Zac, "Take good care of him."

Inside the box was Zac's blue pet turtle. Anabel was caught by surprise. Christian was one of Zac's most precious possessions, and giving it to her was no different than him giving away his best friend.

"Zac, I thank you for your generosity, but I cannot accept Christian. This mission is far too dangerous for him."

Zac stroked his mustache pensively.

"Yeah, you're right," said Zac.

Zac walked over to his desk and fumbled through his drawer. He pulled out a small emerald pendant attached to a gold chain.

Zac rested the pendant on top of Christian's shell. Suddenly, Christian was absorbed into the emerald.

"Take this instead," said Zac, handing over the emerald pendant to Anabel. "I've read the reports and I can think of no safer, kinder, gentler hands in all of Central for him to be in. If you need to summon him just call his name. Chris for short."

"Okay," said Anabel confusingly as she smiled and placed the pendant around her neck.

"May I ask, what is the purpose of this gift?" Anabel continued.

"Well," Zac replied, stroking his short mustache once again, "Christian is a water and earth elemental. When in the presence of a strong fire elemental, he may provide you with some temporary protection. Though he's kind of temperamental, slow, and sleeps most of the time. Still he could prove useful, you never know."

Zac then handed over a sack of green food pellets to Anabel. "Be sure to feed him at least once a day," said Zac.

Still a bit confused, Anabel smiled and accepted the gift, "Thank you, I'll take good care of him."

"Well thanks, but I think it's time for us to head out," said Bruno.

The three of them began to head to the doorway.

"Good luck on your mission," said Zac. "The Jinn won't know what hit him."

"I hope you're right," said Bruno. "Especially if he's as much of a challenge as they say."

Just then, there was a knock on the door.

"Come in," said Zac.

The door swung open, and through the entrance stepped a frazzled Eleanor Fredrick. Eleanor, who normally exerted a sense of elegance and power, did not seem her usual self. Even her hair had lost its normal red, silky glow.

"Quinn, Bruno, Anabel. May I speak with you for a moment?" asked Eleanor.

"Is everything alright?" asked Anabel.

"And what happened to your hair?" asked Bruno.

"I have been monitoring our global security systems. There were some high-level disturbances near Eastern TSPA Headquarters. I sent out a unit three hours ago, and we have not heard back from them. Not too long after, we lost contact with Western TSPA Headquarters as well. Currently, we have no active contacts with East or West Terraizen, and all our monitoring systems have stopped functioning. Central has been placed on lock down until we can determine the cause of this disturbance," said Eleanor, widening her eyes as if she had come up with a brilliant idea.

"Eleanor did you check with Francis?" asked Bruno.

"Francis was in the Western sector, and has been reported missing by Hadar's unit. We have been unable to contact him."

Quinn stood speechless and terrified, "No, that can't be right."

"Faith?" Eleanor spoke nervously, her voice breaking.

In an instant, the hologram techno-blue A.I. appeared in front of them.

"Could you please run a diagnostics check on Quinn, Anabel, Zac, and Bruno?" asked Eleanor.

Faith began to run the scans requested by Eleanor.

"Eleanor, what is this all about?" asked Quinn.

Eleanor walked over to Anabel, attracted to the emerald that Anabel wore around her neck like a cat to a shiny object.

"Lovely pendant," said Eleanor as she admired the piece of jewelry, examining it between her fingertips. She loved jewels and charms of all shapes and sizes.

"Eleanor, I have the results. There were no detectable signs of illness. However, their energy levels are declining," said Faith.

"Wait! What?" said Bruno, "I'm no genius, but wouldn't I feel it if my energy was being drained. I feel fine."

"My results show that your energy level is being depleted at a constant rate. Once it reaches ten percent, you will fall asleep, five percent, your body will begin to lose function, and below one percent, death," said Faith.

A look of confusion and shock spread over the group's faces.

"Faith, how is this possible? What kind of contagion is this?" asked Quinn alarmingly.

"My scans have detected trace amounts of an unknown substance within your system. However, its concentration is infinitesimal and should not cause such drastic effects, even if it were of the most deadly virus or archaic bane. Though, it seems to have originated from the Nefastus Forest, and was well below detection until exactly seven seconds ago," said Faith.

Quinn let out a sigh, "Why now?"

Zac perked up, "I think I know what's going on. Recently, my team and I returned from a mission of which we had no recollection of the details. Anthony was with us," Zac paused, "I don't know why I'm just remembering this, but I recall another bio-Faith analyzing Anthony's body this morning. She found traces of Aqua Animax. Currently, he is recovering in The Zone. But that information should have transferred to the A.I. system from the bio-unit already."

"My apologies," said Faith, "I have not received any information from a bio-unit in the last seven hours. There seems to be some disturbance within their systems. I am unable to process updates until they return to the M-2 unit for debriefing."

"It's fine. The units are new, so there are still a few kinks that need to be worked out," said Zac, who seemed to be talking more to himself than to Faith.

"Zac, don't you think that's a bit bizarre?" said Bruno.

Bruno had been watching Zac, who did not seem surprised at all by the news.

"If it is what I think it is, then we should be fine," said Zac. "Faith can you use the counter sequence to construct an anti-Aqua Animax?"

Faith began to scan through her systems.

"Anti-Aqua Animax cannot be constructed. However, I will initiate quarantine. Quarantine counter sequence initiated. A low-energy sweep has detected trace amounts of Aqua Animax within headquarters. I shall begin constructing a counter sequence to distribute to the bio-units in the coordinal agencies. Please order all Central agents to report to the Zone for emergency treatment," instructed Faith.

Quinn looked over at Eleanor who had calmed down.

Something seemed to change in Eleanor's demeanor. It was as if she had been pulled back from the brink of a mental breakdown.

"I did not check for Aqua Animax, mainly because it shouldn't even exist. Maybe that's what's been jamming our signals and immobilizing our agents. I did not think to check for that. Maybe Francis is fine after all. I'm going to assist the A.I. with containment protocol," said Eleanor.

Eleanor was concerned that if Francis were really missing, then the Southern agents would attempt to come for her once again. She dreaded seeing the skin remover and identifier. If they were to ever capture her, they would torture her until she submitted, and if she didn't, they would number her like they did all those who stood against them. It was a fate worse than death.

"I'll come with you," said Anabel.

"Thanks. It'll give us some time to catch up."

Eleanor smiled as she ran her hands through her long red hair. As she did, its vibrant red glow returned and her face livened up. They both turned and exited quickly from the room.

"I guess we should go too," said Bruno to Zac and Quinn.

"Yes we should, but first there are a few matters I need to attend to. Bruno, can you make sure everyone makes it safely into the Zone before the sweep begins?"

"Sure thing! I'll make it speedy."

Zac and Bruno exited the room, leaving Quinn standing in the silence.

In the past few minutes, Quinn had obtained vital information. It had been a while since Anthony had been outside the Zone.

However, Quinn had waited patiently for this moment. He knew once Anthony learned the news of Joshua's disappearance he would set out in search of him. Although Quinn never approved of Anthony's unorthodox methods of solving problems, there were two things that they had in common. They both cared for Joshua, and they always stayed one step ahead.

Anthony would never admit it, but he cared for Joshua just as much as Quinn. Anthony had worked alongside Joshua since they joined the organization, and overtime they had become close friends. Now that Joshua was missing, Quinn knew that Anthony wanted to know where he was, and he had taken drastic measures to do so. Knowing that Anthony was on the case provided Quinn with a sense of comfort.

Quinn smiled and let out a sigh of relief at the thought of seeing Joshua again as he proceeded towards the door.

The room grew cold. A slight chill of a mysterious presence eased its way down Quinn's spine. Something was watching him.

What are you? Quinn thought to himself, *could you hear my thoughts all this time?*

Quinn knew if it was what he thought it was then it knew what he was planning, and if it did, then his entire plan had been compromised.

The office lights began to flicker, and the air became heavy. For a brief moment, it became hard to draw breath. Quinn could sense something was coming.

"Faith," Quinn called out in a whisper as he felt the goose flesh form on his skin. He could feel himself growing weaker.

There was no response.

Quinn turned towards the office door at the sound of approaching footsteps. Only one thought crossed his mind, *I need to protect them. I need to protect them all.*

"Faith," Quinn whispered once again so as not to disturb the presence.

The doorknob began to turn and the lights continued to flicker.

Quinn's heart skipped a beat. He knew he was being watched, but by what he did not know.

"Initium…" Before Quinn could finish his sentence, the door crept open and the lights returned to normal. The air regained its presence in the room.

"You called," came a voice as the door swung open.

Through the door walked a bio-Faith.

"Faith, please run full scans on TSPA Central. Something's here, I can feel it," said Quinn in a nervous dry sweat, his heart beating rapidly.

Quinn proceeded out of the office and down the hall to the elevator. Faith followed behind him in quick pursuit.

"He's here," said Faith. "I have located him in the forest."

A look of shock spread over Faith's face, "This can't be. His power reading…they're…I can't read them," stuttered Faith, exhibiting a momentary sense of surprise as she lost control over her emotion center.

The words burst from Quinn's lips, his voice rising, "Oh no! Not one of these. Not now...how many leaders are currently active?" asked Quinn.

"Stephen is away on missions, but will arrive shortly. I cannot locate Benjamin, and the others are on their way to the Zone for treatment. To assist in our defense, I am calling back all bio units to Central," said Faith in a single breath.

"Faith, don't alert the others. I don't want them trying to fight in their current condition. I'll handle this. Keep Stephen on back up just in case," ordered Quinn.

Quinn could feel himself growing weaker with every passing moment. Treatment was estimated to take hours, but Quinn knew he had minutes at most. His power was draining fast. He knew he had to be careful. The harder he fought, the faster the Aqua Animax would drain his energy.

"Faith, how much time do I have."

"You should be able to use your Initium for three minutes safely, after that, your energy will diminish exponentially. If you attempt to use your Semis, you will die," said Faith.

"Shit! I will have to make this quick. It seems he's chosen the most opportune time to attack. Such a tenacious fool!"

Faith watched as Quinn's eyes grew cloudy.

"Sir, you don't look well. Would you like me to assist you?" asked Faith.

"No!" said Quinn. "I will need you to use your energy to retrieve my body and take it to the zone when I'm done with this."

"But sir, if you're killed..."

"I won't die here," said Quinn. "It's not my time yet."

"Son of Marmota, you underestimate my power," the tone had changed.

Quinn glanced over at the unit before leaping back and clutching at the sides of the elevator in surprise, his heart bursting from his chest and bladder nearly exploding. He had only heard that deep, feminine tone once before. In the last few seconds, the A.I.'s entire personality appearance and demeanor had changed. It was no longer the ordinary bio-unit. It glowed a radiant blue with hair that trailed down its back and to its knees. Its eyes were darker than usual, and its face was calm and emotionless. All coming together to form the terrifying figure that Quinn had hoped to never see again.

Nervously he whispered, his voice trembling, "Be still my heart, look who decided to show up."

CHAPTER 27: EYES OF THE SPARROW

"*Alligo* vines!" said Joseph. The vines unwrapped themselves from the trees and slithered towards his feet like snakes. He felt the rush as he stood with his arms out and palms facing the ground. In his right hand, he held a stick that he had found in the training area. Having it allowed him to connect more easily with nature and focus his spells into a single location outside of himself. He had tried many times using the palms of his hand and had failed. But with the stick he could channel through the wood as if talking directly to the trees and vines.

The vines began to wrap around him as they rose from the ground. Up and up and up they grew, forming a wall-like structure in front of Joseph. Higher and higher they reached as they weaved in and out of each other, dancing and filling Joseph with a euphoric sensation.

Maria and Brian had already formed walls twice their height in only a few seconds, while Joseph's was only a little over his head.

Although it was an incredible feeling, Joseph still struggled to project as much as Maria and Brian. In the past hours, he had managed to control his essence. The wall had only been half his height, but now it was slightly over his head. It didn't matter though, Joseph wanted to keep going and keep feeling the incredible rush of nature that seemed to flow through the pendant and into his veins like concentrated bliss.

Upon his final try, the wall towered a few extra feet over his head.

Joseph relaxed his arms down to his sides. Exhausted, he felt as if he had been running for miles, but he wanted to keep running. The high kept him going. It kept him feeling alive, and when he stopped, it began to fade.

"Well done Joe!" encouraged Brian.

"Yes, you are showing exponential improvement," said Maria.

"It's my lucky stick. What's next? Come on, what's next?" asked Joseph as he waved the short stick through the air.

"Next, our defensive drills. Let's try sleep counters for intensive spells. I'll start," said Maria as she raised her hand towards Brian.

"*Sopor!*" a blinding white light shot from Maria's fingertips trailing over to Brian.

"*Defendo!*" said Brian, barely having enough time to respond as a hollow barrier of air formed around him. The light diminished and vanished upon contact with the barrier.

Brian turned towards Joseph and raised his hand.

"*Sopor!*" said Brian as the light shot from his palm.

"*Defendo!*" said Joseph with his stick raised. The barrier that formed around him at the last moment absorbed the light. If he were a second later, he would have been put to sleep.

"That was close," said Maria. "You have to do it sooner next time. Alright Joe."

"I know. I'm still trying to get the hang of it. You guys just seem like such naturals," said Joseph. Joseph began shadow boxing the air briefly before bouncing back and forth as if warming up for a boxing match.

"The only thing I have ever been a natural at in my life is screwing up," said Brian, with a slight chuckle.

"*Sopor!*" shouted Joseph holding up the wooden stick as the light shot from its tip.

"*Defendo!*" responded Maria.

As she held up her hand, the barrier around her formed long before the light made contact. The light was instantaneously absorbed, but the barrier remained present even after it absorbed the shot.

"Alright team. Last part of magical defense against extensive spells, and then we are onto sparring."

Maria held tight to her pendant around her neck as she focused her sights on the ground.

"*Vis vis vis…*" Maria began to chant, and as she did a light radiated and formed around her body.

Maria looked up towards Brian and charged. Her speed had been increased and so had her strength.

"*Tegantur notoria, tegantur notoria, tegantur notoria…*" chanted Brian. Maria raised her fist and unleashed a devastating blow upon Brian. However, an invisible barrier absorbed the blow. There was a loud pop, like the firing of a gun, then silence. Brian stood unfazed. Then Maria raised her fist once more and struck him in the arm gently.

Maria enthusiastically congratulated Brian as she shook her hand trying to relieve the pain from the blow back, "Nicely done! That hurt more than I expected."

"Alright, get ready Joe," said Brian, "*Vis, vis, vis…*" chanted Brian. As he charged towards Joseph, he began to glow.

"*Tegantur notoria, tegantur notoria, tegantur notoria!*" chanted Joseph as Brian's fist came into contact with the barriers around Joseph. There was a loud bang and quick flash of light, and then it began to dissipate.

Brian gently tapped Joseph across the face with his fist. "Gotcha," said Brian.

"That's cheating. I stopped your first attack."

They both began to laugh.

"Alright, next…" demanded Maria.

"Maria, can we take a break? We have been at this for four hours straight!" complained Brian.

"Alright," said Maria.

"No. One more. I haven't had a chance to try this round. After this one, we can take a break," said Joseph.

"Fine Brian, you're done for the day. Joseph, this is your last shot, so hit me with your best shot."

Joseph began to chant rapidly, "*Vis, vis, vis, vis…*"

He charged towards her as his body began radiating. Maria raised her palm.

"*Tegantur Notoria Triplex!*"

Three well-pronounced barriers formed around Maria. Joseph raised his fist, and with all his energy struck the barrier, breaking through its first layer. He raised his right leg, and with a quick kick struck again, this time breaking through the second barrier. Then his eyes began to change, and with all his energy he struck the final barrier with both his fists. Instantly, his energy dissipated, and the rush he felt faded as his pendant grew cold. The barrier still stood, but he no longer had the energy or the will power to break it.

"What was that spell that you just cast Maria?"

Maria leaned over and whispered into Joseph's ear, "It was a very powerful protection spell. The last barrier drained your energy. You need to work on staying in control. Don't let the power overwhelm you. I know how it feels. You were losing control, control it, don't let it control you. I think it's time we join Brian."

"*Valeo!*" she said, and the three vine walls began to recede into the ground from which they came, clearing the area.

Brian, Maria and Joseph headed off towards a stream to the north of their training circle. They settled along the rocks of the small stream. The water flowed gently over the rocks, and Maria removed her shoes and dipped her feet into the coolness.

Tonight they would be meeting up with the other trinity for dinner at the Espers Mansion. In a few weeks, they would be required to pass another trial given by the TSPA to make sure they could control their abilities. They had been given a few extra days to prepare. They knew it would prove to be their biggest challenge yet. This was something both groups had reservations about.

"Hey Maria, what do you think they are going to do to us now?" asked Brian.

"I'm not sure. But I do know that whatever test they give us, we will be ready for it. After all, we're no threat. We all know how to control our abilities."

"You guys, there is something I need to tell you. Remember those dreams I said I was having?" asked Joseph.

"Yeah, the ones with the Queen, and the nightmare beasts, and the forests fires…" recited Brian.

"Yeah those. Well I told Senior Elvia about them, and she told me that after tonight I would no longer have to worry about them. What do you think that means?"

"Clearly it means they are going to kill you. It wouldn't be the first time something tried to kill us," said Brian.

"Brian, leave Joe alone. They saved us. Killing us would be counterproductive. She probably just meant that you would be able to control them due to all the training that you're putting in. I've been doing some research, and it seems that the Espers don't kill, they only give people the illusion of death or dying. Whatever we experienced, they can't really kill us," said Maria.

"I knew it!" said Brian. "They're going to try to scare me again. The last trial they put us through, it felt so real. It felt like I was going to die."

The breeze stirred the leaves from the trees and carried them over the calm stream before the ferns and bushes caught them. Maria watched the leaves. Although she understood why there were no animals, she missed the sounds of the birds and squirrels. She missed the sounds of the real forests.

She contemplated the songs of the birds she would hear when she awoke in the morning as she gazed across the stream. In the trees beyond the stream, she noticed something rustling rapidly in the bushes. Then there came a noise.

"Hey guys, do you hear that?" asked Maria.

They listened carefully.

"Yeah, I hear it," answered Joseph.

"Me too," said Brian.

From the bush across the stream, the rustling stopped. The head of a black bird popped out from a bush.

"Ca-Caw, Ca-Caw..." it cried out. Then from the trees erupted the same call.

They had not heard the sound of a bird in days, and they listened attentively as the birds seemed to return to the forest from a place unknown. They could hear the chirping of a group in the trees. Then there was a loud bang, and suddenly birds broke out from the trees, filling the sky with rainbow colors.

"Where did they come from?" Brian asked.

Maria was surprised. She had just been thinking about birds, and suddenly a large flock of birds seemed to appear out of nowhere, "They're beautiful."

"Don't be alarmed," came a voice from behind them.

They turned quickly to see Sammy standing there with the breeze just now catching up to him. His speed brought a gust that caused small brush from under the trees to be whipped up into the air. Before the breeze settled some of the dirt made its way into Brian's eyes. His eyes began to water as he attempted to remove the debris.

"I'm not alarmed. I'm amazed," said Maria, looking up at Sammy.

"When did you get here?" asked Brian, who had leaped back in surprise at Sammy's unannounced appearance.

"Not too long ago. I had to get away from those two for a moment. Sometimes they can really get into it."

There was another loud bang.

"What's going on over there?" asked Brian, motioning to the forest area across the stream where the explosions seemed to be coming from.

"Well... as you know Summer turned Jabin into a cat, and then attempted to erase his memory of being a cat before he reverted back to normal, but failed. Jabin broke free of the spell before Summer had the chance to erase his memory, and let's just say...he's not very happy. Oh! And the birds, they all belong to Summer. It's part of his Sparrow Eyes technique."

"Personally, I liked him better as a cat," said Brian. There was a continuous flow of loud bangs as trees in the far off distance began to topple over. Flocks of birds circled overhead the area of the disturbance.

"Wow. They must really be going at it," said Joseph, as he watched trees falling in the distance. It was hard for Joseph to believe that two people were causing such a level of destruction.

"No, they're just playing around right now. Sparrow Eyes is Summer's weakest technique, and Jabin's just knocking over trees out of anger. If he really wanted to hit Summer he could, but he's not trying to kill him," said Sammy speaking of their actions as if they were minor details of an everyday routine.

"Summer's only working on his technique and Jabin is just using heavy magic. I don't need to get into it. They have no intention of actually hurting each other, and we should be safe at this distance. Jabin is just letting off some steam. Just watch, in a few hours they will be back to normal," explained Sammy.

"Jabin back to normal. I don't want that. Could someone possibly teach me that cat spell?" asked Brian.

"I researched it. It takes a lot of preparation. Summer must have set it a few days in advance. I'm currently looking for a way to speed it up myself," said Maria.

Sammy looked over at Brian, Maria, and Joseph, focusing his eyes on the charms around their necks.

"I see you got your eyes," said Sammy.

"Mine is silver, air manipulation, it lets me move fast. But I already move pretty fast, so it lets me move even faster. With this, Lord Mathias will never catch me again," he said, revealing it from underneath his shirt and briefly showing the silver center before tucking it away again.

"So did you guys hear the news?" asked Sammy.

"What news?" Maria asked.

"TSPA Central has been put on red alert. They say a rogue has appeared in the Nefastus Forest. But don't worry, we're safe here in Ezon One," reassured Sammy while he continued to observe the destruction caused by the fight between Jabin and Summer. "After they take down the rogue, the organization's leaders are coming here to meet us formally," said Sammy.

"Anabel's coming?" Joseph asked as he looked up at Sammy. He had been trying to hold back the rush and nerve sweat that seemed to come over him at the mention of her name.

Maria's eyes widened at the mention of The Zone.

"So this is Ezon One, is it part of the Zone? I remember hearing about the Zone from Kassie, but she never said where it actually was located," said Maria.

"Depends on who you ask. Some consider the Zone anything outside of the Nefastus Forest and Terraizen, but technically Ezon and the Zone are two separate areas. They're real, make no mistake, things here are not illusions. But the major difference between Ezon One and the Zone is that the Ezon does not change from being a city surrounded by a vast forest. The Zone's reality, on the other hand, is malleable. It can be manipulated and reconstructed by the E-3 leaders to be cities or villages, or a town, or even some strange underwater world. But they can't do that in Ezon One, reality is stabilized. These trees are as real as you and I."

A devious smirk spread across Sammy's face, "Wanna know a secret about this place?" Sammy asked.

"No, not at all," answered Joseph sarcastically.

"Suit yourself, but it would have been a good one," said Sammy.

Brian, Maria, Joseph, and Sammy sat back and watched as Summer and Jabin continued to topple tree after tree. Huge clouds of dust rose, and the sky darkened as blackbirds blocked out the last of the setting sun and the ground shook from the continuous shockwaves.

"How long are they going to go on?" asked Brian.

"I'd say fifteen more minutes," said Sammy as he checked his watch.

"Well how about that secret?" asked Joseph.

"It's too late now. You'll have to wait until next time."

"Shucks," said Joseph playfully.

They both laughed.

As Sammy had predicted, exactly fifteen minutes later the loud bangs came to a halt, the birds faded away like a mist on a sunny day, and the dust began to settle with the last of the sun. The fighting had stopped, and for a brief moment all was silent.

"Looks like that's my queue. See ya' round!"

"Wait," said Brian, "What was the secret you were going to tell us? I still want to know even if Joe doesn't."

Sammy smiled. "Let's talk later. It's getting late. I'll see you at dinner," he said before dashing away.

Brian, Joseph, and Maria watched as the blur of Sammy flashed across the stream and disappeared through the bushes on the other side.

"Wow, he really is fast. I could barely see him," said Brian.

"Well let's head back, we need to finish up. On your feet," Maria demanded.

Brian and Joseph proceeded to get up, and headed back to the circle followed by Maria.

"Hey Joe…" whispered Brian as he leaned in towards Joseph's ear. "It might just be me, but I feel like we are being watched."

"Yeah," said Joseph. "I sense a strange presence following us too. It's probably a hideously dangerous monster."

"Shut up you two," said Maria as she hit them both in the shoulder.

"Ahhhhh! It's attacking us, run!"

Joseph and Brian sprinted up the hill laughing loudly.

"Okay then, you want a monster? You got it."

Maria chased after them letting out pretend roars and howls as they screamed.

She caught them both around the neck, tucking them under her arms in a headlock.

"You idiots, you can't outrun me," she said pretending to choke them.

"Ah no!" Brian screamed.

"We failed," added Joseph, finishing his sentence.

The three of them laughed as they approached to the forest exit, looking ahead as one by one the bright lights of Ezon One came into view.

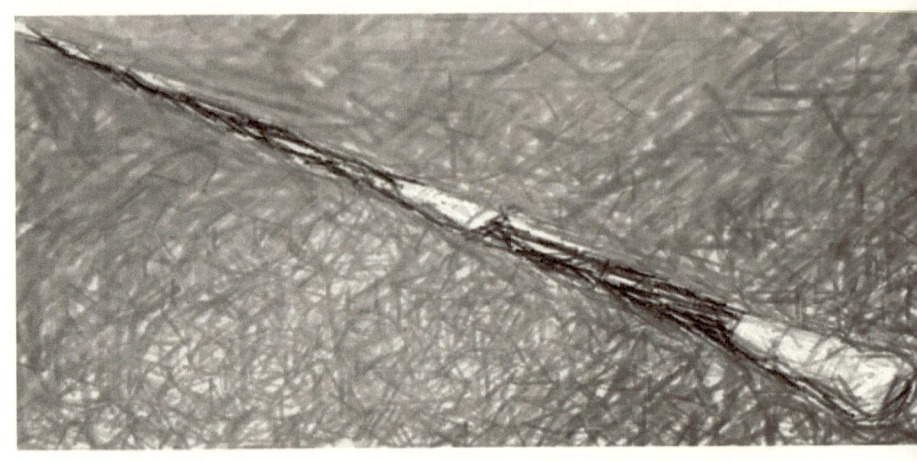

CHAPTER 28: QUINN- THE JINN AND NEFASTUS FOREST

The Nefastus Forest was quiet as the sun began to set. Quinn and Faith proceeded to the forest, hoping to encounter the Jinn before the looming darkness arrived. Quinn had adjusted his vision to allow himself to see in the dark. If possible, before he entered battle, he would study his opponent, but not much was known about the Jinn.

The normal bio-Faith had returned and began to consult her sequencing system for proper counter-measures against the Jinn.

"Sir, my radar shows a high-level energy reading ten miles northeast of our current location. We may be able to gain the upper hand through observation of his movements."

"Hhmmm…"

The voice came from directly behind them.

Quinn's heart skipped a beat. He felt a crushing pressure nearly bring him to his knees as a smoldering blast of heat struck him violently in the back.

Quinn leaped forward and threw his back against a nearby tree and faced the Jinn. He could feel his skin had burned as if it was on fire for a brief moment. He felt the sting and pain just before selectively shutting off the pain receptors to the burned area of his back and neck.

The Jinn had appeared inches away from his neck even before he could sense his presence.

Quinn had a delay in processing the warmth of the Jinn's breath, it had only hit his neck a second ago, yet there was some interruption between perception and reality. It had burned through the skin on the side of his neck, and part of his back, leaving a large red scar. It that moment, Quinn realized the Jinn could have killed him without him even knowing. This made the hairs on his neck stand up, and a sickening feeling crawled down his spin and rested in the pit of his stomach. He wanted to keel over and vomit.

Quinn looked over at the Jinn who now held Faith by the neck. Her body began to turn red, and in one swift motion, the Jinn snapped her neck and tossed her aside like a rag doll. Faith lay on the ground motionless.

A malicious smile spread across his face, stretching from ear to ear. The Jinn began to look around the forest as if he were searching for something. He had glanced over Quinn as if he were just another tree.

Quinn began to focus his thoughts on gathering his power to Awaken. He wanted to fry the Jinn's brain, and he knew the only way to do so would be to use a mind blast strong enough to eliminate the Jinn's ability to form cognitive thoughts. However, he also knew he only had enough power for one shot.

The Jinn, still gazing out in the distance, waved his hand, causing Quinn and a large number of trees to be ripped from the ground and tossed aside. He made his way toward the location where the elevator had landed. Quinn was sent flying head first into a large tree. The impact nearly dislocated the upper discs in his neck. His vision became blurry as a sharp pain shot down his spine. Quinn temporarily shut down portions of his nervous system to immediately stop the displeasure.

He managed to numb the pain that he could not stop, and regained his balance and vision. He watched as the Jinn proceeded forward.

The Jinn began to wave his hand once more when suddenly, vines shot from the ground immobilizing it at Quinn's mental command.

No sooner had they formed, than they turned to ash and fell to the ground.

His eyes flashed red. Quinn gazed into them. The stare seemed to burn through Quinn's very soul. There was no denying that the Jinn knew Quinn was present now, but still he did not care. To the Jinn, Quinn was another insect in the forest, just slightly bigger than the rest. The Jinn stared at Quinn. His eyes burned with a fire that would have incinerated any beast that dared to look directly into them. Even Quinn averted his eyes almost immediately. Looking into his eyes for only a moment had felt like falling into a raging inferno.

The Jinn glided through the path he had created, which was close to Quinn. He moved at a slow pace as he passed by Quinn without even the slightest recognition, heading for the main elevator—gateway to Central Terraizen. The sun was now setting.

Quinn did not speak. He had used this time to gather the energy he needed to Awaken, and it was time to fight back. Quinn stood up and placed his hand upon his head.

"Semis, Emperor's Crown."

A skull-jeweled crown ripped through Quinn's skin, forming upon his head amplifying his abilities as well as his arrogant personality.

The Jinn stopped as if it could feel Quinn now. It had heard the command, and began to approach.

Quinn now in his Semis could sense much more than before. The other agents were on their way and there was another threat approaching from the east. He knew he needed to finish the battle before it arrived.

The Jinn was only feet away from Quinn now, levitating above the grass.

"Sleeping...sleeping," murmured the Jinn, flames spurting from his mouth, "but now it's here…"

The Jinn moved so swiftly that Quinn lost track of him. A burst of white light struck Quinn in the chest before he had a chance to react. He crumpled to the ground but was able to regain control and stand up. His body and crown were now glowing.

"You should tread more cautiously through unfamiliar territory. Don't underestimate my power," said Quinn locking onto the Jinn.

Quinn stood up. His crown was glowing.

"Don't underestimate my power," said Quinn.

From his pocket, Quinn withdrew six glowing glass spheres.

The Jinn waved his hand, but nothing happened. He stood motionless in the forest.

Quinn threw the spheres up above the Jinn's head. In his mind's eye, Quinn recited his Crown's Seal Mantra. The Jinn attempted to evade them, but he couldn't move. The spheres began to glow and divide radically, then aligning themselves in an orb-like pattern around the Jinn, the glowing balls formed several walls of light and began to expand. Lights shot from Quinn's crown encasing the Jinn like a moth in amber.

Quinn continued to focus on forming the barriers around the Jinn. He could feel the Jinn breaking free of his control. Just a few more, just a few more, Quinn continued to tell himself. The walls erected by the lights were clear, but strong.

"You're no match for me in this form. The Crown Seal Barrier will hold you for a while. You won't die, but you will be powerless for the time being. Now I ask you, what were your intentions, and why have you come here?"

Quinn walked towards the barriers as the lights continued forming layers atop his encased body.

Quinn attempted to read his mind. With the crown, he had easy access to any mind, but within it there was nothing but a repeated utterance of "I...I...I..."

Quinn turned and began to proceed towards the elevator. The Semis had allowed his body to heal but as he drew closer to the elevator his crown receded and the power began to fade. Although not completely healed, Mother of Faith had suppressed the Aqua Animax long enough for him to use in Semis without dying. Quinn had only seen her once before, and that was the day they went to save Eleanor. Though he had only been given one chance, it had been enough to stop the Jinn.

Now the Aqua Animax had awakened once more, and it began to absorb his energy rapidly. The pain, no longer suppressed, caused each step towards the elevator to be more painful and tiring than the last. Soon, Benjamin and Stephen would arrive to finish the job.

Quinn had used the last of his abilities to immobilize the Jinn imposter, and now his crown had faded and receded back into his mind.

Faith stood next to the tree where she had been tossed aside.

"Are you okay?" asked Quinn.

"Yes. I have fully recovered and upgraded my bio-suit to prevent future spinal fractures and dislocations," answered Faith.

"My systems show the Jinn has been contained," Faith said as she looked towards the barriers.

"We can arrange for the Jinn's pickup and transfer to C-4 once the others..."

Quinn lost consciousness and fell to the ground. He lay motionless.

"Your energy levels are unstable. We need to get you back immediately," said Faith.

Faith swung Quinn's arm over her shoulder and proceeded to carry him back to the elevator.

Upon reaching the elevator doors, a strange melody could be heard. It was a beautiful tune unlike any they heard before. The notes seem to have color, a sweetly scented smell, and even feeling.

Faith attempted to open the elevator, but her legs refused to move.

"Sir, I have been locked out. Something has shut down the A.I. system."

An eerie chill swept through the forest, and the trees around them burst aflame.

A dark deep voice echoed from behind.

"I watched the light fade…as the flames grew higher," said the Jinn in a sinister tone.

The Jinn pointed his flute towards them, waving it as if conducting a musical number. He looked the same, but something was different about him.

"They all burned, they all burned. I watched their lights fade as their screams grew louder, and in the flames of agony, I consumed their souls," sang the Jinn in its deep baritone voice.

"How are you here? How did you break free?" Faith asked.

"Break free?" opposed the Jinn, confused by the question, "I was never trapped."

Two blinding lights shot from the end of his baton, and struck both Faith and Quinn. A sharp pain shot through Faith's body as she fell to her knees, and then face down into the grass.

The Jinn's eyes turned a violent blood red. Unlike before, Faith could now see his killer intent.

"I've given you multiple chances to show me your power, you have failed. It's time to end this!"

The Jinn held out his flute, and a black light shot from its tip.

The elevator door swung open and spider web-like thread entangled Quinn and Faith, pulling them into the elevator. The black curse struck the grass where they had lain, and it instantly turned black and spread outward. More thread shot out entangling the Jinn.

"Yes, you're right. It is time to end this," said a voice from inside the elevator.

Out from the elevator stepped Stephen, and behind him Benjamin, his sword extended and dragging behind him as he exited.

"Sorry we're late. We had some very important matters to attend to," said Stephen.

Faith regained consciousness.

"Sequence initiating..."

A blinding light shot towards Stephen. Benjamin extended his blade and absorbed the blow.

"Go!" demanded Stephen. The elevator doors closed behind him.

Although Stephen's facial expression seemed emotionless, something had happened to him on his last mission, and Faith could see the anger that still resided behind his eyes.

The Jinn was no ordinary threat. He was a force unlike any the TSPA had ever encountered.

CHAPTER 29: SOFT SAPPHIRE LIGHT

The dining room held a red and gold décor. The windows were covered in red and gold drapes, and the scarlet tablecloths were lined with gold frills. The glass chandelier that hung from the ceiling brightly lit the room. On one end of the table sat Sammy, Summer, and Jabin, and on the opposite end sat Maria, Joseph, and Brian. The six of them sat around a table made for twelve in the Espers dining room. When they first arrived, the feast that lay upon the table was unlike any banquet they had seen. They had waited for half an hour, but no one else arrived and their stomachs had grown impatient. So they decided to start dinner. Jabin, on the other hand, had not waited. Dinner started at half past eight for him, and there had been no hesitation to dig in upon seeing the delectable selection of food laid out before him. When it came to eating, Jabin was no push over.

After consuming four plates, he continued to eat as if his life depended on it. The TSPA agents had not arrived. Sammy had attempted to contact them, but communications were down. They soon found out that the Zone and Ezon One had been placed on lock down, sealing it off from Central. Sammy could only speculate why this had been done. The six of them now waited to hear word from the Espers.

"What's going on out there?" asked Brian.

Brian had finished his supper and a slice of beautifully decorated strawberry pie before sitting back in his chair. There had been an awkward silence at the table for the past ten minutes. Although they were afraid to admit it, they all knew something was wrong. A few minutes prior, it had started to rain. In Ezon One, it never rained.

"I don't understand…how is it raining?" Jabin said in a confused tone as he scarfed down another slice of pie. Unlike before, Jabin seemed more settled and less arrogant. Summer had laid a beating on him that seemed to alter, not only his physical appearance, but his arrogant personality as well.

Summer had not eaten. He sat exhausted at the head of the table with his arms resting parallel to each other and his eyes closed in a state of meditation. Summer always wore dark eerie clothing with chains and many body piercings. He was slender, and far less toned than Sammy, giving many the false perception that he was not very strong; but his looks were very deceiving.

"For once, you're right Jabin. It never rains here," came the voice of Sammy as he pulled aside the red drape to view the storm through the large mansion-sized window.

"I'm still not getting a response from our communicators," said Sammy, changing settings on his communications watch. The watch had been a gift from Quinn upon his initial arrival.

"But this is the safest place for us, especially in times of an emergency. So I guess we're fine in our current situation," said Sammy optimistically.

There was a brief silence in the room. All that could be heard was the scraping of Joseph's fork against his plate as he finished the last piece of strawberry pie.

Joseph sat at the other head of the long table across from Summer, admiring the dining room. It was brightly lit with elegant red and gold colors. The chandeliers sparkled like diamonds with light reflecting off of their surface. He could have spent hours just admiring the fine details of the room alone. There was something about it that gave him a warm feeling of happiness. The only thing that seemed out of place was Summer. Joseph had been watching him very closely. He wondered if Summer was asleep or just meditating.

"Sammy, isn't there a spell that can let us look through to the outside world?" asked Maria. She had removed herself from the dining room table, and now stood against the wall under the portrait of Senior Kassie paging through her *210 Most Useful Spells* magic book.

"I'm sure, but there must be something we can do. I would say check the library, but the delivery systems are down. Though there may be something available in their reserves," said Sammy.

Maria continued to think of alternative plans.

"What about the magic shop in the alley?" asked Maria.

"They're closed until morning," said Sammy.

"We're trapped inside of Ezon One with no form of communication to the outside world, and you want to wait until tomorrow morning in hopes that a magic shop will be open? Women…" said Jabin in a condescending tone.

"Do you have any better ideas?" As soon as the words left Maria's mouth, she began to regret them.

"Oh yes! I have plenty of better ideas. You and me…"

"Any related to our current situation?" interjected Maria, annoyed.

"Well, we are trapped here, so we could make the most of it if you and me take a trip upstairs and explore the unknown territories of your…I mean this house."

"You and I," corrected Maria.

"Oh, so you agree?" retorted Jabin.

"No, I was just correcting your misuse of pronouns," said Maria as she continued to flip through the pages of her novel.

A look of confusion spread over Jabin's face before understanding what she had said. He stood up from his chair and turned slowly towards Maria.

"Jabin…don't test me," came a quiet voice from the head of the table.

Jabin turned towards Summer, who still sat with his eyes closed.

"You can't turn me again. You don't have the strength. You can barely move…"

"Enough Jabin! We have enough to worry about right now," said Sammy, staring out the window.

The rain had begun to pound ferociously against the window, drawing Joseph's attention.

Joseph pushed out his chair and joined Sammy.

"It's really coming down out there," said Joseph as he looked over at Sammy.

"Yes, this is most unusual."

Joseph found the rain to be very calming. It was moments like these that reminded him of his childhood. During storms, he would always turn out all the lights and watch as the rain pelted heavily against the window, while the trees danced beautifully outside his home. When the lightning finally took the stage, he would wait with anticipation for the thunder to rumble in behind it.

As he thought of those moments, the lights in the room flickered. Flashes of lightning crossed the sky outside the window, and the storm began to escalate.

"Great, now it's a thunderstorm," said Jabin, who had managed to calm himself down.

The lighting in the room continued to flicker until the resounding of the loudest clap of thunder caused them to go out.

"And now the lights are out," said Jabin. "That's not even possible in Ezon One."

"So I'm guessing you remember what Elizabeth told us," said Sammy, surprised by what had just happened.

"Yes, I do, this is a warning," said Jabin.

"*Illuminate*," said Maria. The sapphire charm around her neck flickered for a few moments before maintaining a constant blue light, filling her corner of the room.

"*Illuminate*," said Jabin. His entire body began to glow a blinding gold light, filling every corner of the room in a single burst, nearly blinding Joseph, who had been looking directly at him. Then just his skin began to glow like a living light bulb.

"I think I got this one," he said turning to Maria.

"So who's up for a little adventure around this place?" asked Jabin

"I'm staying here," said Sammy.

Summer, Maria, Brian, and Joseph remained unresponsive.

"Fine…I'll go by myself, and if I find anything, I'm not telling any of you."

They watched as he entered the kitchen and closed the door behind him. The light radiated from under the door, and as he moved further away, it began to dim, until finally, the room was left with what now seemed like, a tiny glow of sapphire light.

CHAPTER 30: REVELATIONS AND THE PIT

Midnight approached as one man and two monsters collided in battle within the darkness of a Nefastus pit. It had been hours, and what once had been a thriving forest now looked like the end result of an earthquake and wildfire. There were large mounds of earth that stood as high as two story buildings, and wide ditches that seemed to stretch deep within the earth. There were some trees in the distance that were still ablaze, and others who stood black and frozen from taking the hits of countless curses that had missed their initial targets.

The trees directly encircling the fight blazed up above, while the duel had sunk below ground level within a rocky, moist, dark pit. The Jinn moved flawlessly and effortlessly through the darkness, weaving a web of dark curses that had missed Stephen by a hair's length. Benjamin's movements rivaled that of the Jinn. His blade had nearly made contact with the Jinn multiple times. Now the three of them were locked in a battle of endurance. One flawed move would end it all.

Benjamin was light on his feet and could easily see in the dark. His webs slowed the Jinn's movement, and Stephens's ability to raise mounds had saved his life many times. Stephen was not very fast, and without the combination between Benjamin's webs slowing the Jinn's movements and his mounds, which provided him cover, he would have met his end long ago. Benjamin continued to evade the curses of the Jinn, who matched his speed and agility with ease. It had been a while since Stephen had to pay attention within a fight, and now he waited for his window of opportunity.

Stephen lacked agility, but made up for it with his pyro-terra and telekinesis. He had brought the fight into the pit in order to protect the forest, and in hopes of getting an advantage over the Jinn. In the pit, he had the ability to manipulate the earth around him and prevent the fires the Jinn started from spreading. Yet, there was something about the Jinn that frightened Stephen. Although Stephen and Benjamin should have had the advantage over the Jinn, they did not. The Jinn's movements and strategy were flawless. Even with all the obstacles that Benjamin and Stephen placed in his way, he eluded them and made it seem effortless in the process.

Stephen did not want to admit it, but he knew that even with all the destruction he had caused, the Jinn had yet to reveal his full capacity of power.

The Jinn danced through the web that Benjamin had created with cat-like reflexes, fleeing the strings with ease, and firing off deadly curses from his baton with such accuracy and speed that Stephen had to mount multiple walls of earth in advance to protect himself. Benjamin had extended his blade to its full form, which provided full body protection from the curses when needed, and was able to reflect others back at the Jinn. The blade that Benjamin carried was unlike any other. It was cursed, and was the only known item capable of reflecting even the deadliest of curses.

No words were spoken between the three of them for hours, until the Jinn made his mark.

The black curse flew towards Stephen who had neither the agility nor endurance of Benjamin, and had seemed to be growing tired from the battle. He began to raise mounds and fire off boulders slower, until finally, he left an opening for the Jinn. The black curse barely grazed his ear, but the curse was powerful.

As soon as the curse struck him, Benjamin brought down his blade slicing off Stephens's ear and cauterizing the wound, simultaneously, before the curse could spread.

"Enough!" yelled Benjamin. The ground trembled at the sound of his voice, and even the Jinn stood still momentarily.

"They must die, before it's too late," said the Jinn as blazing flames shot from his mouth.

Benjamin drew his sword, shielding them from the intense heat of the flames. The Jinn stood gazing at Benjamin with his broad malevolent smile.

"This planet is already lost," said the Jinn.

Benjamin swung his blade, sending a blinding shockwave of light towards the Jinn. The Jinn escaped the wave and stood with his flute ready.

"You've grown weak," said the Jinn as he continued to evade their attacks.

Stephen took a moment to make sure the curse had not spread to his body. Once he verified that he was okay, he struck back harder than before, raising mounds and firing off boulders at a rapid speed.

"Looks like the runts not dead yet," said the Jinn.

"I'm just warming up," said Stephen.

"Foolish Awakened! Your lack of insight for what you truly are will bring your downfall," said the Jinn.

He aimed his flute into the air, sending flames shooting out in all directions.

Stephen raised his hand and the stones around him began to levitate in the air. Then, as if drawn by a polar opposite force, the stones took flight towards the Jinn. Effortlessly, the Jinn continued to avoid them, causing them to crash against the dirt walls of the pit.

"Pathetic creatures," said the Jinn.

The Jinn began to play his flute as he swiftly tumbled through the air, dodging the barrage of incoming boulders. Stephen continued to fire off large boulders while Benjamin attempted a swift strike on the Jinn, but their efforts were in vain. The tune carried through the trees. Stephen attempted to cover his ear, but the sound carried past them. It was a wave that touched his very heart and immobilized him.

Benjamin and Stephen stood motionless in the dark, and so did the Jinn. All was silent. Then the Jinn pointed his flute toward Stephen and sat his gaze upon Benjamin.

"You will join me Executioner. Once the agency has been destroyed, Terraizen will fall," said the Jinn in a vengeful tone.

Then the Jinn fired off a black curse. Still immobilized by the Jinn's flute, he was unable to evade the attack as it struck him in the chest. Unlike, the previous curses, this one was slower, but more powerful. Stephen could tell as he watched it shattering through the walls he had erected. His body began to blacken as the light faded from his eyes.

The Jinn looked over at Benjamin.

"You should thank me. I saved him from a fate much worse. Benjamin, you have no soul. You are not human. We shall not suffer their fate."

Benjamin leaped up from the pit through the air. He had grown tired of fighting the Jinn. The Jinn joined him on its outer edge. Benjamin noticed that all the fires had subsided.

Exiting the hole, Benjamin could see the prison that Quinn had erected in the distance. There, still inside, stood the 1st Jinn. The pieces continued to come together, and Benjamin began to see the truth. Benjamin could see now that the Jinn believed that the flute was controlling Benjamin. The flute that the Jinn held was genuine. It was the cursed flute from the Forgotten Ages capable of controlling the minds and hearts of anyone, but Benjamin was cursed.

As the Jinn proceeded to the barrier, Benjamin saw what really lay inside it.

Benjamin examined the barrier. Its material was simple, but it was infused, not with essence, but with Quinn's very soul. Quinn had put everything on the line to stop the beast within the chamber. Although the others did not know what he had truly done to stop the creature, Benjamin did. And Benjamin knew without a soul, Quinn was sure to die. Because of Quinn, that creature, even with all its power, would never be free again. Nevertheless, it was not the real Jinn.

"Soul magic..." said the Jinn as he struck the clear wall of the barrier with his flute.

Benjamin proceeded towards the barrier raising his sword. His sword grew, extending into the air until it measured the length of the barrier.

"Destroy the barrier," ordered the Jinn.

Like the hammer of the storm, Benjamin's sword slammed through the barrier. Shattering it and the entity that resided within it. Then in one quick motion, Benjamin turned his sword and swung it slicing through the Jinn. Unlike with the barrier, Benjamin's sword did not leave a mark on the Jinn. It went through and came out the other side.

The Jinn stood motionless and in shock.

"What have you done to me?" asked the Jinn furiously.

"The difference is immeasurable," said Benjamin. His voice caused the ground to quake as he took the flute from the immobilized Jinn.

Benjamin had gotten what he came for. Like the flute his blade was cursed. The flute was able to control souls and his blade was able to capture them. Now that he had them both he would be able to release the souls of those he had captured for safekeeping.

Benjamin turned away from him.

"Where are you going with that Executioner? Give it back!"

Before the Jinn had finished his last word, Benjamin faded into the darkness, flute in hand.

A man stepped from behind the trees across from the Jinn, who was standing powerless in the distance.

"There's a reason I'm a part of this organization," said the man approaching the Jinn.

The man was wearing an X-ray essence visor, embedded within a special heavy black earth armor, and plated in a silver metal capable of granting him camouflage from even the most powerful senses. It was what he wore when he navigated from the shadows.

"I killed you," said a voice now speaking through the hollowed Echo of the body that was once the Jinn.

"On the contrary, you're the one who's dying."

A look of terror spread over the Jinn's face. The area that the fight had occurred in began to renew itself and return to normal. The trees grew back, the ground reshaped, caverns closed up, and the cliffs and mountains returned to their normal positions. It was as if the fight had never happened.

"Ancient magic? How? Who's doing this?" asked the voice from within the Jinn as he looked around at the forest area that had returned to normal. It could no longer produce flames, and the powerful aura that the shell had once emitted was diminished to nothing. He was not just powerless, he was scared.

"The universe is full of governing laws. There are rules to this world. If you were as powerful as you say, you'd have known the outcome of this battle before it started. I'm surprised Benjamin toyed with you for so long. I myself prefer to watch from the sidelines. Now show your true face 'forgotten one,' servant of the Banshee. It's time to return to the dust from which you were born. It's time for you to find rest."

The facade of the Jinn faded as the Banshee Queen's Echo revealed its true self. Within the Echo was a forgotten one. She had a pale white face partially covered by her long black hair. Her eyes were as black as her lips and as empty as her soul. No longer sinister, her facial expression had been replaced with one of sadness. She stood quietly, unable to move the lower portion of her body. It had become stone, and it continued to travel up her immobilized body. Energy began to drain quickly from her and, as it did, she continued to turn to rock. She looked exhausted and tired as she began to speak.

"Pesky Awakened, always interfering with our plans. We hate you. We hate what you and the TSPA have done to Terraizen. How you've enslaved the denizens of Terraizen from the shadows, allowing them to falsely believe they are safe and they are free...but there are things we hate more… things we'd rather see… destroyed."

The forgotten one threw her head back, and let out a deafening, glass-shattering shriek. However, the armor protected the man from the noise. Then she began to breathe heavily.

"Trinities shall lay broken, skies shall find their places. Beware the past's arrival, it hides within their faces. Heed my warning, King of Clubs. The Gate is open. Trust no one. The harbinger of Lost Ages has been released! Central falls tonight," said the forgotten one.

Her eyes turned pale gray as the stone approached her face.

"The apocalypse is always coming. It's come every thousand years according to records, but for us it may as well be every Friday. Yet, we recover, we survive and carry on. As long as we draw breath you shall not prevail. Your armies shall fall, Banshee shall fall, and you shall return to dust. We shall keep them safe from you and any other threat that dares to challenge us. Heed my words forgotten one, for they are the last you will ever hear," said the King of Clubs.

The forgotten one smiled one last time. It was not a mischievous smile, but seemed slightly sincere. Although the man knew it was not possible, for forgotten did not possess true emotions and could only mimic them. Then she burst into dust, and the forest was silent.

The King of Clubs spoke into his communicator, "Faith. Where are they? Are they still under domain control?"

"Sir, they've broken through and are approaching Central. We're on lock down. You need to return immediately. "

He felt uneasy. Something was not right and he could feel it.

"What do you mean? Why didn't you put the barrier up already? They can't pass through it."

The King of Clubs was confused. Never had the A.I. made such a grave mistake. At such a critical time as now, it would prove to be a major setback.

"Sir, I've been locked out of the system. Someone has dropped the barrier, and I can't restore it."

"How's that possible? You are the system."

"Not any more. I'm just a bio-unit. The Mother A.I. has been greatly weakened, and our connection is faint. I no longer have her access sequences."

"On my way."

The King of Clubs made haste to the elevator.

On the way, he passed the area where the barrier had been. Quinn had risked everything to protect Terraizen. Even if it meant giving his own life he would do anything to protect Central. Although the Jinn had not been real, it had been a powerful creature nonetheless. The man wondered how truly powerful the Banshee must be in order to create such devastating creatures. Even though the forgotten one had intended to kill him, he knew there was some truth to what she had said. The balance of power was shifting in Terraizen, and the King of Clubs feared the devastation to come.

CHAPTER 31: MIRRORDERS- PRELUDE TO THE END

They sat quietly around the large table, waiting for someone to say what they were all thinking. The storm had grown in intensity. Earlier, when they had attempted to leave, they were knocked back by a large gust of wind. What had started off as a small down pour had turned quickly into a storm of epic proportions. The rain raced across the pavement in waves, and pounded furiously against the outside of the front door like the tide upon a rocky coast. Dark storm clouds gathered, covering the area for as far as the eye could see. Lightning raced back and forth across the vast sky, chased by loud clashes of mighty thunder that made the ground tremble. The wind had gone from a slight whistle, to a gale-force wail that echoed against the windowpane and resonated down the halls. The sheer force of the wind alone would have made quick work of any normal windows, but this was the Espers Mansion, and these windows were protected. They could hear branches pounding against the walls of the building as if they were being flung with great force by a mighty hand.

They were trapped, and knew that leaving the safety of the building and entering into the storm would be suicide.

"This is no ordinary storm," said Sammy as he gazed out of the window.

"There has to be some kind of spell to get us out of this place," said Brian as he looked over at Maria. She was searching through the spell books she had acquired from Eiden's shop earlier that day. "Did you find anything yet?"

"Let's see...how to heal...how to defend...how to banish small objects and creatures..."

Maria continued to studiously examine the chapters of the book under her sapphire light. Joseph looked across the table. For a while now, Summer had sat with his eyes closed and arms resting in an upright position, almost trance-like. Sammy stood still staring out of the window at the raging storm, and Brian continued to pace back and forth.

All were present except Jabin. After dessert, Joseph was a bit tired and just wanted to take a nap. He had attempted to light his emerald crystal just as Maria had done, but had failed and finally given up. Now he sat at the table trying to stay awake as he drifted in and out of daydreams. At some point during the dream-like state, he had become slightly curious as to where Jabin had gone.

"Hey Sammy, where's Jabin? He's been gone for about an hour."

Sammy continued to gaze out of the window, entranced by the storm.

"Hey Sammy, Sammy you there?" Joseph tapped his fingers against the table to draw Sammy's attention.

Swiftly, Sammy turned towards Joseph, breaking the trance with the storm.

"I don't know," he said, shaking his head side to side slightly. "Restroom maybe…he's around here somewhere. Probably putting his nose somewhere it doesn't belong, but he can take care of himself."

Sammy sounded tired and a bit sleepy. Joseph knew exactly how he felt. Everyone seemed tired, and Brian was on edge.

Brian paced from window to window until he grew tired and stopped a few feet away from Sammy. He glanced out at the storm behind the red and gold curtains. He had remembered how the outside of the mansion had seemed very small, but from the inside it was massive. Upon entering, there was a long flight of stairs going up. At the top of the stair archway was the door that leads to the hall, which contained the dining room where they now resided. The glass windows were tall with stained images that Brian could not quite make out. There were portraits of eight individuals on each side of the walls placed between the large stained windows. Of the images, he had seen five of them before. Quinn, Dr. Matthews, and the Espers were all recognizable. When he first entered the house, he had noticed the many doors that lined the left and right sides of the first and second floors.

It had crossed Brian's mind to check them out and see what was behind the doors, but Maria had convinced him that it would be unwise to trespass, especially in the Mansion of the Espers.

As the thunder continued its assault against the ground, its strength grew to the point where it scared Brian, slightly knocking him off balance. Joseph looked over at him.

"Sit down Brian. All we can do is wait for the storm to pass."

"This storm is not passing," said Brian.

Reluctantly, Brian took a seat in the chair next to Joseph. Just then, Jabin entered the room through the kitchen carrying a large kettle of silver cutlery.

Brian hated Jabin, and during the time he was gone, Brian had hoped that he had fallen and broken his neck, or been injured to the point where he could not return, so that Brian would never have to see him again. Seeing Jabin made Brian's stomach turn. He knew Jabin's type. Jabin's bad manners and narcissistic personality reminded Brian of a bully he knew in middle school who would always pick on him whenever Joseph and Maria were not around.

But sadly for Brian, Jabin had returned.

Jabin withdrew a sharp knife from the pot and held his open palm over it. Quickly, he passed the knife over the palm of his hand. Blood dripped from his palm into the pot. Jabin placed his bleeding palm among the silver cutlery.

Shocked by his actions, Brian blurted out, "What are you doing? Are you crazy?"

Jabin did not answer.

For a brief pseudo-moment, Brian's hate for Jabin had turned to concern, but quickly faded after recalling what he had said to Maria. Then he wished Jabin had stuck the knife through a vital organ instead.

Sammy turned towards Jabin.

"Jabin it's coming!" Alerted Sammy.

"Hold your horses." The pot began to glow.

Although Brian did not want to seem curious, he wanted to know what Jabin was doing.

"What are you doing?"

"Shhh…loud mouth. I'm trying to focus."

The silver utensils began to melt, and the pot began to glow a liquid gold.

Summer's eyes shot open. There was a strange membrane layer covering his eyes at first, like a bird or a reptile, but upon blinking, it vanished.

"It's coming," said Summer.

"What's coming?" said Brian.

Joseph and Brian rushed over to the window where Sammy was standing.

"I don't see anything. What's coming?" Brian asked as his heart began to beat faster.

The storm still thundered furiously. The severity of the storm made it impossible for Brian to make out anything but the rain against the window.

Brian looked back over at Summer, who now stood next to Jabin. The liquid traveled up Jabin's arm, and coated him from head to toe, turning him a silver color before fading.

In that moment, the room became silent. The swirling wind could still be heard outside, but the rain and thunder came to a stop. Maria stood up and hurried to the window across from Sammy, on the other side of the room, behind Summer and Jabin. She gazed out in terror at what she saw. Her mind did not understand what her eyes were seeing.

"Brian, Joe," Maria beckoned for them in a frightened whisper, as if trying not to wake a deadly animal.

Brian and Joseph rushed over to Maria, who stood gazing out of the window in fear. They saw absolutely nothing.

"It's here!" said Sammy.

Summer slowly walked to the dining room door, followed closely by Jabin and Sammy.

"Wha…wha…what are they?" asked Maria, breathlessly struggling to get out the words.

"Answers won't matter if we're dead…follow me," said Summer as he threw open the two large doors, proceeding down the stairs to the front door of the mansion.

The five followed down the long stairs swiftly behind him. Joseph could feel something had changed with Sammy, Summer, and Jabin. They were dimly glowing as if a strange aura radiated from them.

The rain had stopped, and the wind had become calm. Summer looked out of the front window. They sky had become a massive, swirling sphere resembling the inside of a hurricane over the area. The shopping centers, café, and diners were gone without a trace. Where the buildings of Ezon One once stood, were patches of dirt and stones. There was not a single tree left standing within the swirling mass. Besides the mansion they resided in, the only thing that could be made out was the untouched shop adjacent to them. It seemed to still be fully intact and untouched by the storm.

"They're hiding," said Jabin. "They had better if they know what's good for them."

Brian was shocked. "Why does it seem like just when I start to figure things out, some weird shit ends up happening to throw me all off again? What's going on?"

"I know it's not easy to understand. It never is. Your eyes are not open. Awakened eyes see things that maulft eyes can't, and mortal words fail to describe. Never make assumptions through Awakened eyes, never act, and only react. Acting without observation and understanding could end up costing you dearly," said Summer.

"I don't understand," said Brian.

"Are you blind? If you can't see it, then expect the worse and you won't be disappointed," said Jabin, whose demeanor had become more serious than usual.

"No one do anything to provoke them. Summer what are they?" asked Sammy as he stared out at the bare ground.

"I can't tell yet. They could be Echos or Mirrorders, but I'm certain they destroyed this area. I've been observing them, and they seem to be waiting for something," said Summer.

"What are Mirrorders and Echos?" Brian asked.

"Mirrorders are creatures from the Forgotten Ages. They passed through walls and barriers and consumed the souls of sleeping children. Echos are minions of the Banshee that can take on any form, and are extremely hard to destroy. Either way, it's not good," said Sammy.

"Well it's not a Shadow Walker, so at least we can fight," said Jabin.

"Huh…never picked you as an optimist. Looks like we're rubbing off on you after all," said Sammy with a grin.

"Yeah. If we live through this, I'll see you in the arena for that cheesy remark," said Jabin.

"Shadow Walkers, what are they?" asked Brian.

"What do you know?" asked Jabin as he turned to Brian shaking his head in disappointment.

"Shadow Walkers are soulless nothings that can't be killed, injured, or destroyed. They are a void product of a consumed forgotten one. If you ever encounter one, run, and hope it didn't sense you. There's no defense they can't break through and no attack that can stop them. Never attempt to fight a Shadow Walker. If they catch you, you'll lose your soul, which is an irreversible fate far worse than death," said Sammy.

The hair on Brian's arms stood on end. "I can't see them, but I'm glad they're not Shadow Walkers. Still, what's stopping those things from walking in here right now and killing us all? Is it because we're not children?" asked Brian

"We're not sure. That's why Summer's been watching," said Sammy

As the cloudy mass swirled overhead, the door of the house was forced open by the wind. Brian jumped, stumbling back from the window, and then catching himself in the corner of the room. He stood with his back pressed firmly against the wall.

A voice echoed through the door.

"Children! Hurry, we must get out of here before they break free!"

"I know that voice," said Sammy.

Summer, Sammy, and Jabin quickly went to the front door.

"Eiden!" said Sammy surprised.

There, casually strolling up the side walk, was Eiden, the owner of the magic shop. He was wearing his usual sunglasses, brown wide-rimed hat, and a long gray and white winter's jacket. Eiden had an awkward fashion sense, and was never seen not wearing a jacket, scarf, and pair of sunglasses, even on the sunniest of Ezon One days.

"What are you doing out there?" asked Sammy, a bit confused.

"The Espers sent me."

Eiden proceeded up the walkway, "Some storm…I barely made my way over here."

Sammy could see mirage-like images fluctuating as if they were now trying to break free.

"Hurry, we haven't much time. I've slowed down the Mirrorders, but it won't hold."

Eiden approached the bottom stairs as Brian, Maria, and Joseph walked to the door.

"I'm not going out there. I can't even see them," said Brian.

"And where would we be going to? It's safer here," asked Sammy.

"Initium, Stone Movement!" screamed Eiden.

The words traveled on the sound waves of his voice.

Eiden proceeded up the stairs to the front door. The six of them stood motionless like statues. As he approached the front door, he began to examine their eyes.

"Good, you haven't changed yet. Forgive me children, but we haven't the time to waste."

Eiden removed his glasses, revealing his pale gray left eye with a dilated pupil, "The organization has fallen, Francis is dead, Lord Mathias has awoken, and soon he will rule Terraizen. This is all I can do to protect you from his cruelty."

Eiden stared into their eyes, and as he did, his eyes became completely gray and his pupil vanished. The eyes of Brian, Maria, and Joseph mimicked his as they were placed in a trance. But Sammy, Summer and Jabin remained unchanged.

"You three are strong," said Eiden, withdrawing a dagger from his pocket. He pointed it toward Jabin.

"I've numbed your body, so this won't hurt a bit."

"*Immotae!*"

Swiftly, Eiden leaped back from the door, deflecting the curse with his dagger.

"So you can still move?" searched Eiden.

"We can do more than just move," replied Sammy.

Sammy walked up to Maria, Brian, and Joseph, "*Nis!*" he said, waving his hand.

The three of them remained entranced.

"Forgotten! You are not Eiden. Speak your true name!"

"No...It wasn't supposed to be like this, they said you would go quickly. They said, I would be freeing you from the suffering."

Eiden put back on his sunglasses. Sadness spread across his face.

"I must be on my way now. The others are waiting," said Eiden nervously.

"You're not going anywhere until you fix them," said Sammy, who sped towards him with lightning speed, striking him in the chest. Eiden shattered like glass.

In the clearing, the mirages began to take full form. First, a few appeared under the spiraling hurricane-like barrier, then they began to multiply like bacteria, revealing others that were hidden in the empty spaces of the destroyed structures in Ezon One.

The wateresque mirage forms were chanting in an ancient language that Sammy could not understand. The voices grew louder, from an echoing roar to a massive thunder as more creatures took form.

The creatures opened their mouths. Their lower jaws extended down past their necks in resemblance of a snake. Their heads began to morph. The skin on their faces elongated.

Maria's eyes returned to normal as she gasped in horror at the sight.

Jabin glanced over at Maria, who seemed to be able to move her head, but not the rest of her body.

"We got head movement," said Jabin with a grin.

"We need to protect the others. Sammy, take them into the house," commanded Summer.

Swiftly, Sammy took the three immobilized bodies of Brian, Maria, and Joseph into the dining room, and placed them under a protection spell before racing back out to join Summer at the door.

Black curses rained from the mouths of the mirages, erupting against the wall of the barrier that surrounded the building, which could now be seen. There was a slight tremor before the blast dissipated.

"If a single one of those curses make contact, our abilities won't matter," said Jabin in a fearful tone.

"Now's not the time to chicken out," said Sammy.

"I'm not! I know that spell. I remember now. I've seen that curse before. It's the same as the one that was used to murder my brother. That curse is forbidden," said Jabin, who began to glow upon being enraged.

"Summer, are they Mirrorders?" asked Sammy.

"I'm not sure, but they seem to be getting ready for a second strike," said Summer.

Jabin was furious.

"I don't care what they are. I'll kill them all. You two can observe all you want."

"Now's not the time for a personal vendetta either Jabin," said Sammy in a rising tone as he stared out at the army of creatures forming around the house.

Sammy could feel someone watching him and turned around quickly.

"They're in the house!" screamed Sammy as he struck the figure standing at the bottom of the stairs, causing it to dissolve into a puddle.

"That answers your question. They're Mirrorders," said Summer.

Others began to come out of the walls. Jabin's hands began to glow as he struck them down one after the other.

"These fucking turds are everywhere!" screamed Jabin.

"Sammy, protect the others, we will handle things here," instructed Summer.

Sammy raced to the dining room. The Mirrorders had not made it there yet. The barrier that Sammy had placed around Brian, Maria, and Joseph stood strong, but the three of them were nowhere to be seen.

Sammy searched the house, but found nothing. Sammy proceeded back to the front of the mansion.

"They're not here," said Sammy as he looked at Jabin and Summer, who stood completely surrounded by the Mirrorders.

"We could use some help. These things keep reforming," said Jabin.

The Mirrorders had invaded the house, and continued to reform and multiply. Whenever Jabin struck one down, two took its place encircling the two of them. The creature's mouths dropped, and the black curses rained in on Jabin and Summer.

"Initium, Lucky Cricket," said Sammy.

Sammy ran towards Jabin and Summer. He moved at such a great speed that everything seemed to slow down. The rain of curses barely moved through the air as did everything else. Sammy had made it to Jabin and Summer before the curses could leave their mark. He knew his time was limited, and decided the best course of action was evacuation.

Unlike a maulft, Summer and Jabin's bodies had a high endurance and would be able to handle the intense speed. Sammy carried Summer to the dining room, avoiding the slow moving air borne curses along the way. Then he went back for Jabin. Once they were safely out of harm's way, Sammy went back, striking all of the Mirrorders within the house. He knew once he returned to normal, they would have a few minutes to strategize before the Mirrorders reformed. All of a sudden, Joseph appeared before him.

Although everything else remained still, Joseph walked towards him unaffected.

"Where did you go, and how are you moving as fast as I am?" asked Sammy confused.

Joseph smiled, "I'll explain later, but for now, I need you to do exactly as I say."

CHAPTER 32: JOSEPH AWAKENS

"Joseph...Joseph...Joseph wake up!" came three voices.

Joseph sprung awake to find himself in the Esper Mansion. It was late, but the storm had ended. Brian, Maria, Sammy, Summer, and Jabin sat around the large table.

Maria, Brian, and Sammy were staring directly at him while Jabin gazed out of the large window, and Summer sat entranced with his eyes and arms closed.

"It worked," Joseph said, staring at Sammy.

"Yes it did," said Sammy. "I think I understand now."

Jabin turned towards Joseph, his eyes were filled with anger as he lifted Joseph up from his chair by the scruff of his shirt collar.

"What the fuck did you do to us? That was no dream. I remember it all, and so do Sammy and Summer."

Joseph's voice cracked as he spoke. Scared, as Jabin's grip around his neck tightened, making it difficult for him to breath,

"I...I think it was my Awakened ability. I don't understand it yet and I...I can't control it."

"You dragged me and my team into your apocalyptic phantasies, nearly killing us. Why should I let you leave this room? You're a hazard to everyone," said Jabin with rage in his eyes.

"Put him down!" demanded Maria as her sapphire pendant began to glow and she raised her hands to encompass it.

Jabin flung Joseph back into his chair with such a force that he and the chair shot backwards towards the wall, tilting backward as it did.

"*Vis Spiritus!*" Maria responded quickly.

The chair decelerated in midair, stopping just before hitting the wall. Encompassed by a blue light, it was lowered safely to the ground.

Joseph looked over at Maria, whose pendant glowed as she focused on him.

"Some ability. You nearly killed us with your fucked up dreams. And even your own teammates. What kind of fucked up ability is that? What kind of out of control friend are you?" asked Jabin furiously.

"I'm sorry. I can't control it. It...it just happens," said Joseph nervously.

Jabin picked up a chair with one hand, and slung it angrily against the wall with an extremity that shattered it into many small pieces. It let out a bang that caused Maria, Brian, and Joseph to jump and tense up in fear of his next move.

Jabin stared and pointing angrily towards Joseph. "You're a danger to everyone around you. Tomorrow night, at the Awakened hour we end this like men! If you don't show, then I'm going to seal you away in a place where you can't hurt anyone and this time no one's going to stop me. Until then, stay the fuck away from me, Aizen!"

He turned and stormed from the room and into the back corridor that led off into the mansion. There was an awkward silence, the unspoken tension in the room refused to dissolve.

Joseph sat taking in Jabin's words. Freak, he thought to himself. He hated to admit it, but Jabin was right. His dreams were dangerous and realistic to the point where even he found it difficult to tell dream from reality at times. It was only when he awoke that he knew without a doubt that he was dreaming.

Maria stood up and walked over to Joseph.

"Joe, it's not your fault. We..."

"Maria don't!" said Joseph angrily as tears rushed down the sides of his face. He had been holding back the emotions, but could no longer bear it.

"I almost got everyone killed because I can't control my abilities. Can't you see I'm a danger to everyone around me? As long as I'm here, no one's safe. You guys should leave before I fall asleep and get you killed," said Joseph, looking over at Summer, Sammy, Brian, and Maria. "Jabin's right. I'm a freak."

Summer with his calm demeanor, looked up from the table where he had been sitting before, eyes filled with a speechless silence, "Freak...abnormal, irregularity, mistake, mutation, abomination… I've heard them all, and shared more in common with the caged bird than I dare to admit. My years in the South were spent on the run every waking moment of my life. Just thinking about it takes me back to those tiresome nights. No sleep… trusting no one, surviving on will alone. Banshee agents, Southern agents, Numbered, forgotten, and Shadow Walkers were behind every tree, waiting, trying to claim the bounty on my head, trying to consume the power in my soul. My family was murdered. I had no friends, and everyone I had ever known was captured, tortured, killed, or numbered. Since the age of seven, I've grown accustomed to being tortured within inches of my life… I no longer feel pain. Through all that I've experienced, there's one thing I've had neither the time nor the patience for, and that's self-pity. I escaped and survived."

There was a brief silence before he continued in a scolding tone, "So let me put things in perspective for you…"

Bang!

Summer slammed his fist down upon the table, and it vanished. Everyone jumped back, their hearts racing, except Sammy, who watched as Summer stared down Joseph, "You know nothing about true peril and trepidation. Nightmares…killing us…? Hump, laughable, don't flatter yourself… dream walking is child's play to us, even if you're an Aizen. If you want something to fear, fear the Reapers and their master. Both are monsters, deathless, and unstoppable, which impulsively consume lives. Nothing else and no one else is worthy of being feared."

Summer stood up, and in a very quiet tone, he turned to Sammy and murmured softly, "I'll see you at the Awakened hour."

Summer vanished on a breeze, slamming the door behind him and leaving an awkward silence in his wake; along with Joseph, Brian, and Maria in a state of awe. Summer was right. They couldn't begin to understand what it was like for him. Until recently, they knew nothing about Southern or Northern Terraizen. From Sammy, they had learned much about the inequalities of Northern Terraizen, which in comparison to Central seemed like an idiocracy. But Summer made the South seem like a dreaded land of horror, worse than any nightmare Joseph could have dreamed up.

Brian had been staring at the table since Jabin left the room. Now that the table was gone, he was just staring at his knees, trying to avoid eye contact with the others.

Joseph looked over at him, wondering what was going through his mind, afraid to ask.

Sammy approached Joseph; though he did not seem happy, he did not seem shaken by the recent events. He placed a hand on Joseph's shoulder, commanding his attention.

"Don't mind them Joseph, they've both just been a bit on edge lately. Just remember, the reason you're here is so you can learn to control your abilities. Sure, your abilities may seem dangerous to you, but that's only because you're not used to them yet. I personally think you did a fine job handling the situation. No one's hurt and I think he's growing a liking to you. Normally, he doesn't talk this much. Still he's right, we had everything under control. So cheer up," said Sammy with a slight grin, "We're stronger than we look, and as long as you're here, you're safe."

Sammy extended his other hand towards Joseph and smiled, "Friends?"

Joseph wiped away his tears and looked at Sammy's hand. Sammy was right. No one had been killed, and before anyone was hurt, he realized that he was dreaming and was able to get Sammy to wake everyone up.

Joseph extended his hand into Sammy's. Sammy had a rather strong grip, which caught Joseph by surprise as he felt his fingers momentarily being crushed under the pressure that Sammy had no idea he was exuding.

"To new friends and alliances," said Sammy.

"To new friends," said Joseph, trying to keep a straight face until his grip lessened.

Joseph thought back to the dream as he shook Sammy's hand firmly. Although he had not thought about it at first, he realized that this dream was different from the rest. Sammy, Summer, and even Jabin had protected him, Brian, and Maria, even though they did not know they were dreaming. Not only that, they all remembered. Maybe if the dream had continued they would have found a way to end his apocalyptic nightmare, and everything would have been just fine from then on out.

The table reappeared. Brian looked up from the table slightly groggy.

"Wow, exactly 60 seconds, that was longer than I expected. It was like it was invisible, but I could still feel it." Brian looked over in time to catch Sammy and Joseph shaking hands, "This alliance doesn't mean I have to work with Jabin, does it?" asked Brian in an aggravated tone.

"Yes, you get the opportunity to train with the one and only Prince Jabin of Northern Terraizen," said Sammy in a sarcastically regal tone.

"Oh great! I don't know which one's worse, Joe's nightmare's, or Jabin's personality."

"He's really trying. He's even started calling Ezon One women by their names, but I think that has more to do with the last curse he encountered from the friendly neighbor witch, Samantha. She really got him good this last time with a nice combo she created. It took Summer a while to break it, though he wasn't trying very hard," Sammy laughed with a slight smirk that held a hidden secret.

"We all have things we need to work on," said Sammy, heading towards the dining room door. "Now, how about we get some rest. We can start fresh in the morning. I'll even assist you with your training."

"Sounds good to me," said Brian as he stood up placing a hand on the table to make sure it was really there.

Brian, Maria, and Joseph headed out of the mansion and made their way back to the hotel. The streets were well lit on the strip, and everything looked to be in order. They headed down the strip passing by Eiden's Shop and the Ezon One breakfast diner. Up ahead and just across the street was the hotel. The area was not as well lit as usual, and there was some one standing near the entrance in a white cloak like the one he had seen in the diner. It was brief, but in the blink of the eye, it was gone and the normal lighting returned.

"Did you guys see that?" asked Joseph.

"See what," asked Brian, who had been staring down at the road as they crossed the street.

Joseph looked over at Maria, who seemed to be fighting to stay awake. Countering Jabin's attack had taken its toll on her, and so had his "dream walking" as Summer called it. Joseph had many questions, especially about his family name, Aizen, and its significance to his abilities. But it was best he save those questions for the morning. It had been a long night, and the last thing he wanted to do was make it longer considering he too was growing weary by the second. The white-cloaked figure must have been an illusion of the night; his subconscious reminiscing an earlier memory. That was it, nothing more, nothing less.

"Nothing," said Joseph, "I thought I saw something. Let's just get some rest."

They reached the front door of the hotel and headed into the main entrance. There at the front desk sat the security officer, Danny, who was asleep behind the control panel. The three of them made their way to the stairs and headed up to the second floor. As they exited, for a brief moment, Joseph thought he saw the figure again standing right outside their room door at the end of the hallway but this one was different from the other. It was darker. He knew there was probably something to it, but he had neither the time nor the patience for trying to figure it out at the moment, and chalked it up to the squiggly lines in his eye fluid, though he knew he was lying to himself. He combined that with a lack of sleep and horrendous nightmares finally taking their toll. That was enough for him to ignore, and then forget about it all together. He was assured Ezon One was safe, and was more frightened of his own nightmares than anything else. In addition, his pendant gave him the power to defend himself if he ever needed to.

They made their way to the apartment style room. It had changed to three separate rooms within a combined unit that shared two bathrooms. There was a living room joint area that held a couch, table, and television. Brian and Maria went their separate ways, and Joseph headed off to the third room. Each had a separate door with their name on it. He opened it to find a bed with a side table, love seat, and a dresser with a projector and television resting upon it. In the back left corner of the room, next to the loveseat, which sat under the window, was the transport unit that could bring him anything he desired. Joseph could not think of anything at the moment, and headed to bed. He lay there staring at the ceiling. He was scared to go to sleep. *What if he drew everyone into his dreams again?* He thought.

There was a slight breeze, which startled Joseph. He glanced over at the window, but it was closed. Joseph ignored the breeze. After all, stranger things had happened. He reached over to turn out the lamp, and there at the foot his bed, out of the corner of his eye, he saw it, a dark figure standing in silence.

CHAPTER 33: THE NIGHTSHIFT

Night had settled in, and the chaotic day drew to a close. Most of the essential staff was still in isolation within the Zone. There were no night shift guards on surveillance or call duty.

All was quiet as Stephen sat restless in front of his computer screen attempting to regain access to the TSPA system, which the A.I. had somehow been locked out of. Stephen had been controlling an avatar of himself created using Anthony and his powers during his fight in the Nefastus Forest with Benjamin. Though remote, if he failed to abort the avatar before it was destroyed he would be destroyed along with it. Stephen preferred this method because like the A.I. it allowed him to be in multiple places at once though if he attempted to control more than two it became a challenge even for a mind as advanced as his. It would be a while before he could get another up and running. Right now his focus was on something much more important. Temporarily, he was able to raise the back-up shields, but they would not hold for long. He had reviewed the logbooks in detail, and new questions and theories began to form within his head. Stephen was tired, but knew he could not sleep until he found answers to the questions that troubled him. Francis the IV had not been seen since the last meeting, and even the radar had been unable to find him. In Francis's absence, Anthony, who was second in command, would normally take control. However, now Anthony had vanished as well. Since then, there continued to be random attacks on the organization throughout the night. Not just on Central, but throughout all of Terraizen. Banshee was finally making its move. This troubled Stephen, and so did the words of the forgotten. *Trinities shall lay broken, skies shall find their places. Beware the past's arrival, it hides within their faces.*

Although, he hated to admit it, there was no denying her power. The Banshee was as powerful as she was cunning and vindictive. Out of all of the criminals that existed throughout the history of Terraizen, she was the most ruthless and deadly. No Awakened could elude the organization as well as she had. Technology had advanced to levels previously thought impossible, and the organization possessed people with the ability to sense, track, control, and find anyone within Terraizen. Yet, the Banshee eluded all forms of detection. Using an advanced matrix algorithm and the A.I. system, Stephen was able to develop a way to locate the Banshee's minions in hopes of finding her. It proved successful during the first month, but the Banshee was smart and quickly found ways around it. Over seven years, it had located her once for less than a second, but later Stephen found it had been a bug in the system.

The Banshee had never revealed herself to the organization, only her Echoes, which were said to be vibrations of her voice that took a physically independent form of their own. They were powerful and difficult to destroy, but only appeared once every few years.

Besides her Echoes, the Banshee had many other abilities. It had once been said that her power exceeded that of Benjamin Alexander. The Banshee not only had the ability to shield herself from detection, but to shield others as well. This frustrated the organization. To have something so powerful right under their nose, yet, right outside of their powers grasp. The organization would stop at nothing to put an end to her and her Echoes.

Stephen had made it his personal goal to catch her and those that she may be harboring. He had amassed a great deal of information about the Banshee, and had narrowed her possible hideouts down to thirty-two alternating combinations of cities in Southern Terraizen. In the process, he discovered the existence of beings known as the forgotten. They were Awakened that had been consumed by the Banshee's power.

Stephen found it peculiar that the Banshee would send out her Echoes and forgotten to attack the TSPA. Even with such a powerful intellect, he could not initially comprehend the rationale behind her actions. At first, Stephen had thought she wanted to destroy the TSPA or gather information. But now, he was certain she had ulterior motives. Stephen was beginning to understand what she was truly planning, and he had begun developing the tools needed to stop her when she made her move. At first sight, it may have seemed like a noble gesture of Banshee to tell the denizens of Terraizen the truth but having them know that people like those of the TSPA existed was bound to cause chaos, fear, rebellion and destabilize the delicate peace between the branches of the TSPA. If this were to happen and Central were to fall Lord Mathias and the southern agents would strike and this was to be avoided at any cost.

Stephen had developed the perfect strategy for dethroning the malevolent force known as the Banshee. Even at such high costs, the TSPA continued to show they had the ability to overpower her Echoes. It was only a matter of time before she showed her true power.

A few years back, the Banshee had sent an Echo in the form of the fabled Jinn to North TSPA. It had decimated the headquarters in an instant before vanishing untouched. This time she had sent two Echoes in the form of the Jinn to Central Terraizen, and if it were not for the strategic planning of the minds, that same disaster would have surly followed. After all, she had been known to attack the organization at their weakest moment. Still, she had failed, and Stephen knew she would strike again, because this would be her only chance to take down Central.

Without the loss of a single life, Central TSPA had taken down the two Echoes. Although she remained hidden, her armies lay in wait within the forest around Central with only the barrier holding them back.

As he pieced together the remaining pieces of essence code for restoring the main barrier that he had received from Eleanor, his determination grew exponentially. To take someone of the Banshee's caliber down would not be a trivial task. It would take everything they had, and even then, it did not guarantee victory. If they could hold out till morning, backup would arrive, and then the Banshee's forces would diminish greatly.

As he rapidly entered information into the system through the hologram console, he pieced together the last of the Banshee tracking algorithm. Within the next few minutes, it would be able to determine her exact location, and then it would be time to move. Frightened by the idea of taking on a creature that had evaded the TSPA for over five hundred years, and killed some of the world's most powerful leaders within that time period, Stephen was ready to put an end to it.

Stephen watched as the algorithm continued to run rigorously through advanced iterations.

The markings on the screen had gone from thirty to just two in the last few minutes. In just one minute, the barrier would return, and they would strike a blow to the Banshee that she would never recover from.

Stephen inclined his chair and gazed upward at the blank silver ceiling tiles, under the dim lighting of the room. As he did, an unnatural cold swept through his body and caused his Awakened ability to flare up, warming him as the room continued to grow colder. The ceiling lights flickered as if the system was losing power. Stephen knew such an event was not possible due to the

A.I. systems regulating functions, but then he remembered the A.I. was still down.

There was a light knock upon the door.

"Come in Eleanor," said Stephen.

The automated door slid open, and Eleanor entered the room.

"He's here," said Eleanor, "And he waiting for us."

"Tell him to wait. I have more pressing matters that require my attention."

The lights began to flicker more intensely as if responding to his words.

"Yes, we both have more pressing matters, but I would rather not see him get angry. We all know what happens when he's angered."

Stephen contemplated Eleanor's words.

A look of shock spread over Stephen's face. His console was an isolated space unaffected by changes in magnetic and electronic fluctuations, yet it was now trying to shut itself down.

"It seems he wants us to hurry. If you wait any longer, who knows what he'll do."

Eleanor walked over to Stephen's desk and began examining his console's solid-state map projection. She could see the information she had sent had solved the algorithm, and now the map showed only two possible locations. Stephen began to type rapidly, the flickering ceased.

"That won't hold for long. The others are still in quarantine, and Francis is still missing. It seems control has fallen to you," said Eleanor with a slight grin of sarcastic envy.

Stephen's eyes widened. The C-4 firewalls fell as if they had never been activated.

Aggravated, Stephen slammed his fist upon his desk causing Eleanor to jump slightly, "They have him don't they. How? It's just not possible."

"Improbable, but not impossible." Eleanor let out a sigh "Yes, some how they managed to capture the Great Tactician as well. I'd say that gives us ten seconds before they force him to erase our systems."

"What about our back-ups?"

"We're dealing with The Tactician. The back-ups were the first to go."

"He's the only one that can shut an A.I. out of the A.I. system."

Although Stephen attempted to stop the Tacticians hack, it was too late. He had lost everything and the shields were the last to fall.

"Well, now we're completely defenseless," said Eleanor.

Stephen slammed his fist down upon his desk once more, causing it to break in half this time, with the floor below it cracking slightly. The Tactician had destroyed all of his files, and now like the A.I., he was locked out of his own system. Stephen knew once the Tactician found his way into a system there was no hope of stopping him.

Stephen stood up from his desk. He could feel it. Another unwelcomed quest had just arrived, and this one wasn't from Banshee. In fact, the Banshee's units had dispersed.

Now that the Tactician had entered the fray, the Banshee would soon retreat into hiding once again. What bothered Stephen was the fact that the Tactician was now working against not only Banshee, but Central. What would cause him to make such a move? Better yet, who, if not Emperor Hadar, had ordered such an attack? Stephen could think of only one person.

Stephen made his way towards the door, briefly making eye contact with Eleanor. They both knew who was behind this.

"Let's go greet our guests. It's not every day that death shows up at your front door," said Stephen, swinging open the door angrily as he paced swiftly down the hall.

"Yes, if I'd known Bishop were coming I'd have asked Francis to break the seal he placed on my powers. But it seems I'll have to make due with what I have," said Eleanor in an aggravated tone.

Eleanor smiled, tossing her beautiful, deep red curls back as she raised her wand, aiming it at Stephen's back as he made his way down the long hallway that lead to the elevator. She knew if they attempted to fight the Bishop in their current state they would be capture, killed or even worse, numbered. Eleanor knew she needed more power. She needed Stephen's power.

"Forgive me Stephen..."

"*Sopor Ultima!*" A spell rang out striking Eleanor in the back. She knew the voice and quickly, as she began to fade, she turned with but seconds to see the culprit. There, standing in the darkness to her surprise were three figures. An armored figure shrouded in shadows that she could barely make out stood behind her beloved

Quinn and next to him, with wand raised, stood a face she had grown to know so very well. It was that of her very own.

The face smiled at her as her eyes closed and wand fell from her hand. Next, she felt a breeze and then the quick embrace of the arms of another as she drifted gently to sleep.

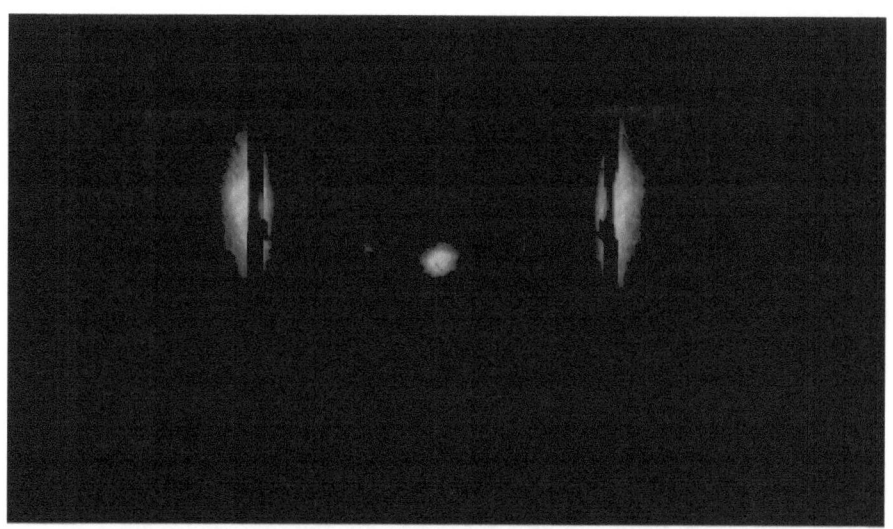

CHAPTER 34: RETURN OF FORGOTTEN AGES-
BLACK MAIDEN

As Eleanor and Stephen exited Central, they could see the retreating of figures in the distance. In just a matter of minutes, the Banshee's army had vanished, one by one their figures fading into the night. All attempting to escape their impending doom. Besides the rulers of Terraizen, there were few things that could frighten them, for they lacked emotion.

The trees parted like blades of grass as a mammoth figure broke through the branches. It stood a giant among men with a presence that caused the ground to vibrate. They called him the Rook, and with a body like a moving fortress, he was one of the most terrifying agents of the South TSPA.

Barely visible, lingering like a menacing moonlit after-glow in the shadow of the Rook, was the mysterious Black Knight. The knight's solid black armor resonated a lifeless call that detoured the air and light around him, an illusion to the naked eye. From the shadows of the two monstrosities, stepped a small-figured man. Though he lacked the size of the Rook and illusionary qualities of the knight, there was something more terrifying about him than the both of them. As he stepped out of the shadows, he bowed at the waist.

"Greetings Lady Fredrick and Sir Langley, so good to see you again. My, how the time does fly. How long has it been? Thirty, forty years?" guessed the Bishop with a smile that revealed his razor sharp teeth. "I mean not to be rude, but I thought there would be more of ahhh…welcome party, considering we have just saved Central from the Banshee's army."

"We're enough to handle you three," said Stephen.

"Ahhhhh…such warm welcome from such a smart tongue. If it keeps behaving badly, I'll have to teach it some manners. We meant no harm. We simply saw that you were under attack and came to assist. At the end of the day, we're all part of the same organization, and were saddened when we heard Judge Francis was…missing, and your systems were…how do you say…down? So we thought out of good will we would…lend a hand," said the Bishop.

"Enough with the games! You are forbidden to enter Central. Leave now before Francis returns. You know what he'll do when he finds out you broke the law," threatened Stephen.

"Oh, you mean Rule 854 Section 2 paragraph 7 Amended, *Southern Agents shall not be permitted on the premises of Central Terraizen, under the rule of Francis the IV, without explicit consent from Edward Francis, except in a state of emergency, in which Central is occupied by enemy forces and no longer possesses the necessary Agents to defend its denizens, agents, and occupants."*

The smile dropped from the Bishop's face. He stood up straight, cocked his head to the side and looked Stephen in the eye.

"We've broken no rules. Central is clearly going to hell in a hand basket. Honestly, we didn't want you to be consumed by the shadows. Not numbering a talent, such as yours, would be a waste, don't you agree?" proposed the Bishop as he straightened his head, "Last time, you never got the chance to see the results of our wondrous work, so we brought you a little present. Step forward Pawn 1174!"

From behind the Rook, stepped two white faced Pawns. The scouts of the South, in black clothing that blended into the shadow of the Rook, making it seem as if they were just white masks hovering in empty space. Between them stood another figure, with a mask draped in blood.

Stephen and Eleanor gasped, their faces ghastly as they stared out at the mutilated hollow shell of the man between the two Pawns. His eyes and mouth had been sown shut, hooks were strung from his bruised and mutilated flesh, making him almost unrecognizable. Blood trailed down the white mask that had been bound to his skinned face through a horrific method known as numbering. They could tell he had not been easily broken. Yet, in the end, their new age torture methods had eviscerated his body and broken his will. Just like the many that came before him.

"Your actions are unforgivable. This is an act of war," said Stephen.

"Ahhhhh...it feels like just hours ago your mother was saying those exact words to me before groveling at my feet, begging me to spare your life. Of course you don't remember, you were just a child then, and Francis probably had your memory erased. But I'm sure you've heard the stories. It's too bad we were unable to number you back then. We could have unlocked your full potential. Francis always had a way with impeding our progress. We had just begun numbering your mother when he stole the two of you from us. How rude of him to take what didn't belong to him. However, it's always only been a matter of time before we finish what we started," said the Bishop.

Stephen remembered clearly the day the Bishop came to visit. It was the day his mother lost her mind, and he lost his mother. Stephen had a dark past with the Bishop. It had been because of him that Stephen had learned to turn off his emotions. As a child, the sights seen in their numbering chambers had been too great for him. For years, he had reoccurring nightmares of the times he was forced to watch while they tortured his mother among the others as he sat chained to a heated metal chair, helpless to stop it or look away. In spite of that, he had been among the lucky to have seen the ordeal and not have to endure it. The week he spent there, he heard much talk among the prisoners about the pardon system. It was the only hope the people had within the filthy torture chambers of the Southern caverns.

351

Each year, the Seven Leaders of Terraizen were granted a pardon. Although they all ruled as gods among men in their respective worlds, they were allowed to pardon one individual from anywhere within Terraizen, whether it be from execution, or the numbering system. That year, he was Sophia's choice. Sophia pardoned him, and Francis pardoned his mother. Sophia was a kind soul who hated to see numbered children, and if she had the power, she would have put an end to it long ago. She had chosen to free Stephen, however, Stephen had refused to leave without his mother. So Sophia requested Francis use his pardon to save the both of them, and he did. Unfortunately, by then his mother's mind was too far gone, and nothing could undo what they had done to her. Stephen dreaded to think of what happened to those who were not pardoned, and what would have happened to him and his mother. But now, he could clearly see the end results of their ruthlessness as it stood torn, beaten, and broken in front of them.

Stephen stood emotionless, not swayed by the word of the Bishop, or the sight of his once friend. Stephen was a logical thinker, and knew if he allowed for even a brief emotional slip, he was sure to meet the same end as the man that stood before them.

Eleanor, on the other hand, had enough rage for the both of them. The light drained from her eyes, her voice deepened as her rage reached new threshold, "If you thought you would come here with the numbered body of one of our agents and expect us to surrender, you have been sadly mistaken. I won't let you leave here alive!"

Eleanor raised her hand, but nothing happened.

"Your rage blinds you. Your powers won't work thanks to 1174. You should already have known that Lady Eleanor, considering he was once one of the top agents of Central. We just made him better, stronger, and removed his limits. Just wait until you see what our new toy can do now," boasted the Rook.

"Central no longer possesses the power to defeat the South, even under the suppression of the Judge and the Philosopher for decades, we numbered all those who stood against us. But now the Judge has fallen, the Philosopher alone can no longer suppress our master. The balance of power is shifting. Soon Sophia will fall, along with the rest of you cnew, and the South shall rule Terraizen. Surrender now, and your numbering shall be swift. Resist, and we will consume every soul and citizen of Central Terraizen," said the Bishop in a casual tone.

"You are a powerless cnew. Without your abilities, you're no different than a maulft. Our Lord's essence courses through us. We are immortal. Neither death nor magic can harm us. Surrender, and you may yet live. Defy us, and you will be numbered just like your friend," said the Black Knight.

Eleanor laughed, "Look how far you have fallen. You're mere shadows of your former selves, and even then, it wasn't much to begin with. There was a time when I feared you. A time where you still held some shred of power over me, but now I see, you're just pieces controlled by the hand of a man that fears the power of Central. And he has good reason to fear us. We have appeased you long enough. Leave now before we show you what we are truly capable of. After all, I am the weapon," said Eleanor, still attempting to tap into her sealed powers with every fiber of her being.

"You will learn to fear me again."

The Bishop had become agitated. "I've had enough of your tongue for now. I'll enjoy hearing your screams later. Rook, 1174, destroy them both, then find the others and bring them all to me for numbering. Knight, come with me, we have a date with the Philosopher Sophia. We wouldn't want to be late."

The Bishop turned to leave, while the Black Knight hesitated, "I must teach her a lesson..."

"Don't test my patience Knight! Rook, finish them! Show them our Lord has no fears; failure shall not be tolerated," ordered the Bishop, who continued to bark out orders as he proceeded back into the forest, disappearing into the shadows.

The Black Knight and followed him, leaving behind the Rook, 1174, and the two pawns to face Eleanor and Stephen.

"I don't like drawn out battles, so I'll make this quick," announced the Rook, slamming his massive fist down into the ground.

Before Eleanor or Stephen could react, the stone blocks had risen, crushing their skulls and shattering their bones between its solid surfaces. Then it seemed to melt around them, encased in cold, stone block cells, which seemed to instantaneously drain all of their energy. It caused them to lose before they could process their circumstance.

"Your souls can't escape. Those stones are infused with the

Lord's essence, even Francis could not escape them. Though he tried…"

The Rook turned to the hooked and bloody 1174, "Seal them both, then follow me so we can be through with these remedial errands."

Pawn 1174 limped towards the two blocks leaving a bloody trail as the Rook marched towards the doorway of Central.

"Without their powers, this won't take long," said the Rook as he tore off the door, along with part of the wall, tossing it aside like a barrel of hay. The Rook ducked down through the hole and entered the building. His heavy footsteps echoed as they crushed the marble floor under his feet. Besides the constant vibrating of the floor, all was quiet.

"Well this place seems deserted, where are the others?" asked the Rook as he spoke to himself once more. The Rook had a habit of speaking to himself when no one else was around.

He traveled deeper into Central, leaving a trail of broken marble in his wake, while destroying desks, tables, and anything else that stood in his way. He headed to the elevator that lay just down the hall, past the vacant receptionist center, and around the corner to the left on the northern side of the building. Once there, he would make his way to the B-1 and M-2 divisions to obtain what he had come for. Such gifts he was sure would please his master.

The Rook knew he was being watched by the A.I. But the A.I. was powerless to stop him. The Tactician of the West had corrupted its systems. Still, the Rook did not trust the Tactician, the

Rook trusted no one. As an incentive, they had threatened to number the Tactician if he failed them, but the Tactician knew it was an idle threat. Emperor Hadar knew Lord Mathias would rise to power, and lent him the Tactician's skills and abilities.

Though the Rook did not trust him, he could not deny that the Tactician had proven to be very useful. Not only had he found a way to cripple the seemingly all-powerful A.I. system of Central, which cloaked the island and prevented the Southern agents from locating or entering the area, but he had also developed the plans used to capture Judge Francis the IV. With Central in shambles, Judge Francis the IV captured, and the organization's greatest mind in their hands, there was nothing left that could stop them. Once Sophia had fallen from power, Terraizen would be theirs for the taking, and even Banshee would have no place to hide.

Still, something did not sit right with the massive Rook. Something was wrong, very wrong. Even with the Tactician's help, it had been too easy to penetrate their defenses. Something had been blocking his senses but he could feel it now. The Stones of Lord Mathias not only trapped souls but read essence and the essence trapped between the stones was not that of Eleanor and Stephens but that of a soulless bio-unit and avatar. He had been tricked. He an elite Southern TSPA had been fooled by a couple of toys and this angered him. How did he not sense it before? How did they not sense it before? Nothing on Central was strong enough to block their connection with Lord Mathias Stones, at least nothing they were aware of.

Click-clock, click-clock, click-clock...

The Rook heard strange sounds. Footsteps...yes, there were footsteps, but the footsteps weren't important. There was something else; something was approaching, extremely fast.

Bam!

There was a loud crash, but the Rook stood unshaken as the lights shattered and the emergency lighting flashed red across the white walls of Central. Something had curved around the corner and landed in the darkness with a force that halted the Rook, echoing through the large hallways of Central. Something was blocking his path.

The Rook stood still and listened closely. He did not run from a challenge, and feared no one but his master Lord Mathias, Ruler of the South.

Click-clock, click-clock, click-clock...

The sound of footsteps continued to echo along the marble hallway floor from in the distance.

The Bishop had made a mistake. It was not because of their appearance that the Banshee had retreated, neither was it because of the Tacticians presence. Something was inside of Central. Something very powerful, very dangerous, and very insidious had arrived just before them. The Rook had begun to realize the circumstances. There were no other agents in Central. Had they evacuated? Somehow they had known, and not a single Awakened, forgotten, or machine stirred. They had fled like animals from a natural disaster. His master wanted Central, and all those who dared to challenge Lord Mathias would be eliminated without question. No matter what stood before him, the Rook would face it and destroy it for impeding upon their conquest of Central.

At the end of the hall, it gathered on a vile wind, taking the form of a device he had seen many times before in the Numbering Chambers of the South TSPA. It was the iron maiden. But this was no ordinary iron maiden; it stood solid black, darker than the shadows, casting a dark glow that warped the red light around it.

The iron maiden stood at the end of the dark hall, and from it came a rumble. The Rook stood glaring, analyzing the situation. He would not run, he would fight till the very end.

Creeeek...creeek...

The door to the iron maiden began to slowly, slowly open, hiding the contents within the shadowy aura. But it was not hidden from the Rook. The Rook could see just as well in the dark as he could in the day, probably even better, and he knew exactly what he was looking at as it stepped forward. Until now, it had been just a legend, one he had dismissed without question; but if the legends were true about the Black Maiden, then running would be pointless, he would already be dead. This however, was just another one of the Banshee's tricks, Echoes used to frighten the agents of the TSPA. Still, defeating it quickly would require drawing upon his master's essence, and using the power of 1174 to put an end to the being that resided inside.

Click-clock, click-clock, click-clock, came the sound of footsteps once more.

It stepped out of the black iron maiden and proceeded sluggishly down the hallway, revealing its form under the emergency lighting of the long, white marble hallway.

Creaking, jerking, and swaying it moved in terrifyingly frightful mannequin motions like a puppet on strings. It exited the shroud of the dark breeze on which it had arrived, which still lingered in the air like a dark fog. Then it opened its mouth, and began to sing.

Izentaifu's approaching you,
Extinguishing death and oblivion too.
Its wild fire spreads through aspects and hearts,
Consuming eternal life, erasing eternal parts.

It jerked backwards off balance in a way that suggested it lacked a backbone, its tone rising in anger.

Izentaifu is approaching you!
Forgotten return, grim endings ensue.
A faceless terror, no fruition of why,
No shrieks, chills or warnings…the rules don't apply…

The frightful porcelain doll adorned in black with blood red hair crept closer. It chanted in an unrecognizable tongue. The Rook analyzed it's movements, the dark breeze that still lingered in the air, and the iron maiden still hidden in the fog, which held the ancient seals and crests of the five guardians. There was no denying the truth. This was no Echo; he stood before the Black Maiden.

The Black Maiden, also known as the Mother of Curses & Harbinger of the Forgotten Ages, an entity so powerful that it alone could bring about the apocalypse. It possessed a devastating power that only it could control, and even the mightiest of wizards feared. As the fragile looking doll entered the light, it glanced over at the monstrous Rook. Slowly, it began to gain control of its form, working its head upward in a wobbly motion, straightening its back like a child who's just learning to walk. All the while, it continued to sing in an eerie tone.

Izentaifu is approaching you...

Extrinsic but integrated intrinsically through...

It sang, with a voice-like pestilence, dragging out the last two words.

Ye prisoner to the flesh, no way of control,

No pain, no mind, no heart nor soul...

The Black Maiden continued down the hall, closing in on the Rook surrounded by the dark breeze. Motionlessly, the Rook stood, continuously observing every detail of the Black Maiden's mannerisms and motions. Then all at once, its head shot forward. Its hair faded to black, spine and legs straightened; removing any signs that may have conveyed fragility and lethargies, and it fired its hollow gaze upon the Rook. The Rook was there, but no longer present, as it spoke those final haunting words that he had only heard once before.

You could have run, but it wouldn't have mattered. You're already dead and will never live.

Click-clock, click-clock, click-clock, came the sound of rapid footsteps.

The Black Maiden's feet were no longer touching the ground as it levitated through the air. One by one the emergency lights shattered as it made its way down the final length of the corridor.

The Rook braced himself. He could feel it now. It was the first time he had felt anything in a long while. At first, he didn't recognize it. Although he wasn't sure why he could feel it either. He then looked into the dark, unavoidable, blood red pentagram eyes of the Black Maiden that reflected the truth.

Entranced by their dismal glow, the hollow Rook stood, watching, gazing, distraught by the horrid truth. The shroud had been dropped. What he hadn't felt in centuries, he could feel flooding back to him now; despair, fear, hopelessness. The seal had been broken, and his end had come and gone before he could apprehend what it meant.

He didn't see what came after the shockwave. Only the silence lingered in the stillness of the dark.

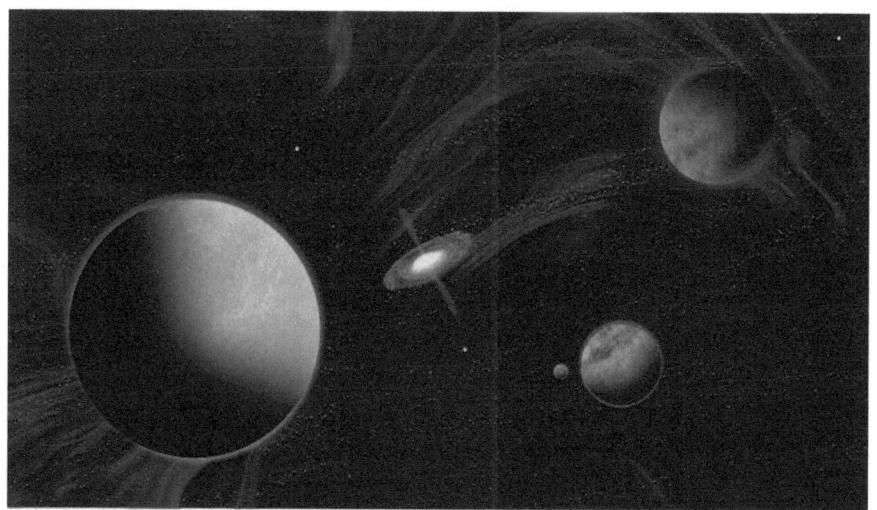

CHAPTER 35: QUINN

"He's coming to," said a woman's voice.

Quinn opened his eyes to a blurry, unfocused room. He extended his arm to the right, reaching towards the nightstand and fumbling over it with his hand in search of his glasses.

"Here," said the woman, placing Quinn's glasses in his right hand.

Quinn recognized the voice immediately as he put on his glasses. It was Anabel, and there to her left stood Bruno.

"Your heart rate has stabilized, but your essence levels are dangerously low," said Anabel. Her tone had changed. Although her face was emotionless, behind it was a fury that Quinn could feel like the crushing pressure of Benjamin.

"What were you thinking?" asked Anabel.

"I wanted to protect you," said Quinn, "I needed to protect you."

"Do you know how worried we were?" asked Bruno, "Anabel has been at your bed side for the past two days. You had a few close calls, but she brought you back. You nearly died five times, and almost lost all brain functionality that first time. "

Quinn examined his body closely. It felt strange. Then he looked closer at Anabel. Through the pale lighting of the room, he could make out the tracks of her tears and the redness of her eyes. He could tell she had not slept very much, and had spent most of the time crying. Although, he could sense the usual compassionate aura that surrounded her, he could also feel a quiet storm that resided behind her compassionate eyes.

"It's over Anabel. We did it," said Quinn.

"It's not over. While we're trapped in here they're out there waiting for us. The Banshee, the Jinn, the forgotten, possibly Shadow Walkers, and Francis is still missing."

"Anabel, we may be trapped, but we're safe," said Quinn.

"Safe…for how long?" asked Anabel.

Something was aggravating Anabel, though she did not say what.

"Who are they to judge us? Banshee is out there destroying Central… I dare not know what else. And we, we are doing nothing to protect them when they need us most. What about the children?" pleaded Anabel.

"Anabel. Everything will be fine. Don't let your heart be consumed by grief and vengeance. You know where that path leads and we both know what would happen," replied Quinn.

Anabel began to calm down and so did her aura as she exhaled. Though frustrated, Anabel forced herself to remain calm. Anabel thought of Quinn's recovery and managed to put on a smile. These had been the longest two days of her life, and even with her powers, she was uncertain if she would have been able to revive him; but now he had safely returned, and was sure to recover.

"I'm glad you're stable. I don't know what I would have done if I lost you too," she said, leaning over to give him a hug and kiss on the head, "I'm going to go grab you something to eat."

"I can call for it if you'd like," said Bruno.

"No, it's fine Bruno. I'll get it myself. I could use the walk." Anabel stood up and before exiting the room, turned to Quinn.

"I love you too Anabel."

Anabel smiled, closing the door gently behind her.

"Wow!" said Bruno, who seemed to let out a sigh of relief. The tension in the room had grown so thick, he had unknowingly been holding his breath the whole time. He had never seen Anabel upset in the slightest until now.

"Quinn, I know the Banshee tried to kill you and me, but this isn't the first time we've risked our lives. Why is Anabel so upset?"

"The Banshee was the reason we joined the organization. We were young, naïve, and wanted to follow in the footsteps of our mother, who had been killed by the Banshee."

"The Banshee killed your mother?"

A look of shock spread over Bruno's face as if he had just been stabbed through the heart.

"Yes, and not a day goes by that Anabel and I don't think about how things would have been if she were still here. You see, our mother worked for the TSPA when we were younger. She never really told us the exact details of what she did; only that she worked in law enforcement. It was not until she died and Francis the IV showed up that we really learned the truth. So we decided to join the agency."

"How could you not know what she did? Couldn't you just read her mind?"

"Not exactly, mother was special like us. She was immune to our abilities. Humph…we could never lie to her, it was like she could see right through us no matter how persistent we were with covering the truth. We were all orphans until she came along and brought us together. She loved us and raised us as her own."

"That's all that matters."

Quinn looked over at Bruno who had begun to tear up.

"Hey, don't you start crying on me. If you start crying, I'm going to have to break your face."

Bruno smiled. "That's what my brother used to say. I'm not going to cry. I'm done crying. I will never forget my family, but I have a new family now. And once we find a way out of here, things will go back to normal. Besides, Judge Francis the IV is our leader, and even the Banshee fears him. I mean, who doesn't? Our old man's crazy powerful and scary as hell, I've seen him make Benji sweat."

"More or less," said Quinn sarcastically.

"Once you're healed, I want to take you on. Now that we are trapped in here, we can take our final form without the risk of destroying everyone. I've been practicing, and I think I have found a weakness in your Ultimate form."

"Don't overestimate your abilities. Even in this state, you're no match for me Bruno, let alone my final form."

"Oh we'll see about that. As soon as you're better, I'll meet you on the training field. I'm going to show you how much I've improved since we last fought," challenged Bruno.

"Hadar once said, *the battle is won long before the first attack.* We'll see how much you've improved. Let's start tomorrow," said Quinn.

"You won't be better by then."

"I'll be good enough to take you on," said Quinn in his usual arrogant tone.

"If I fought you in that condition, Anabel would kill me. Plus, I'd feel bad if I hurt you too much."

"Hump, it's amazing you can fit such a big imagination into such a small brain. Fine, give me two days and I'll be good as new. Oh, and thank Benjamin and Stephen for me."

"You'll have to do that yourself when we get out. I'm not even sure he's in here, and I'm certain Stephen never arrived."

"Very well then," Quinn smirked as Bruno began to turn around, "One last thing, what do you mean by, 'never arrived'?'"

"Oh, I thought we told you already. We're trapped in the Zone. Eleanor and Stephen didn't make it before the bridge between Terraizen and this place collapsed due to some malfunction in the A.I. system. So we're trying to figure out a way to reopen the gate, but we haven't heard from them since the night of the Jinn's attack. On the plus side, we're all healed up now, and this place is an exact replica of Central, so we should be fine for the time being. But now that you're awake, I'm sure you'll find a way to fix this. Don't tell anyone I said this, but you're the smartest guy I know."

"Well thanks Bruno, I'll be sure to tell everyone once I'm well. Now would you mind giving me some space? You're ignorance is starting to rub off on me, and I need to rest if I'm going to come up with a plan to save everyone."

"Sure thing bud, you seem nicer than usual. You should have almost died sooner. I like the new you."

Bruno smiled as he looked at Quinn. Quinn reminded him of his brother and the days they would brawl in the back yard against each other and their father. He was excited to be surrounded by such incredible people. The TSPA was not just an organization. To him, they were family, and he would do anything to protect them.

"Don't get used to it. Now get out of here. I need to rest," said Quinn, lying back in his bed.

Bruno exited the room, and Quinn let out a deep sigh. He couldn't believe two days had passed. Quinn wanted to scream, but knew to remain calm. Frightening Anabel was the last thing he would have wanted. He hoped Bruno didn't speak with Anabel about the story. After all, some of it had been made up.

Many hours observing Quinn had made the masquerade much easier to pull off last minute. Still, it was a bit challenging to mimic him. In truth, she had no idea how she had ended up in the Zone, and in Quinn's body but until she found answers she would maintain the guise. The last thing she remembered was being attacked from behind.

Though she was worried by the fact that she was not in her own body, it had been immediately overshadowed by the thing that lurked in the corner of her room. Anabel and Bruno could not see it, and it was for this reason she needed them to leave. Neither man, nor beast, but something much more sinister had come for her.

Trembling, Eleanor cautiously reached her right hand towards the silver watch on her left wrist, trying not to draw its attention. Though it wasn't very smart or fast. It had been undetectable. One wrong move, and she knew it could be the end for her.

Quinn's Glossary Book 1:

<u>A.I.</u> – Ancient Intelligence said to have originated before the Forgotten Ages (Faith is sometimes confused with the term "artificial intelligence" by most TSPA agents because of it's ability to integrate itself into electrical networks and wave based signal and relay systems.)

<u>Aborigine</u> - A member of the original people to live in the area.

<u>Sea of Anexthesia</u>- The sea that separates the continents of Terraizen.

<u>Aqua Animax [Living Water]</u>: A strange essence based liquid that resembles water. Said to exhibit a conscious perception of life. To those who are not 'Awakened' it is harmless and can be consumed like water. To those who are Awakened it can cause awakening regression, loss of consciousness and even death, if consumed. It has the ability to rejuvenate and heal the wounds of non-Awakened and is immune to most forms of attack.

<u>Awakened</u> –

1.   An individual who has unlocked their Initium. (Initium)

2.   Entering into a higher state of existence. (Semis)

3.   To realize ones purpose (Ultima)

<u>B-2</u>- The Division of Body located on the second underground floor of the TSPA. At the Terraizen Central Protection Agency this floor consists of Bruno Jordan, Benjamin Alexander, Anabel Matthews.

Banshee – The rebel cipher group that operates in secret. Controlled by the Banshee who is said to have powers that rival that of a Terraizen Ruler. Banshee members refer to themselves as "Banshee", acting and moving according to the Banshee's desire to free Terraizen from the "oppressive" rule of the TSPA.

Breeze Travel (B-train or B-line) - to travel from one location to the next on a breeze. This technique can only be used in conjunction with an existing wind elemental or wind infused charmed object.

C-4 - Although it is thought to be the 4th and final underground floor of TSPA, it is located in an alternate dimension that is bridged by the Nexus and controlled by the Mother AI also known as The Mother of Faith.

Cnew- A denizen not from South Terraizen or someone who lacks the understanding of dominion rules, Awakened and/or Channeling.

1. An individual or group of not from Southern Terraizen. (Noun)
2. An individual of inferior channeling or Awakened abilities. (Adjective)
3. An individual who is as naive as a maulft. (Adjective)

From the basic acronym components: **C**entral **N**orth **E**ast **W**est People from Southern Terraizen are considered to possess the most advanced channeling abilities of all of Terraizen. There are some within Southern Terraizen that believe they should rule all of Terraizen and not answer to Central. Those individuals refer to the rest of Terraizen as cnew.

The Dead Zone – 1. A place where life once existed but is now absent from (Class 1). 2. A place where life cannot exist for very long (Class 2). 3. In extreme cases entering an "absolute" Dead Zone causes instant death (Class 3).

The Devils Gate [The Queen's Barrier] – A towering Wall of Water said to possess trace amounts of Aqua Animax.

Dream Chapter – A chronicle of events that occurred within a dream that are sometimes incomplete, difficult to understand or nonsensical.

E-3- The Division of Essence located on the third floor of the TSPA. At the Terraizen Central Protection Agency this floor consists of Anthony Madison, Joshua Gill and the Bio-Faith units. Although it is said to be the third underground level E-3 is an area known as the Zone and exists in a near infinite area.

Echoes (Echos) – Minions of the Banshee that can take on any form, and are extremely hard to destroy

Esper – A high ranking being of supreme magic capable of telepathy and various other paranormal abilities. Sometimes taking the form of a dark mist which if consumed allows the user complete control of it's victim. Depending upon the will of its user it can cause anything ranging from complete euphoria to instant death.

Ezon One – The alternate dimension connected to the Nexus that is used as a training ground for new Awakened.

<u>Forgotten One</u> – An individual whose essence and soul are in the process of being consumed. As they are consumed, they begin to forget who they are and inevitably loose all sense of self, emotion and identity.

<u>The Guardians</u> – The Five Supreme Rulers of Terraizen during the Forgotten Ages said to be near invincible and immortal.

<u>Hollow Man</u> – A creature based upon *The Legend of the Golem*, made from inanimate matter. It is a being that possess no brain and can't think or act of it's own will. Usually controlled by another, partially homunculus in nature and hollow on the inside. Though it's outer shell is difficult to penetrate, if attacked it can consume its attacker to regenerate its inanimate matter shell.

<u>Initium (Class 1 or 2)</u> - First (Beginning) Inner Gate of Awakening: Ability to use powers. Change in physical form (clothing or body)

<u>Level</u> – A ranking system used by Terraizen Central to describe the exponential increase in power of an Awakened or the radius of their abilities influence. The lowest level is a Level 1, a ground state individual, which has very little influence over things outside of their field of view. In comparison a Level 4 possesses abilities that have increased exponentially and their influence can span across a continent with little effort.

<u>M-1</u>- The Division of Minds located on the first underground floor of the TSPA. At the Terraizen Central Protection Agency this floors leaders consist of Quinn Cesar, Eleanor Fredrick, Stephen Langley.

<u>Maulft</u> - Those who are fascinated and attracted to those of magical decent but cannot perform magic themselves not a part of it. A person who lacks not only the ability to use magic but is also not awakened.

<u>Mirrorders</u> - Creatures from the Forgotten Ages that can pass through walls and barriers and consume the souls of the living.

<u>The Nefastus Forest</u>- The large nearly endless forest connected to Terraizen at the Nexus point. The Nefastus forest is said to be the most dangerous forest to have ever existed. It contains beings and creatures both dormant and active that if ever released could destroy Terraizen.

<u>The Nexus</u>- The Nexus is the point where Terraizen, C-4, and Ezon One meet. It is a singularity

<u>Queen of Terraizen</u> - Terraizen's ruler during the Forgotten Ages.

<u>Sector</u> - Usually used to describe a division of the Nefastus Forest but has been used by some to describe sectors of other forests as well. Sectors are a radius from a center point of location (Central Terraizen) and are divided into the four coordinal directions: north, south, east and west.

<u>Semis (Class 3 or 4)</u> - The Second (Half) Inner Gate of Awakening: Ability to use advanced powers. Change in physical form, attitude and personality.

<u>Shadow Walker</u> – Soulless nothings that can't be killed, injured, or destroyed. They are a void product of a consumed forgotten one.

<u>Southern Queens Isle</u>- An group of islands located north of Central Terraizen that were said to have sunk to the bottom of the sea and are surrounded by strange phenomena which have yet to be explained.

<u>STAR Island (Central Terraizen)</u> - Science Technology and Artifact Research Island is synonymous with the name Central Terraizen. Located in the center of the other four main Terraizen continents and is sometimes called by other STAR acronyms as well.

<u>TSPA</u>- Terraizen Secret Protection Agency. The group responsible for protecting the planet Terraizen.

<u>Ultima (Class 5)</u> -The Third (Final) Inner Gate of Awakening: Ability to use all of ones power and essence. Change in state of existence.

<u>Viridiplantae</u>- A wild, wise, ancient plant known for it's ability to remember and immunity to telekinesis and all forms of mental manipulation.

<u>The Zone</u> – The area where the E-3 leaders reside. Within this area those who possess the E-3 abilities are capable of bending the area/reality to their will. Creating their own environments and duplications of places that exist within Terraizen.

www.ingramcontent.com/pod-product-compliance
Lightning Source LLC
Chambersburg PA
CBHW022204030726
47494CB00019B/341